Desire

passionate and dramatic love stories

A Tangled Affair
Fiona Brand

The Paternity Promise
Merline Lovelace

Mills ❤ Boon™

First Published 2012
First Australian Paperback Edition 2012
ISBN 978 1 743 06133 6

Published by
Harlequin Mills & Boon®
Level 5
15 Help Street
CHATSWOOD NSW 2067
AUSTRALIA

® and ™ are trademarks owned by Harlequin Enterprises Limited or its corporate
affiliates and used by others under licence. Trademarks marked with an ® are registered
in Australia and in other countries. Contact admin_legal@Harlequin.ca for details.

Cover art used by arrangement with Harlequin Books S.A.. All rights reserved.

Printed and bound in Australia by
McPherson's Printing Group

A Tangled Affair
Fiona Brand

Mills & Boon™
pure reading pleasure

FIONA BRAND

lives in the sunny Bay of Islands, New Zealand. Now that both her sons are grown, she continues to love writing books and gardening. After a life-changing time in which she met Christ, she has undertaken study for a bachelor of theology and has become a member of The Order of St. Luke, Christ's healing ministry.

Dear Reader,

The second story in The Pearl House series centres on Lucas Atraeus and Carla Ambrosi—both gorgeous and high profile, but actually pretty nice beneath all the media hype. They've chosen to keep their passion secret because of the tension and hurt surrounding Constantine Atraeus and Sienna Ambrosi's broken engagement two years previously.

With a wedding for Sienna and Constantine suddenly in the mix, all the obstacles to true love and happiness for Carla and Lucas finally seem to be dissolved. But Lucas has other ideas.

Wary of a past mistake and the fatal attraction to Carla that has seen him breaking every one of the emotional rules he had sworn to live by—and the streak of niceness that makes it hard for him to say no to women and fluffy pets—Lucas needs a foolproof strategy. But no matter what lengths he goes to to finish things with his ex, Lucas can't seem to stay away from an unexpectedly vulnerable Carla. Let's face it, he's dazzled. To the extent that he has to ask himself the question...

What if, this time, the fatal attraction is the real thing?

Fiona Brand

DEDICATION

For the Lord. Thank you.

The kingdom of heaven
is like a merchant in search of fine pearls.
—*Matthew* 13:45

One

The vibration of Lucas Atraeus's cell phone disrupted the measured bunch and slide of muscle as he smoothly bench-pressed his own weight.

Gray sweatpants clinging low on narrow hips, broad shoulders bronzed by the early morning light that flooded his private gym, he flowed up from the weight bench and checked the screen of his cell. Few people had his private number; of those only two dared interrupt his early morning workout.

"*Si.*" His voice was curt as he picked up the call.

The conversation with his older brother, Constantine, the CEO of The Atraeus Group, a family-owned multibillion-dollar network of companies, was brief. When he terminated the call, Lucas was grimly aware that within the space of a few seconds a great many things had changed.

Constantine intended to marry in less than a fortnight's

time and, in so doing, he had irretrievably complicated Lucas's life.

The bride, Sienna Ambrosi, was the head of a Sydney-based company, Ambrosi Pearls. She also happened to be the sister of the woman with whom Lucas was currently involved. Although *involved* was an inadequate word to describe the passionate, addictive attraction that had held him in reluctant thrall for the past two years.

The phone vibrated again. Lucas didn't need to see the number to know who the second caller was; his gut reaction was enough. Carla Ambrosi. Long, luscious dark hair, honey-tanned skin, light blue eyes and the kind of taut, curvy body that regularly disrupted traffic and stopped him in his tracks.

Desire kicked, raw and powerful, almost overturning the rigid discipline he had instilled in himself after his girlfriend had plunged to her death in a car accident almost five years ago. Ever since Sophie's death he had pledged not to be ruled by passion or fall into such a destructive relationship ever again.

Lately, a whole two years lately, he had been breaking that rule on a regular basis.

But not anymore.

With an effort of will he resisted the almost overwhelming urge to pick up the call. Seconds later, to his intense relief, the phone fell silent.

Shoving damp, jet-black hair back from his face, he strolled across the pale marble floor to the shower with the loose-limbed power of a natural athlete. In centuries past, his build and physical prowess would have made him a formidable warrior. These days, however, Medinian battle was fought across boardroom tables with extensive share portfolios and gold mined from the arid backbone of the main island.

In the corporate arena, Lucas was undefeated. Relationships, however, had proved somewhat less straightforward.

All benefit from the workout burned away by tension and the fierce, unwanted jolt of desire, he stripped off his clothes, flicked the shower controls and stepped beneath a stream of icy water.

If he did nothing and continued an affair that had become increasingly irresistible and risky, he would find himself engaged to a woman who was the exact opposite of the kind of wife he needed.

A second fatal attraction. A second Sophie.

His only honorable course now was to step away from the emotion and the desire and use the ruthless streak he had hammered into himself when dealing with business acquisitions. He had to form a strategy to end a relationship that had always been destined for disaster, for both of their sakes.

He had tried to finish with Carla once before and failed. This time he would make sure of it.

It was over.

Lucas was finally going to propose.

The glow of a full moon flooded the Mediterranean island of Medinos as Carla Ambrosi brought her rented sports car to a halt outside the forbidding gates of Castello Atraeus.

Giddy delight coupled with nervous tension zinged through her as the paparazzi, on Medinos for her sister's wedding to Constantine Atraeus tomorrow, converged on the tiny sky-blue car. So much for arriving deliberately late and under cover of darkness.

A security guard tapped on her window. She wound the glass down a bare two inches and handed him the cream-colored, embossed invitation to the prewedding dinner.

With a curt nod, he slid the card back through the narrow gap and waved her on.

A flash temporarily blinded her as she inched the tiny rental through the crush, making her wish she had ignored the impulse that had seized her and chosen a sensible, solid four-door sedan instead of opting for a low-slung fun and flimsy sports car. But she had wanted to look breezy and casual, as if she didn't have a care in the world—

A sharp rap on her passenger-side window jerked her head around.

"Ms. Ambrosi, are you aware that Lucas Atraeus arrived in Medinos this morning?"

A heady jolt of anticipation momentarily turned her bones to liquid. She had seen Lucas's arrival on the breakfast news. Minutes later, she had glimpsed what she was sure must be his car as she had strolled along the waterfront to buy coffee and rolls for breakfast.

Flanked by security, the limousine had been hard to miss but, frustratingly, the darkly tinted windows had hidden the occupants from sight. Breakfast forgotten, she had both called and texted Lucas. They had arranged to meet but, frustratingly, a late interview request from a popular American TV talk-show host had taken that time slot. With Ambrosi's new collection due for release in under a week, the opportunity to use the publicity surrounding Sienna's wedding to showcase their range and mainstream Ambrosi's brand had been pure gold. Carla had hated canceling but she had known that Lucas, with his clinical approach to business, would understand. Besides, she was seeing him tonight.

Another camera flash made the tension headache she had been fighting since midafternoon spike out of control. The headache was a sharp reminder that she needed to slow down, chill out, de-stress. Difficult to do with the type A personality her doctor had diagnosed just over two years ago, along with a stomach ulcer.

The doctor, who also happened to be a girlfriend, had

advised her to lose her controlling, perfectionist streak, to stop micromanaging every detail of her life including her slavish need to color coordinate her wardrobe and plan her outfits a week in advance. Her approach to relationships was a case in point. Her current system of spreadsheet appraisal was hopelessly punitive. How could she find Mr. Right if no one ever qualified for a second date? Stress was a killer. She needed to loosen up, have some fun, maybe even consider actually sleeping with someone, before she ended up with even worse medical complications.

Carla had taken Jennifer at her word. A week later she had met Lucas Atraeus.

"Ms. Ambrosi, now that your sister is marrying Constantine, is there any chance of resurrecting your relationship with Lucas?"

Jaw tight, Carla continued to inch forward, her heart pounding at the reporter's intrusive question, which had been fired at her like a hot bullet.

And which had been eating at her ever since Sienna had broken the news two weeks ago that she had agreed to marry Constantine.

Tonight, though, she was determined not to resent the questions or the attention. After two years of avoiding being publicly linked with Lucas after the one night the press claimed they had spent together, she was now finally free to come clean about the relationship.

The financial feud that had torn the Atraeus and Ambrosi families apart, and the grief of her sister's first broken engagement to Constantine, were now in the past. Sienna and Constantine had their happy ending. Now, tonight, she and Lucas could finally have theirs.

A throaty rumble presaged the glare of headlights as a gleaming, muscular black car glided in behind her.

Lucas.

Her heart slammed against the wall of her chest. He was staying at the *castello,* which meant he had probably been at a meeting in town and was just returning. Or he could have driven to the small town house she and Sienna and their mother were renting in order to collect her. The possibility of the second option filled her with relieved pleasure.

A split second later the way ahead was clear as the media deserted her in favor of clustering around Lucas's Maserati. Automatically, Carla's foot depressed the accelerator, sending her small sports car rocketing up the steep, winding slope. Scant minutes later, she rounded a sweeping bend and the spare lines of the *castello* she had only ever seen in magazine articles jumped into full view.

The headlights of the Maserati pinned her as she parked on the smooth sweep of gravel fronting the colonnaded entrance. Feeling suddenly, absurdly vulnerable, she retrieved the flame-red silk clutch that matched her dress and got out of the car.

The Maserati's lights winked out, plunging her into comparative darkness as she closed her door and locked the car.

She started toward the Maserati, still battling the aftereffects of the bright halogen lights. The sensitivity of her eyes was uncomfortably close to a symptom she had experienced two months ago when she had contracted a virus while holidaying with Lucas in Thailand.

Instead of the romantic interlude she had so carefully planned and which would have generated the proposal she wanted, Lucas had been forced into the role of nursemaid. On her return home, when she had continued to feel offcolor, further tests had revealed that the stomach ulcer she thought she had beaten had flared up again.

The driver's side door of the car swung open. Her pulse rate rocketed off the charts. Finally, after a day of anxious waiting, they would meet.

Meet.

Her mouth went dry at a euphemism that couldn't begin to describe the explosive encounters that, over the past year, had become increasingly intense.

The reporter at the gate had put his finger on an increasingly tender and painful pulse. Resurrect her relationship with Lucas?

Technically, she was not certain they had ever had anything as balanced as a relationship. Her attempt to create a relaxed, fun atmosphere with no stressful strings had not succeeded. Lucas had seemed content with brief, crazily passionate interludes, but she was not. As hard as she had tried to suppress her type A tendencies and play the glamorous, carefree lover, she had failed. Passion was wonderful, but she *liked* to be in control, to personally dot every *i* and cross every *t*. For Carla, leaving things "open" had created even more stress.

Heart pounding, she started toward the car. The gown she had bought with Lucas in mind was unashamedly spectacular and clung where it touched. Split down one side, it revealed the long, tanned length of her legs. The draped neckline added a sensual Grecian touch to the swell of her breasts and also hid the fact that she had lost weight over the past few weeks.

Her chest squeezed tight as Lucas climbed out of the car with a fluid muscularity she would always recognize.

She drank in midnight eyes veiled by inky lashes, taut cheekbones, the faintly battered nose, courtesy of two seasons playing professional rugby; his strong jaw and firm, well-cut mouth. Despite the sleek designer suit and the ebony seal ring that gleamed on one finger, Lucas looked somewhat less than civilized. A graphic image of him naked and in her bed, his shoulders muscled and broad, his skin dark against crisp white sheets, made her stomach clench.

His gaze captured hers and the idea that they could keep the chemistry that exploded between them a secret until after the wedding died a fiery death. She wanted him. She had waited two years, hamstrung by Sienna's grief at losing Constantine. She loved her sister and was fiercely loyal. Dating the younger and spectacularly better looking Atraeus brother when Sienna had been publicly dumped by Constantine would have been an unconscionable betrayal.

Tonight, she and Lucas could publicly acknowledge their desire to be together. Not in a heavy-handed, possessive way that would hint at the secretive liaison that had disrupted both of their lives for the past two years, but with a low-key assurance that would hint at the future.

As Ambrosi's public relations "face," she understood exactly how this would be handled. There would be no return to the turgid headlines that had followed their first passionate night together. There would be no announcements, no fanfare…at least, not until after tomorrow's wedding.

Despite the fact that her strappy high heels, a perfect color match for the dress, made her more than a little unstable on the gravel, she jogged the last few yards and flung herself into Lucas's arms.

The clean scent that was definitively Lucas, mingled with the masculine, faintly exotic undernote of sandalwood, filled her nostrils, making her head spin. Or maybe it was the delight of simply touching him again after a separation that had run into two long months.

The cool sea breeze whipped long silky coils of hair across her face as she lifted up on her toes. Her arms looped around his neck, her body slid against his, instantly responding to his heat, the utter familiarity of broad shoulders and sleek, hard-packed muscle. His sudden intake of breath, the unmistakable feel of him hardening against the soft contours of her belly filled her with mindless relief.

Ridiculous tears blurred her vision. This was so *not* playing it cool, but it had been two months since she had touched,
kissed, made love to her man. Endless days while she had
waited for the annoying, debilitating ulcer—clear evidence
that she had not coped with her unresolved emotional situation—to heal. Long weeks while she had battled the niggling
anxiety that had its roots in the disastrous bout of illness in
Thailand, as if she was waiting for the next shoe to drop.

She realized that one of the reasons she had not told Lucas
about the complications following the virus was that she had
been afraid of the outcome. Over the years he had dated a
string of gorgeous, glamorous women so she usually took
great care that he only ever saw her at her very best. There
had been nothing pretty or romantic about the fever that had
gripped her in Thailand. There had been even less glamour
surrounding her hospital stay in Sydney.

Lucas's arms closed around her, his jaw brushed her cheek
sending a sensual shiver the length of her spine. Automatically, she leaned into him and lifted her mouth to his, but
instead of kissing her, he straightened and unlooped her
arms from his neck. Cold air filled the space between them.

When she moved to close the frustrating distance he
gripped her upper arms.

"Carla." His voice was clipped, the Medinian accent
smoothed out by the more cosmopolitan overtones of the
States, but still dark and sexy enough to send another shiver
down her spine. "I tried to ring you. Why didn't you pick
up the call?"

The mundane question, the edged tone pulled her back to
earth with a thump. "I switched my phone off while I was
being interviewed then I put it on charge."

But it had only been that way for about an hour. When
she had left the private villa she was sharing with her mother
and Sienna, she had grabbed the phone and dropped it in her

purse. His hands fell away from her arms, leaving a palpable chill in place of the warm imprint of his palms. Extracting the phone from her clutch, she checked the screen and saw that, in her hurry, she had forgotten to turn it on.

She activated the phone, and instantly the missed calls registered on the screen. "Sorry," she said coolly. "Looks like I forgot to turn it back on."

She frowned at his lack of response. With an effort of will, she controlled the unruly emotions that had had the temerity to explode out of their carefully contained box and dropped the phone back in her clutch. So, okay, this was subtext for "let's play it cool."

Fine. Cool she could do, but not doormat. "I'm sorry I missed meeting you earlier but you've been here most of the day. If you'd wanted we could have met for lunch."

A discreet thunk snapped Carla's head around. Automatically, she tracked the unexpected sound and movement as the passenger door of the Maserati swing open.

Not male. Which ruled out her first thought, that the second occupant of the Maserati, hidden from her view by darkly tinted windows, was one of the security personnel who sometimes accompanied Lucas.

Not male. Female.

Out of nowhere her heart started to hammer. A series of freeze frames flickered: silky dark hair caught in a perfect chignon; a smooth, elegant body encased in shimmering, pale pearlized silk.

She went hot then cold, then hot again. She had the abrupt sensation that she was caught in a dream. A *bad* dream.

She and Lucas had an agreement whereby they could date others in order to distract the press and preserve the privacy she had insisted upon. But not here, not now.

Jerkily, Carla completed the movement she realized Lucas wanted from her: she stepped back.

She focused on his face, for the first time fully absorbing the remoteness of his dark gaze. It was the same cool neutrality she had seen on the odd occasion when they had been together and he'd had to take a work call.

The throbbing in her head increased, intensified by a shivery sensitivity that swept her spine. Her fingers tightened on her clutch as she resisted the sudden, childish urge to hug away the chill.

She drew an impeded breath. Another woman? She had not seen that coming.

Her mind worked frantically. No. It couldn't be.

But, if she hadn't felt that moment of heated response she *could* almost think that Lucas—

Emotion flickered in his gaze, gone almost before she registered it. "I believe you've met Lilah."

Recognition followed as Lilah turned and the light from the portico illuminated delicate cheekbones and exotic eyes. "Of course." She acknowledged Ambrosi's spectacularly talented head designer with a stiff nod.

Of course she knew Lilah, and Lilah knew her.

And all about her situation with Lucas, if she correctly interpreted the sympathy in Lilah's eyes.

Confusion rocked her again. How dare Lucas confide their secret to anyone without her permission? And Lilah Cole wasn't just anyone. The Coles had worked for Ambrosi's for as long as Carla could remember. Carla's grandfather, Sebastien, had employed Lilah's mother in Broome. Lilah, herself, had worked for Ambrosi for the past five years, the last two as their head designer, creating some of their most exquisite jewelry.

Lilah's smile and polite greeting were more than a little wary as she closed the door of the Maserati and strolled around the front of the car to join them.

The sudden uncomfortable silence was broken as the front

door of the *castello* was pushed wide. Light flared across the smooth expanse of gravel, the soft strains of classical music filtered through the haze of shock that still held Carla immobile.

A narrow, well-dressed man Carla recognized as Tomas, Constantine's personal assistant, spoke briefly in Medinian and motioned them all inside.

With a curt nod, Lucas indicated that both Carla and Lilah precede him. Feeling like an automaton, Carla walked toward the broad steps, no longer caring that the gravel was ruining her shoes. Exquisite confections she had chosen with Lucas in mind—along with every other item of jewelry and clothing she was wearing tonight, including her lingerie.

With each step she could feel the distance between them, a mystifying cold impersonality, growing by the second. When his hand landed in the small of Lilah's back, steadying her as she hitched up her gown with a poised, unutterably graceful movement, Carla's heart squeezed on a pang of misery. In those few seconds she finally acknowledged the insidious fear that had coexisted with her need to be with Lucas for almost two years.

She knew how dangerous Lucas was in business. As Constantine's right hand, by necessity he had to be coldly ruthless.

The other shoe had finally dropped. She had just been smoothly, ruthlessly dumped.

Two

Tucking a glossy strand of dark hair behind her ear—hair that suddenly seemed too lush and unruly for a formal family occasion—Carla stepped into the disorienting center of what felt like a crowd.

In reality there were only a handful of people present in the elegant reception room: Tomas and members of the Atraeus family including Constantine, his younger brother, Zane, and Lucas's mother, Maria Therese. To one side, Sienna was chatting with their mother, Margaret Ambrosi.

Sienna, wearing a sleek ivory dress and already looking distinctly bridal, was the first to greet her. The quick hug, the moment of warmth, despite the fact that they had spent most of the morning going over the details of the wedding together, made Carla's throat lock.

Sienna gripped her hands, frowning. "Are you okay? You look a little pale."

"I'm fine, just a little rushed and I didn't expect the media ambush at the gates." Carla forced a bright smile. "You know me. I do thrive on publicity, but the reporters were like a pack of wolves."

Constantine, tall and imposing, greeted her with a brief hug, the gesture conveying her new status as a soon-to-be member of Medinos's most wealthy, powerful family. He frowned as he released her. "Security should have kept them at bay."

His expression was remote, his light gray gaze controlled, belying the primitive fact that he had used financial coercion and had even gone so far as kidnapping Sienna to get his former fiancée back.

"The security was good." Carla hugged her mother, fighting the ridiculous urge to cling like a child. If she did that she would cry, and she refused to cry in front of Lucas.

A waiter offered champagne. As she lifted the flute from the tray her gaze clashed with Lucas's. Her fingers tightened reflexively on the delicate stem. The message in his dark eyes was clear.

Don't talk. Don't make trouble.

She took a long swallow of the champagne. "Unfortunately, the line of questioning the press took was disconcerting. Although I'm sure that when Lucas arrived with Lilah any misconceptions were cleared up."

Sienna's expression clouded. "Don't tell me they're trying to resurrect that old story about you and Lucas?"

Carla controlled her wince reflex at the use of the word *resurrect*. "I guess it's predictable that now that you and Constantine have your happy ending, the media are looking to generate something out of nothing."

Sienna lifted a brow. "So, do they need a medic down at the gates?"

"Not this time." Lucas frowned as Carla took another

long swallow of champagne. "Don't forget I was the original target two years ago, not the media."

And suddenly the past was alive between them, vibrating with hurtful accusations and misunderstandings she thought they had dealt with long ago. The first night of unplanned and irresistible passion they'd shared, followed by the revelation of the financial deal her father had leveraged on the basis of Sienna's engagement to Constantine. Lucas's accusation that Carla was more interested in publicity and her career than she had been in him.

Carla forced herself to loosen her grip on the stem of her glass. "But then the media are so very fascinated by your private life, aren't they?"

A muscle pulsed along the side of his jaw. "Only when someone decides to feed them information."

The flat statement, correct as it was, stung. Two years ago, hurt by his comments, she had reacted by publicly stating that she had absolutely no interest in being pursued by Lucas. The story had sparked weeks of uncomfortable conjecture for them both.

Sienna left them to greet more arrivals. Her anger under control, Carla examined the elegant proportions of the reception room, the exquisite marble floors and rich, Italianate decor. "And does that thought keep you awake at night?"

Lucas's gaze flared at her deliberate reference to the restless passion for her that he had once claimed kept him awake at nights. "I'm well used to dealing with the media."

"A shame there isn't a story. It could have benefited Ambrosi's upcoming product launch." She forced a brilliant smile. "You know what they say, any publicity is good publicity. Although in this case, I'm sure the story wouldn't be worth the effort, especially when it would involve dragging *my* private life through the mud."

Lucas's expression shuttered, the fire abruptly gone. "Then I suggest you sleep easy. *I* don't kiss and tell."

The sense of disorientation she had felt the past few minutes evaporated in a rush of anger. "Or commit to relationships."

"You were the one who set the ground rules."

Suddenly Lucas seemed a lot closer. "You know I had no other option."

His expression was grim. "The truth is always an option."

Her chin jerked up. "I was protecting Sienna and my family. What was I supposed to do? Turn up with you at Mom and Dad's house for Sunday dinner and admit that I was—"

"Sleeping with me?"

The soft register of his voice made her heart pound. Every nerve in her body jangled at his closeness, the knowledge that he was just as aware of her as she was of him. "I was about to say dating an Atraeus."

Sienna returned from her hostess duties to step neatly between them. "Time out, children."

Lucas lifted a brow, his mouth quirking in the wry half smile that regularly made women go weak at the knees. "My apologies."

As Constantine joined them, Lucas drew Lilah into the circle. "I know I don't need to introduce Lilah."

There was a moment of polite acknowledgment and brief handshakes as Lilah was accepted unconditionally into the Atraeus fold. The process of meeting Maria Therese was more formal and underlined a salient and well-publicized fact. Atraeus men didn't take their women home to meet their families on a casual basis. To her best knowledge, until now, Lucas had never taken a girlfriend home to meet his mother.

Lucas's *girlfriend*.

Lilah was smiling, her expression contained but lit with an unmistakable glow.

A second salient fact made Carla stiffen. A few months ago, while stuck overnight together at a sales expo in Europe, she and Lilah had discussed the subject of relationships. At age twenty-nine, despite possessing the kind of sensual dark-haired, white-skinned beauty that riveted male attention, Lilah was determinedly single.

She had told Carla a little of her background, which included a single mother, a solo grandmother and ongoing financial hardship. Born illegitimate, Lilah had early on given herself a rule. No sex before marriage. There was no way she was going to be left holding a baby.

While Carla had stressed about finding Mr. Right, Lilah was calmly focused on marrying him, her approach methodical and systematic. She had moved on a step from Carla's idea of a spreadsheet and had developed a list of qualifying attributes as precise and unwavering as an employment contract. Also, unlike Carla, Lilah had *saved* herself for marriage. She was that twenty-first century paragon: a virgin.

The simple fact that she was on Medinos with Lucas, thousands of miles from her Sydney apartment and rigorous work schedule, spoke volumes.

Lilah did not date. Carla knew that she occasionally accompanied a gay neighbor to his professional dinners and had him escort her to charity functions she supported. But their relationship was purely friendship, which suited them both. That was all.

Carla took another gulp of champagne. Her stomach clenched because the situation was suddenly blindingly obvious.

Lilah was dating Lucas because she had chosen him. He was her intended husband.

Anger churned in Carla's stomach and stiffened her spine. She and Lucas had conducted their relationship based on a set of rules that was the complete opposite of everything that

Lilah was holding out for: no strings, strictly casual and, because of the family feud, in secrecy.

An enticing, convenient arrangement for a man who clearly had never had any intention of offering *her* marriage.

Waiters served more chilled champagne and trays of tiny, exquisite canapés. Carla forced herself to eat a tiny pastry case filled with a delicate seafood mousse. She continued to sip her way through the champagne, which loosened the tightness of her throat but couldn't wash away the deepening sense of hurt.

Lilah Cole was beautiful, elegant and likable, but nothing could change the fact that Lilah's easy acceptance into the Atraeus fold should have been *her* moment.

The party swelled as more family and friends arrived. Abandoning her champagne flute on a nearby sideboard, Carla joined the movement out onto a large stone balcony overlooking the sea.

Feeling awkward and isolated amidst the crowd, she threaded her way through the revelers to the parapet and stared out at the expansive view. The breeze gusted, laced with the scent of the sea, sending coils of hair across her cheeks and teasing at the flimsy silk of her dress, briefly exposing more leg than she had planned.

Lucas's gaze burned over her, filled with censure, not the desire that had sizzled between them for the past two years.

Cheeks burning, she snapped her dress back into place, her mood plummeting further as Lilah joined Lucas. Despite the breeze, Lilah's hair was neat and perfect, her dress subtly sensual with a classic pureness of line that suddenly made Carla feel cheap and brassy, all sex and dazzle against Lilah's demure elegance. Her cheeks grew hotter as she considered what she was wearing under the red silk. Again, nothing with any degree of subtlety. Every flimsy stitch was designed to entice.

She had taken a crazy risk in dressing so flamboyantly, practically begging for the continuation of their relationship. After the distance of the past two months she should have had more sense than to wear her heart on her sleeve. Jerking her gaze away, she tried to concentrate on the moon sliding up over the horizon, the churning floodlit water below the *castello*.

A cool gust of wind sent more hair whipping around her cheeks. Temporarily blinded, she snatched at her billowing hemline. Strong fingers gripped her elbow, steadying her. Heart-stoppingly familiar dark eyes clashed with hers. Not Lucas, Zane Atraeus.

"Steady. I've got you. Come over here, out of the wind before we lose you over the side."

Zane's voice was deep, mild and low-key, more American than Medinian, thanks to his Californian mother and upbringing. With his checkered, illegitimate past and lady-killer reputation, Zane was, of the three brothers, definitely the most approachable and she wondered a little desperately why she hadn't been able to fall for him instead of Lucas. "Thanks for the rescue."

He sent her an enigmatic look. "Damsels in distress are always my business."

The warmth in her cheeks flared a little brighter. The suspicion that Zane wasn't just talking about the wind, that he knew about her affair with Lucas, coalesced into certainty.

He positioned her in the lee of a stone wall festooned with ivy. "Can I get you a drink?"

A reckless impulse seized Carla as she glanced across at Lucas. "Why not?"

With his arm draped casually across the stone parapet behind Lilah, his stance was male and protective, openly claiming Lilah as his, although he wasn't touching her in any way.

Unbidden, a small kernel of hope flared to life at that

small, polite distance. Ten minutes ago, Carla had been certain they were an established couple; that to be here, at a family wedding, Lucas would have had to have slept with Lilah. Now she was abruptly certain they had not yet progressed to the bedroom. There was a definite air of restraint underpinning the glow on Lilah's face, and despite his possessive stance, Lucas was preserving a definite distance.

A waiter swung by. Zane handed her a flute of champagne. "Do you think they've slept together?"

Carla's hand jerked at the question. Champagne splashed over her fingers. She dragged her gaze from the clean line of Lucas's profile and glanced at Zane. His expression was oddly grim, his jaw set. "I don't know why you're asking me that question."

Zane, who hadn't bothered with champagne, gave her a steady look, and humiliation curled through her. He knew.

Carla wondered a little wildly how he had found out and if everyone on the balcony knew that she was Lucas's ditched ex.

Zane's expression was dismissive. "Don't worry, it was a lucky guess."

Relief flooded her as she swallowed a mouthful of champagne. A few seconds later her head began to spin and she resolved not to drink any more.

Zane's attention was no longer on her; it was riveted on Lilah and realization hit. She wasn't the only one struggling here. "You want Lilah."

The grim anger she had glimpsed winked out of existence. "If I was in the market for marriage, maybe."

"Which, I take it, you're not."

Zane's dark gaze zeroed in on hers, but Carla realized he still barely logged her presence. "No. Are you interested in art?"

Carla blinked at the sudden change of subject. "Yes."

"If you want out of this wind, I'll be happy to show you the rogue's gallery."

She had glimpsed the broad gallery that housed the Atraeus family portraits, some painted by acknowledged masters, but hadn't had time to view them. "I would love to take a closer look at the family portraits."

Anything to get her off the balcony. "Just do me one favor. Put your arm around my waist."

"And make it look good?"

Carla's chin jerked up a fraction. "If you don't mind."

The unflattering lack of reaction to her suggestion should have rubbed salt into the wound, but Carla was beyond caring. She was dying by inches but she was determined not to be any more tragic than she had to be.

Lucas's gaze burned over her as she handed her drink to a waiter then allowed Zane's arm to settle around her waist. As they strolled past Lucas, she was forcibly struck by the notion that he was jealous.

Confusion rocked her. She hadn't consciously set out to make Lucas jealous; her main concern from the moment she had realized that Lucas and Lilah were together had been self-preservation. Lucas being jealous made no sense unless he still wanted her, and how could that be when he had already chosen another woman?

Carla was relieved when Zane dropped his arm the second they were out of sight of the balcony. After a short walk through flagged corridors, they entered the gallery. Along one wall, arched windows provided spectacular views of the moonlit sea. The opposite wall was softly lit and lined with exquisite paintings.

The tingling sense of alarm, as if at some level she was aware of Lucas's displeasure, continued as they strolled past rank after rank of gorgeous rich oils. Most had been painted pre-1900s, before the once wealthy and noble Atraeus family had fallen on hard times. Lucas's grandfather, after discovering an obscenely rich gold mine, had since purchased most of the paintings back from private collections and museums.

The men were clearly of the Atraeus bloodline, with strong jaws and aquiline profiles. The women, almost without exception, looked like Botticelli angels: beautiful, demure, virginal.

Zane paused beside a vibrant painting of an Atraeus ancestor who looked more like a pirate than a noble lord. His lady was a serene, quiet dove with a steely glint in her eye. With her long, slanting eyes and delicate bones, the woman bore an uncanny resemblance to Lilah. "As you can see it's a mixture of sinners and saints. It seemed that the more dissolute and marauding the Atraeus male, the more powerful his desire for a saint."

Carla heard the measured tread of footsteps. Her heart sped up because she was almost sure it was Lucas. "And is that what Atraeus men are searching for today?"

Zane shrugged. "I can't speak for my brothers. I'm not your typical Atraeus male."

Her jaw tightened. "But the idea of a pure, untouched bride still has a certain appeal."

"Maybe." He sent her a flashing grin that made him look startlingly like the Atraeus pirate in the painting. "Although, I'm always willing to be convinced that a sinner is the way to go."

"Because that generally means no commitment, right?"

Zane's dark brows jerked together. "How did we get on to commitment?"

Carla registered the abrupt silence as if whoever had just entered the gallery had seen them and stopped.

Her heart slammed in her chest as she caught Lucas's reflection in one of the windows. On impulse, she stepped close to Zane and tilted her head back, the move flirtatious and openly provocative. She was playing with fire, because Zane had a reputation that scorched.

Lucas would be furious with her. If he *was* jealous, her behavior would probably kill any feelings he had left for her, but she was beyond caring. He had hurt her too badly for her to pull back now. "If that's an invitation, the answer is yes."

Zane's gaze registered unflattering surprise.

Minor detail, because Lucas was now walking toward them. Gritting her teeth, she wound her finger in Zane's tie, applying just enough pressure that his head lowered until his mouth was mere inches from hers.

His gaze was disarmingly neutral. "I know what you're up to."

"You could at least be tempted."

"I'm trying."

"Try harder."

"Damn, you're type A. No wonder he went for Lilah."

Carla's fingers tightened on his tie. "Is it that obvious?"

"Only to me. And that's because I'm a control freak myself."

"I am *not* a control freak."

He unwound her fingers from his tie. "Whatever you say."

Cut adrift by Zane's calm patience, Carla had no choice but to step back and in so doing almost caromed into Lucas.

She flinched at the fiery trail of his gaze over the shadow of her cleavage, her mouth, the impression of heat and desire. If Zane hadn't been there she was almost certain he would have pulled her close and kissed her.

Lucas's expression was shuttered. "What are you up to?"

Carla didn't try to keep the bitterness out of her voice. "*I'm* not up to anything. Zane was showing me the paintings."

"Careful," Zane intervened, his gaze on Lucas. "Or I

might think you have a personal interest in Carla, and that couldn't possibly be, since you're dating the lovely Lilah."

A sharp pang went through Carla at the tension vibrating between the brothers, shifting undercurrents she didn't understand.

Spine rigid, she kept her gaze firmly on Zane's jaw. She hadn't liked behaving like that, but at least she had proved that Lucas did still want her. Although the knowledge was a bitter pill, because his reaction repeated a pattern that was depressingly familiar. In establishing a stress-free liaison with him based on her rules, she had somehow negotiated herself out of the very things she needed most: love, companionship and commitment.

Lucas had wanted her for two years, but that was all. The relationship had struggled to progress out of the bedroom. Even when she had finally gotten him to Thailand for a whole four-day minibreak, the longest period of time they had ever spent together, the plan had crashed and burned because she had gotten sick.

She wondered in what way she was lacking that Lucas didn't want a full relationship with her? That instead of allowing them to grow closer, he had kept her at an emotional arm's length and gone to Lilah for the very things that Carla needed from him.

She glanced apologetically at Zane in an effort to defuse the tension. "It's okay, Lucas and I are old news. If there was anything more we would be together now."

"Whereas marriage *is* Lilah's focus," Zane said softly.

Lucas frowned. "Back off, Zane."

Confusion gripped Carla along with another renegade glimmer of hope at Lucas's reaction. She was tired of thinking about everything that had gone wrong, but despite that, her mind grabbed on to the notion that maybe all he was doing *was* dating Lilah on a casual basis. Just because Lilah wanted marriage didn't necessarily mean she would get what she wanted.

Grimly, she forced herself to study the Atraeus bride in the painting again. It was the perfect reality check.

Her pale, demure gown was the epitome of all things virginal and pure. Nothing like Carla's flaming red silk dress, with its enticing glimpse of cleavage and leg. The serene eighteenth-century bride was no doubt every man's secret dream. A perfect wife, without a flirty bone in her body. Or a stress condition.

Lucas's gaze sliced back to Carla. "I'll take you back to the party. Dinner will be served in about fifteen minutes."

He *was* jealous.

The thought reverberated through her, but for the first time in two years what Lucas wanted wasn't a priority. *Her* rules had just changed. From now on it was commitment or nothing.

Her chin firmed. "No. I have an escort. Zane will take me back to the party."

For a long, tension-filled moment Carla thought Lucas would argue, but then the demanding, possessive gleam was replaced by a familiar control. He nodded curtly then sent Zane a long, cold look that conveyed a hands-off message that left Carla feeling doubly confused. Lucas didn't want her, but neither did he want Zane anywhere near her.

And if Lucas no longer wanted her, if they really were finished, why had he bothered to search her out?

Three

Lucas Atraeus strode into his private quarters and snapped the door closed behind him. Opening a set of French doors, he stepped out onto his balcony. The wind buffeted the weathered stone parapet and whipped night-dark hair around the obdurate line of his jaw. He tried to focus on the steady roar of the waves pounding the cliff face beneath and the stream of damp, salty air, while he waited for the self-destructive desire to reclaim Carla to dissolve.

The vibration of his cell phone drew him back inside. Sliding the phone out of his pocket, he checked the screen. Lilah. No doubt wondering where he was.

Jaw clenched, he allowed the call to go through to his voice mail. He couldn't stomach talking to Lilah right at that moment with his emotions still raw and his thoughts on another woman. Besides, with a relationship based on a few phone calls and a couple of conversations, most of them purely work based, they literally had nothing to say to each other.

The call terminated. Lucas found himself staring at a newspaper he had tossed down on the coffee table, the one he had read on the night flight from New York to Medinos. The paper was open at the society pages and a grainy shot of Carla in her capacity as the "face" of Ambrosi Pearls, twined intimately close with a rival millionaire businessman.

Picking up the newspaper, he reread the caption that hinted at a hot affair.

He had been away for two months but by all accounts she had not missed him.

Tossing the newspaper down on the coffee table, he strode back out onto the balcony. Before he could stop himself, he had punched in her number on his phone.

Calling her now made no kind of sense.

He held the sleek phone pressed to his ear and forced himself to remember the one overriding reason he should never have touched Carla Ambrosi.

Grimly, he noted that the hit of old grief and sharp-enough-to-taste guilt still wasn't powerful enough to bury the impulse to involve himself even more deeply in yet another fatal attraction.

When he had met Carla, somehow he had stepped away from the rigid discipline he had instilled in himself after Sophie's death.

The car accident hadn't been his fault, but he was still haunted by the argument that had instigated Sophie's headlong dash in her sports car after he had found out that she had aborted his child.

Sophie had been beautiful, headstrong and adept at winding him around her little finger. He should have stopped her, taken the car keys. He should have controlled the situation. It had been his responsibility to protect her, and he had failed.

They should never have been together in the first place.

They had been all wrong for each other. He had been disciplined, work focused and family orientated. Sophie had skimmed along the surface of life, thriving on bright lights, parties and media attention. Even the manner in which Sophie had died had garnered publicity and had been perceived in certain quarters as glamorous.

The ring tone continued. His fingers tightened on the cell. Carla had her phone with her; she should have picked up by now.

Unless she was otherwise occupied. *With Zane.*

His stomach clenched at the image of Carla, mouthwateringly gorgeous in red, her fingers twined in Zane's tie, poised for a kiss he had interrupted.

He didn't trust Zane. His younger brother had a reputation with women that literally burned.

The call went through to voice mail. Carla's voice filled his ear.

Despite the annoyance that gripped him that Carla had decided to ignore his call, Lucas was riveted by the velvet-cool sound of the recorded message. The brisk, businesslike tone so at odds with Carla's ultrasexy, ultrafeminine appearance and which never failed to fascinate.

During the two months he had been in the States he had refrained from contacting Carla. He had needed to distance himself from a relationship that during an intense few days in Thailand had suddenly stepped over an invisible boundary and become too gut-wrenchingly intimate. Too like his relationship with Sophie.

Carla, who was surprisingly businesslike and controlled when it came to communication, had left only one text and a single phone message to which he had replied. A few weeks ago he had seen her briefly, from a distance, at her father's funeral, but they hadn't spoken.

That was reason number two not to become involved with Carla.

The ground rules for their relationship had been based on what she had wanted: a no-strings fun fling, carried out in secret because of the financial scandal that had erupted between their two families.

Secrecy was not Lucas's thing, but since he had never planned on permanency he hadn't seen any harm in going along with Carla's plan. He had been based in the States, Carla was in Sydney. A relationship wasn't possible even if he had wanted one.

The line hummed expectantly.

Irritated with himself for not having done it sooner, Lucas terminated the call.

Grimly, he stared at the endless expanse of sea, the faint curve of the horizon. Carla not picking up the call was the best-case scenario. If she had, he was by no means certain he could have maintained his ruthless facade.

The problem was that, as tough and successful as he was in business, when it came to women his track record was patchy.

As an Atraeus he was expected to be coolly dominant. Despite the years he had spent trying to mold himself into the strong silent type who routinely got his way, he had not achieved Constantine's effortless self-possession. Little kids and fluffy dogs still targeted him; women of all ages gravitated to him as if they had no clue about his reputation as The Atraeus Group's key hatchet man.

Despite the long list of companies he had streamlined or clinically dismantled, he couldn't forget that he had not been able to establish any degree of control over his relationship with Sophie.

Jaw taut, Lucas padded inside. He barely noticed the

warm glow of lamplight, the richness of exquisite antiques and jewel-bright carpets.

His gaze zeroed in on the newspaper article again. A hot pulse of jealously burned through him as he studied the Greek millionaire who had his arm around Carla's waist.

Alex Panopoulos, an archrival across the boardroom table and a well-known playboy.

Given the limited basis of Lucas's relationship with Carla, they had agreed it had to be open; they were both free to date others. Like Lucas, Carla regularly dated as part of her career, although so far Lucas had not been able to bring himself to include another woman in his life on more than a strictly platonic basis.

Panopoulos was a guest at the wedding tomorrow.

Walking through to the kitchen, he tossed the paper into the trash. His jaw tightened at the thought that he would have fend off the Greek, as well.

He guessed he should be glad that it was Zane Carla seemed to be attracted to and not Panopoulos.

Zane had been controllable, so far. And if he stepped over the line, there was always the option that they could settle the issue in the old-fashioned way, down on the beach and without an audience.

Dinner passed in a polite, superficial haze. Carla made conversation, smiled on cue, and avoided looking at Lucas. Unfortunately, because he was seated almost directly opposite her, she was burningly aware of him through each course.

Dessert was served. Still caught between the raw misery that threatened to drag her under, and the need to maintain the appearance of normality, Carla ate. She had reached the dessert course when she registered how much wine she had drunk.

A small sharp shock went through her. She wasn't drunk, but alcohol and some of the foods she was eating did not mix happily with an ulcer. Strictly speaking, after the episode with the virus and the ulcer, she wasn't supposed to drink at all.

Setting her spoon down, she picked up her clutch and excused herself from the table. She asked one of the waitstaff to direct her to the nearest bathroom. Unfortunately, since her grasp of Medinian was far from perfect, she somehow managed to take a wrong turn.

After traversing a long corridor and opening a number of doors, one of which seemed to be the entrance to a private set of rooms, complete with a kitchenette, she opened a door and found herself on a terrace overlooking the sea. Shrugging, because the terrace would do as well as a bathroom since all she required was privacy to take the small cocktail of pills her doctor had prescribed, she walked to the stone parapet and studied the view.

The stiff sea breeze that had been blowing earlier had dropped away, leaving the night still, the air balmy and heavily scented with the pine and rosemary that grew wild on the hills. A huge full moon glowed a rich, buttery gold on the horizon.

Setting her handbag down on the stone pavers, she extracted the MediPACK of pills she had brought with her, tore open the plastic seal and swallowed them dry.

Dropping the plastic waste into her handbag, she straightened just as the door onto the terrace popped open. Her chest tightened when she recognized Lucas.

"I hope you weren't expecting Zane?"

"If I was, it wouldn't be any of your business."

"Zane won't give you what you want."

Carla swallowed to try and clear the dry bitterness in her

mouth. "A loving relationship? The kind of relationship I thought we could have had?"

He ignored the questions. "You should return to the dining room."

The flatness of Lucas's voice startled her. Lucas had always been exciting and difficult to pin down, but he had also been funny and unexpectedly tender. This was the first time she had ever seen this side of him. "Not yet. I have a…headache, I need some air." Which was no lie, because the headache was there, throbbing steadily at her temples.

She pretended to be absorbed by the spectacular view of the crystal-clear night and the vast expanse of sea gleaming like polished bronze beneath the moon. Just off the coast of Medinos, the island of Ambrus loomed, tonight seemingly almost close enough to touch. One of the more substantial islands in the Medinos group, Ambrus was intimately familiar to her because her family had once owned a chunk of it.

"How did you know these are my rooms?"

She spun, shocked at Lucas's closeness and what he'd just said. "I didn't. I was looking for a bathroom. I must have taken a wrong turn."

The coolness of his glance informed her that he didn't quite believe her. Any idea that Lucas would tell her that he had made a mistake and that he desperately wanted her back died a quick death.

A throb of grief hit her at the animosity that seemed to be growing by the second and she pulled herself up sharply. She had run the gamut of shock and anger. She was not going to wallow in self-pity.

It was clear Lucas wasn't going to leave until she did, so she picked up her bag and started toward the door.

Instead of moving aside, Lucas moved to block her path. "I'm sorry you found out this way. I did try to meet with you before dinner."

Her heart suddenly pounding off the register, she stared rigidly at his shoulder. "You could have told me when I called to cancel and given me some time. Even a text would have helped."

His dark brows jerked together. "I'm not in the habit of breaking off relationships over the phone or by text. I wanted to tell you face-to-face."

Her jaw tightened. It didn't help that his gaze was direct, that he was clearly intent on softening the blow. The last thing she wanted from Lucas was pity. "Did Lilah fly in with you?"

"She arrived this afternoon."

Relief made her feel faintly unsteady. So, Lilah hadn't been with Lucas in the limousine.

As insignificant as that detail was, it mattered, because when she had seen the limousine she had been crazily, sappily fantasizing about Lucas and the life they could now share. Although she should have known he hadn't arrived with Lilah, because there hadn't been any media reports that he had arrived at the airport with a female companion.

Lucas's gaze connected with hers. "Before you go back inside, I need to know if you intend to go to the press with a story about our affair."

Affair.

Her chin jerked up. For two years she had considered they had been involved in a relationship. "I'm here for Sienna's wedding. It's her day, and I don't intend to spoil it."

"Good. Because if you try to force my hand by going public with this, take it from me, I'm not playing."

Comprehension hit. She had been so absorbed with the publicity for Ambrosi's latest collection and the crazy rush to organize Sienna's wedding that she had barely had time to sleep, let alone think. When Sienna married Constantine, Carla would be inextricably bound to the Atraeus family.

The Atraeus family were traditionalists. If it were discovered that she and Lucas had been seeing each other secretly for two years, he would come under intense pressure from his family to marry her.

Now the comment about her looking for his rooms made sense.

What better way to force a commitment than to arrange for them both to be found together in his rooms at the *castello?* Anger and a burning sense of shame that he should think she would stoop that low sliced through her. "I hadn't considered that angle."

Why would she when she had assumed Lucas wanted her?

He ignored her statement. "If it's marriage you want, you won't get it by pressuring me."

Which meant he really had thought about the different ways she could force him to the altar. She took a deep breath against a sharp spasm of hurt. "At what point did I ever say I was after marriage?"

His gaze bored into hers, as fierce and obdurate as the dark stone from which the fortress was built. "Then we have an understanding?"

"Oh, I think so." She forced a bright smile. "I wouldn't marry you if you tied me up and dragged me down the aisle. Tell me," she said before she could gag her mouth and instruct her brain to never utter anything that would inform Lucas just how weak and vulnerable she really was. "Did you ever come close to loving me?"

He went still. "What we had wasn't exactly about love."

No. Silly her.

"There's something else we need to talk about."

"In that case, it'll have to wait. Now I really do have a headache." She fumbled in her clutch, searching for the painkillers she'd slipped in before she'd left the villa, just in case. In her haste the foil pack slipped out of her fingers and dropped to the terrace.

Lucas retrieved the pills before she could. "What are these?"

He held the foil pack out of her reach while he read the label. "Since when have you suffered from headaches?"

She snatched the pills from his grasp. "They're a leftover from the virus I caught in Thailand. I don't get them very often."

She ripped the foil open and swallowed two pills dry, grimacing at the extra wave of bitterness in her mouth when one of the pills lodged in her throat. She badly needed a glass of water.

Lucas frowned. "I didn't know you were still having problems."

She shoved the foil pack back in her clutch. "But then you never bothered to ask."

And the last thing she had wanted to do was let him know that she had been so stressed by the unresolved nature of their relationship that she had given herself an even worse stomach ulcer than she had started with two years ago.

After the growing distance between them in Thailand, she hadn't wanted to further undermine their relationship or give him an excuse to break up with her. Keeping silent had been a constant strain because she had wanted the comfort of his presence, had *needed* him near, but now she was glad she hadn't revealed how sick she really had been. It was one small corner of her life that he hadn't invaded, one small batch of memories that didn't contain him.

She felt like kicking herself for being so stupid over the past couple of months. If Lucas had wanted to be with her he would have arranged time together. Once, he had flown into Sydney with only a four-hour window before he'd had to fly out again. They had spent every available second of those four hours locked together in bed.

Cold settled in her stomach. In retrospect, their relationship had foundered in Thailand. Lucas hadn't liked crossing the line into caring; he had simply wanted a pretty, adoring lover and uncomplicated sex.

Lucas was still blocking her path. "You're pale and your eyes are dilated. I'll take you home."

"No." She stepped neatly around him and made a beeline for the open door. Her heart sped up when she realized he was close behind her. "I can drive myself. The last thing I want is to spend any more time with you."

"Too bad." His hand curled around her upper arm, sending a hot, tingling shock straight to the pit of her stomach as he propelled her into the hall. "You've had a couple of glasses of wine, and now a strong painkiller. The last thing you should do is get behind the wheel of that little sports car."

She shot him a coolly assessing look. "Or talk to the paparazzi at the gate."

"Right now it's the hairpin bends on the road back to the villa that worry me."

Something snapped inside her at the calm, matter-of-fact tone of his voice, as if he was conducting damage control in one of his business takeovers. "What do you think I'm going to do, Lucas? Drive off one of your cliffs into the sea?"

Unexpectedly his grip loosened. Twisting free, she grasped the handle of the door to the suite she had briefly checked out before, thinking it could be a bathroom. It was Lucas's suite, apparently. Forbidden territory.

Flinging the door wide, she stepped inside. She was about to prove that at least one of Lucas's fears was justified.

She was going to be her control-freak, ticked-off, stressed-out self for just a few minutes.

She was going to behave badly.

Four

The paralyzing fear that had gripped Lucas at the thought of Carla driving her sports car on Medinos's narrow roads turned to frustration as she stepped inside his suite.

Grimly, he wondered what had happened to the dominance and control with which he had started the evening.

Across boardroom tables, he was aware that his very presence often inspired actual fear. His own people jumped to do his bidding.

Unfortunately, when it came to Carla Ambrosi, concepts like power, control and discipline crashed and burned.

He closed the door behind him. "What do you think you're doing?"

Carla halted by an ebony cabinet that held a selection of bottles, a jug of ice water and a tray of glasses. "I need a drink."

Glass clinked on glass, liquid splashed. His frustration deepened. Carla seldom drank and when she did it had always been in moderation. Tonight he knew she'd had champagne, then wine with dinner. He had kept a watch on her intake, specifically so he could intervene if he thought she was in danger of drinking too much then making a scene. He had been looking for an opportunity to speak to her alone when she had walked out halfway through dessert. Until now he had been certain she wasn't drunk.

He reached her in two long strides and gripped her wrist. "How much have you had?"

Liquid splashed the front of her dress. He jerked his gaze away from the way the wet silk clung to the curve of her breasts.

Her gaze narrowed. A split second later cold liquid cascaded down his chest, soaking through to the skin.

Water, not alcohol.

Time seemed to slow, stop as he stared at her narrowed gaze, delicately molded cheekbones and firm jaw, the rapid pulse at her throat.

The thud of the glass hitting the thick kilim barely registered as she curled her fingers in the lapel of his jacket.

"What do you think you're doing?" His voice was husky, the question automatic as he stared at her face.

"Conducting an experiment."

Her arms slid around his neck; she lifted up onto her toes. Automatically, his head bent. The second his mouth touched hers he knew it was a mistake. Relief shuddered through him as her breasts flattened against his chest and the soft curve of her abdomen cradled his instant arousal.

His hands settled at her waist as he deepened the kiss. The soft, exotic perfume she wore rose up, beguiling him, and the fierce clamp of desire intensified. Two months. As intent as he had been on finishing with Carla, he didn't know how he had stayed away.

No one else did this to him; no one came close. To say he

made love with Carla didn't cover the fierceness of his need or the undisciplined emotion that grabbed at him every time he weakened and allowed himself the "fix" of a small window of time in her bed.

Following the tragedy with Sophie, he had kept his liaisons clear-cut and controlled, as disciplined as his heavy work schedule and workout routines. He had been too shell-shocked to do anything else. Carla was the antithesis of the sophisticated, emotionally secure women he usually chose. Women who didn't demand or do anything flamboyant or off-the-wall.

He dragged his mouth free, shrugged out of his jacket then sank back into the softness of her mouth. He felt her fingers dragging at the buttons of his shirt, the tactile pleasure of her palms sliding over his skin.

Long, drugging minutes passed as he simply kissed her, relearning her touch, her taste. When she moved restlessly against him, he smoothed his hands up over her back, knowing instinctively that if she was going to withdraw, this would be the moment.

Her gaze clashed with his and he logged her assent. It occurred to Lucas that if he had been a true gentleman, he would have eased away, slowed things down. Instead he gave into temptation, cupped her breasts through the flimsy silk of bodice and bra. She arched against him with a small cry. Heat jerked through him when he realized she had climaxed.

Every muscle taut, he swept her into his arms and carried her to the couch. Her arms wound around his neck as she pulled him down with her. At some point his shirt disappeared and Carla shimmied against him, lifting up the few centimeters he needed so he could peel away the flimsy scrap of silk and lace that served as underwear.

He felt her fingers tearing at the fastening of his trousers. In some distant part of his mind the fact that he didn't have a condom registered. A split second later her hands closed around him and he ceased to think.

Desire shivered and burned through Carla as Lucas's hands framed her hips. Still dazed by the unexpected power of her climax, she automatically tilted her hips, allowing him access. Shock reverberated through her when she registered that there was no condom.

She hadn't thought; he hadn't asked. In retrospect she hadn't wanted to ask. She had been drowning in sensation, caught and held by the sudden powerful conviction that if she walked away from Lucas now, everything they had shared, everything they had been to each other would be lost. She would never touch him, kiss him, make love with him again, and that thought was acutely painful.

It was wrong, crazily wrong, on a whole lot of levels. Lucas had broken up with her. He had chosen someone else.

His gaze locked with hers and the steady, focused heat, so utterly familiar—as if she really was the only woman in the world for him—steadied her.

Emotion squeezed her chest as the shattering intensity gripped her again, linking her more intensely with Lucas. She should pull back, disengage. Making love did not compute, and especially not without a condom, but the concept of stopping now was growing progressively more blurred and distant.

She didn't want distance. She loved making love with Lucas. She loved his scent, the satiny texture of skin, the masculine beauty of sleek, hard muscle. The tender way he touched her, kissed her, made love to her was indescribably singular and intimate. She had never made love with another man, and when they were together, for those moments, he was *hers*.

Sharp awareness flickered in his gaze. He muttered something in rapid, husky Medinian, an apology for his loss of control, and a wild sliver of hope made her tense. If Lucas had wanted her badly enough that he hadn't been able to stop long enough to take care of protection, then there had to be a future for them.

With a raw groan he tangled his fingers in her hair, a glint of rueful humor charming her as he bent and softly kissed her. Something small and hurt inside her relaxed. She wound her arms around his neck, holding him tight against her and the hot night shivered and dissolved around them.

For long minutes Carla lay locked beneath Lucas on the couch. She registered the warm internal tingle of lovemaking. It had been two months since they had last been together, and she took a moment to wallow in the sheer pleasure of his heat and scent, the uncomplicated sensuality of his weight pressing her down.

She rubbed her palms down his back and felt his instant response.

Lucas's head lifted up from its resting place on her shoulder. The abrupt wariness in his gaze reflected her own thoughts. They'd had unprotected sex once. Were they really going to repeat the mistake?

A sharp rap at the door completed the moment of separation.

"Wait," Lucas said softly.

She felt the cool flutter as he draped her dress over her thighs. Feeling dazed and guilty, Carla clambered to her feet, snatched up her panties and her bag and found her shoes.

"The bathroom is the second on the left."

Her head jerked up at the husky note in his voice, but Lucas's expression was back to closed, his gaze neutral.

He was already dressed. With his shirt buttoned, his jacket on, he looked smoothly powerful and unruffled, exactly as he had before they had made love. Somewhere inside her the sliver of hope that had flared to life when they had been making love died a sudden death.

Nothing had changed. How many times had she seen him distance himself from her in just that way when he had left her apartment, as if he had already separated himself from her emotionally?

As if what they had shared was already filed firmly in the past and she had no place in his everyday life.

The moment was chilling, a reality check that was long overdue. "Don't worry, I'll find it. I don't want anyone to know I was here, either." Her own voice was husky but steady. Despite the hurt she felt oddly distant and remote.

She stepped into the cool, tiled sanctuary of the bathroom and locked the door. After freshening up she set about fixing her makeup. A sharp rap on the door made her jerk, smearing her mascara.

"When you're ready, I'll take you home."

"Five minutes. And I'll take myself home."

She stared at her reflection, her too pale skin, the curious blankness in her eyes as if, like a turtle retreating into its shell, the hurt inner part of her had already withdrawn. With automatic movements, she cleaned away the smear and reapplied the mascara.

When she stepped out of the bathroom the sitting room was empty. For the first time she noticed the fine antiques and jewel-bright rugs, the art that decorated the walls and which was lit by glowing pools of light.

Lucas stepped in from the terrace, through an elegant set of French doors.

She met his gaze squarely. "Who was at the door?"

"Lilah."

Oh, good. Her life had just officially gone to hell in a handbasket. "Did she see me?"

"Unfortunately."

Lucas's choice of word finally succeeded in dissolving the curious blankness and suddenly she was fiercely angry. "What if I'm pregnant?"

A pulse worked in his jaw. "If you're pregnant, that changes things—we'll talk. Until you have confirmation, we forget this happened."

When Carla woke in the morning, the headache was still nagging, and she was definitely off-color. She stepped into the shower and washed her hair. When she'd soaped herself, she stood beneath the stream of hot water and waited to feel better.

She spread her palm over her flat abdomen, a sense of disorientation gripping her when she considered that she could be pregnant.

A baby.

The thought was as shocking as the fact that she had been weak enough to allow Lucas to make love to her.

If she was pregnant, she decided, there was no way she could terminate. She loved babies, the way they smelled, their downy softness and vulnerability, the gummy smiles—and she would adore her own.

Decision made. If—and it was a big *if*—she was pregnant she would have the child and manage as a single parent. Lucas wouldn't have to be involved. There was no way she would marry him without love, or exist in some kind of twilight state in his life that would allow him discreet access while he married someone else.

Turning off the water, she toweled herself dry, belted on a robe and padded down to breakfast. Her stomach felt vaguely nauseous and she wasn't hungry, but she forced herself to chew one of the sweet Medinian rolls she had enjoyed so much yesterday.

Half an hour later, she checked on Sienna, who was

smothered by attendants, then dressed for the wedding in an exquisite lilac-silk sheath. She sat for the hairdresser, who turned her hair into a glossy confection of curls piled on top of her head, then moved to another room where a cosmetician chatted cheerfully while she did her makeup.

Several hours later, with the wedding formalities finally completed and the dancing under way, she was finally free to leave her seat at the bridal table. Technically, as the maid of honor, her partner for the celebration was Lucas, who was the best man. Mercifully, he was seated to one side of the bride and groom, and she the other, so she had barely seen him all evening.

As she rose from the table and found the strap of her purse, which was looped over the back of her seat, lean brown fingers closed over hers, preventing her from lifting up the bag.

A short, sharp shock ran through her at the pressure. Lucas released his hold on her fingers almost immediately.

He indicated Constantine and Sienna drifting around the dance floor. "I know you probably don't want to dance, but tradition demands that we take the floor next."

She glanced away from the taut planes of his cheekbones and his chiseled jaw, the inky crescents of his lashes. In a morning suit, with its tight waistcoat, he looked even more devastatingly handsome than usual. "And is that what you do?" she said a little bitterly. "Follow tradition?"

Lucas waited patiently for her to acquiesce to the dance. "You know me better than that."

Yes, she did, unfortunately. As wealthy and privileged as Lucas was, he had done a number of unconventional things. One of them was to play professional rugby. Her gaze rested on the faintly battered line of his nose. An automatic tingle of awareness shot through her at the dangerous, sexy edge it added to features that would otherwise have been *GQ* perfect.

His gaze locked on hers and, as suddenly as if a switch had been thrown, the sizzling hum of attraction was intimately, crazily shared.

Her breath came in sharply. Not good.

Aware that they were now under intense scrutiny from guests at a nearby table, including Lilah, Carla placed her hand on Lucas's arm and allowed him to lead her to the dance floor.

Lucas's breath feathered her cheek as he pulled her close. "How likely is it that you are pregnant?"

She stiffened at the sudden hot flood of memory. On cue the music changed, slowing to a sultry waltz. Lucas pulled her into a closer hold. Heat shivered through her as her body automatically responded to his touch. "Not likely."

Since the virus she had caught in Thailand she hadn't had a regular cycle, mostly because, initially, she had lost so much weight. She had regained some of the weight but she hadn't yet had a period. Although she wasn't about to inform Lucas of that fact.

"How soon will you know?"

"I'm not sure. Two weeks, give or take."

"When you find out, one way or the other, I want to be informed, but that shouldn't be a problem. As of next week, I'm Ambrosi's new CEO."

She stumbled, missing a step. Lucas's arm tightened and she found herself briefly pressed against his muscular frame. Jerkily, she straightened, her cheeks burning at the intimate brush of his hips, a stark reminder of their lovemaking last night. "I thought Ben Vitalis was stepping in as CEO."

Lucas's specialty was managing hostile acquisitions. Since her family, embattled by long-term debt, had voluntarily offered The Atraeus Group a majority shareholding of Ambrosi Pearls, the situation was cut-and-dried. Lucas shouldn't have come within a mile of Ambrosi.

Unless he viewed *her* as a problem.

Her chin jerked up as another thought occurred to her. "You told Constantine about us."

His brows jerked together. "No."

Relief flooded her. The thought that Lucas could have revealed their relationship now, when it was over, would have finally succeeded in making her feel cheap and disposable.

She drew in a steadying breath. "When was the decision made?"

"A few weeks ago, when we knew Ambrosi was in trouble."

"It's not necessary for you to come to Sydney. In the unlikely event that there is a baby, I will contact you."

His glance was impatient. "The decision is made."

She drew an impeded breath at the sudden graphic image of herself round and heavy with his child. She didn't think a pregnancy was possible, but clearly Lucas did.

The music wound to a sweeping, romantic halt. There was a smattering of applause. Carla allowed Lucas to complete the formalities by leading her off the dance floor.

The rest of the evening passed in a haze. Carla danced with several men she didn't know, and twice with Alex Panopoulos, an Ambrosi client she'd had extensive dealings with in Sydney. The wealthy owner of a successful chain of high-end retail stores, Alex was a reptile when it came to women. He was also in need of a public relations officer for a new venture and spent the first dance fishing to see if she was available. Halfway through the second dance, Lucas cut in.

His gaze clashed with hers as he spun her into a sweeping turn. "Damn. What are you doing with Panopoulos?"

"Nothing that's any of your business. Why? Do you think

I'm in danger of meeting a man who might actually propose?"

"Alex Panopoulos is a shrewd operator. When he marries, there will be a business connection."

She stared at the clean line of his jaw. "Are you suggesting that all he wants is an affair?"

His grip on her fingers tightened. "I have no idea what Panopoulos wants. All I know is that when it comes to women he doesn't have a very savory reputation."

"I'm surprised you think I need protection."

"Trust me, you don't want to get involved with Panopoulos."

Dragging free of his gaze, she stared at the muscular column of his throat. "Maybe he wanted something from me that has nothing to do with sex? Besides, you're wasting your breath trying to protect me. From now on, who I choose to be with is none of your business."

"It is if you're pregnant."

The flash of possessive heat in his gaze and the tightening of his hold finally succeeded in making her lose her temper. "I might have some say in that."

Five

Lucas leaned against the wall in a dim alcove, arms folded over his chest as he observed the final formality of the wedding, the throwing of the bouquet.

Zane joined him, shifting through the shadows with the fluid ease that was more a by-product of his time spent on the streets of L.A. than of the strict, conventional upbringing he'd received on Medinos. He nodded at Carla, who was part of a cluster of young women gathered on the dance floor. "Not your finest hour. But, if you hadn't rescued her, I was thinking of doing it myself."

"Touch Carla," Lucas said softly, "and you lose your hand."

Zane took a swallow of beer. "Thought so."

Lucas eyed his younger brother with irritation. Four years difference and he felt like Methuselah. "How long have you known?"

"About a year, give or take."

The bouquet arced through the air straight into Carla's hands. Lucas's jaw tightened as she briskly handed it to one of the pretty young flower girls and detached herself from the noisy group. She made a beeline for her table, picked up the lilac clutch that went with her dress, and made her way out of the *castello's* ballroom.

Lucas glanced at Zane. "Do me a favor and look after Lilah for me for the rest of the evening."

Zane's expression registered rare startlement. "Let me get this right, you won't let me near Carla, but with Lilah it's okay?"

Lucas frowned at his turn of phrase, but his attention was focused on the elegant line of Carla's back. "The party's almost over. An hour, max."

"That long."

Impatiently, he studied the now empty hallway. "She'll need a ride back to the villa."

"Not a problem. Aunts at six o'clock." With a jerk of his chin, indicating direction, Zane snagged his beer and made a swift exit.

Pushing away from the wall, Lucas started after Carla, and found himself the recipient of a shrewd glance from his mother and steely speculation from a gaggle of silver-haired great-aunts.

He groaned inwardly, annoyed that he had dropped his guard enough that not only Zane but his mother had become aware of his interest in Carla. The last thing he needed was his mother interfering in his love life.

Seconds later, he traversed the vaulted hallway and stepped outside onto the graveled driveway just as the sound of Constantine and Sienna's departing helicopter cut the air.

The sun was gone, the night thick with stars, but heat still flowed out of the sunbaked soil as he strode toward Carla.

The ambient temperature was still hot enough that he felt uncomfortable in his suit jacket.

A stiff sea breeze was blowing, tugging strands loose from the rich, dark coils piled on top of Carla's head, making her look sexily disheveled. The breeze also plastered her dress against her body, emphasizing just how much weight she had lost.

His frown deepened. A regular gym bunny, Carla had always been fit and toned, with firm but definite curves. The curves were still there but if he didn't miss his guess she had dropped at least a dress size. After the virus she had picked up in Thailand, weight loss was understandable, but she should have regained it by now.

She spun when she heard the crunch of gravel beneath his shoes. A small jolt went through him when he registered the blankness of her gaze.

Carla didn't do sad. She had always been confident, sassy and adept at using her feminine power to the max. For Carla, masculine conquest was as natural as breathing. He had assumed that when their relationship was at an end she would have a lineup of prospective boyfriends eager to fill the gap.

In that moment it hit him forcibly that as similar as Carla was to Sophie with her job and her lifestyle, there were some differences. Sophie had been immature and self-centered, while Carla was fiercely loyal to her sister and her family, to the point of putting her own needs aside so as not to hurt Sienna. Even though that loyalty had clashed with what he had wanted, he had respected it. It also occurred to him that in her own way, Carla had been fiercely loyal to him. She had dated other men, but only ever in a business context for Ambrosi Pearls.

Broodingly, he considered the fact that Carla had been a virgin the first time they had made love, that she had never slept with anyone but him. He realized he had conveniently pushed the knowledge aside because it hadn't fitted the picture of Carla he had wanted to see.

He had been the one who had held back and played it safe, not Carla, and now the sheer intimacy of their situation kept hitting him like a kick to the chest.

He should let her go, but the shattering fact that he could have made her pregnant had changed something vital in his hard drive.

They were linked, at least until he had ascertained whether or not she was carrying his child. Despite his need to end the relationship, he couldn't help but feel relieved about that fact. "The limousines are gone. If you want a lift, I'll drive you."

"That won't be necessary." Carla extracted a cell phone from her clutch. "I'll get a taxi."

"Unless you've prebooked, with all the guests on Medinos for the wedding, you'll have difficulty getting one tonight."

She frowned as she flipped the phone closed and slipped it back in her clutch. "Then I'll ask Constantine."

He jerked his head in the direction of the helicopter, which was rapidly turning into a small dot on the horizon. "Constantine is on honeymoon. I'll take you."

Her glare was pointed. "I don't understand what you're doing out here. Shouldn't you be looking after your new girlfriend?"

"Zane's taking care of Lilah." Before she could argue, he cupped her elbow and steered her in the direction of the *castello's* stable of garages.

She jerked free of his hold. "Why doesn't Zane take me home and you go and take care of Lilah?"

His jaw clamped. "Do you want the lift or not?"

She stared at a point somewhere just left of his shoulder. Enough time passed that his temper began to spiral out of control.

Carla shrugged. "I'll accept a lift because I need one, but please don't touch me again."

"I wasn't trying to 'touch' you."

Her gaze connected with his, shooting blue fire. "I know what you were doing. The same thing you tried to do on the dance floor. Save it for Lilah."

He suppressed the cavemanlike urge to simply pick her up and carry her to the car. "You don't look well. What's wrong with you?"

"Nothing that a good night's sleep won't fix." Her gaze narrowed. "Why don't you say what's really bothering you? That, with all the paparazzi still on the loose, you can't take the risk that I might give them a story? And I think we both know that I could give them quite a story, an exposé of the *real* Lucas—"

Lucas gave in to the caveman urge and picked her up. "Did I mention the paparazzi?"

She thumped his shoulder with her beaded purse. "Let me down!"

Obligingly, he set her down by the passenger door of the Maserati. He jerked the door open. "Get in. If you try to run I'll come after you."

"There has to be a law against this." But she climbed into the sleek leather bucket seat.

"On Medinos?" Despite his temper, Lucas's mouth twitched as he slid behind the wheel and turned the key in the ignition. For the first time in two months he felt oddly content. "Not for an Atraeus."

Carla's tension skyrocketed when, instead of responding to her request and parking out on the street, Lucas drove into the cobbled driveway of the villa. At that point, he insisted on taking the house key from her and unlocked the door. When she attempted to close the door on him, he simply stepped past her and walked into the small, elegant house, switching on lights.

A narky little tension headache throbbing at her temples, Carla made a beeline for the bathroom, filled the glass on the counter with water and took her pills. Refilling the glass, she sat down on the edge of the bath and sipped, waiting to feel better.

A sharp rap on the bathroom door made her temper soar. She had hoped Lucas would take the hint and leave, but apparently he was still in the house. Replacing the glass on the counter, she checked her appearance then unlocked the door and stepped out into the hall.

He was leaning against the wall, arms crossed over his chest. She tried not to notice that, though he was still wearing his jacket, his tie and waistcoat were gone and several buttons of his shirt were undone revealing a mouthwatering slice of bronzed skin. "I'm fine now. You can leave."

She stepped past him and headed for the front door. Her spine tightened as Lucas followed too close behind, and she remembered what had happened the last time they had been alone together.

Note to self, she thought grimly as he peeled off into the sitting room and picked up his tie and waistcoat, *do not allow yourself to be alone with Lucas again.*

Opening the front door, she stood to one side, allowing him plenty of space. "Thank you for the lift."

He paused at the open door, making her aware of his height, the width of his shoulders, the power and vitality that seemed to burn from him. "Maybe you should see a doctor."

"If I need medical help, I'll get it for myself." She glanced pointedly at her wristwatch, resisting the urge to squint because one of the annoying symptoms of the headache now seemed to be that her eyes were ultrasensitive to light.

Not good. Her doctor had warned her that stress could

cause a viral relapse. With her father's funeral, Sienna's wedding and the breakup with Lucas, she was most definitely under stress.

His hand landed on the wall beside her head. Suddenly he was close enough that his heat engulfed her, and his clean, faintly exotic scent filled her nostrils.

Grimly, she resisted the impulse to take the half step needed, wrap her arms around his neck and melt into a goodnight kiss that would very likely turn into something else. "Um, shouldn't you be getting back to Lilah?"

For the briefest of moments he hesitated. His gaze dropped to her mouth and despite the tiredness that pulled at her, she found herself holding her breath, awareness humming through every cell of her being.

He let out a breath. "We can't do this again."

"No." But it had been an effort to say that one little word, and humiliation burned through her that, despite everything, she was still weak enough to want him.

His hand closed into a fist beside her head, then he was gone, the door closing gently behind him.

Carla leaned her forehead against the cool cedar of the door, her face burning.

Darn, darn, darn. Why had she almost given in to him? Like a mindless, trained automaton responding to the merest suggestion that he might kiss her.

After the stern talking-to she had given herself following the episode on the dance floor, she had succeeded in making herself look needy, like a woman who would do anything to get him back into her bed.

The pressure at her temples sharpened. Feeling more unsteady by the second, as if she was coming down with the flu, Carla walked to her bedroom. The acute sensitivity of her eyes was making it difficult to stand being in a lit room. No doubt about it, the virus had taken hold.

Removing her jewelry, she changed into cool cotton drawstring pants and a tank. She pulled on a cotton sweatshirt and cozy slippers against the chill and walked through to the bathroom. After washing and moisturizing her face, she pulled the pins out of her hair, which was an instant relief.

A discreet vibration made her frown. Her cell phone had a musical ring tone, and so did Sienna's. Margaret Ambrosi didn't own a cell, which meant the phone must belong to Lucas.

She padded barefoot into the sitting room in time to see the phone vibrate itself off the coffee table and drop to the carpet. A small pinging sound followed.

Carla picked up the phone. Lucas had missed a call from Lilah; now he had a text message, also from Lilah.

Fingers shaking slightly, she attempted to read the text but was locked out. A message popped up requesting she unlock the phone.

Not a problem, unless Lucas had changed his PIN since the last time they had dated.

Not dated, she corrected, her mood taking another dive. *Slept together.*

The last time he had stayed over at her apartment, before the holiday in Thailand, Lucas had needed to buy a new phone. The PIN he had used had been her birth date. At the time she had been ridiculously happy at his sentimental streak. She had taken it as a definite, positive *sign* that their relationship was progressing in the right direction.

She held her breath as she keyed in the number. The mail menu opened up.

The message was simple and to the point. Lilah was waiting for Lucas to call and would stay up until she heard from him.

The sick feeling in her stomach, the prickling chill she'd felt when he had broken up with her the previous night, came back at her full force. If she'd needed reinforcement of her decision to stay clear of Lucas Atraeus, this was it.

He was involved with someone else. He had *chosen* someone else, and the new woman in his life was waiting for him.

Closing the message, she replaced the phone on the coffee table and walked back to the bathroom. She switched off lights as she went, leaving one lamp burning in the sitting room for her mother when she came home. The relief of semidarkness was immense.

In the space of the past few minutes, she realized, the throbbing in her head had intensified and her skin hurt to touch. She swallowed another headache tablet, washing it down with sips of water. The sound of the doorbell jerked her head up. The sharp movement sent a stab of hot pain through her skull.

Lucas, back for his phone.

Setting the glass down, she walked back out to the hall, which was lit by the glow from the porch light streaming through two frosted sidelight windows. The buzzer sounded again.

"Open up, Carla. All I want is my phone."

That particular request, she decided, was the equivalent of waving a red rag at a bull. "You can have the phone tomorrow."

"I still have the key to this door," he said quietly. "If you don't unlock it, I'll let myself in."

Over her dead body.

"Just a minute." Annoyed with herself for forgetting to reclaim the key, she reached for the chain and tried to engage it. In her haste it slipped from her fingers.

She heard Lucas say something short and sharp. Adrenaline pumped. He knew she was trying to chain the door against him. The metallic scrape of a key being inserted into the lock was preternaturally loud as she grabbed the chain again.

Before she could slot it into place the door swung open, pushing her back a half step. Normally, the half step back wouldn't have fazed her, but with the weird shakiness of the virus she was definitely not her normal, athletic self and had to clutch at the hall table to help with her balance. Something crashed to the floor; glass shattered. She registered that when she had grabbed at the table her shoulder must have brushed against a framed watercolor mounted on the wall.

Lucas frowned. "Don't move."

Ignoring him, she bent down and grasped the edge of the frame.

Lean fingers curled around her upper arms, hauling her upright. "Leave that. You'll cut yourself."

Too late. Curling her thumb in against her palm, she made a fist, hiding a tiny, stinging jab that as far as she was concerned was so small it didn't count as a cut. She blinked at the bright porch light. "I didn't give you permission to come in, and you don't have the right to give me orders."

"You *did* cut yourself." He muttered something in Medinian. She was pretty sure it was a curse word. "Give me the watercolor before you do any more damage."

Her grip on the watercolor firmed, even though his request made sense. If she got blood on the painting it would be ruined. "I don't need your help. Get your phone and go."

"You look terrible."

"Thanks!"

"You're as white as a sheet."

He released her so suddenly she swayed off balance. By the time she recovered he had laid claim to her sore thumb and was probing at the small cut. But she still had the painting. "Neat trick."

His gaze was oddly intent. "There doesn't seem to be any glass in it."

He wrapped a handkerchief around her thumb and closed her fingers around it to apply pressure. "How long have you been sick?"

Her jaw tightened. She was being childish, she knew, but she hated being sick. It literally brought out the worst in her. "I'm not sick. Like I said before, all I need is a good night's sleep, so if you don't mind—"

The brush of his fingers against her temple as he pushed hair away from her face distracted her.

"Does that hurt? Don't answer. I can see that it does."

He leaned close. Arrested by his nearness, she studied the taut line of his jaw, suddenly assaulted by a myriad of sensations—the heat from Lucas's body, the clean scent of his skin, the rasp of his indrawn breath. That was one of the weird things about the virus: it seemed to amplify everything, hearing, scent, emotions, as if protective layers had been peeled away, leaving her senses bare and open.

In a slick move, he took the watercolor while her attention was occupied by the intriguing shape of his cheekbones, which were meltdown material.

A small sound informed her that he had placed the painting on the hall table. Out of nowhere her stomach turned an uncomfortable somersault. "I think I'm going to be sick."

His hand closed around her upper arm, and the heat from his palm burned through the cotton sweatshirt. Then they were moving, glass crunching under the soles of her slippers as he guided her out of the entrance hall into the sitting room. Another turn and they were in the bathroom.

Long minutes later, she rinsed her mouth and washed her face. She had hoped that Lucas would have left, but he was leaning against the hallway wall looking patient and composed and drop-dead gorgeous. In contrast she felt bedraggled and washed-out and as limp as a noodle.

Disgust and a taut, burning humiliation filled her. It was a rerun of Thailand, everything she had never wanted to happen again.

He folded his arms across his chest. "I'm guessing this is a relapse of the virus."

Keeping one hand on the wall for steadiness, she made a beeline for her bedroom. "Apparently. This is the first recurrence I've had." Her head spun and for a split second she thought she might be sick again, although she was fairly certain there was nothing left in her stomach. Two more wavering steps then the blissful darkness of her bedroom enfolded her. "Don't turn on the light. And don't come in here. This is *my* room." And as such it was off-limits to men who didn't love her.

"You should have told me you were still ill."

Her temper flashed, but if it was measured on a color spectrum it would have been a washed-out pink, not the angry red it had been earlier in the evening. She didn't have the energy for anything more and she was fading fast. "I didn't *know* I was still ill."

"That's some temper you've got."

Her teeth would have gritted if she'd had the strength. "Inherited it from my mother." She dragged her coverlet back. "She'll be home soon." The thought filled her with extreme satisfaction. She hadn't been able to kick Lucas's butt out, but Margaret Ambrosi would. Especially if she found him in her little girl's room.

Gingerly she sat on the side of the bed. Now that the stomach issue was over her attention was back on her head, which was pounding. What she needed was another painkiller, because the last one had just been flushed.

Dimly, she registered that despite her express order, Lucas *was* in her room. "I told you not to be here."

He crouched down and eased her slippers off her feet. "Or what? You'll lose that famous temper?"

"That's right." A shiver went through her at the burning heat of his hands on her feet. The chill on her skin made her realize that the next stage of the virus was kicking in. Oh, goody, she thought wearily, Antarctic-cold shivers followed by sweats that rivaled burning desert sands. Exactly how she always wanted to spend a Saturday night.

"I'll take the risk. I survived Thailand, I can survive this."

He pulled her to her feet. Her nose bumped against his shoulder. Automatically, she clutched his lean waist and leaned into his comforting strength. She inhaled, breathing in his scent, and for a crazy moment all she wanted to do was rest there.

A split second later, the sheet peeled back, Lucas eased her into bed and pulled the sheets and coverlet over her.

With a sigh, she allowed her head to sink into the feather pillow. "All I need is another one of the painkillers on the bathroom vanity and some water and I'll be fine." It was surrender, she knew it, but she really did need the pill.

She registered his near silent footfalls as he walked to the bathroom, the hiss of water as he filled the glass, then he was back. His arm came around her shoulders as he propped her up so she could take the pill and drink the water. When she was finished he set the glass down on her bedside table.

She settled back on the pillows. "You know what? You're good at this."

"I had lots of practice in Thailand. Do you need anything else?" His voice was closer now, the timbre low and deliciously gruff.

It was the kind of velvety masculine rumble that, if they had been in bed together, would have invited a snuggling session. Then suddenly she remembered. Lucas was with Lilah now; he no longer wanted her. If he felt anything for her, it had to be pity. A weak, watered-down version of fury roared through her.

She peeled her lids open and peered at Lucas, ready to read him the riot act, then forgot what she was about to say because there was a strange, intent expression on his face. "Nothing. You can leave. Phone's on the coffee table. That was what you came for, wasn't it?"

He was so close she could feel the heat blasting off his body, see his gaze sliding over her features, cataloging her white face and messy hair. For shallow, utterly female reasons she wished that her face was glowing instead of chalky-white and that she had taken the time to brush her hair. Mercifully, the strong painkiller finally kicked in, taking the heat out of the ache in her head and dragging her down into sleep. "I don't want you here."

It was a lie. The virus had made her so weak that she was fast losing the strength to keep up the charade, even to herself.

"I'm staying until I know you'll be all right."

"I would like you to leave. Now." The crisp delivery she intended was spoiled by the fact that the words ran together in a drunken, blurred jumble.

She was certain the soft exhalation she heard had something to do with amusement, which made her even more furious. The mattress shifted as he planted a hand on either side of her head and leaned close. "What are you going to do if I don't? Make me leave?"

For a crazy moment she thought he was actually flirting with her, but that couldn't be. "Don't have to," she mumbled, settling the argument. Her eyelids slid closed. "You've already gone."

Silence settled around her, thick, heavy, as the sedative effect of the pills dragged her down.

"Do you want me back?"

The words jerked her awake, but they had been uttered so quietly she wasn't sure if she had imagined them or if Lucas had actually spoken.

She could see him standing in her bedroom doorway. Maybe she had been dreaming, or worse, hallucinating. "I took codeine, not truth serum."

"It was worth a try."

So he *had* asked the question.

She pushed up on one elbow. The suspicion that he was sneakily trying to interrogate her while she was drowsy from the pills solidified. Although she couldn't fathom why he would be interested in what she really thought and felt now. "I don't know why you're bothering. Thank you for helping me, but please leave now."

He shook his head. "You're...different tonight."

Different? She had been dumped. She had committed the cardinal sin of making love with her ex and could quite possibly be pregnant.

"Not different." Turning over, she punched the pillow and willed herself to go to sleep. "Real."

Six

Ten days later, Carla strolled into the Ambrosi building in Sydney.

When she reached her office, her assistant, Elise, a chirpy blonde with a marketing degree and a formidable memory for names and statistics, was in the process of hanging up the phone. "Lucas wants you in his office. *Now*."

A jolt of fiery irritation instantly evaporated the peace and calm of four days spent recuperating at her mother's house, the other five in the blissful solitude of the Blue Mountains at a friend's holiday home. "Did he say why?"

Elise looked dreamily reflective. "He's male, hot *and* single. Does it matter?"

Nerves taut, Carla continued on to her desk and deliberately took time out to examine the list of messages and calls Elise had compiled in her absence. Keeping her bag hooked over her shoulder, she checked her calendar and noted she had two meetings scheduled.

When she couldn't stall any longer, she strolled to Sienna's old office, frowning at the changes Atraeus money had already made to her family's faltering business. Worn blue carpet had been replaced with a sleek, dove-gray weave. Fresh paint and strategically placed art now graced walls that had once been decorated solely with monochrome prints of Ambrosi jewelry designs.

Feeling oddly out of place in what, from childhood, had been a cozily familiar setting, she greeted work colleagues.

Directing a brittle smile at Sienna's personal assistant, Nina—Lucas's PA now—she stepped into the elegant corner office.

Lucas, broad shouldered and sleekly powerful in a dark suit with a crisp white shirt and red tie, dominated a room that was still manifestly feminine as he stood at the windows, a phone held to one ear.

His gaze locked with hers, he terminated the call. "Close the door behind you and take a seat."

Suddenly glad she had made an extra effort with her appearance, she closed the door. The sharp little red suit, with its short skirt and fitted V-necked jacket, always made her feel attractive and energized. It probably wasn't the best idea for dealing with Lucas, but she hadn't worn it for him. She had a job interview at five with Alex Panopoulos, and she needed to look confident and professional. His upmarket Pan department stores were branching into jewelry manufacture and he had been chasing her all week to come in for an interview.

She hated the idea of leaving Ambrosi Pearls, but she had to be pragmatic about her position. When Constantine had offered the company back to Sienna on her wedding day they had held a family meeting. In essence, they had agreed to honour their debts, so the transfer of the company to The Atraeus Group had gone through as planned. With Sienna's marriage to Constantine binding both families together, combined with Constantine's assurance that he would keep the company intact, it had seemed the most sensible solution.

As a consequence, Carla now owned a block of voting shares. They would assure her of an income for the rest of her life, but they gave her no effective power. Her current personal contract as Ambrosi Pearls's public relations executive was up for renewal directly after Ambrosi's new product launch in a week's time. She didn't anticipate that Lucas would renew it. Her tenure as "The Face of Ambrosi" was just as shaky, but as she provided that service for free to help the company save money, it was no skin off her nose if Lucas no longer wanted her face on the posters.

Annoyance flickered in Lucas's gaze when she didn't immediately sit. He replaced the phone on its base. "I didn't expect you back in so soon."

She lifted a brow. "I felt okay, so there was no point in staying at home."

"I've been trying to reach you all week. Why didn't you return my calls?"

She shrugged. "I was staying with friends and didn't take my phone." She had left the phone at her apartment on purpose. The last thing she had needed was to have a desperately low moment and make the fatal mistake of trying to call or text Lucas.

There was a small charged silence. "How are you?"

"Fine. A couple of days in bed and the symptoms disappeared." She smiled brightly. "If that's all…"

"Not exactly." His gaze rested on her waist, where the jacket cinched in tight. "Are you pregnant?"

Despite her effort at control, heat flooded her cheeks. "I don't know yet. I have a test kit, but it's early to get an accurate reading."

"When will you know?"

She frowned, feeling distinctly uncomfortable with the subject and the way he was regarding her, as if she was a concubine who had somehow escaped the harem and he had ownership rights. "I should know in another couple of days. But whether I'm pregnant or not, it needn't concern you."

Actually, she could find out right that minute if she wanted. The test kit had said a result could be obtained in as early as seven days. She had studied the instructions then chucked the box in the back of one of her drawers. She still felt too raw and hurt to face using the kit and discovering that not only had she lost Lucas, her life was about to take a huge, unplanned turn. In a few days, when she felt ready, she would do the test.

Anger flickered in his gaze. "You would abort the child?"

"No." She felt shocked that he had even jumped to that conclusion. If there was a child, there was no way she would do anything other than keep the baby and smother it with love for the rest of its life. "What I meant is that *if* there is a child, I've decided that you don't have to worry, because you don't need to be involved, or even acknowledge—"

"Any child of mine would be acknowledged."

The whiplash flatness of his voice, as if she had scraped a raw nerve, was even more shocking. Carla sucked in a breath and forced herself to loosen off the soaring tension. She was clearly missing something here. "This is crazy. I don't know why we're discussing something that might never happen. Is that all you wanted to know?"

"No." He propped himself on the edge of the desk. "Have a seat. There's something else we need to discuss."

There were three comfortable client seats; she chose the one farthest away from Lucas. The second she lowered herself into the chair she regretted the decision. Even though he wasn't standing, Lucas still towered over her. "Let me guess—I'm fired in a week's time? I'm surprised it took you so long to get around to—"

"I'm not firing you."

Carla blinked. Constantine had fired Sienna almost immediately, although his reasons had been understandable. Continuing on as CEO of a company in Sydney while he was based in Medinos had not been viable.

His gaze flicked broodingly over the crisp little suit. "Do you always dress like that for work?"

His sudden change of tack threw her even more off balance. She realized that from his vantage point he could see more than the shadowy hint of cleavage that was normally visible in the vee of the jacket. She squashed the urge to drag the lapels together. "Yes. Is there a problem?"

He crossed his arms over his chest. "Nothing that an extra button or a blouse wouldn't fix."

She shot to her feet. "There is nothing wrong with what I'm wearing. Sienna was perfectly happy with my wardrobe."

He straightened, making her even more aware of his height, the breadth of his shoulders, the incomprehensible anger simmering behind midnight-dark eyes.

"Sienna was female."

"What has that got to do with anything?"

"From where I'm standing, quite a lot.

She didn't know what was bothering him. Maybe a major deal had fallen through, or even better, Lilah had dumped him. Whatever it was she would swear that he was behaving proprietorially, but that couldn't be. He had dumped her without ceremony; he had made it clear he didn't want her. To add insult to injury, the tabloids were having a field day reporting his relationship with Lilah.

His gaze dropped once again to the vee of her jacket. "Who are you meeting today?"

Temper soaring at the lightning perusal, the even more pointed innuendo, she reeled off two names.

"Both male," he said curtly.

"Chandler and Howarth are contemporaries of my father! And I resent the implication that I would resort to using sex to make sales for Ambrosi, but if you prefer I could turn up for work in beige. Or, since this conversation is taking a medieval turn, maybe you'd prefer sackcloth and ashes."

His mouth twitched at the corners and despite her spiraling anger she found herself briefly mesmerized by the sudden jolt of charm. Lucas was handsome when he was cool and ruthless, but when he smiled he was drop-dead gorgeous in a completely masculine way that made her go weak at the knees and melt.

"You don't own anything beige."

"How would you know?" she pointed out, glad to get her teeth into something that could generate some self-righteous anger.

She wasn't vengeful, nor did she have a desire to hurt Lucas. It was simply that she was black-and-white in her thinking. They were either together or they weren't, and she couldn't bear the underlying invitation in his eyes, his voice, to be friends now that he had decreed their relationship was over. "As I recall, you were more interested in taking my clothes off than noticing what I was wearing. You had no more interest in my wardrobe than you had in any other aspect of my life."

His brows jerked together. "That's not true. You were the one who decreed we had to live separate lives."

Her hands curled into fists. "Don't say it didn't suit you."

"It did, at the time."

"Ha!" But the moment of triumph was hollow. She just wished she had realized she wasn't built for such a shallow, restricted relationship.

Pointedly, she checked her wristwatch. "I have a meeting in ten minutes. If there's nothing else, I need to go. With the product launch in two days' time, there's a lot to do."

"That's what I wanted to talk to you about. We've made some changes to the arrangements for the launch party. Nina will be heading up the team running the promotion."

Not fired, Carla thought blankly. Sidelined.

She took a deep breath and let it out slowly, but when she spoke her voice was still unacceptably husky. "Some product launch without the most high-profile component, or have you forgotten that I'm 'The Face of Ambrosi'?"

Broodingly, Lucas surveyed Carla's perfect face, exquisite in every detail from exotic eyes to delicate cheekbones and enticing mouth. Add in the outrageously sexy tousle of dark hair trailing down her back and she was spectacularly irresistible.

Ambrosi had cut costs and cashed in on Carla's appeal, but he found himself grimly annoyed every time he noticed one of the posters. "It's hard to miss when your face is plastered all over the front of the building."

And in every one of the perfumed women's magazines he had been forced to flick through since he'd stepped into Sienna Ambrosi's front office.

Triumph glowed briefly in her gaze. "You can't sideline me. I have to be there." She began ticking off all the reasons he couldn't surgically remove her from the campaign.

His frustration levels increased exponentially with every valid reason, from interviews with women's magazines to a promotional stunt she had organized.

"I have to be there—it's a no-brainer. Besides, the costuming has all been completed to my measurements."

He cut her off in midstream. "No."

Carla's eyes narrowed. "Why not?"

Not a subject he was prepared to go live on, he thought, gaze fixed on the sleek fit of her red suit.

Every time he saw one of the posters, he had to fight the irrational urge to rip it down. The idea that Carla would do a promotional show in the transparent, pearl-encrusted creation he had viewed in front of an audience filled with voyeuristic men was the only no-brainer in the equation.

Over his dead body.

He felt as proprietary as he imagined a father would feel keeping his daughter from hormonal teenage boys. Not that his feelings were remotely fatherly. She could threaten and argue all day; it wasn't going to happen.

"You haven't been well, and you could be pregnant," he said flatly. "I'll do the interviews, and I've arranged for a model to take your place for the promotion. Nina is hosting the promotional show. Elise will take care of the styling."

Styling. He gripped the taut muscles at his nape. A week ago he didn't even know what that meant.

"I'm so well I'm jumping out of my skin. I'm here to work. The launch is *my* project."

"Not anymore."

Silence hung heavy in the air. Somewhere in the office a clock ticked; out on the street someone leaned on a car horn. Carla groped for the fire-engine-red bag that matched her suit.

Lucas's stomach clenched when he saw tears glittering on her lashes. Ah, damn… He resisted the sudden off-the-wall urge to coax her close and offer comfort. He had expected opposition—a fight—but he hadn't been prepared for this level of emotion. Somewhere in the raft of detail involved with taking over Ambrosi and figuring out how to handle Carla, he had forgotten how passionately intense and protective she was about her family and the business. Although how he could forget a detail that had seen *him* sidelined in Carla's life, he didn't know. "Carla—"

"Don't." She turned on her heel.

Jaw clenched against the need to comfort her and soothe away the hurt, he reached the door first. His hand landed on the cream-and–gilt-detailed panel of the door, preventing her from opening it. "Just one more thing. My mother and Zane fly in tomorrow. I've organized a press conference to promote The Atraeus Group's takeover of Ambrosi and the product launch, then a private lunch. As a family member and PR executive your presence is required at both."

She stared blankly ahead. "Will Lilah be there?"

"Yes."

Lucas had to restrain himself from going after Carla as she strode out of his office. His jaw tightened as he noted the outrageously sexy red heels and the enticing sway of her hips as she walked. The fact that he had lost his temper was disturbing, but ten days kicking his heels while she had disappeared off the radar had set him on edge. The second he had seen her in the red suit he had lost it. He had been certain she wasn't wearing anything but a bra under the tight little jacket, and he had been right.

Closing the door, he prowled back to the window and held aside the silky curtains that draped the window, feeling like a voyeur himself as he watched Carla stroll out onto the street and climb into the sports car that was waiting for her.

He had questioned her assistant extensively about her meetings, then, dissatisfied with her answers, had looked both Chandler and Howarth up on the internet.

Elise had been correct in her summation. Both men were old enough to be her father. Unfortunately, that didn't seem to cut any ice with him. They were men, period.

At a point in time when he should have been reinforcing

the end of their relationship by keeping his distance, he had never felt more possessive or jealous.

Instead of moving to Sydney, he should have stepped back and simply kept in touch with Carla. If she was pregnant, whether she told him or not, he would soon have known. Instead he had grabbed at the excuse to be close to her.

The fact that he had lost control to the extent that he had made love to Carla after they had broken up, *without protection,* still had the power to stun him.

Worse, he found the idea that they could have made a baby together unbearably sexy and appealing.

Maybe it was a kickback to his grief and loss over Sophie, but a part of him actually hoped Carla was pregnant.

He dropped the curtain as the taxi merged into traffic. Broodingly, he reflected that when it came to Carla Ambrosi, he found himself thinking in medieval absolutes.

For two years one absolute had dominated: regardless of how risky or illogical the liaison was, he had wanted Carla Ambrosi.

Despite breaking up and replacing her with a new girlfriend—a woman he had not been able to bring himself to either touch or kiss—nothing had changed.

Seven

Carla checked the time on the digital clock in her small sports car. She had ten minutes to reach Alex Panopoulos's office and rush hour was in full swing, the traffic already jammed.

On edge and impatient, Carla used every shortcut she knew, but even so she was running late when she reached the dim underground garage.

Late for an interview that was becoming increasingly important, she grabbed her handbag and portfolio and exited the car.

Her heels tapped on concrete as she strode to the elevator, just as a sleek dark car cruised into a nearby space. The tinted driver's side window was down, giving her a shadowy glimpse of the driver. The car reminded her of the vehicle Lucas's security detail used when he was in town.

Frowning, she stepped into the elevator and keyed in the PIN she had been given. She punched the floor number, then wished she hadn't as the doors slid shut, nixing her view of the driver before he could climb out of the car. Maybe she was paranoid, or simply too focused on Lucas, but for a split second she had entertained the crazy thought that the driver could be Lucas.

She kept an eye on the floor numbers as they lit up. She caught her reflection in the polished steel doors. The scene with Lucas accusing her of dressing to entice replayed in her mind.

Hurt spiraled through her that he clearly had such a bad opinion of her and was so keen to get rid of her that he had replaced her both personally and professionally. She wondered if he intended to escort Lilah to the event, then grimly decided that of course he would.

As a publicity stunt, the move couldn't be faulted. The media would love Lilah fronting for Ambrosi and the further evidence of her close relationship with Lucas. Ambrosi couldn't ask for a better launch gimmick…except maybe an engagement announcement at the launch party.

Her chest squeezed tight on a pang of misery. Suddenly, that didn't seem as ludicrous or far-fetched as it should, given that Lucas and Lilah had only been publicly dating for a couple of weeks. Lucas was legendary for his ruthless efficiency, his unequivocal decisions. If he had decided Lilah was the one, why wait?

The elevator doors opened onto a broad carpeted corridor. Discreetly suited executives, briefcases in hand, obviously leaving for the day, stepped into the elevator as she stepped out.

The receptionist showed her into Alex's office.

Twenty minutes later, the interview over, Carla stepped out of the lift and strode to her car. She had been offered the job of PR executive for Pan Jewelry, but she had turned it down. Five minutes into the interview she had realized that

Alex hadn't wanted her expertise; he had wanted to utilize her connection with the Atraeus family. Apparently, he could double his profit base in two years if they allowed Pan to trade in the luxury Atraeus Resorts.

She had been prepared to withstand his smooth charm, possibly even reject an attempt at seduction. She had done that before, on more than one occasion. Alex had made it clear he was prepared to deal generously with her in terms of position and salary, including a free apartment, if she came to him.

Stomach churning at the sexual strings that were clearly attached to his offer, and because she had missed lunch, Carla tossed her portfolio and purse on the backseat of her car. Flipping the glove box open, she found the box of cookies she kept there for just such an emergency. Part of the reason she had ended up with an ulcer was that she had a high-acid system. She had to be careful of what she ate, and of not eating at all. Stress coupled with an empty stomach was a definite no-no. Popping a chunk of the cookie in her mouth, she drove out of the parking garage.

The car she had thought could possibly belong to Lucas's security guy was no longer in its space, but, as she took the ramp up onto the sunlit street, the distinctive dark sedan nosed in behind her.

Spine tingling with a combination of renewed anger and the flighty, unreasoning panic of knowing someone was following her—no matter how benign the reason—she sped up. The car stayed with her, confirming in her mind that it *was* one of Lucas's men snooping on her.

Still fuming at his high-handed behavior, she pulled into her apartment building. When the sedan slid past the entrance and kept on going, she reversed out and made a beeline for Lucas's inner-city apartment.

Twenty minutes later, after running the gauntlet of a concierge and one of Lucas's security detail, she pressed the buzzer on Lucas's penthouse door.

It swung open almost immediately. Lucas was still dressed in the dark pants and white shirt he had worn to the office that morning, although minus the tie and with the shirt hanging open to reveal a mouthwatering slice of taut and tanned torso. He leaned one shoulder against the door-jamb, unsubtly blocking her from barging into his apartment.

"Tell me that wasn't you following me."

"It wasn't me following you. It was Tiberio."

"In that case, do you really want to have this discussion in the hallway, where anyone can overhear?"

Cool amusement tugged at his mouth. "I rent the entire floor. The other three apartments are all occupied by my people."

"Let me rephrase that, then. Do you really want to have this discussion where your employees can overhear what I'm about to say?"

His jaw tightened, but he stepped back, leaving her just enough room to march past him. She was in the hallway, strolling across rug-strewn wooden floors into an expansive, airy sitting room before she had time to consider the unsettling fact that Lucas might not be alone. With his shirt hanging open and his sleeves unbuttoned it was highly likely he had company.

Her stomach churned at the thought. She'd had plenty of time on the drive over to consider that Lilah could be here.

She breathed a sigh of relief when she registered that the sitting room, at least, was unoccupied, although that didn't rule out the bedrooms. Until that moment she hadn't known just how much she dreaded seeing Lilah in Lucas's home, occupying the position in his life that until a few days ago she had foolishly assumed was hers.

Fingers tightening on her purse, she surveyed the sitting room with its eclectic mix of artwork and sculpture. Some she knew well; at least two she had never seen. "Nice paintings."

But then that had been one of the things that had attracted her to Lucas. He wasn't stuffy with either his thinking or his enjoyment of art.

As her gaze was drawn from one new painting to the next, absorbing the nuances of line, form and color, her stomach tensed. "A new artist?"

"You know me." His gaze was faintly mocking as he walked through an open-plan dining area to a modern kitchen and opened the fridge. "I'm always on the lookout for new talent."

It occurred to her that the artist could be Lilah, who painted in her spare time, and jealousy gripped her. Before she could stop herself she had stepped closer to the nearest of the new paintings, so she could study the signature. S. H. Crew, not L. Cole.

Her knees felt a little shaky as she moved on to the next painting, also by S. H. Crew. For some odd reason, the thought that Lilah might appeal to Lucas on a creative, spiritual level was suddenly more sharply hurtful than her physical presence would have been.

Lucas loomed over her, the warm scent of his skin, the faint undernote of sandalwood, making her pulse race. "Is it safe to give you this?"

"Not really." Jaw clenching against an instant flashback of the scene on Medinos when she had dashed water over Lucas, and the lovemaking that had followed, she took the glass of ice water. She strolled the length of the sitting room and drifted into a broad hall that served as a gallery. She sipped water and pretended to be interested in the paintings that flowed along a curving cream wall that just happened to lead to the master bedroom. "So why did you have me followed?"

He strolled past her and stood, arms folded over his chest, blocking her view of his bedroom. "I wanted to see what you were up to. Tell me," he said grimly, "what did Panopoulos offer you?"

She blinked at the mention of Panopoulos's name, but it went in one ear and out the other. She was consumed with suspicion because Lucas clearly did not want her to see into his bedroom, and the notion that Lilah was there, maybe even in his bed, was suddenly overwhelming.

Setting the water down on a narrow hall table she marched past him. Lucas's hand curled around her arm as she stepped through the door, swinging her around to face him, but not before she had ascertained that his bedroom was empty. And something else that made her heart slam hard against the wall of her chest.

What he hadn't wanted her to see. A silk robe she had left at his apartment by mistake the last time she had been here almost three months ago, and which was exactly where she had left it, draped over the back of a chair. The aquamarine silk was wildly exotic, sexy and utterly feminine. No woman would have missed its presence or significance and allowed it to remain. The robe was absolute proof that Lilah had never been in Lucas's bedroom.

Her heart beat a queer, rapid tattoo in her chest. "You haven't slept with her yet."

Lucas let her go, his gaze glittering with displeasure. "Maybe I was in the process of getting rid of your things before I invited her over."

Anger flaring, she backed up a half step. The cool solidity of the door frame stopped her dead. "I'm here now, you can hand it to me personally."

"Is that a command, or are you going to ask me nicely?"

Wary of the banked heat in Lucas's gaze, which was clearly at odds with the coolness of his tone, she controlled her temper with difficulty. "I just did ask you nicely."

"I'm willing to bet you were nicer to Alex Panopoulos when you walked into his office in that suit. Did you finally agree to sleep with him?"

"*Sleep* with him?" The words came out as an incredulous yelp. She couldn't help it, she was so utterly distracted by the fact that Lucas thought she could be even remotely interested in Alex Panopoulos, a man she barely tolerated for the sake of business. "Well, I haven't jumped into his bed, yet. Does that make you feel better about me?"

Hot anger simmered through her, doubly compounded by the humiliating fact that Panopoulos *had* wanted to sleep with her.

With a suddenness that shocked her, Lucas leaned forward and kissed her. The sensual shock of the kiss, even though she had half expected it and had goaded him into it, sent a wave of heat through Carla. Until that moment, she hadn't understood how much she had wanted to provoke him, how angry she was at his defection. She was also hurt that he still didn't know who she was after more than two years, and evidently didn't have any interest in knowing, when she was deeply, painfully in love with him.

She blinked, dazed. At some point, she realized, probably that first time they had met, something had happened. After years of dating men and knowing they weren't right, she had taken one look at Lucas and chosen him.

That was why she had broken almost every personal rule she'd had and slept with Lucas in the first place, then continued with the relationship when she knew any association with him would hurt her family. If she had been sensible and controlled she would have stepped back and waited. After all, if a relationship had legs it should stand the test of a little time. But she hadn't been able to wait. She had wanted him, needed him, right then, the same way she needed him now.

Two years. She blinked at the immensity of her self-deception. She had buried the in-love thing behind the pretense that theirs was a modern relationship between two overcommitted people with the added burden of some crazy family pressures. Anything to bury the fact that the sporadic interludes with Lucas in no way satisfied her need to be loved.

Her arms closed convulsively around his neck. She shouldn't be kissing him now, not when she wanted so much more, but in that moment she ceased to care.

"What's wrong?" Lucas pulled back, his gaze suddenly heart-stoppingly soft. "Am I hurting you?"

"No." *Yes.* Her hands tangled in the thick black silk of his hair and dragged his mouth back to hers. "Just kiss me."

Long minutes later they made it to the bed. She dragged his shirt off his shoulders and tossed it aside. Her palms slid across his sleek, heavy shoulders and muscled chest. Giddy pleasure spun through her as he removed her clothing, piece by piece, and she, in turn, removed his.

Time seemed to slow, then stop as she fitted herself against him and clasped his head, pulling his mouth to hers, needing him closer, needing him with her. Late-afternoon sun slanted through the shutters, tiger striping his shoulders as his gaze linked with hers and she suddenly knew why making love with Lucas had always been so special, so important. For those few minutes when they were truly joined it was as if he unlocked a part of himself that normally she could never quite reach, and he was wholly hers. In those few moments she could believe that he did love her.

Cool air swirled around naked skin as he sheathed himself. Relief shivered through her as they flowed together. She was utterly absorbed by the feel of him inside her, his touch and taste, the slow, thorough way he made love to her, as if he knew her intimately, as if they did belong together.

Aside from those few minutes on Medinos it had been long months since they had last made love, and she had missed him, missed this. As crazy as it seemed, despite everything that had gone wrong, everything that was still wrong, this part was right.

His head dipped, she felt the softness of his lips against her neck. Her stomach clenched, the slowly building tension suddenly unbearable as she tightened around him. She felt his raw shudder. In that moment her own climax shimmered through her with an intense pleasure that made tears burn behind her lids, and the room spun away.

Long minutes later the buzzer at the front door jerked her out of the sleepy doze she had fallen into. With smooth, fluid movements, Lucas rolled out of bed, snagged his clothes off the floor and walked through to the adjoining bathroom. Seconds later, he reappeared, fastening dark trousers around narrow hips as he strolled to the door.

Carla didn't wait to see who it was. Snatching up her clothes, including her bra, which had ended up hooked over a bedside lamp, she hurried into the bathroom to freshen up and change. Her clothes were crumpled and her hair was a tumbled mass, but she couldn't worry about that. Her priority was to leave as quickly as possible.

Slipping into her shoes, she searched and found her bag on the floor just outside the bedroom door. She must have dropped it when Lucas had kissed her there. Her cheeks burned with embarrassment as she marched through the sitting room where Lucas was talking in low, rapid Medinian to two of his security personnel.

Lucas said her name. She ignored him and the curious looks of the men, in favor of sliding through the open door and making a dash for the elevator.

Relief eased some of her tension when she saw that the doors were open. Jogging inside, she jabbed the ground floor button as Lucas appeared in the corridor.

"Wait," he said curtly.

The doors closed an instant before he reached the elevator. Heart pounding, Carla examined her reflection in the mirrored rear wall and spent the few seconds repairing her smudged mascara. She winced at her swollen lips and the pink mark on her neck where Lucas's stubble must have grazed her. She looked as if she had just rolled out of bed.

The elevator stopped with a faint jolt. Shoving her mascara back in her bag, Carla strolled quickly through the foyer, ignoring the concierge, who stared at her with a fascinated expression.

She almost stopped dead when she saw Lilah sitting in a chair, flipping through a magazine, obviously waiting. Pretending she hadn't noticed her, Carla quickened her step. Now the two security staff talking with Lucas in hushed, rapid Medinian made sense. Lilah had wanted to go up to Lucas's apartment, but they had known Carla was there.

Mortified, she dimly registered Lilah's white face, the shock in her eyes, as she pushed the foyer doors wide. The sound of traffic hit her like a blow. The sun, now low on the horizon, shone directly in her eyes, dazzling her, a good excuse for the tears stinging her eyes. Her throat tightened as she started down the front steps.

As she stepped onto the sidewalk a hand curved around her arm, stopping her in her tracks.

Her heart did a queer leap in her chest as she spun. "Lucas."

Eight

Carla wrenched free. Lucas was still minus his shirt, his hair sexily tangled. If she looked rumpled, he definitely looked like he had just rolled out of the love nest. "How did you get down so fast?"

"There's a second, private lift."

Her fingers tightened on the strap of her bag. "More to the point, why did you bother?"

His gaze narrowed. "I won't glorify that with an answer. What did you think you were doing running out like that?"

Now that the initial shock of Lucas chasing after her was over, she was desperate to be gone. She needed to be alone so she could stamp out the crazy notion that kept sliding into her mind that there was still a chance for them. She had to get it through her skull that there was no hope. She was the one who got lost in useless emotion, while Lucas remained coolly elusive.

Her gaze flashed. "We were finished, weren't we?" *In*

more ways than one. "Or was there something else you wanted?"

Heat burned along his cheekbones. "You know I never viewed you that way."

"How, then?"

He said something low and taut in Medinian that she was pretty sure was a swear word or phrase of some kind. Not for the first time it occurred to her that for her own peace of mind she really should learn some of that language.

His palm curved around the base of her neck, his fingers tangling in her hair. A split second later his mouth closed over hers.

A series of flashes, the slick, motorized clicking of a high-speed camera jerked them apart. A reporter with an expensive-looking camera had just emerged from a parked car.

A shudder of horror swept Carla. When the press recognized her they would put one and one together and make seven. Before she arrived back at her apartment they would have her entangled in a second-time-around affair with Lucas. By morning they would have her cast off and pregnant or, more probably, since Lucas was involved with Lilah, caught up in some trashy love triangle.

Most of it, unfortunately, was embarrassingly true.

A strangled sound jerked her head around. Bare meters away, directly behind Lucas, Lilah was caught in an awkward freeze-frame.

Carla's stomach lurched as if she'd just stepped into a high-speed elevator on its way down. That was a definite "go" on the love triangle.

Lilah spun on her heel and walked quickly away.

With a final, manic series of clicks the reporter slid back into the car from which he had emerged. With a high-pitched whine reminiscent of a kitchen appliance the tiny hatchback sped away.

Lucas swore softly, this time in English, and released his grip on her nape. His gaze was weary. "Did you know he was out here?"

Her temper soared at what she could only view as an accusation. She gestured at her crumpled clothing and hair, the smeared makeup. "Do I look like I'm ready to be photographed by some sleazy tabloid reporter?"

Lucas's brows jerked together. "You did it once before."

A tide of heat swept her at his reference to her admittedly outrageous behavior in making their first breakup public and the resulting scandal that had followed. "You deserved that for the way you treated me."

"I apologized."

He had apologized. And she had forgiven him, then continued to sleep with him. There was a pattern there, somewhere.

His head jerked around as he spotted Lilah climbing into a small sedan. Slipping a cell phone out of his pants pocket, he punched in a number.

Carla blinked at his sudden change of focus. Feeling oddly deflated and emptied of emotion, she rummaged in her purse to find her car keys. "Before you ask the question, the reporter didn't follow me. Why would he? I'm not your girlfriend."

Lucas frowned and gave up on the call, which clearly wasn't being picked up.

He was no doubt calling Lilah, trying to soothe her hurt and explain away his mistake. Despite the fact that Carla knew she was the one in the wrong for sleeping with Lucas, she found she couldn't bear the thought of Lucas trivializing what they had just shared.

He had the nerve to try the phone number again.

A red mist swam before her eyes. Before she even registered what she was about to do, her hand shot out, closed around the phone and she flung it as hard as she could onto the road. It bounced and flew into several pieces. A split second later a truck ran over the main body of the phone, smashing it flat.

There was a moment of silence.

Lucas's expression was curiously devoid of emotion. "That was an expensive phone."

"So sue me, but I find it insulting and objectionable that the man I've just slept with should phone another woman in my presence. You could have at least waited until I had left."

His gaze narrowed. "My apologies for accusing you of calling the press in. I forgot about Lilah."

"Something you seem to be doing a lot lately. I don't know what you're doing out here with me when you should be concentrating on getting back with her."

A swirling breeze started up, making her feel chilled. She rubbed at the gooseflesh on her arms, suddenly in urgent need of a hot bath and an early night. Technically, she was still recovering from the viral relapse and under doctor's orders to take it easy, not that she would tell Lucas that. She was supposed to take an afternoon nap if she could fit it in. Ha!

She started toward her car. Lucas stepped in front of her, blocking her path.

She stared at his sleek, bare shoulders and muscled chest, the dark line of hair that arrowed down to the waistband of his pants. She was tired, and her body still ached and throbbed in places from what they had done in his penthouse apartment. What they had done was *wrong,* but that didn't stop the automatic hum of desire.

"I have no plans on 'getting back' with Lilah. Do you intend to sleep with Panopoulos?"

She went still inside at the first part of that sentence, although she felt no sense of surprise that Lucas was breaking up with Lilah. If he could gravitate back to her so easily then clearly there wasn't much holding them together. Then a second thunderbolt hit her.

Lucas was jealous.

Make that *very* jealous. She didn't know why she hadn't seen it before, but the knowledge demystified his overbearing reaction to her job interview with Alex Panopoulos. It also cast a new light on the dictatorial way he had decided that she would no longer be "The Face" or act in the promotional play she had planned to stage as part of Ambrosi's product launch. She had thought he was downgrading her both personally and professionally because he didn't want her, but the opposite was true.

A glow of purely feminine pleasure soothed over the hurt he had inflicted by demoting her. The launch was *her* baby. She had meticulously planned every detail, always shooting for perfection, and she needed to be there to make sure everything went smoothly. She still didn't like what he had done, but she understood his reasoning now and, because it involved his emotions for her, she would allow him to get away with being so high-handed.

Her chin came up at the question about Alex Panopoulos, although it no longer had any sting. "You're not my boyfriend," she said flatly. "You have no right to ask that question."

Maybe not. But that situation was about to change.

Lucas's jaw locked as he controlled the surge of cold fury at the thought of Carla and Panopoulos together. When he had asked her before she had said she hadn't slept with him, and he believed her, but he knew Alex Panopoulos. He was wealthy and spoiled and used to having what he wanted. If he wanted Carla, he wouldn't give up.

His hands curled into fists at the almost overwhelming urge to simply pick Carla up and carry her back up to his apartment and his bed. Instead, he forced himself to still-ness as Carla climbed behind the wheel of her sports car and shot away from the curb.

He was finished with caveman tactics. Finesse was now required.

He examined his options as he took the stairs into his apartment building and strode through the foyer. They were not black-and-white, exactly, but close.

He stepped into the elevator, which Tiberio was holding for him. It was a fact that ever since he had first seen Carla he hadn't been able to keep his hands off her. His attempt to create distance and sever their relationship had backfired. Instead of killing his desire, distance had only served to in-crease it to the point that the very thing he had been trying to avoid happened: he lost control.

He could deny the story the tabloids would print and which would no doubt hit the stands by morning, or he could allow the story to stand. If he took the second option, Car-la's name would be dragged through the mud. He would not allow that to happen.

Until that afternoon, he had been certain about the one thing he didn't want: a forced marriage to Carla Ambrosi.

But that had been before she had waved Alex Panopou-los in his face.

The elevator door slid open. Jaw tight, Lucas strode to his apartment and waited for Tiberio to swipe the key card.

He walked through to his bedroom, every muscle lock-ing tight as he studied the rumpled bed. He picked up the sexy, exotic silk wrap, his fingers closing on the silk. Her delicate feminine scent still clung to the silk, the same scent that currently permeated the very air of his room and would now be in his bed.

If she had wanted to force his hand, he reflected, she could have done it at the beginning, when the media had published the story about the first night they had spent together. Instead, she had walked away from him. He was the one who'd had to do the running.

He had gotten her back, but only after weeks of effort. His fingers tightened on the silk. It was an uncomfortable fact that he wanted Carla more now than he had in the beginning. With each encounter, instead of weakening, his need had intensified.

Now Panopoulos had entered the picture.

Alex was a clever man who had leveraged a modest fortune into an impressive retail empire. Lucas was aware that he wouldn't miss the opportunity to enhance his bid to place his stores in Atraeus resorts by marrying close to his family.

Lucas reached for his cell phone, and remembered that Carla had destroyed it. He shook his head at the irrational urge to grin. The destruction of personal property, especially his, shouldn't be viewed as sexy.

He found the landline then, irritated because his directory had been on his dead cell and he had to ring his PA on Medinos to find the unlisted number. Frustrating minutes later, he made the call. Panopoulos picked up almost immediately.

Lucas's message was succinct and direct.

If Panopoulos offered Carla any kind of position within his company, or laid so much as a finger on her, he would lose any chance at a business alliance with The Atraeus Group. Lucas would also see to it personally that a lucrative business deal Panopoulos was currently negotiating with a European firm The Atraeus Group had a stake in, deVries, would be withdrawn.

Panopoulos's voice was clipped. "Are you warning me off because Constantine is now married to Carla's sister?"

"No." Lucas made no effort to temper the cold flatness of his reply. "Because Carla Ambrosi is mine."

The instant he said the words satisfaction curled through him. Decision made.

Carla was his. Exclusively his.

He was over making excuses to be with her. He wanted her. And he would do what he had to to make sure that not Panopoulos or any other man went near her again.

Terminating the call, Lucas propped the phone back on its rest.

Panopoulos was smart; he would back off. Now all Lucas had to do was talk to Lilah, then deal with the press and Carla.

Carla wouldn't like his ultimatum, but she would accept it. The damage had been done in the instant the reporter had snapped them on the street.

The following morning, after a mostly sleepless night, Carla dressed for the scheduled press conference and luncheon with care. Bearing in mind the elegance of the restaurant Lucas had booked, she chose a pale blue dress that looked spectacular against her skin and hair. It was also subtly sexy in the way it skimmed her curves and revealed a hint of cleavage. High, strappy blue heels made her legs look great, and a classy little jacket in powder-blue finished off the outfit.

Normally she would dress in a more low-key way for a press conference, but any kind of meeting with Lucas today called for a special effort. The heels were a tad high, but that wasn't a problem; she had learned to balance on four-inch stilettos from an early age. She figured that by now that particular ability was imprinted in her DNA.

She decided to leave her hair loose, but took extra care with her makeup in an effort to hide the faint shadows under her eyes.

Minutes later, after sipping her way through a cup of coffee, she stepped out of her apartment. As she locked the door, she noticed a familiar sleek sedan parked across the entrance to her driveway, blocking her in. Her tiredness evaporated on a surge of displeasure.

As she marched toward the car she could make out the shadowy outline of a man behind darkly tinted windows. It would be one of Lucas's security team, probably the guy who had tailed her to her interview with Alex Panopoulos.

Temper escalating, she bent down and tapped on the passenger-side window. Tinted glass slid down with an expensive hum. Glittering dark eyes locked with hers and a short, sharp jab of adrenaline shot through her. Lucas.

Dressed in a gray suit with a metallic sheen and a black T-shirt, his hair still damp from his shower, Lucas looked broodingly attractive. His hair was rumpled as if he'd run his fingers through it. He looked edgy and irritable, the shadow on his jaw signaling that he hadn't had time to shave.

The irritating awareness that still dogged her despite her repeated efforts to reprogram her mind kicked in, making her belly clench and her jaw set even tighter. "What are you doing here?"

"Keeping the press off." Lucas jerked his head in the direction of a blue hatchback parked on the opposite side of the street.

With an unpleasant start, Carla recognized the reporter who had snapped them outside Lucas's apartment the previous evening. "He wouldn't be here if he wasn't following you."

"He arrived before I did."

Her stomach sank. That meant the press would be going

all out with whatever story they could leverage out of that kiss. "Even more reason for you not to be here."

He leaned over and opened the passenger door. "Get in."

Carla gauged the time it would take to dash to her small garage, open the door and back her convertible out. With the reporter just a few fast steps away it would be no contest.

The flash and whir of the camera sent a second shot of adrenaline zinging through her veins as she slid into the passenger seat and slammed the door. The thunk of the locks engaging coincided with the throaty roar of the engine as the vehicle shot away from the curb. Seconds later, they were on the motorway heading into town and forced to an agonizing crawl by rush-hour traffic.

Carla relaxed her death grip on her purse, strapped on her seat belt and checked the rearview mirror. Anything but acknowledge the fact that she was once more within touching distance of Lucas Atraeus.

And riding in his car.

Although this wasn't his personal car. His taste usually ran to something a little more muscular and a lot faster, like the Maserati, but the intimacy still set her on edge and recalled one too many memories she would rather forget.

The first time they had made love had been in a car.

Two years ago he had given her a lift home from a dinner at a restaurant, a family meet-and-greet following Constantine and Sienna's first engagement.

Accepting a lift with Lucas, when she had expected to be delivered home the same way she had arrived, via hired limousine service, had seemed safe despite his bad-boy reputation with the tabloids. Plus there was the fact that recently he had been photographed on two separate occasions, each time with a different gorgeous girl.

Despite telling herself that he was clearly not on the hunt, when she slid into his car, she had felt a deliciously edgy kind of thrill. Lucas was gorgeous in a dangerous, masculine way, so she was more than a little flattered to be singled out for his attention.

It had taken a good half hour to reach her apartment during which time Lucas had played cruising music and asked her about her family and whether or not she was dating.

When they'd reached her place it was pitch-dark. Instead of parking out on the street, Lucas had driven right up to her garage door and parked beneath the shelter of a large shade tree. An oak overhung the driveway and blocked the neighbor's view on one side. Her security lights had flicked on as Lucas turned off the engine, although they remained encapsulated in darkness since the garage blocked the light from reaching the car.

With the music gone, the silence took on a heavy intensity, and her stomach had tightened on a kick of nerves because she knew in that moment that despite her frantic reasoning to the contrary, he *did* want to kiss her. If Lucas was just dropping her home, he wouldn't have driven right into her driveway, and so far up it that the car was partially concealed.

He had barely touched her all night, although she had been aware that he had been watching her and, admittedly, she had played to her audience.

But all of the time she had flirted and played she had been on edge in a feminine way, her nerves tingling. She was used to being pursued, that went with the fashion industry and the PR job. But Lucas was in a whole different league and she hadn't made up her mind that she wanted him to catch her.

She had turned her head, bracing herself for the jolt of eye contact, and his mouth caught hers, his tongue siding right in. A burning shaft of heat shot straight to her loins and she went limp.

Long seconds later, he had released her mouth. She gulped in air and then his mouth closed on hers again and she was sinking, drowning. Her arms closed convulsively around his neck, her fingers tangling in his hair, which was thick and silky and just long enough to play with. Not a good idea, since playing with Lucas Atraeus was the dating equivalent of stroking a big hunting cat, but the second he had touched her, her normal rules had evaporated.

She'd felt the zipper of her silk sheath being eased down her spine, the hot shock of his fingers against the bare skin of her back.

He'd muttered something in Medinian, too thick and rapid for her to catch, and lifted his head, jaw taut. "Do you want this?"

She realized he was holding on to control by a thread. The realization of his vulnerability was subtly shocking.

From the first her connection with Lucas had been powerful. Cliché or not, she had literally glanced across the restaurant and been instantly riveted.

Head and shoulders above most of the occupants of the room, all three Atraeus brothers had been compelling, but it had been Lucas's faintly battered profile that had drawn her.

She had let out a shuddering breath, abruptly aware of what he was asking. Not just a kiss. Somehow they had already stepped way beyond a kiss.

He'd bent his head as if he couldn't bear not to touch her. His lips feathered her throat, sending hot rills of sensation chasing across her skin, and abruptly something slotted into place in her mind.

She had been twenty-four, and a virgin, not because she had been consciously celibate but for the simple reason that she had never met anyone with whom she wanted to be that intimate. No matter how much she liked a date, if they couldn't knock her sideways emotionally, she refused to allow anything more than a good-night kiss.

Making love with Lucas Atraeus hadn't made sense for

a whole list of logical reasons. She barely knew him, and so there was no way she could be in love, but instead of recoiling, she'd found herself irresistibly compelled to throw away her rule book. On an instinctive level, with every touch, every kiss, Lucas Atraeus felt utterly right. "Yes."

A car horn blasted, shattering the recall, jerking Carla's gaze back to the road.

"What's wrong?"

Lucas's deep, raspy voice sent a nervy shock wave through her. His gaze caught hers, dispatching another electrical jolt. "Nothing."

His phone vibrated. He answered the call, his voice low. A couple of times his gaze intercepted hers and that weird electrical hum of awareness zapped her again, so she switched back to watching the wing mirror. Once she thought she spotted the blue hatchback and she stiffened, but she couldn't be certain.

"He's not behind us. I've been checking."

Which raised a question. "You said he got to my place before you did, so how did you know he was there?"

Constantine inched forward in traffic, braked, then reached behind to the backseat and handed her a newspaper, which had been folded open.

The headline, Lightning Strikes Twice for Atraeus Hatchet Man, sent her into mild shock, although she had been expecting something like it.

They hadn't made the front page, but close. A color photo, which had been taken just as Lucas had kissed her, was slotted directly below the story title.

Her outrage built as she skimmed the piece. According to the reporter, the romantic fires had been reignited during a secret tryst while she'd been on Medinos. An "insider" had supplied the tidbit that the wedding had literally thrown them together and they were now a hot romantic item. Again.

Although the speculation that Lucas would pop the question was strictly lighthearted. According to the "source," if Carla Ambrosi hadn't had what it took to keep Atraeus interested the first time around, the "reheat" would be about as exciting as day-old pasta.

Carla dropped the newspaper as if it had scorched her fingers. The instant she had seen her name coupled with Lucas's she should have known better than to read on.

Two years ago when Lucas had finished with her after that one night, she had been angry enough to go to the press. They'd had a field day with speculation and innuendo. Her skin was a lot thicker now, but the careless digging into her personal life, and the outright lies, still stung.

Reheat.

Her jaw tightened. If she ever found out who the cowardly "insider" was, the next installment of that particular story could be printed in the crime pages.

Folding the newspaper, she tossed it on the backseat. "You should have called me. You didn't have to show up on my doorstep."

Making it look like there really was substance to the story.

"If I'd called, you would have hung up on me."

She couldn't argue with that, because it was absolutely true.

Lucas signaled and made a turn into the underground parking garage beneath the Ambrosi building.

Carla was halfway out of the car, dragging her bag, which had snagged on a tiny lever at the base of the seat, when movement jerked her head up. A man with a camera loomed out of the shadows, walking swiftly toward them. Not the guy in the blue hatchback, someone else. The pale gleam of a van with its garish news logo registered in the background.

Lucas, who had walked around to open her door, said

something curt beneath his breath as she yanked at the strap. The bag came free and she surged upright.

"Smile, Mr. Atraeus, Ms. Ambrosi. Gotcha!"

The camera flashed as she lurched into Lucas.

The touching was minimal—her shoulder bumped his, he reached out to steady her—but the damage was done. In addition to the kiss outside Lucas's apartment the tabloids now had photos of Lucas picking her up from her apartment then delivering her to work.

The day-old pasta had just gotten hotter.

Nine

When Carla stepped out of her office to attend the press conference later on that morning, one of Lucas's bodyguards, Tiberio, was waiting for her in the corridor.

Lucas wasn't in the office. He had left after dropping her off that morning, so there was no one to interpret. After a short, labored struggle with Tiberio's fractured English, Carla finally agreed that, yes, they would both follow Lucas's orders and Tiberio could drive her to the press conference and see her safely inside.

On the way down to the parking garage, she decided that she was secretly glad Lucas had delegated Tiberio to mind her. She had been dreading dealing with the paparazzi when she arrived at the five-star hotel where the press conference was being held.

To her surprise, Tiberio opened the door on a glossy black limousine, not the dark sedan Lucas's security usually drove. When she slid into the leather interior, she was startled to discover that Lucas was already ensconced there, a briefcase open on the floor, a sheaf of papers in his hand.

The door closed, sealing her in. Lucas said something rapid to Tiberio as he slid behind the wheel. There was a discreet thunk, followed by the low hum of the engine.

She depressed the door handle, when it wouldn't budge, her gaze clashed with Lucas's. "You locked it."

His expression was suspiciously bland. "Standard security precaution."

Daylight replaced the gloom of the parking garage as they glided up onto the street. Her uneasiness at finding Lucas in the car coalesced into suspicion; she was beginning to feel manipulated. "Tiberio said you had ordered him to mind me, that he was supposed to drop me at the press conference. He didn't say we would be traveling together."

Lucas, still dressed in the silver-gray suit and black T-shirt he had been wearing that morning, but now freshly shaved, retrieved a cell phone from his briefcase. "Is there a problem with going together?"

She frowned. "After what happened, wouldn't it be the smart thing to arrive separately?"

Lucas's attention was centered on what was, apparently, a swanky new phone. "No."

Her frustration spiked as he punched in a number and lifted the phone to his ear then subsided just as quickly as she listened to his deep voice, the liquid cadences of his rapid Medinian. Reluctantly fascinated, she hung on every word. He could be reciting a grocery list and she could still listen all day.

Minutes later, the limousine pulled into a space outside the hotel entrance. When she saw the media crush, she experienced a rare moment of panic. Publicity was her thing; she had a natural bent for it. But not today. "Isn't there a back entrance we can use?"

Lucas, seemingly unconcerned, snapped his phone closed and slipped it into his pocket.

She flashed him an irritated look. "The last thing we need right now is to be seen arriving together, looking like we *are* a couple."

"Don't worry, the media will be taken care of. It's all arranged."

Something about his manner brought her head up, sharpened all her senses. "What do you mean, 'arranged'? If the media doesn't see me for a few days, the story will die a death."

"No, it won't," Lucas said flatly. "Not this time."

The door to the limousine popped open. Lucas exited first. Reluctantly Carla followed, stepping into the dusty, steamy heat of midtown Sydney.

The media surged forward. To Carla's relief they were instantly held at bay by a wall of burly men in dark suits.

Lucas's hand landed in the small of her back, the heat of his palm burning through her dress, then they were moving. Carla kept her spine stiff, informing Lucas that she wasn't happy with either the situation or his touch, which seemed entirely too intimate.

The glass doors of the hotel threw a reflection back at her. Lucas stood tall and muscled by her side, his gaze with that grim, icy quality that always sent shivers down her spine. With the other men flanking them in a protective curve, she couldn't help thinking they looked like a trailer for a gangster flick.

The doors slid open, and the air-conditioned coolness of the hotel foyer flowed around her as they walked briskly to a bank of elevators. A security guard was holding an empty elevator car. Relief eased some of her tension as they stepped inside.

Before the doors could slide closed a well-dressed female reporter, microphone in hand, cameraman in tow, side-stepped security and grabbed the door, preventing it from closing.

"Mr. Atraeus, Ms. Ambrosi, can you confirm the rumor that Sienna Atraeus is pregnant?"

There was a moment of confusion as security reacted, forcing the woman and her cameraman to step back.

Lucas issued a sharp order. The doors snapped closed and she found herself alone with Lucas as the elevator lurched into motion.

Carla's stomach clenched at the sudden acceleration.

Sienna pregnant.

"Constantine phoned me earlier to let me know that Sienna was pregnant and that it was possible the story had been leaked."

A hurt she had stubbornly avoided dealing with hit her like a kick in the chest.

She didn't begrudge Sienna one moment of her happiness, but it was a fact that she possessed all the things that Carla realized *she* wanted. Not necessarily right now, but some-time in the future, in their natural order, and with Lucas.

But Lucas was showing no real signs of commitment.

Blankly, she watched floor numbers flash by. If she were pregnant she had to assume there would be no marriage, no happy ending, no husband to love and cherish her and the child.

She became aware the elevator had stopped. She sucked in a deep breath, but the oxygen didn't seem to be getting through. Her head felt heavy and pressurized, her knees wob-bly. Not illness, just good old-fashioned panic.

Lucas took her arm, holding her steady. The top of her head bumped his chin, the scrape of his stubbled jaw on the sensitive skin of her forehead sending a reflexive shiver through her. She inhaled, gasping air like a swimmer surfacing, and his warm male scent, laced with the subtle edge of cologne, filled her nostrils.

Lucas said something curt in Medinian. "Damn, you *are* pregnant."

A split second later the elevator doors slid open.

Fingers automatically tightening around the strap of her handbag, which was in danger of sliding off her shoulder, she stepped out into a broad, carpeted corridor. Lucas's security, who must have taken another elevator, were waiting.

Lucas's hand closed around her arm. "Slow down. I've got you."

"That's part of the problem."

"Then deal with it. I'm not going away."

She shot him an icy glare. "I thought leaving was the whole point?"

He traded a cool glance but didn't reply because they had reached the designated suite. A murmur rippled through the room as they were recognized, but this time, courtesy of the heavy presence of security, there was no undisciplined rush.

Tomas, Constantine's PA, and Lucas's mother, Maria Therese, were already seated. Carla took a seat next to Lucas. Seconds later, Zane escorted Lilah into the room.

Her stomach contracted as the questions began. The presence of a mediator limited the topics to the Atraeus takeover of Ambrosi, Ambrosi's new collection and the re-creation of the historic Ambrosi pearl facility on the Medinian island of Ambrus. However, when Lucas rose to his feet, indicating that the press conference was over, a barrage of personal questions ensued.

Lucas's fingers laced with hers, the contact intimate and unsettling as he pulled her to her feet. When she discreetly tried to pull free, wary of creating even more unpleasant speculation, he sent her a warning glance, his hold firming.

As they stepped off the podium the media, no longer quietly seated, swirled around them. The clear, husky voice of a well-known television reporter cut through the shouted questions. A microphone was thrust at Lucas's face.

The reporter flashed him a cool smile. "Can you confirm or deny the reports that you've resumed your affair with Carla?"

Lucas pulled her in close against his side as they continued to move at a steady pace. His gaze intersected with hers, filled with cool warning. "No official statement has been issued yet, however I can confirm that Carla Ambrosi and I have been secretly engaged for the past two years."

The room erupted. Lucas bit out a grim order. The security team, already working to push the press back, closed in, forcing a bubble of privacy and shoving Carla up hard against Lucas. His arm tightened and she found herself lifted off her feet as he literally propelled her from the room.

Shock and a wave of edgy heat zapped through her as she clung to his narrow waist and scrambled to keep her balance. Seconds later they were sealed into the claustrophobic confines of what looked like a service elevator, still surrounded by burly security.

Carla twisted, trying to peel loose from his hold. Lucas easily resisted the attempt, tightening his arms around her. In the process she ended up plastered against his chest. The top button of her dress came unfastened and his hand, which was spread across her rib cage, shifted up so that his thumb and index finger sank into the swell of one breast.

As if a switch had been thrown, she was swamped by memories, some hot and sensuous enough that her breasts tightened and her belly contracted, some hurtful enough that her temper roared to life.

Lucas's gaze burned over the lush display of cleavage where the bodice of her dress gaped. "Keep still," he growled.

But she noticed he didn't move his hand.

She was *not* enjoying it. After the humiliation of the previous evening the last thing she needed was to be clamped against all that hot, hard muscle, making her feel small and wimpy and tragically easy. Unfortunately, her body wasn't in sync with her mind. She couldn't control the heat flushing her skin or the automatic tightening of her nipples, and Lucas knew it.

The doors slid open. Before she could protest, they were moving again, this time through the lower bowels of the hotel. A door off a loading bay was shoved wide and they spilled out onto a walled parking area where several vehicles, including a limousine, were parked.

Her fury increased. Here was the back entrance she had needed an hour ago.

Hot, clammy air flowed around her as she clambered into the limousine, clutching her purse. Lucas slid in beside her, his muscled thigh brushing hers. She flinched as if scalded and scooted over another few inches.

His gaze flashed to hers as they accelerated away from the curb. "All right?"

His calm control pushed her over the edge. She reached for her seat belt and jammed the fastenings together. "Secretly *engaged?*"

A week ago an engagement was what she had longed for, what she would have *loved*. "Correct me if I'm wrong, maybe I blacked out at some stage, but I don't ever remember a proposal of marriage."

She caught Tiberio's surprised glance in the rearview mirror.

Lucas's expression was grim. A faint hum filled the air as a privacy screen slid smoothly into place, locking them into a bubble of silence.

She stared at Lucas, incensed. Thanks to the mad dash

through the hotel, her hair had unwound and was now cascading untidily down her back, and she was perspiring. In contrast, Lucas looked cool and completely in control, his suit *GQ* perfect. "An engagement is the logical solution."

"It's damage control, and it's completely unnecessary." She remembered her gaping bodice and hurriedly refastened the button. "I may not be pregnant."

Her voice sounded husky and tight, even to herself, and she wondered, a little wildly, if he could tell how much she suddenly wanted to be pregnant.

"Whether you're pregnant or not is a consideration, but it isn't an issue, yet."

Something seized in her chest, her heart. For a crazy moment she considered that he was about to admit that he was in love with her, that he didn't care if she was pregnant or not, he couldn't live without her. Then reality dissolved that fantasy. "But what the newspapers are printing is. Do you know how humiliating it is to be offered a forced marriage?"

Irritation tinged with outrage registered in his expression. "No one's *forcing* you to do anything. Marriage as an option can't be such a shock. Not after what happened on Medinos. And last night."

"Well, I guess that puts things in perspective. It's a *practical* option."

Her mood was definitely spiraling down. Practicality spelled death for all romance. Cancel the white wedding with champagne and rose petals. Bring on the registry office and matching gray suits.

"I wouldn't propose marriage if I didn't *want* to marry you."

Her gaze narrowed. "Is that the proposal?"

His expression was back to remote. "It isn't what I had planned, but, yes."

"Uh-huh." She drew a deep breath and counted to ten.

"The biggest mistake I made was in agreeing to sleep with you."

Suddenly he was close, one arm draped behind her, his warm male scent laced with the enticing cologne stopping the breath in her throat. "On which occasion?"

She stared rigidly ahead, trying to ignore the heated gleam in his eyes, the subtle cajoling that shouldn't succeed in getting her on side, but which was slowly undermining her will to resist.

That was the other thing about Lucas, besides the power and influence he wielded in the business world. When he wanted he could be stunningly seducingly attentive. But this time she refused to be swayed by his killer charm. "All of them."

He wound a strand of her hair around one finger and lightly tugged. She felt his breath fanning her nape. "That's a lot of mistakes."

And she had enjoyed every one of them.

She resisted the urge to turn her head, putting her mouth bare inches from his and letting the conversation take them to the destination he was so blatantly angling for—a bone-melting kiss. "I should never have slept with you, period."

He dropped the strand of hair and sat back, slightly, signaling that he had changed tack. "Meaning that if you had played your cards right," he said softly, "you could have had marriage in the beginning?"

Ten

Like quicksilver the irresistible pull of attraction was gone, replaced by wrenching hurt. "Just because I didn't talk about marriage, that didn't mean I thought it would never be on the agenda for us. And what is so wrong with that?"

Silence vibrated through the limousine. She saw Tiberio glance nervously in the rearview mirror. She turned her head to watch city traffic zip by and registered that her stomach felt distinctly hollow.

Glancing at her watch, she noted the time. She'd only had coffee for breakfast and it was after one. She would be eating lunch soon, which would fix the acid in her stomach, but she couldn't wait that long. Fumbling in her purse, she took out the small plastic bag that contained a few antacid tablets and a couple of individually packaged biscuits. After unwrapping a slightly battered biscuit, she took a bite.

"Marriage is on the agenda now," Lucas reminded her. "I need an answer."

She hastily finished the biscuit and stuffed the plastic bag back in her purse.

Lucas watched her movements with an annoyed fascination. "Do you usually eat when marriage is being proposed?"

"I was hungry. I needed to eat."

"I'll have to remember that should I ever have occasion to propose again."

She closed the flap on her purse. Maybe it was childish not to tell him that she had ended up with an ulcer, but it was no big deal and she was still hurt that he hadn't ever bothered to check up on her after he had deposited her on the plane home from Thailand. The memory of his treatment of her, which had been uncharacteristically callous, stiffened her spine. "I don't know why you want marriage now when clearly you broke up with me because you didn't view me as 'wife' material."

His gaze was unwavering, making her feel suddenly uncomfortable about giving him such a hard time.

"As it happens, you've always fulfilled the most important requirement."

She was suddenly, intensely conscious of the warmth of his arm behind her. "Which is?"

Her breath seized in her throat as Lucas cupped her chin with his free hand. She had a split second to either pull back or turn her head so his mouth would miss hers. Instead, hope turned crazy cartwheels in her stomach, and she allowed the kiss.

Long, breathless minutes later he lifted his head. "You wanted to know why marriage is acceptable to me. This is why."

His thumb traced the line of her cheekbone, sending tingling heat shivering across the delicate skin and igniting a familiar, heated tension. His mouth brushed hers again, the kiss lingering. The stirring tension wound tighter. Reflexively, she leaned closer, angling her jaw to deepen the kiss. Her hand slid around to grip his nape and pull him closer still.

When he finally lifted his head, his gaze was bleak. "Two months without you was two months too long. What happened on Medinos and in my apartment is a case in point. I want you back."

Carla released her hold on his nape and drew back. Her mouth, her whole body, was tingling.

It wasn't what she wanted to hear, but the hope fizzing inside refused to die a complete death.

Lucas had tried to end their relationship; it hadn't happened. She hadn't chased him. If he had truly wanted an end, she was in no doubt that he would have icily and clinically cut her out of his life.

He hadn't been able to because he couldn't resist her.

He might label what held them together as sex; she preferred to call it chemistry. There was a reason they were attracted to each other that went way beyond the physical into the area of personality and emotional needs. Despite their difficulties and clashes, at a deep, bedrock level she knew they were perfect for each other.

That they had continued their relationship for two years was further proof that whatever he either claimed or denied, for Lucas she was different in some way. She knew, because she had made it her business to check. Lucas was only ever recorded by the tabloids as having one serious relationship before her, a model called Sophie, and that had been something like five years ago. The fact that he wanted the marriage now, when a pregnancy was by no means certain, underlined just how powerfully he did want her.

It wasn't love, but everything in her shouted that it had to be possible for the potent chemistry that had bound Lucas to her for the past two years to turn to love.

She was clutching at straws. Her heart was pounding and her stomach kept lurching. There was a possibility that Lucas might never truly love her, never fully commit himself to the relationship. There was a chance she was making the biggest mistake of her life.

But, risky or not, if she was honest, her mind had been made up the second she'd heard his announcement to the press.

She loved Lucas.

If there was a chance that he could love her, then she was taking it.

Lucas activated the privacy screen. When it opened, he leaned forward and spoke in rapid Medinian to Tiberio. He caught the skeptical flash of his chief bodyguard's gaze in the rearview mirror as he confirmed that they would be making the scheduled stop at the jewelers.

However, the wry amusement that would normally have kicked up the corners of his mouth in answer to Tiberio's pessimism was absent. When it came to Carla, he was beginning to share Tiberio's doubts. She hadn't said yes, and he was by no means certain that she would.

Carla, who was once again rummaging in her handbag, stiffened as the limousine pulled into the cramped loading bay of a downtown building. "This isn't the restaurant."

Lucas climbed out as Tiberio opened the door then leaned in and took Carla's hand. "We have one stop to make before lunch."

As Carla climbed out he noted the moment she spotted the elegant sign that indicated this was the rear entrance to the premises of Moore's, a famous jeweler. A business that just happened to be owned by The Atraeus Group.

Her expression was accusing. "You had this all planned."

"Last night you knew as well as I that the story would go to press."

Her light blue gaze flashed. Before she could formulate an argument and decide to answer his proposal with a no, Lucas propelled her toward the back entrance.

Frustration welled that he hadn't been able to extract an answer from her *and* that he couldn't gauge her mood, but he kept a firm clamp on his temper. An edgy, hair-trigger temper that, until these past two weeks, he hadn't known existed.

He offered her his arm and forced himself to patience when she didn't immediately take it.

Clear, glacial-blue eyes clashed with his. "What makes you think I'm actually going to go through with this?"

Lucas noted that she stopped short of using the word *charade.* "I apologize for trying to bulldoze you," he said grimly. "I realize I've mishandled the situation."

He had used business tactics to try to maneuver Carla into an engagement. He had assumed that when he proposed marriage she would be, if not ecstatic, then, at least, happy.

Instead, she was decidedly *unhappy,* and now he was being left to sweat.

He acknowledged that he deserved it. If patience was now required to achieve a result, then he would be patient. "The ring is important. I need you to come inside and choose one."

"I suppose we need one because we've been *secretly engaged* for two years, so of course you would have loved me enough to buy a ring."

Ignoring Tiberio's scandalized expression, he unclenched his jaw. *"Esattamente,"* he muttered, momentarily forgetting his English. "If you don't have a ring, questions will be asked."

"So the ring is a prop, a detail that adds credence to the story."

The door popped open. A dapper gray-haired man, ele-

gant in a dark suit and striped tie, appeared along with a security guard. "Mr. Atraeus," he murmured. "Ms. Ambrosi.
My name is Carstairs, the store manager. Would you like
to come this way?"

Keeping his temper firmly in check, Lucas concentrated
on Carla. If she refused the ring, he would arrange for a selection to be sent to his apartment and she could choose one
there. What was important was that she accept his proposal,
and that hadn't happened yet. "Are you ready?"

Her eyes clashed with his again, but she took his arm.

Jaw clenched, Lucas controlled his emotions with a forc-
ible effort. Fleetingly, he registered Tiberio's relief, an exaggerated expression of his own, as he walked up the steps
and allowed Carla to precede him into the building.

She would say yes. She had to.

The turnaround was huge, but now that he had made the
decision that he wanted her in his life permanently, he felt
oddly settled.

Like it or not he was involved, his feelings raw, possessive. Sexually, he had lost control with Carla from the beginning, something that had never come close to happening
with any other woman.

It was also a blunt fact that the thought of Carla with Panopoulos, or any man, was unacceptable. When he had walked
into that particular wall, his reaction had cleared his mind.
Despite everything that could go wrong with this relationship, Carla was his.

If he had to be patient and wait for her, then he would
be patient.

Carla stepped into the room Carstairs indicated, glad for
a respite from the odd intensity of Lucas's gaze and her own
inner turmoil. For a fractured moment, she had been an inch
away from giving up on the need to pressure some kind of

admission out of Lucas and blurting out "yes." She would marry him, she would do whatever he wanted, if only he would keep on looking at her that way. But then the emotional shutters she had never been able to fathom had come crashing down and they had ended up stalemated again.

The room was an elegant private sitting room with sleek leather couches offset by an antique sideboard and coffee tables. Classical music played softly. The largest coffee table held a selection of rings nestled in black velvet trays.

Carstairs, who seemed to be staring at her oddly, indicated that she take a seat and view the rings, then asked if she would like coffee or champagne. Refusing either drink with a tight smile, she sat and tried to concentrate on the rings. Lucas, who had also refused a drink, paced the small room like an overlarge caged panther, then came to stand over her, distracting her further.

His breath stirred her hair as he leaned forward for a closer look. Utterly distracted by his closeness, she stared blindly at the rings, dazzled by the glitter but unable to concentrate, which was criminal because she loved pretty jewelry. "I didn't think you were interested in jewelry."

"I'm interested in you," he said flatly. "This one."

He picked out a pale blue pear-shaped stone, which she had noticed but bypassed because it occupied a tray that contained a very small number of exquisite rings, all with astronomical price tags.

He handed it to her then conferred briefly with Carstairs. "It's a blue diamond, from Brazil. Very rare, and the same color as your eyes. Do you like it?"

She studied the soft, mesmerizing glow of the diamond, but was more interested in the fact that he had picked the ring because it matched her eyes. She slipped the ring on her finger. Wouldn't you know, it was a perfect fit and it looked even better on. "I love it."

His gaze caught hers, held it, and for a moment she felt absurdly giddy.

"Then we'll take it." He passed Carstairs his credit card.

Yanking the ring off, she replaced it on its plush velvet tray and pushed to her feet, panic gripping her. "I haven't said yes yet."

Lucas said something in rapid Medinian to Carstairs. With a curt bow, the store manager, who could evidently speak the language, left the room, still with Lucas's card, which meant Lucas was buying the ring, regardless. Simultaneously, an elegant older woman in a simple black dress collected the remaining trays and made a swift exit along with Tiberio, leaving them alone. The blue ring, she noticed, was left on the coffee table.

In the background the classical music ended. Suddenly the silence was thick enough to cut.

Carla shoved to her feet and walked to the large bay window. She stared out into the tiny yard presently dominated by the limousine, and the issue she'd been desperate to ignore, which had hurt more than anything because it had cut into the most tender part of her, surfaced. As hard as she had tried for two years to be everything Lucas could want or need, it hadn't been enough. When the pressure had come on to commit, he hadn't wanted *her*. He had wanted Lilah, who in many ways was her complete opposite: calm, controlled and content to keep a low profile.

In retrospect, maybe she had tried too hard and he hadn't ever really seen her, just the glossy, upbeat side that was always "on." The one time he had truly seen her had been in Thailand. She had been too sick to try to be anything but herself, and he had run a mile. "What about Lilah?"

"I spoke to Lilah last night. Zane is taking care of her."

She met his gaze in the window. "I thought you were in love with her."

He came to stand behind her. "She was my date at the wedding, that was all. And, no, we didn't sleep together. We didn't kiss. I didn't so much as hold her hand."

Relief made Carla's legs feel as limp as noodles. He pulled her back against him in a loose hold, as the palm of one hand slid around to cup her abdomen.

"Marriage wasn't on my agenda, with anyone, but the situation has…changed. Don't forget it's entirely possible you're pregnant."

Lucas's hold tightened, making her intensely aware of his hard, muscled body so close behind her. Their reflection bounced back at her, Lucas large and powerfully male, herself paler and decidedly feminine. "I can't marry solely for a baby that might not exist! There has to be something more. Sienna is married to a man she loves. A man who loved her enough that he kidnapped her—"

"Are you saying you want to be *kidnapped?*"

She stared at the dark, irritable glitter of Lucas's eyes, the tough line of his jaw. Her own jaw set. "All I'm saying is that Constantine loves Sienna. It matters."

There was an arresting look in his eyes. "You love me."

Eleven

Carla inhaled sharply at the certainty in Lucas's voice, feeling absurdly vulnerable that, after two years of careful camouflage, she was so transparent now. She was also hurt by his matter-of-fact tone, as if her emotional attachment was simply a convenience that smoothed his path now. "What did you expect, that I was empty-headed enough that I was just having sex with you?"

"Meaning that was how I was with you?" His grip on her arms gentled. "Calm down. I didn't know until that moment. I'm…pleased."

"Because it makes things easier?"

"We're getting married," he said flatly. "This is not some business deal."

He didn't make the mistake of trying to kiss her. Instead he released her, walked over to the coffee table and picked the ring up.

The diamond shimmered in the light, impossibly beautiful, but it was the determined set to Lucas's jaw, the rock-solid patience in his gaze, that riveted her. "What if I'm not pregnant?"

"We'll deal with that possibility when we get to it."

Her jaw tightened. She didn't want to create difficulties, but neither could she let him put that ring on her finger without saying everything that needed to be said. "I'm not sure I want marriage under these conditions."

"That's your choice," he said flatly, his patience finally slipping. "But don't hold out for Alex Panopoulos to intervene. As of yesterday he has reviewed his options."

The sudden mention of Panopoulos was faintly shocking. "You warned him off."

"That's right." Lucas's voice was even, but his expression spoke volumes, coolly set with a primitive gleam in his eyes that sent a faint quiver zapping down her spine.

Just when she thought Lucas was cold and detached he proved her wrong by turning distinctly male and predatory.

It wasn't much, it wasn't enough, but it told her what she needed to know: Lucas was jealous. Given his cool, measured approach to every other aspect of his life, if he was jealous then he had to feel something powerful, something special, for her.

It was a leap in the dark. Marriage would be an incredible risk, but the past two years had been all about risk and she had already lost her heart. It came down to a simple choice. She could either walk away and hope to fall out of love with Lucas or she could stay and hold out for his love.

Her chin came up. When it came down to it she wasn't a coward. She would rather try and fail than not try at all.

"Okay," she said huskily, and extended her hand so he could slide the ring on her finger.

The fit was perfect. She stared at the fiery blue stone, her chest suddenly tight.

Lucas lifted her fingers to his lips. "It looks good."

The rough note in his voice, the unexpected caress, sent a shimmering wave of emotion through her. "It's beautiful."

He bent his head. Before she could react, he kissed her on the mouth. "I have good taste."

Despite her effort to stay calm and composed and not let Lucas see how much this meant to her, a wave of heat suffused her cheeks. "In rings or wives?"

He grinned quick and hard and dropped another quick kiss on her mouth. "Both."

Lucas shepherded Carla into the backseat of the limousine, satisfaction filling him at the sight of the ring glowing on her finger.

She loved him.

He had suspected it, but he hadn't known for sure until she had said the words. Her emotional involvement was an element he hadn't factored in when he had decided on marriage. He had simply formulated a strategy and kept to it until she had capitulated.

Now that he knew she loved him and had agreed to marry him, there would be no reason to delay moving her in with him. No reason to delay the wedding.

Marriage.

Since Sophie's death, marriage had not been an option, because he had never gotten past the fact that he still felt responsible for the accident.

It had taken a good year for the flashbacks of the accident to fade from his mind, another six months before he could sleep without waking up and reliving that night.

Sometimes, even now, he still woke up at night, reliving their last argument and trying to reinvent the past. He had avoided commitment for the simple reason that he knew his own nature: once he did commit he did so one hundred percent and he was fiercely protective. The night Sophie had died, he had been blindsided by the fact that she had aborted his child. He'd allowed her to throw her tantrum and leave. Maybe he was overcompensating now, but he would never allow himself, or any woman he was with, to be put in that situation again.

Until Carla, he had avoided becoming deeply involved with anyone. The week in Thailand had been a tipping point. Caring for Carla in that intimate situation had pushed him over an invisible boundary he had carefully skirted for five years. He hadn't liked the intense flood of emotion, or the implications for the future. He knew the way he was hardwired. For as long as he could remember he had been the same: when it came to emotion it was all or nothing.

Now that Carla had agreed to marry him and it was possible that he would be a father, if not in the near future, then sometime over the next few years, he was faced with a double responsibility. He could feel the possessiveness, the desire to cushion and protect already settling in.

With Sophie he hadn't had time to absorb the impact of her pregnancy because it had been over before he had known about it. She hadn't given him a chance. With Carla the situation was entirely different. He knew that she would never abort their child. She would extend the same fiercely protective, single-minded love she gave her family to their baby.

Any child Carla had would be loved and pampered. Unlike Sophie, she would embrace the responsibility, the chills and the spills.

It was an odd moment to realize that one of the reasons he wanted to marry Carla was that he trusted her.

During the drive to the restaurant Lucas had booked, Carla wavered between staring with stunned amazement at the engagement ring and frantically wondering what Lucas's mother was going to think.

Like every other member of the Atraeus family, Maria Therese would know that Carla and Lucas had more than a hint of scandal in their past. Plus, the first and only time they had met, Lucas had been dating Lilah.

Lucas, who had been preoccupied with phone calls for the duration of the short trip to the restaurant, took her arm as she exited the limousine. "Now that we're engaged, there is one rule you will follow—don't talk to the press unless you've cleared it with me."

Carla stiffened. "PR is my job. I think I can handle the press."

Lucas nodded at Tomas, who was evidently waiting for them at the portico of the restaurant. "PR for Ambrosi is one thing. For the Atraeus family the situation is entirely different."

"I think I can be trusted."

His glance was impatient. "I know you can handle publicity. It's the security aspect that worries me. Every member of my family has to take care, and situations with the press provide prime opportunities for security breaches. If you're going to be talking to the press, a security detail needs to be organized. And by the way, I've booked you into the hotel for the launch party. We leave first thing in the morning."

Carla stopped dead in her tracks, a small fuzzy glow of happiness expanding in her chest. Lucas had obviously taken care of that detail before he had asked her to marry him, righting a wrong that had badly needed fixing. She knew she wouldn't be in charge of running the show, but that was a mere detail. She would still be able to make sure everything came off perfectly and that was what mattered. She was finally starting to believe that this marriage could work. "My contract as Ambrosi's public relations executive is up for renewal next week."

"It's as good as signed."

"That was almost too easy."

His arm slid around her waist, pulling her in against his side as they walked into the restaurant. "I was going to renew it anyway. You're damn good at the job, and besides, I want you to be happy."

Her happiness expanded another notch. It wasn't perfection yet—she still had to deal with that emotional distance thing that Lucas constantly pulled—but it was inching closer.

Maria Therese, Zane and Lilah were already seated at the table. Carla's stomach plunged as Lucas's mother gave her a measuring glance. With her smooth, ageless face and impeccable fashion sense, the matriarch of the Atraeus family had a reputation for being calm and composed under pressure. And with her late husband's affairs, there had been constant media pressure. "Does your mother know how long we've been involved?"

"You're an Ambrosi and my future wife. She'll be more than happy to accept you into the family."

Carla's stomach plunged. "Oh, good. She knows."

The resort chosen for the product launch was Balinese in style. Situated in its own private bay with heavy tropical gardens, it was also stunningly beautiful.

The hotel foyer was just as Carla remembered it when she had originally investigated the resort for the launch party. Constructed with all the grandeur of a movie set, it was both exotic and restful with a soaring atrium and tinkling fountains.

When Carla checked in at the front desk, however, she found that the guest room that had originally been booked for her had been canceled and there were no vacancies. Every room had been booked for the launch.

Lucas, casual in light-colored pants and a loose gauzy white shirt that accentuated his olive skin and made his shoulders look even broader, slipped his platinum card across the counter. "You're sharing with me. The suite's in my name."

So nice to be told. Even though she understood that Lucas was behaving this way because he was still unsure of her and he wanted to keep her close, there was no ignoring that it was controlling behavior. Pointedly ignoring the interruption, she addressed the receptionist. "Are you sure there are no rooms left? How about the room that was originally booked for Lilah Cole?"

Lilah had originally been slated to attend the launch. As the head designer she had a right to be there, but she had pulled out at the last minute.

The receptionist dragged her dazzled gaze off Lucas. "I'm sorry, ma'am, there was a waiting list. The room has already been allocated."

Carla waited until they were in the elevator. The feel-good mood of the two-hour drive from Sydney in Lucas's Ferrari was rapidly dissolving. Maybe it was a small point since they were engaged, but she would like to have been asked before Lucas decided she would be sharing his room. Lucas's controlling streak seemed to be growing by leaps and bounds and she was at a loss to understand why. She had agreed to marry him; life should be smoothing out, but it wasn't. Lucas was oddly silent, tense and brooding. Something was wrong and she couldn't figure out what it was.

Lucas leaned against the wall, arms folded over his chest, his gaze wary. "It's just a hotel room. I assumed you would want to share."

"I do."

Lucas frowned. The relaxed cast to his face, courtesy of an admittedly sublime night spent together in his bed, gone. "Then what's wrong? You already know that Lilah and I were not involved."

"It's not Lilah—"

The doors slid open. A young couple with three young children were waiting for the elevator.

Lucas propelled her out into the corridor. "We'll continue this discussion in our room."

Their luggage had already been delivered and was stacked to one side, but Carla barely registered that detail. The large airy room with its dark polished floors, teak furniture and soaring ceilings was filled with lush bouquets of roses in a range of hues from soft pinks to rich reds. Long stemmed and glorious, they overflowed dozens of vases, their scent filling the suite.

Dazed, she walked through to the bedroom, which was also smothered with flowers. An ice bucket of champagne and a basket crammed with fresh fruit and exquisitely presented chocolates resided on a small coffee table positioned between two chairs.

Lucas carried their bags into the bedroom. The second he set them down she flung her arms around him. "I'm sorry. You organized all this—it's beautiful, gorgeous—and all I could do was complain."

His arms closed around her, tucking her in snugly against him. The comfort of his muscled body against hers, the enticement of his clean scent, increased her dizzy pleasure.

The second she had seen what Lucas had done, how focused he was on pleasing her, the notion that there was something wrong had evaporated. Now she felt embarrassed and contrite for giving him such a hard time.

Carla spent a happy hour rearranging the flowers and unpacking. By the time she had finished laying out her dress for the evening function, Lucas had showered, changed into a suit and disappeared, called away to do a series of interviews.

A knock on the door made her frown. When she opened it a young woman in a hotel uniform was standing outside with a hotel porter. After a brief conversation she discovered that Lucas had arranged for the items to be delivered for her perusal. Anything she didn't want would be returned to the stores.

Feeling a bit like Alice falling down the rabbit hole, Carla opened the door wider so the porter could wheel in a clotheshorse that was hung with a number of plastic-shrouded gowns. At the base of the clotheshorse were boxes of shoes from the prominent design stores downstairs. She signed a docket and closed the door behind the hotel employees.

A quick survey of the gowns revealed that while they were all her size and by highly desirable designers, they were definitely not her style. Two had significantly high necklines, one a soft pink, the other an oyster lace. Both were elegant and gorgeously detailed, but neither conformed to her taste. The pink was too ruffled, like a flapper dress from the 1920s, and the oyster lace was stiffly formal and too much like a wedding gown.

The other boxes contained matching shoes and wraps and matching sets of silk underwear. She couldn't help noticing that none of the shoes had heels higher than two inches.

As dazzled as she was by the lavish gifts, nothing about any of them fitted her personality or style. Each item was decidedly conventional and, for want of a better word, boring, like something her mother would have worn.

Her pleasure in unwrapping the beautiful things was dissolving by the second. Aside from the underwear, which was sexy and beautiful, it was clear that Lucas had had one thought in mind when he had had the things sent up: he was trying to tone her down. That brought them back to the original problem. Despite the engagement, Lucas still didn't accept her for who she was. If he couldn't accept her, she didn't see how he could ever love her.

She found her phone and jabbed in the number of Lucas's new phone. He picked up on the second ring, his voice impatient.

She cut him off. "I'm not wearing any of these dresses you've just had sent up."

"Can we discuss this later?" The register of his voice was low, his tone guarded, indicating that he wasn't alone.

Carla was beyond caring. "I'm discussing it now. I resent the implication that I dress immodest—"

"When did I say—"

"I'm female and, newsflash, I have a *figure*. I do not buy clothes to emphasise sex appeal—"

"Wait there. I'm coming up."

A click sounded in her ear. Heart pounding, she snapped her phone closed, slipped it back in her bag and surveyed the expensive pile of items. Hurt squeezed her chest tight.

She had repacked the shoes and started on the underwear when the door opened.

Lucas snapped the door closed behind him and jerked at his tie. "What's the problem?"

Carla glanced away from the heated irritation in his gaze, his ruffled hair as if he'd dragged his fingers through it, and the sexy dishevelment of the loose tie.

She picked up the pink ruffled number. "This, for starters."

He frowned. "What's wrong with it?"

She draped the gown against her body. "Crimes against humanity. The fashion police will have me in cuffs before I get out of the elevator."

He pinched the bridge of his nose as if he was under intense pressure. "Do you realize that on Medinos, as your future husband I have the right to dictate what you wear?"

For a moment she thought he was joking. "That's *medieval*—"

"Maybe I'm a medieval kind of guy."

She blinked. She had been wanting to breach his inner barriers, but now she was no longer sure she was going to like what she'd find. The old Lucas had been a pussycat compared to what she was now uncovering. "I buy clothes because they make me look and feel good, not to showcase my breasts or any other part of my anatomy. If that means I occasionally flash a bit of cleavage, then you, and the rest of Medinos, are just going to have to adjust."

She snatched up the pink silk underwear, which in stark contrast to the dress was so skimpy it wouldn't keep a grasshopper warm. "Are these regulation?"

He hooked the delicate thong over one long brown finger. "Absolutely."

Carla snatched the thong back and tossed the pink underwear back in its box. Retrieving the list of items she had signed for, she did what she had been longing to do—ripped it into shreds and tossed the pieces at Lucas. The issue of clothing, as superficial as it seemed, ignited the deep hurt that Lucas still viewed her as his sexy, private mistress and not his future wife. "You can have your master plan back."

Lucas ignored the fluttering pieces of paper. "What master plan?"

"The one where you turn me into some kind of perfect stuffed mannequin and put me in a room on Medinos with one of those wooden embroidery frames in my hand."

Lucas rubbed the side of his jaw, his gaze back to wary. "Okay, I am now officially lost."

"I resent being treated as if I'm too dumb to know how I

should dress. This is not digging gold out of rocks or sweaty men building a hotel, this is a *fashion* industry event."

His jaw took on an inflexible look she was beginning to recognize. "We're engaged. Damned if I'm going to let other men ogle you."

She threw up her hands. "You're laying down the law, but you don't even know what I plan to wear tonight."

Marching to the bed, she held up a hanger that held a sleek gold sheath with a softly draped boat-shaped neckline. "It's simple, elegant, shows no cleavage—and, more to the point, I like it."

"In that case, I apologize."

Feeling oddly deflated, she replaced the dress on the bed. When she turned, Lucas pulled her into his arms.

Her palms automatically spread on his chest. She could feel the steady pound of his heart beneath the snowy linen of his shirt, the taut, sculpted muscle beneath. Her heart rate, already fast, sped up, but he didn't try to pull her closer or kiss her.

"It wasn't my intention to upset you, but there is one thing about me that you're going to have to understand—I don't share. When it comes down to it, I don't care what you wear. I just don't want other men thinking you're available. And from now on the press will watch you like a hawk."

"I'm not irresponsible, or a tease." She released herself from his hold. The problem was that she had never understood Lucas's mood swings; she didn't understand him. One minute he was with her, the next he was cut off and distant and she needed to know why, because that distance frightened her. Ultimately it meant it was entirely possible that one day he could close himself off completely and leave her.

She began carefully rehanging the dresses, needing something to do. "Why did you never want any kind of long-term relationship with me? You planned to finish with me all along."

He gripped his nape. "We met and went to bed on the same night. At that point marriage was not on my mind."

"And after Thailand it definitely wasn't."

"I compressed my schedule to be with you in Thailand. Taking further time off wasn't possible."

"What if I'd been *really* ill?"

His gaze flashed with impatience. "If you had been ill, you would have contacted me, but you didn't."

"No."

"Are you telling me you *were* ill and didn't contact me?" he asked quietly.

"Even if I was," she said, folding the oyster silk lingerie into the cloud of tissue paper that filled the box, "you didn't want to know because looking after me in Thailand was just a little too much reality for you, wasn't it?"

"Tell me more about how I was thinking," he muttered. "I'm interested to know just how callous you think I am."

Frustration pulling at her, she jammed the lid on the box. Lucas had cleverly turned the tables on her, but she refused to let up. It suddenly occurred to her that Lucas's behavior was reminiscent of her father's. Roberto Ambrosi had hated discussing personal issues. Every time anyone had probed him about anything remotely personal he had turned grouchy and changed the subject. Attack was generally seen as the most effective form of defense.

She realized now that every time she got close to what was bothering Lucas, he reacted like a bear with a sore head. If he was snapping now, she had to be close. "If I wasn't what you wanted before," she said steadily, "how can I be that person now?"

There was a small, vibrating silence. "Because I realized you weren't Sophie."

Carla froze. "Sophie Warrington?"

"That's right. We lived together for almost a year. She died in a car accident."

Carla blinked. She remembered the story. Sophie Warrington had been gorgeous and successful. She had also had a reputation for being incredibly spoiled and high maintenance. She had lost a couple of big contracts with cosmetic companies because she had thrown tantrums. She had also been famous for her affairs.

Suddenly, Carla's lack of control in the relationship made sense. She was dealing with a ghost—a gorgeous, irresponsible ghost who had messed Lucas around to the point that he had trouble trusting any woman.

Let alone one who not only looked like Sophie but who was caught up in the same glitzy world.

Twelve

Half an hour later, after taking her medication with a big glass of water, she nibbled on a small snack then decided to go for a walk along the beach and maybe have a swim before she changed for the evening function. It wouldn't exorcise the ghost of Sophie Warrington or her fear that Lucas might never trust enough to fall in love with her, but at least it would fill in time.

Winding her hair into a loose topknot, she changed into an electric blue bikini and knotted a turquoise sarong just above her breasts. After transferring her wallet to a matching turquoise beach bag, she slipped dark glasses on the bridge of her nose and she was good to go.

Half an hour later, she stopped at a small beach café, ordered a cool drink and glimpsed Tiberio loitering behind some palms. She had since found out that Tiberio wasn't just a bodyguard, he was Lucas's head of security. That being the case, the only logical reason for him to be here was that Lucas had sent him to keep an eye on her.

Annoyed that her few minutes of privacy had been invaded by security that Lucas hadn't had the courtesy to advise her about, she finished the drink and started back to the resort.

The quickest way was along the long, curving ocean beach, which was dotted with groups of bathers lying beneath bright beach umbrellas. As she walked, she stopped, ostensibly to pick up a shell, and glanced behind. Tiberio was a short distance back, making no attempt to conceal himself, a cell phone held to his ear.

No doubt he was talking to Lucas, reporting on her activities. Annoyed, she quickened her pace. She reached the resort gardens in record time but the fast walk in the humidity of late afternoon had made her uncomfortably hot and sticky. She strode past the cool temptation of a large gleaming pool. Making an abrupt turn off the wide path, she strode along a narrow winding bush walk with the intention of losing herself amongst the shady plantings.

Beneath the shadowy overhanging plants, paradoxically it was even hotter. Slowing down, she unwound her sarong and tied it around her waist for coolness and propped her dark glasses on top of her head.

Footsteps sounded behind her, coming fast. Annoyed, she spun, and came face-to-face with Alex Panopoulos.

Dressed in a pristine business suit, complete with briefcase, his smooth features were flushed and shiny with perspiration.

She frowned, perversely wondering what had happened to Tiberio, and suddenly uncomfortably aware of the brevity of her bikini top. "What are you doing here?"

Alex set his briefcase down and jerked at his edgily patterned tie. "I just arrived and was walking to my chalet when I saw you."

She frowned, disconcerted by the intensity of his expression and the fact that he had clearly run after her. "There was no need. I'll see you tonight at the presentation."

"No you won't. My invitation was rescinded."

"Lucas—"

"Yes," he muttered curtly, "which is why I wanted to talk with you privately."

His gaze drifted to her chest, making her fingers itch with the need to yank the sarong back up. "If it's about the job—"

"Not the job." He stepped forward with surprising speed and gripped her bare arms. This close the sharp scent of fresh sweat and cologne hit her full force.

His gaze centered on her mouth. "You must know how I feel about you."

"Uh, not really. Let me go." She tried to pull free. "I'm engaged to Lucas."

"Engagements can be ended."

A creepy sense of alarm feathered her spine. He wasn't letting go. She jerked back more strongly, but his grip tightened, drawing her closer.

The thought that he might try to kiss her made her stomach flip queasily. Alex had frequently made it clear that he was attracted to her, but she had dismissed his come-ons, aware that he also regularly targeted other women, including her sister, Sienna.

Deciding on strong action, she planted her palms on his chest but, before she could shove, Panopoulos flew backward, seemingly of his own accord. A split second later Lucas was towering over her like an avenging angel.

Alex straightened, his hands curling into fists.

Lucas said something low and flat in Medinian.

Alex flinched and staggered back another step, although Lucas hadn't either stepped toward him or touched him.

Flushing a deep red, Panopoulos lunged for his briefcase and stumbled back the way he'd come.

With fingers that shook slightly with reaction, Carla untied the sarong, dragged it back over her breasts and knotted it. "What did you say to him?"

Lucas's gaze glittered over her, coming to rest on the newly tied knot. "Nothing too complicated. He won't be bothering you again."

"Thank you. I was beginning to think he wasn't going to let go." Automatically, she rubbed at the red marks on her arms where Panopoulos had gripped her just a little too hard.

With gentle movements, Lucas pushed her hands aside so he could examine the marks. They probably wouldn't turn into bruises, but that didn't change the cold remoteness of his expression.

"Did he hurt you?"

"No." From the flat look in his dark eyes, the grim set to his jaw, Carla gained the distinct impression that if Panopoulos had stepped any further over the line than he had, Lucas wouldn't have been so lenient. A small tingling shiver rippled the length of her spine as she realized that Lucas was fiercely protective of her.

It was primitive, but she couldn't help the warm glow that formed because the man she had chosen as her mate was prepared to fight for her. In an odd way, Lucas springing to her defense balanced out the hurt of discovering how affected he'd been by Sophie Warrington. To the extent that his issues with her had permeated every aspect of his relationship with Carla.

His hand landed in the small of her back, the touch blatantly dominant and possessive, but she didn't protest. She was too busy wallowing in the happy knowledge that Lucas hadn't left it to Tiberio to save her. Instead, he had interrupted what she knew was a tight schedule of interviews and come after her himself. Despite the unpleasant shock of the encounter, she was suddenly glad that it had happened.

When they reached the room, Lucas kicked the door shut and leaned back against the gleaming mahogany and drew her close.

Carla, still on edge after the encounter, went gladly. Coiling her arms around his neck, she fitted her body against the familiar planes and angles of his, soaking in the calm reassurance of his no-holds-barred protection.

Tangling the fingers of one hand in her hair, Lucas tilted her head back and kissed her until she was breathless.

When he lifted his head, his expression was grim. "If you hadn't tried to get away from Tiberio, Panopoulos wouldn't have had the opportunity to corner you."

She felt her cheeks grow hot. "I needed some time alone."

"From now on, while we're at the hotel you either have security accompany you, or I do, and that's nonnegotiable."

"Yes."

He cupped her face, his expression bemused. "That was too easy. Why aren't you arguing?"

She smiled. "Because I'm happy."

A faint flush rimmed his taut cheekbones and suddenly she felt as giddy as a teenager.

"Damn, I wish I didn't have interviews." His mouth captured hers again.

She rose up into the kiss, angling her jaw to deepen it. This time the sensuality was blast-furnace hot, but she didn't mind. For the first time in over two years Lucas's kiss, his touch, felt absolutely and completely right.

He wanted her, but not just because he desired her. He wanted her because he *cared*.

* * *

Carla showered and dressed for the launch party. Lucas walked into the suite just as she was putting the finishing touches to her makeup.

"You're late." Pleasurable anticipation spiraled through her as he appeared behind her in the mirror, leaned down and kissed the side of her neck.

His gaze connected with hers in the mirror. "I had an urgent business matter to attend to."

And she had thrown his busy schedule off even further because he'd had to interrupt his meetings to rescue her.

The happy glow that had infused her when he'd read Panopoulos the riot act reignited, along with the aching knowledge that she loved him. It was on the tip of her tongue to tell him just how much when he turned and walked into the bathroom. Instead she called out, "I'll see you downstairs."

Minutes later, with Tiberio in conspicuous attendance, she strolled into the ballroom, which was already filled with elegantly gowned and suited clients, the party well under way.

She threaded her way through the crowd, accepting congratulations and fielding curious looks. When she walked backstage to check on the arrangements for the promotional show, Nina's expression was taut.

She threw Carla a harassed look. "A minor glitch. The model we hired is down with a virus, so the agency did the best they could at short notice and sent along a new girl." She jerked her head in the direction of the curtained-off area that was being used as dressing rooms.

Dragging the curtain back far enough so she could walk through, Carla stared in disbelief at the ultrathin model. She was the right height for the dress, but that was all. Obviously groomed for the runway, she was so thin that the gown, which had originally been custom-made for Carla, hung off her shoulders and sagged around her chest and hips.

Carla's assistant, Elise, was working frantically with pins. The only problem was, the dress—an aquamarine creation studded with hundreds of pearls in a swirling pattern that was supposed to represent the sea—could only be taken in at certain points.

To add insult to injury, the model was a redhead and nothing about the promotion was red. Everything was done in Ambrosi's signature aquamarine and pearl hues. The color mix was subtle, clean and classy, reflecting Ambrosi's focus on the luxury market.

"No," Carla said, snapping instantly into work mode, irritated by the imperfections of the model and the utter destruction of the promotion that had taken her long hours of painstaking time to formulate. "Take the pins out of the dress."

She smiled with professional warmth at the model and instructed her to change, informing her that she would be paid for the job and was welcome to stay the weekend at Ambrosi's expense, but that she wouldn't be part of the promotion that evening.

Clearly unhappy, the model shimmied out of the gown on the spot and walked, half-naked and stiff backed, into a changing cubicle. At that point, another curtain was swished wide, revealing the gaggle of young ballet girls, who were also part of the promotion, in various states of undress.

Tiberio made a strangled sound. Clearly unhappy that he had intruded into a woman's domain, he indicated he would wait in the ballroom.

Elise carefully shook out the gown, examined it for signs of damage and began pulling out the pins she'd inserted. "Now what?" She indicated her well-rounded figure. "If you think I'm getting into that dress, forget it."

"Not you. Me."

Nina looked horrified. "I thought the whole point of this was that you weren't to take part."

Carla picked up the elegant mask that went with the outfit and pressed it against her face. The mask left only her mouth and chin visible.

Her stomach tightened at the risk she was taking. "He won't know."

Thirteen

Carla stepped into the gown and eased the zipper up, with difficulty. The dress felt a little smaller and tighter than it had, because it had been taken in to fit the model who was off sick.

She fastened the exquisite trailing pearl choker, which, thankfully, filled most of her décolletage and dangled a single pearl drop in the swell of her cleavage.

Cleavage that seemed much more abundant now that the dress had been tightened.

She surveyed her appearance in the mirror, dismayed and a little embarrassed by the sensual effect of the too-tight dress.

Careful not to breathe too deeply and rip a seam, she fastened the webbed bracelet that matched the choker and put sexy dangling earrings in her lobes. She fitted the pearl-studded mask and surveyed the result in the mirror.

With any luck she would get through this without being

recognized. A few minutes on stage then she would make her exit and quickly change back into her gold dress and circulate.

Elise swished the curtain aside. "It's time to go. You're on."

Lucas checked his watch as he strolled through the ballroom, his gaze moving restlessly from face to face.

Tiberio had informed him that Carla was assisting the girls backstage with the small production they had planned. He had expected no less. When it came to detail, Carla was a stickler, but now he was starting to get worried. She should have been back in the ballroom, with him, by now.

He checked his watch again. At least Panopoulos was out of the picture. He had made certain of that.

Every muscle in his body locked tight as he remembered the frightened look on Carla's face as she'd tried to shove free of him. When he'd seen the marks on Carla's arms, he had regretted not hitting Panopoulos.

Instead, he had satisfied his need to drive home his message by personally delivering the older man to the airport and escorting him onto a privately chartered flight out.

Panopoulos had threatened court action. Lucas had invited him to try.

Frowning, he checked the room again. He thought he had seen Carla circulating when he had first entered the room, but the gold dress and dark hair had belonged to a young French woman. He was beginning to think that something else had gone wrong since the heart-stopping passion of those moments in their room and she had found something else to fret about.

The radiant glow on her face when he'd left her had hit him like a kick in the chest, transfixing him. He could remember her looking that way when they had first met, but gradually, over time, the glow had gone. He decided it was a grim testament to how badly he had mismanaged their relationship that Carla had ceased to be happy. From now on he was determined to do whatever it took to keep that glow in her eyes.

A waiter offered him a flute of champagne. He refused. At that moment there was a stir at one end of the room as Nina, who was the hostess for the evening, came out onto the small stage.

Lucas leaned against the bar and continued to survey the room as music swelled and the promotional show began. The room fell silent as the model, who was far more mouth-wateringly sexy than he remembered, moved with smooth grace across the stage. *Floor show* wasn't the correct terminology for the presentation but he was inescapably driven to relabel the event.

Every man in the room was mesmerized, as the masked model, playing an ancient Medinian high priestess, moved through the simple routine, paying homage to God with the produce of the sea, a basket of Ambrosi pearls. With her long, elegant legs and tempting cleavage, she reminded him more of a Vegas dancer than any depiction of a Medinian priestess he had ever seen.

His loins warmed and his jaw tightened at his uncharacteristic loss of control. He had seen that dress on the model who was supposed to be doing the presentation. At that point the gown, which was largely transparent and designed so that pearl-encrusted waves concealed strategic parts and little else, had looked narrow and ascetically beautiful rather than sexy. He hadn't been even remotely turned-on.

The model turned, her hips swaying with a sudden sinuous familiarity as she walked, surrounded by a gaggle of young ballet dancers, all carrying baskets overflowing with free samples of Ambrosi products to distribute to clients.

Suspicion coalesced into certainty as his gaze dropped to the third finger of her left hand.

He swallowed a mouthful of champagne and calmly set the flute down. The mystery of his future wife's whereabouts had just been solved.

He had thought she was safely attired in the gold gown, minus any cleavage. Instead she had gone against his instructions and was busy putting on an X-rated display for an audience that contained at least seventy men.

Keeping a tight rein on his temper, he strode through the spellbound crowd and up onto the stage. Carla's startled gaze clashed with his. Avoiding a line of flimsy white pillars that were in danger of toppling, he took the basket of pearls she held, handed them to one of the young girls and swung her into his arms.

She clutched at his shoulders. "What do you think you're doing?"

Grimly, Lucas ignored the clapping and cheering as he strode off the stage and cut through the crowd to the nearest exit. "Removing you before you're recognized. Don't worry," he said grimly, "they'll think it's part of the floor show. The Atraeus Group's conquering CEO carrying off the glittering prize of Ambrosi Pearls."

"I can't believe you're romanticizing a business takeover, and it is *not* a floor show!"

He reached the elevator and hit the call button with his elbow, his gaze skimming the enticing display of cleavage. "What happened to the model I employed?"

"She came down with a virus. The replacement they sent didn't fit the dress. If I hadn't stepped in, the only option would have been to cancel the promotion."

A virus. That word was beginning to haunt him. "And canceling would have been such a bad idea?"

"Our events drive a lot of sales. Besides, I'm wearing a mask. No one knew."

"*I* knew."

She ripped off the mask, her blue gaze shooting fire. "I don't see how."

He took in the sultry display of honey-tanned skin. Cancel the Vegas dancer. She looked like an extremely expensive courtesan, festooned with pearls. *His* courtesan.

It didn't seem to matter what she wore, he reflected. The clothing could look like a sack on any other woman, but on Carla it became enticingly, distractingly sexy. "Next time remember to take off the engagement ring."

The elevator doors opened. Seconds later they had reached their floor. Less than a minute later Lucas kicked the door to their suite closed.

"You realize I need to go back to the party."

He set her down. "Just not in that dress."

"Not a problem, it's not my color." Carla tugged at the snug fit of the dress. Fake pearls pinged on the floor. A seam had given way while Lucas was carrying her, but on the positive side, at least she could breathe now. She eyed Lucas warily. "What do you think you're doing?"

He had draped his suit jacket over the back of a couch, loosened his tie and strolled over to the small business desk in the corner of the sitting room. She watched as he flipped his laptop open. "Checking email."

The abrupt switch from scorching possessiveness to cool neutrality made her go still inside. She had seen him do this often. In the past, usually, just before he would leave her apartment he would begin immersing himself in work—phone calls, emails, reading documents. She guessed that on some level she had recognized the process for what it was; she just hadn't ever bothered to label it. Work was his coping mechanism, an instant emotional off button. She should know. She had used it herself often enough.

She watched as he scrolled through an email, annoyed at the way he had switched from blazing hot to icy cool. Lucas had removed her from the launch party with all the finesse of a caveman dragging his prize back to the fire. He had gotten his way; now he was ignoring her.

The sensible option would be to get out of the goddess outfit, put on another dress and go downstairs and circulate before finding her gold dress and handbag, which she had left backstage. But that was before her good old type A personality decided to make a late comeback.

Ever since she had been five years old on her first day at school and her teacher, Mrs. Hislop, had put daddy's little girl in the back row of the classroom, she had understood one defining fact about herself: she did not like being ignored.

Walking to the kitchenette, she opened cupboards until she found a bowl. She needed to eat. Cereal wasn't her snack of choice this late, but it was here, and the whole point was that she stayed in the suite with Lucas until he realized that she was not prepared to be ignored.

She found a minipacket of cereal, emptied it into the bowl then tossed the packaging into the trash can, which was tucked into a little alcove under the bench.

Lucas sent her a frowning glance, as if she was messing with his concentration. "I thought you were going to change and get back to the party."

She opened the fridge and extracted a carton of milk. "Why?"

"The room is full of press and clients."

She gave him a faintly bewildered look, as if she didn't understand what he was talking about, but inwardly she was taking notes. He clearly thought she was a second Sophie, a party girl who loved to be the center of attention. "Nina and Elise are taking care of business. I don't need to be there."

"It didn't look that way ten minutes ago."

She shrugged. "That was an emergency."

Aware that she now had Lucas's attention, she opened the carton with painstaking precision and poured milk over the cereal. Grabbing a spoon, she strolled out into the lounge, sat on the sofa and turned the TV on. She flicked through the channels till she found a talk show she usually enjoyed.

Lucas took the remote and turned the TV off. "What are you up to?"

Carla munched on a spoonful of cereal and stared at the now blank screen. Before the party she had found reasons to adore Lucas's dictatorial behavior. Now she was back to loathing it, but she refused to allow her annoyance to show. She had wanted Lucas's attention and now she had gotten it. "Considering my future employment. I'm not good with overbearing men."

"You are not going to work for Panopoulos."

She ate another mouthful of cereal. He was jealous; she was getting somewhere. "I guess not, since I have an iron-clad contract I signed only yesterday."

Lucas tossed the remote down on the couch and dispensed with his tie. "Damn. You must be sleeping with the boss."

"Plus, I have shares."

"It's not a pleasing feminine trait to parade your victories." He took the cereal bowl from her and set it down on the coffee table. Threading her fingers with his, he pulled her to her feet.

More pearls pinged off the dress as she straightened. A tiny tearing sound signaled that another seam had given. "You shouldn't take food from a woman who could be pregnant."

His gaze was arrested. "Do you think you are?"

"I don't know yet." She had left the test kit behind. With everything that had happened, taking time out to read the instructions and do the test hadn't been a priority.

"I could get used to the idea." Cupping her face, he dipped his head and touched his mouth to hers.

The soft, seducing intimacy of the kiss made Carla forget the next move in her strategy. Before she could edit her response, her arms coiled around his neck. He made a low sound of satisfaction, then deepened the kiss.

Hands loosely cupping her hips, he walked her backward, kiss by drugging kiss, until they reached the bedroom. She felt a tug as the zipper on the dress peeled down, then a loosening at the bodice. More pearls scattered as he pulled the dress up and over her head and tossed it on the floor.

"The dress is ruined." Not that she really cared. It had only been a prop and it had served its purpose, in more ways than one.

"Good. That means you can't wear it again."

Stepping out of her heels, she climbed into bed and pulled the silk coverlet over her as she watched him undress. With his jet-black hair and broad, tanned shoulders he looked sleek and muscular.

The bed depressed as he came back down beside her. The clean scent of his skin made her stomach clench.

He surveyed the silk coverlet with dissatisfaction. "This needs to go." He dragged it aside as he came down on the bed. One long finger stroked over the pearl choker at her throat down to the single dangling pearl nestled in the shadowy hollow between her breasts. "But you can keep this on."

She had forgotten about the jewelry. Annoyed by the suggestion, which seemed more suited to a mistress than a future wife, she scooted over on the bed, wrapping the coverlet around her as she went. "You just destroyed an expensive gown. If you think I'm going to let you make love to me while I'm wearing an Ambrosi designer orig—"

His arm curled around her waist, easily anchoring her to the bed. "I'll approve the write-off for it."

Despite her reservations, unwilling excitement quivered through her as he loomed over her, but he made no effort to do anything more than keep her loosely caged beneath him.

"Whether we make love or not," he said quietly, "is your decision, but before you storm off, you need to know that I've organized a special license on Medinos. We're going to be married before the week is out."

"You might need my permission for that."

Something flared in his gaze and she realized she had pushed him a little too hard. "Not on Medinos."

"As I recall from Sienna's wedding, I still have to say yes."

Frustration flickered in his gaze and then she finally got him. For two years she had been focused on organizing their time together, taking care of every detail so that everything was as perfect as she could make it, given their imperfect circumstances. Lucas had fallen in with her plans, but she had overlooked a glaring, basic fact. Lucas was male; he needed to be in control. He now wanted her to follow the plan he had formulated, and she was frustrating him.

He cupped her face. "I have the special license. I don't care where we get married, just as long as it happens. Damned if I want Panopoulos, or any man, thinking you're available."

Unwilling delight filtered through the outrage that had driven her ever since she had realized that Lucas had developed a coping mechanism for shutting her out. The incident with Alex seemed a lifetime away, but it had only been hours.

She understood that in Lucas's mind he had rescued her for a second time that day, this time from a room full of men. As domineering and abrasive as his behavior was, in an odd way, it was the assurance she so badly needed that he cared. After watching him detach and walk away from her for more than two years, she wasn't going to freeze him out just when she finally had proof that he was falling for her.

"Yes."

His gaze reflected the same startled bemusement she had glimpsed that afternoon. "That's settled, then."

Warmth flared to life inside her. The happy glow expanded when he touched his lips to hers, the soft kiss soothing away the stress of dealing with Lucas's dictatorial manner. Sliding her fingers into the black silk of his hair, she pulled him back for a second kiss, then a third, breathing in his heat and scent. The kiss deepened, lingered. The silk coverlet slid away and she went into his arms gladly.

Sometime later, she woke when Lucas left the bed and walked to the bathroom, blinking at the golden glow that still flooded the room from the bedside lamp. Chilled without his body heat, she curled on her side and dragged the coverlet up high around her chin.

The bed depressed as Lucas rejoined her. One arm curled around her hips, he pulled her back snug against him. His palm cupped her abdomen, as if he was unconsciously cradling their baby.

Wistfully, her hand slipped over his, her fingers intertwining as she relaxed back into the blissful heat of his body. She took a moment to fantasize about the possibility that right at that very moment there could be an embryo growing inside her, that in a few months they would no longer be a couple, they would be a family. "Do you think we'll make good parents?"

"We've got every chance."

She twisted around in his grip, curious about the bitter note in his voice. "What's wrong?"

He propped himself on one elbow. "I had a girlfriend who was pregnant once. She had an abortion."

"Sophie Warrington?"

"That's right."

"You told me about her. She died in a car accident."

There was silence for a long, drawn-out moment. "Sophie had an abortion the day before she died. When she finally got around to telling me that she'd aborted our child before even telling me she was pregnant, we had a blazing argument. We broke up and she drove away in her sports car. An hour later she was dead."

Carla blinked. She hadn't realized that Lucas had split with Sophie before she had died. She smoothed her palm over his chest. "I'm sorry. You must have loved her."

"It was an addiction more than love."

Something clicked into place in her mind. Lucas had once used that term with regard to her. She hadn't liked it at the time, because it implied an unwilling attraction. "You don't see me as another Sophie?"

His hand trapped hers, holding it pressed against his chest so she could feel the steady thud of his heart. "You are similar in some ways, but maybe that's how the basic chemistry works. Both you and Sophie are my type."

Her stomach plunged a little. There it was again, the unwilling element to the attraction.

She knew he hadn't considered her marriageable in the beginning, because in his mind marriage hadn't fitted with the addictive sexual passion she had inspired in him. Admittedly, she hadn't helped matters. She had been busy trying to de-stress in line with her doctor's orders and keep their relationship casual but organized until the problems between both families had been rectified. In the process she had given him a false impression of her values. He had gotten to know who she really was a little better in the past few days, but that was cold comfort when she needed him to love her.

Fear spiked though her at the niggling thought that, if he

categorized her as being like Sophie, it was entirely possible that he wouldn't fall in love with her, that he would always see her as a fatal attraction and not his ideal marriage partner.

If she carried that thought through to its logical conclusion, it was highly likely that once the desire faded, he would fall for the kind of woman that in his heart he really wanted. "What happens when I get old, or put on weight, or…get sick?"

Physical attraction would fade fast and then where would they be?

She cupped his jaw. "I think I need to know *why* you can't resist me, because if what you feel is only based on physical attraction, it won't last."

He stoked a finger down the delicate line of her throat to her collarbone. "It's chemistry. A mixture of personality and the physical."

She frowned, her dissatisfaction increasing. "If you feel this way about me then how could you have been attracted to Lilah?"

As soon as she said Lilah's name, she wished she hadn't. Despite having Lucas's ring on her finger, she couldn't forget the weeks of stress when Lucas had avoided her then the sudden, hurtful way he had replaced her with Lilah.

"If you're jealous of Lilah, you don't need to be."

"Why?" But the question was suddenly unnecessary, because the final piece of the puzzle had just dropped into place. Lucas hadn't wanted Lilah for the simple reason that he had barely had time to get to know her. She had been part of a coldly logical strategy. An instant girlfriend selected for the purpose of spelling out in no uncertain terms that his relationship with Carla was over.

Fourteen

Carla stiffened. All the comments he'd made about her not needing to worry about Lilah and the quick way he had ended his relationship with her suddenly made perfect sense. "I have no reason to be jealous of Lilah, because you were never attracted to her."

His abrupt stillness and his lack of protest were damning.

"You manufactured a girlfriend." Her throat was tight, her voice husky. "You picked out someone safe to take to the wedding to make it easy to break up with me. You knew that if I thought you had fallen for another woman I would keep my distance and not make a fuss."

He loomed over her, his shoulders blocking out the dim glow from the lamp. "Carla—"

"No." Pushing free of his arms, she stumbled out of bed and struggled into her robe.

She yanked the sash tight as another thought occurred, giving her fresh insight into just how ruthless and serpentine

Lucas had been. "And you didn't pick just anyone to play your girlfriend. You were clever enough to select someone from Ambrosi Pearls, so the relationship covered all bases and would be in my face at work. That made it doubly clear to me that you were off-limits. It also made it look like you wanted her close, that you couldn't bear to have her out of your sight."

The complete opposite of his treatment of her.

Through the course of their relationship she had been separated and isolated from almost every aspect of his personal and business life.

Suddenly the room, with its romantic flowers, her clothes and jewelry draped over furniture and on the floor, emphasized how stupid she had been. Lucas's silence wasn't making her feel any better. "You probably even wanted to push me into leaving Ambrosi, which would get me completely out of your hair."

He shoved off the bed, found his pants and pulled them on. "I had no intention of depriving you of your job."

She stared at him bleakly, uncaring about that minor detail, when his major sin had been his complete and utter disregard for her feelings and her love. "What incentive did you offer Lilah to pose as your girlfriend?"

"I didn't pay Lilah. She knew nothing about this beyond the fact that I asked her to be my date at Constantine's wedding. That was our first, and last, date."

He caught her around the waist and pulled her close. "Do you believe me?"

She blinked. "Do you love me?"

There was the briefest of hesitations. "You know I do."

She searched his expression. It was a definite breakthrough, but it wasn't what she needed, not after the stinging hurt of finding out that he had used Lilah to facilitate getting rid of her.

His gaze seared into hers. "I'm sorry."

He bent and kissed her and the plunging disappointment receded a little. He was sorry and he very definitely wanted her. Maybe he even did love her. It wasn't the fairy tale she had dreamed about, but it was a start.

A few days ago she had been desperate for just this kind of chance with Lucas. Now too she was possibly pregnant. She owed it to herself and to Lucas to give him one more chance.

After an early breakfast, Carla strolled into the conference room Ambrosi had booked for its sales display. Lucas had phone calls to make in their suite, then meetings with buyers. Carla had decided to make herself useful and help Elise put together the jewelry display and set out the sales materials and press kits.

The fact that, if Lilah had been here, setting up the jewelry would have been her job was a reminder she didn't need, but she had to be pragmatic. Lilah was likely to be a part of the landscape for the foreseeable future, and she probably wasn't any happier about the situation than Carla. They would both have to adjust.

Security was already in place and lavish floral displays filled the room with the rich scent of roses. Elise had arranged for Ambrosi's special display cases to be positioned around the room. All that remained was for the jewelry, which was stored in locked cases, to be set out and labeled.

Elise, already looking nervous and ruffled, handed her a clipboard. "Just to make things more complicated, last night Lilah won a prestigious design award in Milan for some Ambrosi pieces. The buzz is *huge*." She snapped a rubber band off a large laminated poster. "Lucas had this expressed from the office late last night." She unrolled the poster, which was a blown-up publicity shot of Lilah, looking ultrasleek and gorgeous in a slim-fitting white suit, Ambrosi pearls at her lobes and her throat. With the pose she had struck and her calm gaze square on to the camera, Carla couldn't help thinking she looked eerily like the Atraeus bride in the portrait both she and Zane had studied at the prewedding dinner.

Elise glanced around the room. "I think I'll put it there, so people will see it as soon as they walk into the room. What do you think?"

Carla stared at the background of the poster. If she wasn't mistaken Lilah's image was superimposed over a scenic shot of Medinos—probably taken from one of the balconies of the *castello*. It was a small point, but it mattered. "Lucas ordered that to be done *late* last night?"

If that was the case, the only window of time he'd had was the few minutes after he had abducted her from the party when he had suddenly lost all interest in her because he had been so absorbed with what he was doing online.

Ordering a poster of the gorgeous, perfect Lilah.

Elise suddenly looked uncertain. "Uh, I think so. That's what he said."

Carla smiled and held out her hand. "Cool. Give the poster to me."

Elise went a little pale, but she handed the poster over.

Carla studied the larger-than-life photo. Her first impulse was to fling it into the ocean so she didn't have to deal with all that perfection. With her luck, the tide would keep tossing the poster back.

"I need scissors."

Elise found a pair and handed them over. Carla spent a happy few minutes systematically reducing the poster to an untidy pile of very small pieces.

Elise's eyes tracked the movement as Carla set the scissors down. She cleared her throat. "Do you want to sort through the jewelry, or would you prefer I did that?"

"I'm here to help. I'll do it."

"Great! I'll do the press kits." She dug in her briefcase. "Here's the plan for the display items. With all of the other publicity about, uh, Lilah, our sales have gone through the roof. We've already received orders from some of the attending clients so some of that jewelry is for clients and not for display. With any luck, they've kept the orders separate."

Carla slowly relaxed, determinedly thinking positive thoughts as she checked off the orders against the packing slip and set those packages to one side. Her mood improved by the second as she began putting the display together, anchoring the gorgeous, intricate pieces securely on black velvet beds then locking the glass cases. Lilah may have designed most of the jewelry, but they were Ambrosi pieces and she was proud of them. She refused to allow any unhappiness she felt about Lilah affect her pride in the family business.

A courier arrived with a package. Elise signed for it, shrugging. "This is weird. All the rest was delivered yesterday."

Carla took the package and frowned. The same courier firm had delivered it, but this one wasn't from the Ambrosi warehouse in Sydney. The package had been sent by another jeweler, the same Atraeus-owned company from which Lucas had purchased her engagement ring. That meant that whatever the package contained it couldn't be either an order for a customer or jewels for the launch.

Anticipation and a glow of happy warmth spread through her as she studied the package. She had her ring, which meant Lucas must have bought her something else, possibly a matching pendant or bracelet.

Her heart beat a little faster. Perhaps even matching wedding rings.

The temptation to open the package was almost overwhelming, but she managed to control herself. Lucas had bought her a gift, his first real gift of love, without pressure or prompting. She wasn't about to spoil his moment when he gave her the special piece he had selected.

She studied the ring on her finger, unable to contain her pleasure. She didn't care about the size of the diamond or the cost. What mattered was that Lucas had chosen it because it matched her eyes. Every time she looked at the ring she remembered that tiny, very personal, very important detail. It was a sign that he was one step closer to truly loving and appreciating her. After what had happened last night, how close they had come to splitting up again, she treasured every little thing that would help keep them together.

Elise finished shoving boxes and Bubble Wrap in the bin liner the hotel had provided. She waggled her brows at the package. "Not part of the display, huh? Looks interesting. Want me to take it to Lucas? I'm supposed to take the Japanese client he's meeting with to the airport in about ten minutes."

"Hands off." Carla's fingers tightened on the package. Despite knowing that Elise was teasing her, she felt ridiculously possessive of whatever Lucas had bought for her.

A split second later, Lucas strolled into the conference room. Immediately behind him, hotel attendants were setting up for morning tea, draping the long tables in white table-cloths and setting out pastries and finger food. Outside, in the lobby, she could hear the growing chatter. Any minute now, buyers and clients would start pouring into the conference room and there would be no privacy. The impulse to thrust the package at Lucas and get him to open it then and there died a death.

Lucas's gaze locked with hers then dropped to the glossy cut-up pieces of poster still strewn across the table. He lifted a brow. "What's that?"

"Your poster of Lilah."

There was a moment of assessing silence.

Lucas was oddly watchful, recognizing and logging the changes in her. As if he was finally getting that she was a whole lot more than the amenable, compartmentalized lover he had spent the past two years holding at a distance.

In that moment Carla knew Lilah had to go completely, no matter how crucial she was to Ambrosi Pearls. If she and Lucas were to have a chance at a successful marriage, they couldn't afford a third person in the equation.

Lucas lifted a brow. "What's in the package?"

"Nothing that won't keep." She pushed the package out of sight in her handbag then briskly swept all the poster fragments into the trash.

Whatever Lucas had bought her, she couldn't enjoy receiving it right at that minute, not with the larger-than-life specter of Lilah still hanging over them.

The weekend finished with a dinner cruise, by the end of which Lucas was fed up with designer anything. Give him steel girders and mining machinery any day. Anything but the shallow, too bright social whirl that was part and parcel of the world of luxury retailing.

He kept his arm around Carla's waist as they stood on the quay, bidding farewell to the final guests.

Carla was exhausted—he could feel it in the way she leaned into him—and her paleness worried him. The last thing she needed was another viral relapse.

He had insisted she fit in a nap after lunch. It had been a struggle to make her let go of the organizational reins, but in the end he had simply picked her up and carried her to their room. He had discovered that there was something about the masculine, take-charge act of picking Carla up that seemed to reach her in a way that words couldn't.

She had been oddly quiet all day, but he had expected that. He had made a mistake with the poster. The second he had walked into the conference room that morning and seen the look on Carla's face he had realized just how badly he had messed up. He had grimly resolved to take more care in future.

Her quietness had carried over into the evening. He had debated having her stay in their suite and rest, but in the end he had allowed her to come on the cruise for one simple reason. If he left her behind, she might not be there when he returned.

Lucas recognized Alan Harrison, a London buyer and the last straggling guest.

He paused to shake Lucas's hand. "Lilah Cole, the name on everyone's lips. You might have trouble holding on to her now, Atraeus. I know Catalano jewelry in Milan is impressed with her work. Wouldn't be surprised if they try and spirit her away from you."

Lucas clenched his jaw as Carla stiffened beside him. "That won't happen for at least two years. Lilah just signed a contract to take on the Medinos retail outlet as well as head up the design team."

"Medinos, huh? Smart move. Pretty girl, and focused. Got her in the nick of time. Another few days and you would have lost her."

Carla waited until Harrison had gone then gently detached herself from his hold. "You didn't tell me you had renewed Lilah's contract."

There was no accusation in her voice, just an empty neutrality, but Lucas had finally learned to read between the lines. When Carla went blank that was when she was feeling the most, and when *he* was being weighed in the balance.

Two years, and he hadn't understood that one crucially important fact. "I offered her the Medinos job a couple of days ago. If I'd realized how much it would hurt you I would have let her go. At the time removing her to Medinos for two years seemed workable, since I'll be running the Sydney office for the foreseeable future and we'll be based here."

"You did that for me." There was a small, vibrating silence and he was finally rewarded with a brilliant smile. "Thank you."

"You're welcome." Grinning, he pulled her into his arms.

Carla slipped out of her heels as she walked into their suite. Her feet were aching but she was so happy she hardly noticed the discomfort.

Lucas had finally crossed the invisible line she had needed him to cross; he had committed himself to her, and the blood was literally fizzing through her veins.

Maybe she should have felt this way when they had gotten engaged, but the reality was that all he'd had to do was say words and buy a ring. As badly as she had wanted to, she hadn't felt secure. Now, for the first time in over two years, she finally did.

The fact that he had arranged for Lilah to work in Medinos because they would be based in Sydney for two years had been the tipping point.

He had made an arrangement to ensure their happiness. He had used the word *they*. It was a little word, but it shouted commitment and togetherness.

Two years in Sydney. Together.

Taking Lucas by the hand, she pulled him into the bedroom, determinedly keeping her gaze away from the bedside bureau where she had concealed the package that had arrived that morning. "Sit down." She patted the bed. "I'll get the champagne."

He shrugged out of his jacket and tossed it over a chair before jerking at his tie. "Maybe you shouldn't drink champagne."

"Sparkling water for me, champagne for you."

"What are we celebrating, exactly?"

"You'll see in a minute."

He paused in the act of unbuttoning his shirt. "You're pregnant."

The hope in Lucas's voice sent a further shiver of excitement through her. Not only did he want her enough that he had bought her a wonderful surprise gift, he really did want their baby. Suddenly, after weeks, years, of uncertainty everything was taking on the happy-ever-after fairy tale sparkle she had always secretly wanted.

Humming to herself, she walked into the kitchen and opened a chilled bottle of vintage French champagne. The label was one of the best. The cost would be astronomical, but this was a special moment. She wanted every detail to be perfect. She put the champagne and two flutes on a tray and added a bottle of sparkling water for herself. On the way to the bedroom, she added a gorgeous pink tea rose from one of the displays.

She set the tray down on the bedside table as Lucas padded barefoot out of the bathroom. In the dim lamp-lit room with his torso bare, his dark dress trousers clinging low on narrow hips, his bronzed, muscular beauty struck her anew and she was suddenly overwhelmed by emotion and a little tearful.

Lucas cupped her shoulders and drew her close. "What's wrong?"

She snuggled against him, burying her face in the deliciously warm, comforting curve of his shoulder. "Nothing, except that I love you."

There was a brief hesitation, then he drew her close. "And I love you."

Carla stiffened at the neutral tone of his voice then made an effort to dismiss the twinge of disappointment that, even now, with this new intimacy between them, Lucas still couldn't relax into loving her.

She pushed away slightly, enough that she could see his face and read his expression, but she was too late to catch whatever truth had been in his eyes when he had said those three little words.

Forcing a bright smile, she released herself from Lucas's light hold, determined to recapture the soft, fuzzy fairy-tale glow. "Time for the champagne."

Lucas took the bottle from her and set it back down on the tray.

He reeled her in close. "I don't need a drink."

His head dipped, his lips brushed hers. She wound her arms around his neck, surrendering to the kiss as he pulled her onto the bed. Long seconds later he propped his head on one elbow and wound a finger in a coiling strand of her hair. "What's wrong? You're like a cat on hot bricks."

Rolling over, Carla opened the bureau drawer and took out the courier package. "This came today."

The heavy plastic rustled as she handed it to Lucas. Instead of the teasing grin she had expected, Lucas's gaze rested on the courier package and he went curiously still.

A sudden suspicion gripped her.

Clambering off the bed she took the package and ripped at the heavy plastic.

"Carla—"

"No. Don't talk." Tension banded her chest as she walked out to the kitchen, found a steak knife in the drawer and slit the plastic open. A heavy, midnight-blue box, tied with a black silk bow, the jeweler's signature packaging, tumbled out of layers of Bubble Wrap onto the kitchen counter.

Not an oblong case that might hold a necklace, or a bracelet. A ring box.

Lucas loomed over her as she tore the bow off. Maybe

it was a set of wedding rings. Lucas wanted an early wedding. It made sense to order the rings from the same place they had bought her engagement ring.

"Carla—"

She already knew. Not wedding rings. She flipped the jewelry case open.

A diamond solitaire glittered with a soft, pure fire against midnight-blue velvet.

Fingers shaking, she slid the ring onto the third finger of her right hand. It was a couple of sizes too small and failed to clear her knuckle. The bright, illusory world she had been living in dissolved.

The ring had never been meant for her. The elegant, classic engagement ring had been selected and sized with someone else in mind.

Lilah.

Fifteen

Carla replaced the ring in its box and met Lucas's somber gaze head-on. "You weren't just dating Lilah to facilitate making a clean break with me, were you? You intended to marry her."

Lucas's expression was calmly, coolly neutral. "I had planned to propose marriage, but that was before—"

"Why would you want to marry Lilah when you still wanted me?" She couldn't say *love,* because she now doubted that love had ever factored in. Lucas had wanted her, period. He had felt desire, passion: lust.

"It was a practical decision."

"Because otherwise you were worried that when Constantine and Sienna tied the knot you might be pressured into marrying me."

Impatience flashed in his gaze. "No one could pressure me into marriage. I wanted you. I would have married you in a New York second."

Realization dawned. "Then lived to regret it."

"I didn't think what we had would last."

"So you tied yourself into an arrangement with Lilah so you couldn't be tempted into making a bad decision."

His brows jerked together. "There was no 'arrangement.' All Lilah knew was that I wanted to date her."

"With a view to marriage."

"Yes."

Because she wouldn't have gone out with him otherwise. Certainly not halfway across the world to a very public family wedding.

Hurt spiraled through her that Lucas hadn't bothered to refute her statement that marrying her would have been a bad decision. And that he had so quickly offered Lilah what she had longed for and needed from him.

Throat tight, eyes stinging, Carla snapped the ring box closed and jammed it back into the courier bag. She suddenly remembered the odd behavior of the manager of Moore's. It hadn't been because their engagement was so sudden, or because of the scandal in the morning paper. The odd atmosphere had been because Lucas had bought *two* engagement rings in the same week for two separate women.

Blindly, she shoved the courier bag at Lucas. "You were going to propose to her *here,* at this product launch." Why else would he have requested the ring be couriered to the hotel?

Carla remembered the flashes of sympathy in Lilah's gaze on Medinos, her bone-white face outside of Lucas's apartment when the reporter had snapped Carla and Lucas kissing. Lilah had expected more than just a series of dates. She wouldn't have been with Lucas otherwise.

"You were never even remotely in love with Lilah."

"No."

Her head jerked up. "Then, why consider marriage?"

His expression was taut. "The absence of emotion worked for me. I wasn't after the highs and lows. I wanted the opposite."

"Because of Sophie Warrington."

"That's right," he said flatly. "Sophie liked bright lights, publicity. She loved notoriety. We clashed constantly. The night of the crash we argued and she stormed out. That was the last time I saw her alive. I shouldn't have let her go, should have stopped her—"

"If she wasn't your kind of girl, why were you with her?"

"Good question," he said grimly. "Because I was stupid enough to fall for her. We were a mismatch. We should never have been together in the first place."

Carla's jaw tightened. "You do still think I'm like her," she said quietly. "Another Sophie."

His expression was closed. "I...did."

The hesitation was the final nail in the proverbial coffin. Her stomach plummeted. "You still do."

"I've made mistakes, but I know what I want," Lucas said roughly.

"Me, or the baby I might possibly be having?" Because if Lucas still didn't know who she was as a person, the baby seemed the strongest reason for marriage. And she couldn't marry someone who saw his attraction to her as a weakness, a character flaw. She stared blankly around the flower-festooned room. "If you don't mind, I'd like to get some sleep."

Stepping past Lucas, she walked into the bedroom and grabbed a spare pillow and blanket from the closet.

"Where are you going?"

"To sleep on the couch."

"That's not necessary. I'll take the couch."

She flinched at the sheer masculine beauty of his broad shoulders and muscled chest. She had fallen in love with a mirage, she thought bleakly, a beautiful man who was prepared to care for her but who, ultimately, had never truly wanted to be in love with her. "No. Right now I really would prefer the couch."

His fingers curled around her upper arms. "We can work this through. I can explain—"

She went rigid in his grip. The pillow and blanket formed a buffer between them that right now she desperately needed because, despite everything, she was still vulnerable. "Let me go," she said quietly. "It's late. We both need sleep."

His dark gaze bored into hers, level and calm. "Come back to bed. We can talk this through."

She fought the familiar magnetic pull, the desire to drop the pillow and blanket and step back into his arms. "No. We can talk in the morning."

A familiar cramping pain low in her stomach pulled Carla out of sleep. A quick trip to the bathroom verified that she had her period and that she was absolutely, positively not pregnant.

Numbly, she walked back to the couch but didn't bother trying to sleep. Until that moment she hadn't realized how much she had desperately needed to be pregnant. If there was a child then there had been the possibility that she could have stayed with Lucas. Now there wasn't one and she had to face reality.

Lucas had broken up with Sophie when she had aborted his child. He had also proposed marriage when he had thought she could be pregnant. For a man who had gone to considerable lengths to cut her out of his life, that was a huge turnaround. She could try fooling herself that it was because he loved her, even if he didn't quite know it, but she couldn't allow herself to think that way. She deserved better.

Now she knew for sure she wasn't pregnant. There were no more excuses.

Her decision made, she opted not to shower, because that would wake Lucas. Instead, she found her gym bag, which was sitting by the kitchen counter and which contained fresh underwear, sweatpants, a tank and a light cotton hoodie. She quickly dressed and laced on sneakers. Her handbag with all her medications was in the bedroom. She couldn't risk getting that, but she had a cash card and some cash tucked in her gym bag. That would give her enough money and the ID she needed to book a flight back to Sydney. She had plenty of medication at home, so leaving the MediPACKs in her purse wasn't a problem. She would collect her hand-bag along with the rest of her luggage from Lucas when he got back to Sydney.

Working quickly, she jammed toiletries into the sports bag. She paused to listen, but there was no sound or move-ment from the bedroom. She wrote a brief note on hotel paper, explaining that she was not pregnant and was there-fore ending their engagement. She anchored the note to the kitchen counter with the engagement ring.

Picking up the sports bag and hooking her handbag over her shoulder, she quietly let herself out of the room.

Within a disorientingly short period of time the elevator shot her down to the lobby. The speed with which she had walked away from what had been the most important adult relationship of her life made her stomach lurch sickly, but she couldn't go back.

She couldn't afford to commit one more minute to a man who had put more creative effort into cutting her out of his life than he ever had to including her.

A small sound pulled Lucas out of a fitful sleep.

Kicking free of the tangled sheet, he pushed to his feet and pulled on the pair of pants he'd left tossed over the arm of a chair.

Moonlight slanted through shuttered windows as he walked swiftly through the suite. His suspicion that the sound that had woken him had been the closing of the front door turned to certainty when he found a note and Carla's engagement ring on the kitchen counter.

The note was brief. Carla wasn't pregnant. Rather than both of them being pushed into a marriage that clearly had no chance of working, she had decided to give him his out.

She had left him.

Lucas's hand closed on the note, crumpling it. His heart was pounding as if he'd run a race and his chest felt tight. Taking a deep breath, he controlled the burst of raw panic.

He would get her back. He had to.

She loved him, of that fact he was certain. All it would take was the right approach.

He had messed up one too many times. With the double emotional hit of discovering that he had intended to propose to Lilah then the shock of discovering that she wasn't pregnant, he guessed he shouldn't be surprised that she had reacted by running.

Like Sophie.

His stomach clenched at the thought that Carla could have an accident. Then logic reasserted itself. That wouldn't happen. Carla was so *not* like Sophie he didn't know how he could have imagined she was in the first place.

But this time he would not compound his mistake by failing to act. He would make sure that Carla was safe. He would not fail her again.

He loved her.

His stomach clenched as he examined that reality. He couldn't change the past; all he could do was try to change the future.

Sliding the note into his pocket along with the ring, he strode back to his room to finish dressing. He pulled on shoes and found his wallet and watch. The possibility that he could lose Carla struck him anew and for a split second he was almost paralyzed with fear. Until that moment he hadn't understood how necessary Carla was to him.

For more than two years she had occupied his thoughts and haunted his nights. He had thought the affair would run its course; instead his desire had strengthened. In order to control what he had deemed an obsession, he had minimized contact and compartmentalized the affair.

The strategy hadn't worked. The more restrictive he had become in spending time with Carla, the more uncontrollable his desire had become.

She wasn't pregnant.

Until that moment he hadn't known how much he had wanted Carla to be pregnant. Since the out-of-control lovemaking on Medinos, the possibility of a pregnancy had initiated a number of responses from him. The most powerful had been the cast-iron excuse it had provided him to bring her back into his life. But as the days had passed, the thought of Carla losing her taut hourglass shape and growing soft and round with his child had become increasingly appealing. Along with the need to keep Carla tied close, he had wanted to be a father.

Pocketing his keys, he strode out of the suite. Frustration gripped him when he jabbed the elevator call button then had to wait. His gaze locked on the glowing arrow above the doors, and he scraped at his jaw, which harbored a five-o'clock shadow.

Dragging rough fingers through his rumpled hair, he began to pace.

He couldn't lose her.

Whatever it took, he would do it. He would get her back.

He recalled the expression on Carla's face when she had found the engagement ring he had ordered for Lilah, her stricken comment that Constantine had wanted Sienna enough that he had kidnapped her.

Raw emotion gripped him.

Almost the exact opposite of his behaviour.

Carla walked quickly through the lobby, which was empty except for a handful of guests checking out. She had wasted frantic minutes checking the backstage area. It had been empty of possessions, which meant either Elise or Nina had her things.

Too fragile to bear the stirring of interest she would cause by waiting inside, she avoided the concierge desk and made a beeline for the taxi stand.

Not having her medication wasn't ideal. She hadn't taken any last night, and now she would go most of the day without them. Antacids would have to do. She could wait out the short flight to Sydney and the taxi ride home, where there was a supply of pills in her bathroom cupboard.

A pale-faced group of guests, obviously catching an early flight out, were climbing into the only taxi waiting near the hotel entrance. Settling her gym bag down on the dusty pavement, she settled herself to wait for the next taxi to turn into the hotel pickup area.

Long seconds ticked by. She glanced in at the empty reception area, her tension growing, not because she was desperate to escape, she finally admitted to herself, but because a weak part of her still wanted Lucas to stride out and stop her from going.

Not that Lucas was likely to chase her.

Shivering in the faint chill of the air, she stared at the bleak morning sky now graying in the east as a cab finally braked to a halt beside her.

She slipped into the rear seat with her bag, requested the cab driver take her to the airport and gave the hotel entrance one last look before she stared resolutely at the road unfolding ahead.

Why would Lucas come after her, when she was giving him the thing he had always valued most in their relationship, his freedom?

Lucas caught the flash of the taxi's taillights as it turned out of the resort driveway and the panic that had gripped him while he'd endured the slow elevator ride turned to cold fear.

Sliding his phone out of his pocket, he made a series of calls then strode back into the hotel and took the elevator to the rooftop.

Seconds later, Tiberio phoned back. He had obtained Carla's destination from the taxi company. She was headed for Brisbane Airport. He had checked with the flight desk and she had already booked her flight out to Sydney.

The quiet, efficient way Carla had left him hit Lucas forcibly. No threats or manipulation, no smashed crockery or showy exit in a sports car, just a calm, orderly exit with her flight already arranged.

He felt like kicking himself that it had taken him this long to truly see who she was, and to understand why she was so irresistible to him. He hadn't fallen into lust with a second Sophie. He had fallen in love for the first time—with a woman who was smart and fascinating and perfect for him.

Then he had spent the past two years trying to crush what he felt for her.

Issuing a further set of instructions, Lucas settled down to wait.

Carla frowned as the taxi took the wrong exit and turned into a sleepy residential street opposite a sports field. "This isn't the way to the airport."

The driver gave her an odd look in the rearview mirror

and hooked his radio, which he'd been muttering into for the past few minutes, back on its rest. "I have to wait for someone."

Carla started to argue, then the rhythmic chop of rotor blades slicing the air caught her attention. A sleek black helicopter set down on the sports field. A tall, dark-haired man climbed out, ducking his head as he walked beneath the rotor blades.

Her heart slammed in her chest. She had wanted Lucas to come after her. Contrarily, now that he was here, all she wanted to do was run.

Depressing the door handle, she pushed the door wide and groped for the cash in the side pocket of her gym bag. She shoved some money at the driver, more than enough to cover his meter, and dragged the sports bag off the back-seat. A split second later the world flipped sideways and she found herself cradled in Lucas's arms.

Her heart pounded a crazy tattoo. The strap of the sports bag slipped from her fingers as she grabbed at his shoulders. "What do you think you're doing?"

His gaze, masked by dark glasses, seared over her face. "Kidnapping you. That's the benchmark, isn't it?"

Her mouth went dry at his reference to the conversation they'd had when she had listed the things Constantine had done that proved his love for Sienna. Her pulse rate ratcheted up another notch.

She stared into the remote blankness of the dark glasses, suddenly terribly afraid to read too much into his words. "If you're afraid I'm going to do something silly or have an accident, I'm not. I'm just giving you the out you want."

"I know. I read the note." He placed her in the seat directly behind the pilot. "And by the way, here it is."

He took out a piece of the hotel notepaper, tore it into

pieces and tossed it into the downdraft of the blades. The scraps of paper whirled away.

"What are you doing now?" she asked as he started to walk away from the chopper.

The noise muffled his reply. "Getting your shoes and makeup and whatever else it is that makes you happy."

Seconds later, he tossed her sports bag on the floor at her feet and belted himself in beside her.

"Where are we going?" She had to yell now above the noise from the chopper.

Lucas fitted a set of earphones over her head then donned a set himself. "A cabin. In the mountains."

A short flight later the helicopter landed in a clearing. Within minutes the pilot had lifted off, leaving them with a box stamped with the resort's logo on the side. Lucas picked it up. She guessed it was food.

Carla stared at the rugged surrounding range of the Lamingtons, the towering gum trees and silvery gleam of a creek threading through the valley below. "I can't believe you kidnapped me."

"It worked for Constantine."

Her heart pounded at his answer. It wasn't quite a declaration of love, but it was close.

She followed Lucas into the cabin, which was huge. With its architectural angles, sterile planes of glass and comfortable leather couches it was more like an upscale executive palace than her idea of a rustic holiday cottage.

He placed the box on a kitchen counter then began unloading what looked like a picnic lunch. A kidnapping, Atraeus-style, with all the luxury trappings.

Frustrated by his odd mood and the dark glasses, she walked outside, grabbed her sports bag and brought it into the house. She could feel herself floundering, unable to ask the questions that mattered in case the hope that had flared to life when he had bodily picked her up and deposited her in the helicopter was extinguished. "It's not as if this is a real kidnapping."

He stopped, his face curiously still. "How 'real' did you want it to be?"

Sixteen

"We're alone. We're together." Lucas reached for calm when all he really wanted was to pull her close and kiss her.

But that approach hadn't worked so far. Carla had actually tried to run from him, which had altered his game plan somewhat. Plan B was open-ended, meaning he no longer knew what he was doing except that he wasn't going to blow this now by resorting to sex. "We can do what we should have done last night and talk this out. Have you eaten?"

"No." She stared absently at the rich, spicy foods and freshly squeezed juice he had set out then began rummaging through her gym bag just in case there was a stray pack of antacids in one of the pockets.

Lucas, intensely aware of every nuance of expression on Carla's face, tensed when she picked up the phone on the counter. "What's wrong? Who are you calling?"

She frowned when the call wasn't picked up. "Elise. She can get me some medication I need."

"What medication?" But suddenly he knew. The small bag of snacks she carried, her preoccupation with what she was eating and the weight loss. "You're either diabetic or you've got an ulcer."

"The second one."

He could feel his temper soaring. "Why didn't you tell me?"

"You weren't exactly over the moon when I got ill in Thailand."

"You had a virus in Thailand."

"And the viral bacteria just happened to attack an area of my stomach that was still healing from an ulcer I had two years ago. Although I didn't find that out until the ulcer perforated and I got to hospital."

He felt himself go ice-cold inside. "You had a perforated ulcer?" For a split second he thought he must have misheard. "You could have died. Why didn't you tell me?"

Her gaze was cool. "After what happened in Thailand I didn't want you to know I was sick again." She shrugged. "Mom and Sienna didn't know about you, so it was hardly likely they would call you. Why would they? You had no visible role in my life."

That was all going to change, he thought grimly. From now on he was going to be distinctly, in-your-face visible.

He felt like kicking himself. In Thailand he had distanced himself from Carla when she was sick because the enforced intimacy of looking after her had made him want a lot more than the clandestine meetings they'd had through the year. Pale and ill, sweating and shivering, Carla hadn't been either glamorous or sexually desirable. She had simply been *his*.

He had wanted to continue caring for her, wanted to keep her close. But the long hours he had spent sitting beside her bed, waiting for her fever to break, had catapulted him back to his time with Sophie.

He had not wanted her to be that important to him. He hadn't wanted to make himself vulnerable to the kind of guilt and betrayal his relationship with Sophie had resulted in. He could admit that now.

"When was the last time you had your medication?"

She punched in another number. "Lunch, yesterday. That's why I'm calling the resort. Either Nina or Elise can go to the suite and find my handbag, which is where I keep my Medi-PACKs. I'm hoping Tiberio or one of your other bodyguards could drive up with it."

"If you think I'm taking two hours to get you the medication you need, think again." Lucas's cell was already in his hand. He speed dialed and bit out commands in rapid Medinian, hung up and slipped the phone back in his pocket. "Our ride will be here in fifteen minutes."

She slipped her phone back in her handbag. "I could have waited. It's not that bad. I just have to manage my stomach for a few weeks."

"You might be able to wait, but *I* can't. What do you think it did to me to hear that you almost died in hospital?"

"I didn't *almost* die." She grimaced. "Although it wasn't pleasant, that's for sure. It wasn't as if I wasn't used to dealing with the ulcer. It just got out of hand."

He went still inside. "How long did you say you had the ulcer?"

"Two years or so."

Around the time they had met. His jaw tightened at this further evidence of how blind he had been with Carla. He knew ulcers could be caused by a number of factors, but number one was stress. In retrospect, the first time they had made love and he had found out she was a virgin he should have taken a mental step back and reappraised. He hadn't done it. He hadn't wanted to know what might hurt or upset

Carla, or literally eat away at her, because he had been so busy protecting himself.

"News flash," she said with an attempted grin. "I'm a worrier. Can't seem to ditch the habit."

He reached her in two steps and hauled her close. "The woman I love collapses because she has a perforated ulcer," he muttered, "and all you can say is that it *wasn't pleasant?*"

Carla froze in Lucas's arms and, like a switch flicking, she swung from depression and despair to deliriously happy. She stared, riveted by his fierce gaze, and decided she didn't need to pinch herself. "You really do love me?" He had said the words last night but they had felt neutral, empty.

"I love you. Why do you think I couldn't resist you?"

"But it did take you two years to figure that out."

"Don't remind me. Tell me how you ended up with the ulcer."

"Okay, here it goes, but now you might fall out of love with me. I'm a psycho-control-freak-perfectionist. I worked myself into the ground trying to lift Ambrosi's profile and micromanage all of our advertising layouts and pamphlets. When I started color coordinating the computer mouses and mouse pads, Sienna sent me to the family doctor. Jennifer gave me Losec and told me to stop taking everything so seriously, to lighten up and change my life. A week later, I met you."

"And turned my life upside down."

"I wish, but it didn't seem that way." She snuggled in close, unable to stop grinning, loving the way he was staring at her so fiercely. "All I knew was that I was running the relationship in the exact opposite way I wanted, supposedly to avoid stress. If you'd arrived in my life a couple of weeks early, you would have met a different woman."

"I fell in love with you. Instantly."

She closed her eyes and basked for just a few seconds. "Tell me again."

"I love you," he said calmly and, finally, he kissed her.

During the short helicopter ride, Lucas insisted on being given a crash course on her condition. When they reached the doctor's office, which was in a nearby town, Carla took Losec and an antibiotic under the eagle eye of both the doctor and Lucas.

At Lucas's insistence, the doctor also gave her a thorough checkup. Twenty minutes later she was given a clean bill of health.

They exited the office and strolled around to the parking lot to wait for the rental vehicle that Tiberio, apparently, had arranged to have delivered.

Lucas had kept his arm around her waist, keeping her close. "How are you feeling?"

"Fine." She leaned on him slightly. Not that she needed the support, but she loved the way he was treating her, as if she was a piece of precious, delicate porcelain. She could get used to it.

Lucas cupped her face, his fingers tangling in her hair. "I need to explain. To apologize."

Carla listened while Lucas explained about how her illness in Thailand had forced him to confront the guilt and betrayal of the past and had pushed him into a decision to break off with her.

His expression was remote. "But as you know, I couldn't break it off completely. When Constantine told me he was marrying Sienna, I knew I had to act once and for all."

"So you asked Lilah to accompany you to the wedding."

"She was surprised. Before that we had only ever spoken on a business level."

"But she guessed what was going on the night before the wedding."

"Only because she saw us together." He pulled her close, burying his face in her hair. "I'm not proud of what I did but I was desperate. I didn't realize I was in love with you until I read the note you left in the hotel room and discovered that you had left me. It was almost too late."

He hugged her close for long minutes, as if he truly did not want to let her go. "I've wasted a lot of time. Two years."

"There were good reasons we couldn't be together in the beginning. Some of those reasons were mine."

He frowned. "Reasons that suited me."

Gripping her hands gently in his, he went down on one knee. "Carla Ambrosi, will you marry me and be the love of my life for the rest of my life?"

He reached into his pocket and produced the sky-blue diamond ring, which he must have been carrying with him all along, and gently slipped it on the third finger of her left hand.

Tears blurred Carla's eyes at the soft gleam in Lucas's gaze, the intensity of purpose that informed her that if she said no he would keep on asking until she was his.

Emotion shimmered through her, settled in her heart, because she *had* been his all along.

"Yes," she said, the answer as simple as the kiss that followed, the long minutes spent holding each other and the promise of a lifetime together.

* * * * *

Don't miss the stories in this mini series!

THE PEARL HOUSE

**Business and passion collide when
two dynasties forge ties bound by love.**

A Breathless Bride
FIONA BRAND
May 2012

A Tangled Affair
FIONA BRAND
July 2012

Mills & Boon™

The Paternity Promise
Merline Lovelace

Mills & Boon™
pure reading pleasure

MERLINE LOVELACE

A career Air Force officer, Merline Lovelace served at bases all over the world. When she hung up her uniform for the last time she decided to combine her love of adventure with a flair for storytelling, basing many of her tales on her own experiences in uniform. Since then she's produced more than ninety action-packed sizzlers, many of which have made the *USA TODAY* and Waldenbooks bestseller lists. Over eleven million copies of her books are available in some thirty countries.

When she's not tied to her keyboard, Merline enjoys reading, chasing little white balls around the fairways of Oklahoma and travelling to new and exotic locales with her handsome husband, Al. Check her website at www.merlinelovelace.com or friend her on Facebook for news and information about her latest releases.

Dear Reader,

When my husband and I spent a week in the small town of Saint-Rémy-de-Provence in the south of France, we absolutely fell in love with the place. And since I'm always on the lookout for exciting locales for books, I knew Saint-Rémy would eventually show up in one.

I didn't, however, expect the road that led my characters there would be so bumpy and pitted with tension, sexual and otherwise. I had great fun overcoming the roadblocks with Grace and Blake—hope you do, too!

All my best, and happy reading,

Merline Lovelace

DEDICATION

To the Elite Eight, and the wonderful times we've shared.
Thanks for giving me such terrific fodder for my books!

One

His fists balled inside the pockets of his tuxedo pants, Blake Dalton forced a smile as he stood amid the wedding guests jamming the black-and-white-tiled foyer of his mother's Oklahoma City mansion. The lavish reception was finally winding down. The newlyweds had just paused in their descent of the foyer's circular marble staircase so the bride could toss her bouquet. The couple were mere moments from departing for their honeymoon in Tuscany.

Blake was damned if he'd block their escape. His twin had waged a tumultuous battle to win the stubbornly independent pilot he'd finally finessed to the altar. Alex had earned these two weeks in Tuscany with his new bride, away from his heavy responsibilities as CEO of Dalton International.

Blake had no problem taking up the slack in his absence. An MBA, a law degree and almost a decade of

handling the corporation's complex legal affairs had
honed the leadership and managerial skills he'd developed as DI's CFO. He and Alex regularly took over sole
control of the multibillion-dollar conglomerate during
each other's frequent business trips.

No, the job wasn't the problem.

Nor was it their mother, who'd waged a fierce and
unrelenting campaign to get her sons married and settled down for over a year now.

Blake's glance cut to the matriarch of the Dalton clan.
Her hair was still jet-black, with only a hint of silver at
the temples. She wore a melon-colored Dior lace dress
and an expression of smug satisfaction as she surveyed
the newly married couple. Blake knew exactly what she
was thinking. One son down, one to go.

But it was the baby peering over his mother's shoulder that made his fist bunch even tighter and his heart
squeeze inside his chest. In the weeks since person or
persons unknown had left the six-month-old on his
mother's doorstep, Molly had become as essential to
Blake as breathing.

DNA testing had proved with 99.99 percent certainty
that the bright-eyed infant girl was a Dalton. Unfortunately, the tests hadn't returned the same accuracy as
to *which* of the Dalton brothers had fathered the baby.
Although even identical twins carried distinctive DNA,
there were enough similarities to fog the question of paternity. The report had indicated a seventy-seven percent probability that Alex was the father, but the issue
couldn't be completely resolved until the lab matched
the father's DNA with that of the mother.

As a result, the Dalton brothers had spent several uncomfortable weeks after Molly's arrival tracking down
the women they'd connected with early last year. Alex's

list had been considerably longer than Blake's, but none of the potential candidates—including the woman who'd just become Ms. Alex Dalton—had proved to be the baby's mother. Or so they'd thought.

A noisy round of farewells wrenched Blake's gaze from the baby. He looked up to find his brother searching the crowd. It was like looking in a mirror. Both he and Alex had their father's build. Like Big Jake Dalton, they carried six feet plus of solid muscle. They'd also inherited their father's electric blue eyes and tawny hair that the hot Oklahoma sun streaked to a dozen different shades of gold.

Blake caught Alex's eye and casually, so casually, shook his head. He had to forcibly blank both his face and his mind to block any more subtle signals. In the way of all twins, the Dalton brothers could pick up instantly on each other's vibes. Time enough for Alex and Julie to hear the news when they got back from Tuscany. By then Blake would have dealt with it. And with the shock and fury it had generated.

He rigidly suppressed both emotions until the newlyweds were on the way to the airport. Even then he did his duty and mingled until the last guests finally departed. His training as an attorney stood him in good stead. No one, not even his mother, suspected there was fury boiling in his gut.

"Whew!" Ebullient but drooping, Delilah Dalton kicked off her heels. "That was fun, but I'm glad it's over. Went off well, don't you think?"

"Very," Blake answered evenly.

"I'm going to check on Molly." She swooped up her shoes and padded on stockinged feet to the circular marble staircase. "Then I'm hitting the tub to soak for an hour. You staying here tonight?"

"No, I'll go back to my place." With a vicious exercise of will, he kept his voice calm. "Would you ask Grace to come down? I'd like to talk to her before I go."

His mother lifted a brow at his request to speak to the woman she'd hired to act as a temporary nanny. In the weeks since a baby had dropped into the lives of all three Daltons, Grace Templeton had proved indispensable. Become almost part of the family. So much so that she'd served as Julie's maid of honor while Blake stood up with Alex as best man.

She'd also started the wheels turning in Delilah's fertile mind. His mother had begun dropping unsubtle hints in recent days about how sweet Grace was. How well she interacted with Molly. And just tonight, how good Blake had looked standing beside her at the altar. The fact that he'd begun to think along those same lines only added to the fury simmering hot and heavy.

"Tell Grace I'll be in the library."

For once Delilah was too tired to pry. She merely waved her shoes and continued up the stairs. "Will do. Just don't keep her too long. She has to feel as whipped as I do."

She was about to feel a whole lot more whipped. Yanking on the ends of his black bow tie, Blake stalked down the hall to the oak-paneled library. The soft glow from the recessed lighting contrasted starkly with his black mood as he retrieved the report he'd stuffed into his pocket more than an hour ago. The facts were no less shattering now than they had been then. He was still trying to absorb their impact when Grace Templeton entered the library.

"Hey, Blake. Delilah said you wanted to talk to me."

His eyes narrowed on the slender blonde, seeing her in a wholly different light. She'd changed from the lilac, off-the-shoulder tea gown she'd worn for the wedding. She'd also released her pale, almost silvery hair from its sophisticated upsweep. The ends now brushed the shoulders of a sleeveless white blouse sporting several large splotches.

"'Scuze the wet spots," she said, brushing a hand down her front with a rueful laugh in her warm brown eyes. "Molly got a little lively during her bath."

Blake didn't respond. He merely stood with his shoulders rigid under his tux as she hitched a hip on the wide, rolled arm of the library's sofa.

"What did you want to talk about?"

Only then did she pick up on his silence. Or maybe it was his stance. Her head tilting, she gave him a puzzled half smile.

"Something wrong?"

He countered her question with one of his own. "Did you happen to notice the man who arrived at the reception just before Alex and Julie left?"

"The guy in the brown suit?" She nodded slowly, still trying to gauge his odd mood. "I saw him, and couldn't help wondering who he was. He looked so out of place among the other guests."

"His name's Del Jamison."

Her brow creased. Blake guessed she was mentally sorting through the host of people she'd met during her stint as Molly's temporary nanny. When she drew a blank, he supplied the details.

"Jamison's a private investigator. The one Alex and I hired to help search for Molly's mother."

She was good, he thought savagely. Very good. Her cinnamon eyes transmitted only a flicker of wariness, quickly suppressed, but she couldn't keep the color from leaching out of her cheeks. The sudden pallor gave him a vicious satisfaction.

"Oh, right." The shrug was an obvious attempt at nonchalance. "He was down in South America, wasn't he? Checking the places where Julie worked last year?"

"He was, but after Julie made it clear she wasn't Molly's mother, Jamison decided to check another lead. In California."

She couldn't hide her fear now. It was there in the quick hitch in her breath, the sudden stillness.

"California?"

"I'll summarize his report for you." Blake used his courtroom voice. The one he employed when he wanted to drive home a point. Cool, flat, utterly devoid of emotion. "Jamison discovered the woman I was told had died in a fiery bus crash was not, in fact, even on that bus. She didn't die until almost a year later."

The same woman he'd had a brief affair with. The woman who'd disappeared from his life with no goodbye, no note, no explanation of any kind. Aided and abetted, he now knew, by this brown-eyed, soft-spoken schemer who'd wormed her way into his mother's home.

And into Blake's consciousness, dammit. Every level of it. As disgusted by her duplicity as by the hunger she'd begun to stir in him, he stalked across the room. She sprang to her feet at his approach and tried to brazen it out.

"I don't see what that has to do with me."

Still he didn't lose control. But his muscles quivered with the effort of keeping his hands off her.

"According to Jamison, this woman gave birth to a baby girl just weeks before she died."

His baby! His Molly!

"She also had a friend who showed up at the hospital mere hours before her death." He planted his fists on the sofa arm, boxing her in, forcing her to lean back. "A *friend* with pale blond hair."

"Blake!" The gold-flecked brown eyes he'd begun to imagine turning liquid with desire widened in alarm. "Listen to me!"

"No, Grace—if that's really your name." His temper slipped through, adding a whiplash to his voice. "You listen, and listen good. I don't know how much you figured you could extort from our family, but the game ends now."

"It's not a game," she gasped, bent at an awkward angle.

"No?"

"No! I don't want your money!"

"What do you want?"

"Just… Just…!" She slapped her palms against his shirtfront. "Oh, for Pete's sake! Get off me."

He didn't budge. "Just what?"

"Dammit!" Goaded, she bunched a fist and pounded his chest. Her fear was gone. Fury now burned in her cheeks. "All I wanted, all I cared about, was making sure Molly had a good home!"

Slowly, Blake straightened. Just as slowly, he moved back a step and allowed her only enough space to push upright. Slapping a rigid lid on his anger, he folded his arms and locked his gaze on her face. Assessing. Considering. Evaluating.

"Let's start at the beginning. Who the hell are you?"

Grace balanced precariously on the sofa arm, her thoughts chaotic. After all she'd been through! So much fear and heartache. Now this? Just when she'd started to breathe easy for the first time in months. Just when she'd thought she and this man might...

"Who are you?"

He repeated the question in what she'd come to think of as his counselor's voice. She'd known Blake Dalton for almost two months now. In that time she'd learned to appreciate his even temperament. She admired even more his ability to smoothly, calmly arbitrate between his more outspoken twin and their equally strong-willed mother.

Oh, God! Delilah!

Grace cringed inside at the idea of divulging even part of the sordid truth to the woman who'd become as much of a friend as an employer. Sick at the thought, she lifted her chin and met Blake's cold, unwavering stare.

"I'm exactly who I claim to be. My name *is* Grace Templeton. I teach...I taught," she corrected, her throat tight, "junior high social studies in San Antonio until a few months ago."

She paused, trying not to think of the life she'd put on hold, forcing herself to blank out the image of the young teens she took such joy in teaching.

"Until a few months ago," Blake repeated in the heavy silence, "when you asked for an extended leave of absence to take care of a sick relative. That's the story you gave us, isn't it? And the principal of your school?"

She knew they'd checked her out. Neither Delilah nor her sons would allow a stranger near the baby unless they'd vetted her. But Grace had become so adept these past years at weaving just enough truth in with the lies that she'd passed their screening.

"It wasn't a story."

Dalton's breath hissed out. Those sexy blue eyes that

had begun to smile at her with something more than friendliness the past few weeks were now lethal.

"You and Anne Jordan were related?"

Anne Jordan. Emma Lang. Janet Blair. So many aliases. So many frantic phone calls and desperate escapes. Grace could hardly keep them straight anymore.

"Anne was my cousin."

That innocuous label didn't begin to describe Grace's relationship to the girl who'd grown up just a block away. They were far closer than cousins. They were best friends who'd played dolls and whispered secrets and shared every event in their young lives, big and small.

"Were you with her when she died?"

The question came at her as swiftly and mercilessly as a stiletto aimed for the heart. "Yes," she whispered, "I was with her."

"And the baby? Molly?"

"She's your daughter. Yours and…and Anne's."

Blake turned away, and Grace could only stare at the broad shoulders still encased in his tux. She ached to tell him she was sorry for all the lies and deception. Except the lies had been necessary, and the deception wasn't hers to tell.

"Anne called me," she said instead. "Told me she'd picked up a vicious infection. Begged me to come. I jumped a plane that same afternoon but when I got there, she was already slipping into a coma. She died that evening."

Blake angled back to face her. His eyes burned with an unspoken question. Grace answered this one as honestly as she could.

"Anne didn't name you as Molly's father. She was almost out of it from the drugs they'd pumped into her.

She was barely coherent… All I understood was the name Dalton. I knew she'd worked here, so…so…"

She broke off, her throat raw with the memory.

"So you brought Molly to Oklahoma City," Blake finished, spacing every word with frightening deliberation, "and left her on my mother's doorstep. Then you called Delilah and said you'd just happened to hear she needed a temporary nanny."

"Which she did!"

He gave that feeble response the disgust it deserved. "Did you enjoy watching my brother and me jump through hoops trying to determine which of us was Molly's father?"

"I told you! I didn't know which of you it was. Not until I'd spent some time with you."

Even then she hadn't been sure. The Dalton twins shared more than razor-sharp intelligence and devastating good looks. Grace could see how her cousin might have succumbed to Alex's charisma and self-confidence. She'd actually figured him for Molly's father until she'd come to appreciate the rock-solid strength in quiet, coolly competent Blake.

Unfortunately, Blake's self-contained personality had made her task so much more difficult. Although friendly and easygoing, he kept his thoughts to himself and his private life private. If he'd had a brief affair with a woman who'd worked for him, only he—and possibly his twin—had known about it.

Grace had hoped the DNA tests they'd run would settle the question of Molly's paternity. She'd been as frustrated as the Dalton brothers at the ambiguous results.

Then they'd launched a determined search for Molly's mother and thrown Grace in a state of near panic. She'd sworn to keep her cousin's secret. She had no choice but to do just that. Molly's future depended on it. Now Blake had unearthed at least a part of that secret. She couldn't tell him the rest, but she could offer a tentative solution.

"As I understand it, Molly's parentage can't be absolutely established unless the father's DNA is matched with the mother's. She…Anne…was cremated. I don't have anything of hers to give you that would provide a sample."

Not a hairbrush or a lipstick or even a postcard with a stamp on it for Molly to cling to as a keepsake. The baby's mother had lived in fear for so long. She'd died the same way, mustering only enough strength at the end to extract a promise from her cousin to keep Molly safe.

"You could test my DNA," Grace said, determined to hold to that promise. "I've read that mitochondria are inherited exclusively through the female line."

She'd done more than read. She'd hunched in front of the computer for hours when not tending to Molly. Her head had spun trying to decipher scientific articles laced with terms like hypervariable control regions and HVR1 base pairs. It had taken some serious slogging, but she'd finally come away with the knowledge that those four-hundred-and-forty-four base pairs determined maternal lineage. As such, they could theoretically be used to trace a human's lineage all the way back to the mitochondrial Eve. The Daltons didn't need to go that far back to confirm Molly's heritage. They just needed to hop over one branch on her family tree.

The same thought had obviously occurred to Blake. His eyes were chips of blue ice as he delivered an ultimatum.

"Damn straight you'll give me a DNA sample. And until the results come back, you'll stay away from Molly."

"What?"

"You heard me. I want you out of this house. Now."

"You're kidding!"

She discovered an instant later that he wasn't. In two strides he'd closed the distance between them and wrapped his fist around her upper arm. One swift tug had her off the sofa arm and marching toward the library's door.

"Blake, for God's sake!" As surprised as she was angry, she fought his grip. "I've been taking care of Molly for weeks now. You can't seriously think I would do anything to hurt her."

"What I think," he returned in a voice as icy as his eyes, "is that there are a helluva lot of holes in your story. Until they're filled in, I want you where I can watch you day *and* night."

Two

"Get in."

Blake held open the passenger door of his two-seater Mercedes convertible. The heat of the muggy July evening wrapped around them, almost as smothering as the worry and fear that clogged Grace's throat.

"Where are we going?"

"Downtown."

"I need to tell Delilah that I'm leaving," she protested. "Get some of my things."

"I'll let my mother know what's happening. Right now all you need to do is plant your behind in that seat."

If Grace hadn't been so stunned by this unexpected turn of events, the brusque command might have made her blink. This was Blake. The kind, polite, always solicitous Dalton twin. In the weeks since she'd insinuated herself into Delilah's home, she'd never known him to be anything but patient with his sometimes overbearing mother, considerate with the servants and incredibly, achingly gentle with Molly.

"Get in."

She got. Even this late in the evening, the pale gray leather was warm and sticky from the July heat. The seat belt cracked like a rifle shot when she clicked it into place.

As the convertible rolled down the curved driveway, Grace fought to untangle her nerves. God knew she should be used to having her life turned upside down without warning. It had happened often enough in the past few years. One call. That's all it usually took. One frantic call from Hope.

No, she corrected fiercely. Not Hope. *Anne.* Although her cousin was dead, Grace had to remember to think and remember and refer to her as Anne.

She made that her mantra as the Mercedes sliced through the night. She was still repeating it when Blake pulled into the underground parking for Dalton International's headquarters building in downtown Oklahoma City. Although the clicker attached to the Mercedes's visor raised the arm, the booth attendant leaned out with cheerful greeting.

"Evenin', Mr. Dalton."

"Hi, Roy."

"Guess your brother 'n his bride are off on their honeymoon."

"Yes, they are."

"Sure wish 'em well." He leaned farther down and tipped a finger to his brow. "How're you doin', Ms. Templeton?"

She dredged up a smile. "Fine, thanks."

Grace wasn't surprised at the friendly greeting. She'd made many a trip to Dalton International's headquarters with Molly and her grandmother. Delilah had turned over control of the manufacturing empire she and Big Jake had scratched out of bare dirt to her sons. That didn't mean she'd surrendered her right to meddle as she saw fit in either DI's corporate affairs or in her sons' lives. So Delilah, with Molly and her nanny in tow, had regularly breezed into boardrooms and conferences. Just as often, she'd zoomed up to the top floor of the DI building, where her bachelor sons maintained their separate penthouse apartments.

The penthouse also boasted a luxurious guest suite for DI's visiting dignitaries. That, apparently, was where Blake had decided to plant her. Grace guessed as much when he stopped at the security desk in the lower lobby to retrieve a key card. Moments later the glass-enclosed elevator whisked them upward.

Once past the street level, Oklahoma City zoomed into view. On previous visits Grace had gasped at the skyline that rose story by eye-popping story. Tonight she barely noticed the panorama of lights and skyscrapers. Her entire focus was on the man crowding her against the elevator's glass wall.

She hadn't been able to tell which Dalton twin was which at first. With their dark gold hair, chiseled chins and broad shoulders, one was a feast for the eyes. Two of them standing side by side could make any woman drool.

It hadn't taken Grace long to separate the men. Alex was more outgoing, with a wicked grin that jump-started female hormones without him half trying. Blake was quieter. Less obvious. With a smile that was all the more seductive for being slow and warm and…

The ping of the elevator wrenched her back to the tor-tuous present. When the doors slid open, Blake grasped her arm again and marched her down a plushly carpeted hall toward a set of polished oak doors.

Okay, enough! Grace didn't get angry often. When she did, her temper flashed hot and fierce enough to burn through the fear still gripping her by the throat.

"That's it!" She yanked her arm free of his hold and stopped dead in the center of the hall. "You hustle me out of your mother's house like a thief caught stealing the silver. You order me into your bright, shiny convertible. You drag me up here in the middle of the night. I'm not taking another step until you stop acting like you're the Gestapo or KGB."

He arched a brow at her rant, then coolly, deliberately shot back the cuff of his pleated tux shirt to check his gold Rolex.

"It's nine-twenty-two. Hardly the middle of the night."

She wanted to hit him. Slap that stony expression right off his too-handsome face. Might have actually attempted it if she wasn't sure she would crack a couple of finger bones on his hard, unyielding jaw.

Besides which, he deserved some answers. The detective's report had obviously delivered a body blow. He'd loved her cousin once.

The fire drained from Grace's heart, leaving only sadness tinged now with an infinite weariness. "All right. I'll tell you what I can."

With a curt nod, he strode the last few feet to the guest suite. A swipe of the key card clicked the lock on the wide oak doors. Grace had visited the lavish guest suite a number of times. Each time she stepped inside, though, the sheer magnificence of the view stopped her breath in her throat.

Angled floor-to-ceiling glass walls gave a stunning, hundred-and-eighty-degree panorama of Oklahoma City's skyline. The view was spectacular during the day, offering an eagle's-eye glimpse of the domed capitol building, the Oklahoma River and the colorful barges that carried tourists past Bricktown Ballpark to the larger-than-life-size bronze sculptures commemorating the 1889 land run. That momentous event had opened some two million acres of unassigned land to settlers and, oh, by the way, created a tent city with a population of more than fifty thousand almost overnight.

The view on a clear summer night like this one was even more dazzling. Skyscrapers glowed like beacons. White lights twinkled in the trees lining the river spur that meandered through the downtown area. But it was the colossal bronze statue atop the floodlit capitol that drew Grace to the windows. She'd been born and bred in Texas, but as a social studies teacher she knew enough of the history of the Southwest to appreciate the deep symbolism in the twenty-two-foot-tall bronze statue. She'd also been given a detailed history of the statue by Delilah, who'd served on the committee that raised funds for it.

Erected in 2002, *The Guardian,* with his tall spear, muscular body and unbowed head, represented not only the thousands of Native Americans who'd been forced from their homes in the East and settled in what was then Indian Territory. The statue also embodied Oklahomans who'd wrestled pipe into red dirt as hard as brick to suck out the oil that fueled the just-born automobile industry. The sons and daughters who lived through the devastating Dust Bowl of the '30s. The proud Americans who'd worked rotating shifts at the Army Air Corps' Douglas Aircraft Plant in the '40s to overhaul, repair and build fighters and bombers. And, most recently, the grimly determined Oklahomans who'd dug through nine stories of rubble to recover the bodies of friends and coworkers killed in the Murrah Building bombing.

Grace and Hope… No! Grace and *Anne* had driven up from Texas during their junior year in high school to visit Oklahoma City's National Memorial & Museum. Neither of them had been able to comprehend how the homegrown terrorist Timothy McVeigh could be so evil, so twisted in both mind and morals. Then, less than a year later, her cousin met Jack Petrie.

Frost coated Grace's lungs. Feeling its sick chill, she wrapped both arms around her waist and turned away from *The Guardian* to face Blake Dalton.

"I can't tell you about Anne's past," she said bleakly. "I promised I would bury it with her. What I *can* say is that you're the only man she got close to in more years than you want to know."

"You think I'm going to be satisfied with that?"

"You have no choice."

"Wrong."

He yanked on the dangling end of his bow tie and threw it aside before shrugging out of his tuxedo jacket. His black satin cummerbund circled a trim waist. The pleated white shirt was still crisp, as might be expected from a tailor who catered exclusively to millionaires and movie stars.

Yet under the sleek sophistication was an edge that didn't fool Grace for a moment. Delilah bragged constantly about the variety of sports Blake and his twin had excelled at during their school years. Both men still carried an athlete's build—lean in the hips and flanks, with the solid chest and muscled shoulders of a former collegiate wrestler.

That chest loomed far too large in Grace's view at the moment. It invaded her space, distracted her thoughts and made her distinctly nervous.

"How many cousins do you have?" he asked with silky menace. "And how long do you think it will take Jamison to check each of them out?"

"Not long," she fired back. "But he won't find anything beyond Anne's birth certificate, driver's license and a few high school yearbook photos. We made sure of that."

"A person can't just erase her entire life after high school."

"As a matter of fact, she can."

Grace moved to the buckskin leather sofa and dropped onto a cushion. Blake folded his tall frame onto a matching sofa separated by a half acre of glass-topped coffee table.

"It's not easy. Or cheap," she added, thinking of her empty savings account. "But you can pull it off with the help of a very smart friend of a friend of a friend. Especially if said friend can tap into just about any computer system."

Like the Texas Vital Statistics agency. It had taken some serious hacking but they'd managed to delete the digital entry recording Hope Patricia Templeton's marriage to Jack David Petrie. By doing so, they'd also deleted the record of the last time Grace had used her maiden name and SSN.

A familiar sadness settled like a lump in Grace's middle. Her naive, trusting cousin had believed Petrie's promise to love and cherish and provide for her every need. As the bastard had explained in the months that followed, his wife didn't require access to their bank account. Or a credit card. Or a job. Nor did she have to register to vote. There weren't any candidates worth going to that trouble for. And they sure as hell didn't need to talk to a marriage counselor, he'd added when she finally realized he'd made her a virtual prisoner.

Financially dependent and emotionally battered, she'd spent long, isolated years as a shadow person. Jack trotted her out when he wanted to display his pretty wife, then shuffled her back into her proper place in his bed. It hadn't taken him long to cut off her ties with her friends and family, either. All except Grace. She refused to be cut, even after Petrie became furious over her meddling. Grace wondered whether those horrific moments when her gas pedal locked on the interstate were, in fact, due to mechanical failure.

Grace and Hope had become more cautious after that. No more visits. No letters or emails that could be intercepted. No calls to the house. Only to a pay phone in the one grocery store where Jack allowed his wife to shop. Even then it had taken a solid year of pleading before Hope worked up the courage to escape.

Grace didn't want to remember the desperate years that followed. The mindless fear. The countless moves. The series of false identities and fake SSNs, each one more expensive to procure than the last. Until finally— *finally!*—a woman with the name of Anne Jordan had found anonymity and a tenuous, tentative security at Dalton International. She'd been just one of DI's thousands of employees worldwide. An entry-level clerk with only a high school GED. Certainly not a position that would bring her into contact with the multinational corporation's CFO.

Yet it had.

"Please, Blake. Please believe me when I tell you Anne wanted her past to be buried with her. All she cared about in her last, agonizing moments was making sure Molly would know her father, if not her mother."

Or more accurately, that her baby would have the name and protection of someone completely unknown to Jack Petrie.

Grace prayed she'd convinced Blake. She hadn't, of course. The lawyer in him wouldn't be satisfied until he'd dug up and turned over every bit of evidence. But maybe she could deflect his inquisition.

"Will you tell me something?"

"Quid pro quo?" His mouth twisted. "You haven't given me much of a trade."

"Please. I…I wasn't able to talk or visit with Anne much in her last year."

She hadn't dared. Jack Petrie was a Texas state trooper, with a cop's wide connections. Grace knew he'd had her under surveillance at various times, maybe even bugged her phone or planted a tracking device on her car, hoping she would lead him to his wife. Grace had imposed on every friend she had, borrowing their cars or using their phones, to maintain even minimal contact with her cousin.

Jack didn't know about Grace's last, frantic flight to California. She'd made sure of that. She'd emptied her savings account, had a friend drive her to the airport and paid cash for a ticket to Vegas. There she'd rented a car for a desperate drive across the desert to the San Diego hospital where her cousin had been admitted.

Five heart-wrenching days later, she'd retraced that route with Molly. Instead of flying back to San Antonio with the baby, though, she'd paid cash for a bus ticket to Oklahoma City.

She hadn't used her cell phone or any credit cards in the weeks since she'd wrangled a job as Molly's temporary nanny. Nor had she cashed the checks Delilah had written for her salary. She'd planned to go back to her teaching job once Molly was settled with her father. The longer she spent with the baby, though, the more painful the prospect of leaving her became.

The thought of leaving Blake Dalton was almost as wrenching. Lately her mind had drifted to him more than it should. Especially at night, after she'd put Molly to bed. The increasingly erotic direction of that drift spurred pinpricks of guilt, then and now.

"Tell me how you and Anne met," she pleaded, reminding herself yet again Blake was her cousin's love, the man she'd let into her life despite all she'd been through. "How... Well..."

"How Molly happened?" he supplied.

"Yes. Anne was so shy around men."

For shy, read insecure and cowed and generally scared *shitless*. Grace couldn't imagine how Blake had breached those formidable barriers.

"Please," she said softly. "Tell me. I'd like to know she found a little happiness before she died."

He stared at her for long moments, then his breath eased out on a sigh.

"I think she was happy for the few weeks we were together. I was never sure, though. Took me forever to pry more than a murmured hello from her. Even after I got her to agree to go out with me, she didn't want anyone at DI to know we were seeing each other. Said it would look bad, the big boss dating a lowly file clerk."

He hooked his wrists on his knees and contemplated his black dress shoes. He must not have liked what he saw. A note of unmistakable self-disgust colored his deep voice.

"She wouldn't let me take her to dinner or to the theater or anywhere we might be seen together. It was always her place. Or a hotel."

It had to be that, Grace knew. Her cousin couldn't take the chance some society reporter or gossip columnist would start fanning rumors about rich, handsome Blake Dalton's latest love interest. Or worse, the paparazzi might snap a photo of them together and post it on the internet.

Yet she risked going to a hotel with him. She'd come out of her defensive crouch enough for that. And when she discovered she was pregnant with his child, she'd had no choice but to run away. She wanted the baby desperately, but she couldn't tell Dalton about the pregnancy. He would have wanted to give the child his name, or at least establish his legal rights as the father. Hope's false IDs wouldn't have held up under legal scrutiny, and her real one would have led Petrie to her. So she'd run. Again.

"Did you love her?"

Damn! Grace hadn't meant to let that slip out. And she sure as heck hadn't intended to feel jealous of her cousin's relationship with this man.

Yet she knew he had to have been so tender with her. So sensitive to her needs. His mouth would have played a gentle song on her skin. His hands, those strong, tanned hands, must have stroked and soothed even as they aroused and...

"I don't know."

With a flush of guilt, Grace jerked her attention back to his face.

"I cared for her," he said quietly, as much to himself

as to her. "Enough to press her into going to bed with me. But when she left without a word, I was angry as well as hurt."

Regret and remorse chased each other across his face.

"Then, when I got the report of the bus accident…"

He stopped and directed a look of fierce accusation at Grace.

"I wasn't with her when it happened," she said in feeble self-defense. "She was by herself, in her car. The bus spun out right in front of her and hit a bridge abutment. She was terrified, but she got out to help."

"And left her purse at the scene."

"Yes."

"Deliberately?"

"Yes."

"Why?"

Grace shook her head. "I can't tell you why. I can't tell you any more than I have. I promised Anne her past would die with her."

"But it didn't," he countered swiftly. "Molly's living proof of that."

She slipped off the sofa and onto her knees, desperate for him to let it go. "She's your daughter, Blake. Please, just accept that and take joy in her."

He was silent for so long she didn't think he would respond. When he did, the ice was back in his voice.

"All I have right now is your word that Anne and I had a child together. I'll send in the DNA sample you offered to provide. Once we have the results, we'll discuss where we go from here."

"Where I need to go is back to your mother's house! She's exhausted from the wedding. She told me tonight she was feeling every one of her sixty-two years. She can't take care of Molly by herself for the next few days."

"I'll help her, and when I can't be there I'll make sure someone else is. In the meantime, you stay put."

He pushed out of the chair and strode to the wet bar built into the far wall. For a moment Grace thought he intended to pour them both a drink to wash down the hurt and bitterness of the past hour, but he lifted only one crystal tumbler from one of the mirrored shelves. He returned with it and issued a terse command.

"Spit."

Three

The melodic chimes of a doorbell pierced Grace's groggy haze. When the chimes gave way to the hammer of an impatient fist, she propped herself up on one elbow and blinked at the digital clock beside the bed.

Oh, God! Seven-twenty! She'd slept right through Molly's first feeding.

She threw the covers aside and was half out of bed before reality hit. One, this wasn't her room in Delilah's mansion. Two, she was wearing only the lavender lace bikini briefs she left on when she'd changed her maid of honor gown. And three, she was no longer Molly's temporary nanny.

Last night's agonizing events came crashing down on her as the fist hammered again. Scrambling, Grace snatched up her now hopelessly wrinkled khaki crops and white blouse. She got the pants zipped and buttoned the blouse on her way to the front door. She had a good idea whose fist was pounding away. She'd spent almost a month now with Blake Dalton's often autocratic, occasionally irascible, always kindhearted mother.

So she expected to see the raven-haired matriarch. She *didn't* expect to see the baby riding on Delilah's chest, nested contentedly in a giraffe sling. Grace gripped the brass door latch, swamped by an avalanche of love and worry and guilt as she dragged her gaze from the infant to her grandmother.

"Delilah, I..."

"Don't you Delilah me!" She stomped inside, the soles of her high-topped sneakers slapping the marble foyer. "Don't you dare Delilah me!"

Grace closed the door and followed her into the living room. She wished she'd taken a few seconds to brush her hair and slap some water on her face before this showdown. And coffee! She needed coffee. Desperately.

She'd tossed and turned most of the night. The few hours she'd drifted into a doze, she'd dreamed of Anne. And Blake. Grace had been there, too, stunned when his fury at her swirled without warning into a passion that jerked her awake, breathless and wanting. Remnants of that mindless hunger still drifted like a steamy haze through her mind as Delilah slung a diaper bag from her shoulder onto the sofa and released Molly from the sling.

Grace couldn't help but note that her employer had gone all jungle today. The diaper bag was zebra-striped. Grinning monkeys frolicked and swung from vines on the baby's seersucker dress. Delilah herself was in knee-length leopard tights topped by an oversize black T-shirt with a neon message urging folks to come out and be amazed by Oklahoma City's new gorilla habitat—a habitat she'd coaxed, cajoled and strong-armed her friends into funding.

"Don't just stand there," she snapped at Grace. "Get the blanket out of the diaper bag."

Even the blanket was a riot of green and yellow and jungle red. Grace spread it a safe distance away from the glass coffee table. Molly was just learning to crawl. She could push herself onto her hands and knees and hold her head up to survey the world with bright, inquisitive eyes.

Delilah deposited the baby on the blanket and made sure she was centered before pointing an imperious finger at Grace.

"You. Sit." The older woman plunked herself down in the opposite chair, keeping the baby between them. "Now talk."

"You sure you wouldn't like some coffee first?" Grace asked with a hopeful glance at the suite's fully equipped kitchen. "I could make a quick pot."

"Screw coffee. Talk."

Grace blew out a sigh and raked her fingers through her unbrushed hair. Obviously Delilah had no intention of making this easy.

"I don't know how much Blake told you…" She let that dangle for a moment. Got no response. "Okay, here's the condensed version. Molly's mother was my cousin. When Anne worked at Dalton International, she had a brief affair with your son. She died before she could tell me *which* son, so I brought Molly to you and finessed a job as her nanny while Alex and Blake sorted out the paternity issue."

Delilah pinned Grace with a look that could have etched steel. "If one of my sons got this cousin of yours pregnant, why didn't she have the guts or the decency to let him know about the baby?"

Grace stiffened. Shielding Hope—*Anne!*—had become as much a part of her as breathing. No one knew what her cousin had endured. And Grace was damned if she'd allow anyone, even the formidable Delilah Dalton, to put her down.

"I told Blake and I'll tell you. Anne had good reasons for what she did, but she wanted those reasons to die with her. She didn't, however, want her baby to grow up without knowing either of her parents."

Delilah fired back with both barrels. "Don't get uppity with me, girl!"

The fierce retort startled the baby. Molly swung her head toward her grandmother, wobbled and plopped down on one diapered hip. Both women instinctively bent toward her, but she was already pushing back onto her knees.

Delilah moderated her tone if not her message. "I'm the one who bought your out-of-work schoolteacher story, remember? I took you into my home. I trusted you, dammit."

Grace didn't see any use in pointing out that she hadn't lied about being a teacher or temporarily out of work. The trust part stung enough.

"I'm sorry I couldn't tell you about my connection to Molly."

"Ha!"

"I promised my cousin I would make sure her child was loved and cared for." Her glance went again to the baby, happily drooling and rocking on hands and knees. Slowly, she brought her gaze back to Delilah. "And she is," Grace said softly. "Well cared for and very much loved."

Delilah huffed out something close to a snort but

didn't comment for long moments. "I pride myself on being a good judge of character," she said at last. "Even that horny goat I married lived up to almost everything I'd expected of him."

Grace didn't touch that one. She'd heard Delilah say more than once she wished to hell Big Jake Dalton hadn't died before she'd found out about his little gal pal. His passing would've been a lot less peaceful.

"Is all this you've just told me true?" the Dalton matriarch demanded.

"Yes, ma'am."

"Molly's mother was really your cousin?"

"Yes."

"Well, I guess we'll have proof of that soon enough. Damned lab is making a fortune off all these rush DNA tests we've ordered lately."

She pooched her lips and moved them from side to side before coming to an abrupt decision.

"I've watched you with Molly. I don't believe you're some schemer looking to extort big bucks from us. You'll have to work to convince Blake of that, though."

"I can't tell him any more than I have."

"You don't know him like I do. He has his ways of getting what he wants. So do I," she added as she pushed out of the chair and adjusted the sling. "So do I. C'mon, Mol, let's go see your daddy."

Without thinking Grace moved to help. Swooping the baby up, she planted wet, sloppy kisses on her cheeks before slipping the infant's feet through the sling's leg openings. While Delilah tightened the straps, Grace folded the jungle blanket back into the diaper bag and handed it to the older woman.

"I'm sorry Blake doesn't want me to help with Molly."

"We'll manage until this mess gets sorted out."

* * *

If it got sorted out. Grace grew more antsy as one day stretched into two, then three.

Blake had her things packed and delivered along with her purse. She tried to take that as a good sign. Apparently he wasn't afraid she would pull a disappearing act like her cousin had.

He didn't contact her personally, though, and that worried Grace. It also caused an annoyingly persistent ache. Only now that she'd been banished from their lives did she realize how attached she'd become to the Daltons, mother and son. And to Molly! Grace missed cooing to the baby and watching her count her toes and shampooing her soft, downy blond hair.

She'd known the time would come when she would have to drop out of Molly's life. The longer she stayed here, the greater the risk Jack Petrie might trace her to Oklahoma City and wonder what she was doing here. Yet she felt a sharp pang of dismay when Blake finally condescended to call a little past 6:00 p.m. with a curt announcement.

"I need to talk to you."

"All right."

"I'm downstairs," he informed her. "I'll be up in a few minutes."

At least she was a little better prepared for this face-to-face than she'd been for their last. Her hair was caught up in a smooth knot and she'd swiped on some lip gloss earlier. She debated whether to change her jeans and faded San Antonio SeaWorld T-shirt but decided to use the time to take deep, calming breaths.

Not that they did much good. The Blake Dalton she opened the door to wasn't one she'd seen before. He'd always appeared at his mother's house in suits or neatly pressed shirts and slacks sporting creases sharp enough to shave fuzz from a peach. Then, of course, there was the tux he'd donned for the wedding. Armani should wish for male models with builds like either of the Dalton twins.

This Blake was considerably less refined. Faded jeans rode low on his hips. A black T-shirt stretched across his taut shoulders. Bristles the same shade of amber as his hair shadowed his cheeks and chin. He looked tough and uncompromising, but the expression in his laser blues wasn't as cold as the one he'd worn at their last meeting, thank God.

"We got the lab report back."

Wordlessly she led the way into the living room. Electric screens shielded the wall of windows from the sun that hadn't yet slipped down behind the skyscrapers. Without the endless view, the room seemed smaller, more intimate. *Too* intimate, she decided when she turned and found Blake had stopped mere inches away.

"Aren't you going to ask the results?"

"I don't need to," she said with a shrug. "Unless the lab screwed up the samples, their report confirms Molly and I descend from the same family tree."

"They didn't screw up the samples."

"Okay." She crossed her arms. "Now what?"

Surprise flickered across his face.

"What'd you expect?" Grace asked, her chin angling. "That I would throw myself into your arms for finally acknowledging the truth?"

The surprise was still there, but then his gaze dropped to her mouth and it took on a different quality. Darker. More intense. As though the idea of Grace throwing herself at him was less of a shock than something to be considered, evaluated, assessed.

Now that the idea was out there, it didn't particularly shock her, either. Just the opposite. In fact, the urge grew stronger with each second it floated around in the realm of possibility. All she had to do was step forward. Slide her palms over his shoulders. Lean into his strength.

As her cousin had.

Guilt sent Grace back a pace, not forward. He'd been Anne's lover, she reminded herself fiercely. The father of her baby. At best, Grace was a problem he was being forced to solve.

"Now you know," she said with a shrug that disguised her true feelings. "You're Molly's father. And *I* know you'll be good with her. So it's time for me to pack and head back to San Antonio. I'll stop by to say goodbye to her on my way out of town."

"That's it?" His frown deepened. "You're just going to drop out of her life?"

"I'll see her when I can."

After she was certain Jack Petrie hadn't learned about her stay in Oklahoma City.

"There are legalities that have to be attended to," Blake protested. "I'll need Molly's birth certificate. Her mother's death certificate."

Both contained the false name and SSN her cousin had used in California. Grace could only pray the documents would be sufficient for Blake's needs. They should. With his legal connections and his family's political clout here in Oklahoma, he ought to be able to push whatever he wanted through the courts.

"I'll send you copies," she promised.

"Right." He paused, his jaw working. "I hope you know that whatever trouble Anne was in, I would have helped her."

"Yes," she said softly. "I know."

His eyes searched hers. "Anne couldn't bring herself to trust me, but you can, Grace."

She wanted to. God, how she wanted to! Somehow she managed to swallow the hard lump in her throat.

"I trust you to cherish Molly."

Saying goodbye to the baby was every bit as hard as it had been to say goodbye to Blake. Molly broke into delighted coos when she saw her nanny and lifted both arms, demanding to be cuddled.

Grace refused to cry until her rental car was on I-35 and heading south. Tears blurred the rolling Oklahoma countryside for the next fifty miles. By the time she crossed the Red River into Texas, her throat was raw and her eyes so puffy that she had to stop at the welcome center to douse them with cold water. Six hours later she hit the outskirts of San Antonio, still mourning her severed ties to Molly and the woman who'd been both cousin and best friend to her since earliest childhood.

Her tiny condo in one of the city's older suburbs felt stale and stuffy when she let herself in. With a gulp, she glanced from the living room she'd painted a warm terra-cotta to the closet-size kitchen. She loved her place, but the entire two-bedroom unit could fit in the foyer of Delilah Dalton's palatial mansion.

As soon as she'd unpacked and powered up her computer, Grace scanned the certificates she'd promised to send Blake. That done, she skimmed through the hundreds of emails that had piled up in her absence and tried to pick up the pieces of her life.

The next two weeks dragged interminably. School didn't start until the end of month. Unfortunately, the open-ended leave of absence Grace had requested had forced her principal to shuffle teachers to cover the fall semester. The best he could promise was hopefully steady work as a substitute until after Christmas.

At loose ends until school started, Grace had to cut as many corners as possible to make up for her depleted bank account. Even worse, she missed Molly more than she would have believed possible. The baby had taken up permanent residence in her heart.

Only at odd moments would she admit she missed Molly's father almost as much as she did the baby. Like everyone else swept up in the Daltons' orbit, she'd been overwhelmed by Delilah's forceful personality and dazzled by Alex's wicked grin and audacious charm. Now that she viewed the Dalton clan from a distance, however, Grace recognized Blake as the brick and mortar keeping the family together. Always there when his mother needed him to pull together the financing on yet another of her charitable ventures. Holding the reins at Dalton International's corporate headquarters while Alex jetted halfway around the world to consult with suppliers or customers. Grace missed seeing his tall form across the table at his mother's house, missed hearing his delighted chuckle when he tickled Molly's tummy and got her giggling.

The only bright spot in those last, endless days of summer was that she heard nothing from Jack Petrie. She began to breathe easy again, convinced she'd covered her tracks. That false sense of security lasted right up until she answered the doorbell on a rainy afternoon.

When she peered though the peephole, the shock of seeing who stood on the other side dropped her jaw. A second later, fear exploded in her chest. Her fingers scrabbled for the dead bolt. She got it unlocked and threw the door almost back on its hinges.

"Blake!"

He had to step back to keep from getting slammed by the glass storm door. Grace barely registered the neat black slacks, the white button-down shirt with the open collar and sleeves rolled up, the hair burnished to dark, gleaming gold by rain.

"Is...?" Her heart hammered. Her voice shook. "Is Molly okay?"

"No."

"Oh, God!" A dozen horrific scenarios spun through her head. "What happened?"

"She misses you."

Grace gaped at him stupidly. "What?"

"She misses you. She's been fretting since you left. Mother says she's teething."

The disaster scenes faded. Molly wasn't injured. She hadn't been kidnapped. Almost reeling with relief, Grace sagged against the doorjamb.

"That's what you came down to San Antonio to tell me?" she asked incredulously. "Molly's teething?"

"That, and the fact that she said her first word."

And Grace had missed both events! The loss hit like a blow as Blake's glance went past her and swept the comfortable living room.

"May I come in?"

"Huh? Oh. Yes, of course."

She moved inside, all too conscious now of her bare feet and the T-shirt hacked off to her midriff. The shirt topped a pair of ragged cutoffs that skimmed her butt cheeks.

The cutoffs were comfortable in the cozy privacy of her home but nothing she would have ever considered wearing while she'd worked for Delilah—or around her son. She caught Blake's gaze tracking to her legs, moving upward. Disconcerted by the sudden heat that slow once-over generated, she gulped and snatched at his reason for being there.

"What did Molly say?"

"We thought it was just a ga-ga," he said with a small, almost reluctant smile. "Mother insisted she was trying to say ga-ma, but it came out on a hiss."

She sounded it out in her head, and felt her stomach go hard and tight.

"Gace? Molly said Gace?"

"Several times now."

"I…uh…"

He waited a beat, but she couldn't pull it together enough for coherence. She was too lost in the stinging regret of missing those first words.

"We want you to come back, Grace."

Startled, she looked up to find Blake regarding her intently.

"Who's *we?*" she stammered.

"All of us. Mother, me, Julie and Alex."

"They're back from their honeymoon?"

"They flew in last night."

"And you…" She had to stop and suck in a shaky breath. "And you want me to come back and pick up where I left off as Molly's nanny?"

"Not as her nanny. As my wife."

Four

Blake could certainly understand Grace's slack-jawed astonishment. He'd spent the entire flight to San Antonio telling himself it was insane to propose marriage to a woman who refused to trust him with the truth.

It was even more insane for him to miss her the way he had. She'd wormed her way into his mother's house and Molly's heart. She'd lied to him—to all of them—by omission if nothing else. Yet the hole she'd left behind had grown deeper with each hour she was gone.

Molly's unexpected arrival had already turned his calm, comfortable routine upside down. This doe-eyed blonde had kicked it all to hell. So he felt a savage satisfaction to see his own chaotic feelings mirrored in her face.

"You're crazy! I can't marry you!"

"Why not?"

She was sputtering, almost incoherent. "Because… Because…"

He thought she might break down and tell him then. Trust him with the truth. When she didn't, he swallowed a bitter pill of disappointment.

"Why don't we sit down?" he suggested with a calm he was far from feeling. "Talk this through."

"Talk it through?" She gave a bubble of hysterical laughter and swept a hand toward the living room. "My first marriage proposal, and he wants to *talk* it though. By all means, counselor, have a seat."

She regrouped during the few moments it took him to move to a sofa upholstered in a nubby plaid that complemented the earth-toned walls and framed prints of Roman antiquities. As she dropped into a chair facing him, Blake could see her astonishment giving way to anger. The first hints of it fired her eyes and stiffened her shoulders under her cottony T-shirt. He had to work to keep his gaze from drifting to the expanse of creamy skin exposed by the shirt's hem. And those legs. Christ!

He'd better remember what he'd come for. He had to approach this challenge the same way he did all others. Coolly and logically.

"I've had time to think since you left, Grace. You're good with Molly. So good both she and my mother have had difficulty adjusting to your absence."

So had he, dammit. It irritated Blake to no end that he hadn't been able to shut this woman out of his head. She'd lied to him and stubbornly refused to trust him. Yet he'd found himself making excuses for the lies and growing more determined by the hour to convince her to open up.

"You're also Molly's closest blood relative on her mother's side," he continued.

As far as he could determine at this point, anyway. He fully intended to keep digging. Whatever it took, however he got it, he wanted the truth.

"That's right," she confirmed with obvious reluctance. "Anne's parents are dead, and she was their only child."

He waited, willing her to share another scrap of information about her cousin. It hit Blake then that he could barely remember what Anne had looked like. They'd been together such a short time—if those few, furtive meetings outside their work environment could be termed togetherness.

Jaw locked, he tried to summon her image. She'd been an inch or two shorter than Grace. That much he remembered. And her eyes were several shades darker than her cousin's warm, caramel-brown. Beyond that, she was a faint memory when compared with the vibrant female now facing him.

Torn between guilt and regret, Blake presented his next argument. "I know you're facing monetary problems right now."

She bolted upright in her chair. "What'd you do? Have Jamison check my financials?"

"Yes." He offered no apology. "I'm guessing you drained your resources to help Anne and Molly. I owe you for that, Grace."

"Enough to marry me?" she bit out.

"That's part of the equation." He hesitated, aware he was about to enter treacherous territory. "There's another consideration, of course. Something frightened Anne enough to send her into hiding. It has to frighten you, too, or you wouldn't have gone to such lengths to protect her."

He'd struck a nerve. He could tell by the way she

wouldn't meet his eyes. Regret that he hadn't been able to shield Anne from whoever or whatever had threatened her knifed into him. With it came an implacable determination to protect Grace. Battling the fierce urge to shake the truth out of her, he offered her not just his name but every powerful resource at his disposal.

"I'll take care of you," he promised, his steady gaze holding hers. "You *and* Molly."

She wanted to yield. He could see it in her eyes. He congratulated himself, reveling in the potent mix of satisfaction at winning her confidence and a primal need to protect his chosen mate.

His fierce exultation didn't last long. Only until she shook her head.

"I appreciate the offer, Blake. You don't know how much. But I can take care of myself."

He hadn't realized until that moment how determined he was to put his ring on her finger. His expression hardening, he played his trump card.

"There's another aspect to consider. Right now, you can't—or won't—claim any degree of kinship to Molly. That could impact your access to her."

Her back went rigid. "What are you saying? That you wouldn't let me see her if I don't marry you?"

"No. I'm simply pointing out that you have no legal rights where she's concerned. Mother's not getting any younger," he reminded her coolly. "And if something should happen to me or Alex…"

He was too good an attorney to overstate his case. Shrugging, he let her mull over the possibilities.

Grace did, with ever increasing indignation. She couldn't believe it! He'd trapped her in her own web of lies and half-truths. If she wanted to see Molly—which she did, desperately!—she would have to play the game by his rules.

But marriage? Could she tie her future to his for the sake of the baby? The prospect dismayed her enough to produce a sharp round of questions.

"What about love, Blake? And sex? And everything else that goes into a marriage? Don't you want that?"

With a smooth move, he pushed off the sofa. Grace rose hastily as well and was almost prepared when he stopped mere inches away.

"Do you?" he asked.

"Of course I do!"

For the first time she saw a glint of humor in his eyes. "Then I don't see a problem. The sex is certainly doable. We can work on the love."

Dammit! She couldn't form a coherent thought with him standing so close. Between that and the blood pounding in her ears, she was forced to fight for every breath. It had to be oxygen deprivation that made her agree to his outrageous proposal.

"All right, counselor. You've made your case. I want to be part of Molly's life. I'll marry you."

She thought that would elicit a positive response. At least a nod. Wasn't that what he wanted? What he'd flown down here for? So why the hell did his brows snap together and he looked as though he seriously regretted his offer?

Let them snap! They'd both gone too far to back down now. But there was one final gauntlet she had to throw down.

"I just have one condition."

"And that is?"

"We play this marriage very low-key. No formal announcement. No fancy ceremony. No big, expensive reception with pictures splashed across the society page."

She paced the room, thinking furiously. She'd covered her tracks in Oklahoma City. She was sure of it. Still, it was best to stick as close to the truth as possible.

"If anyone asks, we met several months ago. Fell in love, but needed time to be sure. Decided it was for real when you flew down here to see me this weekend, so we found a justice of the peace and did the deed. Period. End of story."

She turned, hands on hips, and waited for his response. It was slow coming. *Extremely* slow.

"Well?" she demanded, refusing to let his stony silence unnerve her. "Do we have a deal or don't we?"

He held out a hand. To shake on their bargain, she realized as the full ramifications of what she'd just agreed to sank in. If her cousin's horrific experience hadn't killed most of Grace's girlish fantasies about marriage, this coolly negotiated business arrangement would have done the trick.

Except Blake didn't take the hand she extended. To her surprise, he elbowed her arm aside, hooked her waist and brought her up against his chest.

"If we're going to project a pretense of being in love, we'd better practice for the cameras."

"No! No cameras, remember? No splashy… Mmmmph!"

She ended on a strangled note as his mouth came down on hers. The kiss was harder than it needed to be. It was also everything that she'd imagined it might be! Her blood leaping, she gloried in the press of his body against hers for a moment or two or ten.

Then reality hit. This was payback for the secrets she still refused to reveal. A taste of the sex he'd so generously offered to provide. She bristled, fully intending to jerk out of his hold, but he moved first.

Dropping his arm, he put a few inches between them. He'd lost that granite look, but she wasn't sure she liked the self-disgust much better.

"I'm sorry."

"You should be," she threw back. "Manhandling me isn't part of our deal."

"You're right. That was uncalled for."

It certainly was. Yet for some perverse reason, the apology irritated her more than the kiss.

"Do we need to negotiate an addendum?" she asked acidly. "Something to the effect that physical contact must be mutually agreed to?"

Red singed his cheeks. "Amendment accepted. If you still want to go through with the contract, that is."

"Do you?"

"Yes."

"Then I do, too."

"Fine." His glance swept over her, lingering again momentarily on her legs. "You'd better get changed."

"Excuse me?"

"You scripted the scenario. I flew down to see you. We decided it was for real. We hunted down a justice of the peace. Period. End of story."

She threw an incredulous glance at the window. Rain still banged against the panes. Thunder rumbled in the distance.

"You want to get married *today?*"

"Why not?"

She could think of a hundred reasons, not least of which was the fact that she had yet to completely recover from that kiss.

"What about blood tests?" she protested. "The seventy-two-hour mandatory waiting period?"

"Texas doesn't require blood tests. I've checked."

Of course he had.

"And the seventy-two-hour waiting period can be waived if you know the right people."

Which he did. Grace should have known he would cover every contingency with his usual attention to detail.

"We'll get the marriage license at the Bexar County Courthouse. One of my father's old cronies is a circuit judge. I'll call and see if he's available to perform the ceremony." He pulled out his cell phone. "Pack what you need to take back to Oklahoma with you. We'll arrange for a moving company to take care of the rest."

The speed of it, the meticulous preplanning and swift execution, left her breathless.

"You were that sure of me?" she asked, feeling dazed and off balance.

He paused in the act of scrolling through the phone's address book. "I was that sure of how much you love Molly."

They left for the county courthouse a little more than three hours later. Blake was driving the Lincoln town car his efficient staff had arranged for him. As Grace stared through the Lincoln's rain-streaked window, she grappled with a growing sense of unreality.

Like all young girls, she and her cousin had spent hours with an old lace tablecloth wrapped around their shoulders, playing bride. During giggly sleepovers, they'd imagined numerous iterations of her wedding day. Grace's favorite consisted of a church fragrant with flowers and perfumed candles, a radiant bride in filmy white and friends packed into the pews.

After that came the smaller, more intimate version. Just her, her cousin as her attendant, a handsome groom and the pastor in a shingle-roofed gazebo while her family beamed from white plastic folding chairs. She'd even toyed occasionally with the idea of Elvis walking her down the aisle in one of Vegas's wedding chapels. This hurried, unromantic version had never figured in her imagination, however.

The reality of it hit home when they walked across a rain-washed plaza to the Bexar County Courthouse. The building was listed on the National Register of Historic Places. Unfortunately the recent storm and still ominous thunderclouds hanging low in an angry sky tinted its sandstone turrets to prison-gray. The edifice looked both drab and foreboding as Blake escorted Grace up its granite steps.

The frosted window on the door of the county clerk's office welcomed walk-ins, but the bored counter attendant showed little interest in their application. He cracked a jaw-popping yawn when the prospective bride and groom filled out the application. Five minutes and thirty-five dollars later, they entered the chambers of Judge Victor Honeywell. *His* clerk, at least, seemed to feel some sense of the occasion.

The beaming, well-endowed matron hurried around her desk to shake their hands. "I can't remember the last time we got to perform a spur-of-the-moment wedding. Brides today seem to take a year just to decide on their gown."

Unlike Grace, who had slithered out of her cutoffs and into the white linen sundress she'd picked up on sale a few weeks ago.

Blake, on the other hand, had come prepared for every eventuality, a wedding included. While she'd packed, he'd retrieved a suit bag from the Lincoln. Dark worsted wool now molded his wide shoulders. An Italian silk tie that probably cost more than Grace had earned in a week was tied in a neat Windsor. The clerk's admiring gaze lingered on both shoulders and tie for noticeable moments before she turned to the bride.

"These just came for you."

She ducked behind a side counter and popped up again with a cellophane-wrapped cascade of white roses. Silver lace and sprays of white baby's breath framed the bouquet. A two-inch-wide strip of blue was looped into a floppy bow around the stems.

"The ribbon—such as it is—is the belt from my raincoat," she said, her eyes twinkling. "You know, something borrowed, something blue."

A lump blocked Grace's throat. She had to push air past it as she folded back the cellophane and traced a finger over the petals. "Thank you."

"You're welcome. And this is for you." Still beaming, the clerk pinned a white rose to Blake's lapel. "There! Now I'll take you to Judge Honeywell."

She ushered them into a set of chambers groaning with oak panels and red damask drapes. The flags of the United States and the state of Texas flanked a desk the size of a soccer field. A set of steer horns stretched across an eight-foot swath of wall behind the desk.

"It's Ms. Templeton and Mr. Dalton, Your Honor."

The man ensconced on what Grace could only term a leather throne jumped up. His black robe flapped as he rounded his desk, displaying a pair of hand-tooled cowboy boots. He was at least six-three or four and as whiskery as he was tall. When he thrust out a thorny palm, Blake had to tilt back to keep from getting stabbed by the exaggerated point of his stiff-as-a-spear handle-bar mustache.

"Well, damn! So you're Big Jake Dalton's boy."

"One of them," Blake replied with a smile.

"He ever tell you 'bout the time the two of us busted up a saloon down to Nogales?"

"No, he didn't."

"Good. Some tales are best left untold." Honeywell shifted his squinty gaze to Grace. "I'd warn you against marrying up with any son of Big Jake if they didn't have the prettiest, smartest female in all fifty states for their mama." His nose twitched above the bushy mus-tache. "Speaking of Delilah, is she comin' to witness the ceremony?"

"No, but my brother is."

That was the first Grace had heard of it! She glanced at him in surprise while he confirmed the startling news.

"Alex should be here any moment. He was on final approach when we left the condo. In fact..."

He cocked his head. Grace followed suit and picked up the sound of footsteps in the tiled hallway. A mo-ment later the judge's clerk reappeared with another couple in tow. The tall, tawny-haired male who entered the chambers was a mirror image of Blake. The copper-haired female with him elicited a joyous cry from Grace.

"Julie!"

She took an instinctive step toward the woman she'd grown so close to during her sojourn in Oklahoma. Guilt brought her to a dead stop. Grace hadn't lied to Julie or the Daltons, but she hadn't told the truth, either. Alex and his new wife had to be feeling the same anger Blake had when he'd first discovered her deception.

It wasn't anger she saw in her friend's distinctive green-brown eyes, however, but regret and exasperation.

"Grace, you idiot!" Brushing past Blake, Julie folded Grace into a fierce hug, roses and all. "You didn't need to go through what you did alone. You could have told me. I would've kept your secret."

Limp with relief, Grace gulped back a near sob. "The secret isn't mine to tell."

Her gaze slid to Blake's brother. Alex didn't appear quite as forgiving as his bride. She didn't blame him. She'd watched him interact with Molly these past months, knew he loved the baby every bit as much as Blake did. It had to hurt to transition so abruptly from possible father to uncle. Grace could offer only a soft apology.

"I'm sorry, Alex. I didn't know which of you was Molly's father. Honestly. Not until I'd been in Oklahoma City for a while, and by then you and Julie were, ah, working a separate set of issues."

The hard set to his jaw relaxed a fraction. "That's one way to describe the hell this stubborn woman put me through."

He stood for a moment, studying Grace's face. She braced herself, but his next words didn't carry either the condemnation or the sting she expected.

"Everyone, me included, will tell you that my brother is the better man. But once he sets his mind to something, he can be as ruthless as I am and as hardheaded as our mother. Blake's convinced us this marriage is what he wants. Is it what you want?"

Her fingers tightened on the stem of the roses. Their white velvet scent drifted upward as she turned to her groom. Blake stood tall and seemingly at ease, but his blue eyes were locked on hers.

"Yes," she said after only a minuscule hesitation. "I'm sure."

Was that satisfaction or relief or a brief flash of panic that rippled across his face? Grace was still trying to decide when the judge boomed out instructions.

"All right, folks. Y'all gather round so we can get these two hitched."

Blake held out a hand. Grace laid her palm in his, hoping he couldn't hear the violent thump of her heart against her ribs. As they faced the judge, she reminded herself she was doing this for Molly.

Mostly.

Five

It was actually happening. It was for real. Grace had to fight the urge to pinch herself as Blake slid a band of channel-cut diamonds onto her ring finger. Dazed, she heard the judge's prompt.

"With this ring…"

Her groom followed the cues in a deep, sure voice. "With this ring…"

"I thee wed."

"I thee wed."

The diamonds caught the light from the overhead lighting. Brilliant, multicolored sparks danced and dazzled. Grace couldn't begin to guess how many carats banded her finger. Four? Five? And she couldn't reciprocate with so much as a plain gold band.

"By the authority vested in me by the state of Texas," Judge Honeywell intoned, "I now pronounce you husband and wife."

He waited a beat before issuing another prompt. "Go ahead, Dalton. Kiss your bride."

For the second time that afternoon, Blake slipped an arm around her waist. Grace's pulse skittered. A shiver raced down her spine. Apprehension? Anticipation?

She knew which even before he bent toward her. Her whole body quivered in expectation. He was gentle this time, though. *Too* gentle! She ached to lean into him, but the deal they'd struck kept her rigid. Their marriage was first and foremost a business arrangement, a legal partnership with Molly as the focus. Grace might eventually accept Blake's oh-so-casual offer of sex, but she'd damned well better keep a close watch on her heart.

With that resolve firm in her mind, she accepted the hearty congratulations of Judge Honeywell, another fierce hug from Julie and a kiss on the cheek from her new brother-in-law. At that point Alex produced an envelope from his inside suit coat pocket.

"Mother wanted to be here, but Molly's cutting a tooth and was too fussy to fly. She sent this instead."

Grace took the envelope with some trepidation. Inside was a folded sheet of notepaper embossed with Delilah's raised monogram. Before unfolding the note, she looked a question at Blake. His small shrug told her this was as much a surprise to him as it was to her. Nervously, Grace skimmed the almost indecipherable scrawl.

I can't say I'm happy with the way you decided to do this. We'll discuss it when you get back from France. DI's corporate jet will fly you to Marseille. Contact Madame LeBlanc when you arrive. Blake has her number. Julie, Alex and I will take care of Molly.

For a wild moment Grace thought she was being hustled out of the country so Delilah could hammer some sense into Blake. Then the last line sank in. Julie, Alex and Delilah would care for Molly. She and her groom, apparently, were jetting off to France.

Wordlessly, she handed the note to Blake. After a quick read, he speared a glance at this twin. "Were you in on this?"

"I figured something was up when Mother had me ferry the Gulfstream V down to San Antonio. Where's she proposing it take you?"

"The south of France."

That produced a quick grin. "You get no sympathy from me, Bubba. She sent Julie and me to Tuscany on our wedding night. Good thing we're both pilots and know how to beat jet lag." He winked at his wife before addressing Grace. "Hope you have a passport."

"I do, but…"

But what? She'd decided in a scant few moments to turn her whole world upside down by accepting Blake's proposition. What possible objection could she have to capping an unreal marriage with a fake honeymoon?

"But Blake probably didn't bring his," she finished helplessly.

"He didn't," Julie interjected, fishing in her purse. "I did, however. Delilah had me race over and pick it up from your executive assistant," she explained as she slapped the passport into her brother-in-law's palm. "I forgot I had it until this moment."

He fingered the gold lettering for several moments, then shrugged. "Good thing you're packed," he said to Grace. "I can pick up whatever extras I need when we get to France."

* * *

They said their goodbyes at the airport. Then Alex and Julie boarded the smaller Dalton International jet that had flown Blake to San Antonio and the newly-weds crossed the tarmac to the larger, twin-engine Gulf-stream V.

The captain met them at planeside and tendered his sincere best wishes. "Congratulations, Mrs. Dalton."

"I...uh... Thank you."

Blake stepped in to cover his wife's surprise at hearing herself addressed by her new title. "I understand you just got back from Tuscany, Joe. Sorry you had to make such a quick turnaround."

"Not a problem. Alex and Julie were at the controls for most of the flight back, so the crew is rested and ready to go. We'll top off our gas in New York and have you basking in the sun a mere seven hours after that."

Blake made the swift mental calculation. Three hours to New York. Seven hours to cross the Atlantic. Another hour or more to contact Madame LeBlanc and travel to the villa DI maintained in Provence. Eight hours' time difference.

He was used to transatlantic flights, but he suspected Grace would be dead by the time they arrived at their final destination. Just as well. She could use the next few days to rest and get used to the idea of marriage.

So could he, for that matter. He'd lined up all his arguments, pro and con, before he'd flown down to San Antonio. Then Grace had opened the door in those cut-offs and he'd damned near forgotten every one. Only now could he admit that the hunger she stirred had him twisted in as many knots as her refusal to trust him with the truth. Helluva foundation to build a marriage on, he conceded grimly as he put a hand to the small of her back to guide her up the stairs.

A Filipino steward in a white jacket met them at the hatch, his seamed face creased into a smile. "Welcome aboard, Mr. Blake. I sure wouldn't have bet we'd be flying both you and Mr. Alex on honeymoons in almost the same month."

"I wouldn't have bet on it, either, Eualdo. This is my wife, Grace."

He bowed over her hand with a dignity that matched his years. "It's an honor to meet you, Ms. Grace."

"Thank you."

"If you'll follow me, I'll show you to your seats."

Blake had spent so many in-flight hours aboard the Gulfstream he'd long since come to regard it more as a necessity than a luxury. Grace's gasp when she entered the cabin reminded him not everyone would view it that way.

The interior was normally configured with high-backed, lumbar-support seats and generous workstations in addition to the galley, head and sleeping quarters. For personal or pleasure trips like this, however, the workstations were moved together to form an elegant dining area and the seats repositioned into a comfortable sitting area.

"Good grief." She gazed wide-eyed at the gleaming teak paneling and dove-gray leather. "I hope Dalton International isn't paying for all this."

"You're married to DI's chief financial officer," Blake replied dryly. "You can trust me to maintain our personal expenses separate and distinct from corporate accounts."

She flushed a little, either at the reminder that they'd

just merged or at the unspoken reminder that she *wouldn't* trust him with other, more important matters.

The pink in her cheeks deepened when they passed the open door to the sleeping quarters. A quick glance inside showed the twin beds had been repositioned into a queen-size sleeper complete with down pillows, satiny sheets and a duvet with DI's logo embroidered in gold thread. Blake didn't have the least doubt that Julie and Alex had put those sheets to good use every moment they weren't in the cockpit.

Different couple, completely different circumstances. Blake and *his* bride wouldn't share that wide bed. The reality of the situation didn't block his thought of it, though. Swearing under his breath, Blake was hit with a sudden and all-too-vivid mental image of Grace stretched out with her arms raised languidly above her head, her breasts bare, her nipples turgid from his tongue and his teeth.

"I've got a bottle of Cristal on ice, Mr. Blake."

He blinked away the searing image and focused on Eualdo's weathered face.

"Shall I pour you and Ms. Grace a glass now or wait until after takeoff?"

A glance at his bride provided the answer. She had the slightly wild-eyed look of someone who was wondering just what kind of quicksand she'd stumbled into. She needed a drink or two to loosen her up. So did he. This looked to be a *long* flight.

It wound up lasting even longer than either Blake or the captain had anticipated. When they put down at a small commercial airstrip outside New York City to refuel, a thick, soupy fog rolled in off the Atlantic and delayed their departure for another two hours. The same front that produced the fog necessitated a more northerly route than originally planned.

By the time they gained enough altitude for Eualdo to serve dinner, Grace's shoulders were drooping. The steward's honey-crusted squab on a bed of wild rice and a bottle of perfectly chilled Riesling revived her enough for dessert. When darkness dropped like a stone outside the cabin windows, however, she dropped with it.

The first time her chin hit her chest, she jerked her head up and protested she was wide-awake. The second time, she gave up all attempt at pretense.

"I'm sorry." She dragged the back of her hand across her eyes. "I shouldn't have piled wine on top of champagne. I'm feeling the kick."

"Altitude probably has something to do with that."

Blake's calm reply gave no hint of his thoughts. He'd never seduced a tipsy female, but the idea was pretty damned tempting at the moment.

"It's been a long day. Why don't you go to bed?"

Her glance zinged to the rear of the cabin, shot back. "Aren't you tired?"

"Some." He put the last of his willpower into another smile. "But Eualdo's used to me working my way across the Atlantic."

"On your wedding night?"

He had no trouble interpreting the question behind the question. "He's been with Dalton International for more than a decade," he said calmly. "You don't need to worry about what he'll think. Or anyone else, for that matter."

Her glance dropped to her hands. She played with the band of diamonds, and he added getting the ring resized to his mental list of tasks to be accomplished when they returned to Oklahoma City.

"Go to bed, Grace."

Nodding, she unhooked her seat belt. Blake's hooded gaze followed her progress. When she disappeared inside the stateroom, he downed the dregs of his Riesling and reclined his seat back.

Well, Grace thought as she crawled between the sheets fifteen minutes later, she could imagine worse wedding nights. The social studies teacher in her had read enough ancient history to shudder at some of the barbaric marriage rites and rituals practiced in previous times.

In contrast, this night epitomized the ultimate in comfort and luxury. She was being whisked across an ocean in a private jet. She'd found every amenity she'd needed in the surprisingly spacious bathroom. The cotton sheets were so smooth and soft they felt like whipped cream against her skin. Two million stars winked outside the curved windows built into the bulwark. The only thing she needed to perfect the scene was a groom.

With a vengeance, all those play-wedding scenes she and her cousin had enacted as girls came back to haunt her. Hope's marriage had brought her nothing but heartache and fear. Grace's…

Oh, hell! Disgusted by her twinge of poor-me self-pity, she rolled over and thumped the pillow. She'd made her bed. She'd damned well lie in it.

Now if only she could stop with the nasty urge to march back into the main cabin and reopen negotiations. As Blake had so bluntly suggested, the sex was certainly doable. *More* than doable. The mere thought of his hard, muscled body stretched out beside her, his hands on her breasts, his mouth hot against hers, made the muscles low in Grace's belly tighten.

She clenched her legs, felt the swift pull between her thighs. Need, fierce and raw, curled through her. Her breath got shorter, faster.

This was stupid! Blake was sitting just a few yards away! Two steps to the stateroom door, one signal, silent or otherwise, and he'd join her.

Sex could be enough for now, she told herself savagely. She didn't need the shared laughter, the private smiles, the silly jokes married couples added to their storehouse of memories.

And it wasn't as though she'd arrived at this point unprepared. Teaching high school kids repeatedly reinforced basic truths, including the fact that each individual had to take responsibility for his or her protection during sex. Grace had seen too many bright, talented students' lives derailed by their biological urges. She wasn't into one-night stands and hadn't had a serious relationship in longer than she cared to admit, but she'd remained prepared, just in case.

So why not ease out of bed and take those two steps to the door? Why not give the signal? She and Blake were married, for God's sake!

She kicked off the sheet. Rolled onto a hip. Stopped. The problem was she *wanted* the shared smiles and silly jokes. *Needed* more than casual sex.

"Dammit!"

Disgusted, she flopped down and hammered the pillow again. She was a throwback. An anachronism. And thoroughly, completely frustrated.

She didn't remember drifting off, but the wine and champagne must indeed have gotten to her. She went completely out and woke to a knock on the stateroom door and blinding sunlight pouring through the window she'd forgotten to shade. She squinted owlishly at her watch, saw it was the middle of the night Texas time, and had to stifle a groan when another knock sounded.

"It's Eualdo, Ms. Grace. Mr. Blake said to let you know we're ninety minutes out."

"Okay, thanks."

"I'll serve breakfast in the main cabin when you're ready."

She emerged from the stateroom a short time later, showered and dressed in a pair of white crops and a gauzy, off-one-shoulder top in a flowery print. A chunky white bracelet added a touch of panache. She figured she would need that touch to get through her first morning-after meeting with her groom.

Blake unbuckled his seat belt and rose when she approached. Except for the discarded tie and open shirt collar, he didn't look like a man who'd sat up all night. Only when she got closer did she spot the gold bristles on his cheeks and chin.

"'Morning."

"Good morning," he answered with a smile. "Did you get any sleep?"

"I did." God! Could this be any more awkward? "How about you?"

"All I need is a shower and shave and I'll be good to go. Eualdo just brewed a fresh pot of coffee. I'll join you for breakfast as soon as I get out of the shower."

He started past her, then stopped. A rueful gleam lighting his eyes, he brushed a knuckle across her cheek.

"We'll figure this out, Grace. We just need to give it time."

* * *

Time, she repeated silently as the Gulfstream swooped low over a dazzling turquoise sea in preparation for landing. Despite her inner agitation, the sweeping view of the Mediterranean enchanted her.

So did the balmy tropical climate that greeted them. Grace had watched several movies and travel specials featuring the south of France. She'd also read a good number of books with the same setting, most recently a Dan Brown–type thriller that had the protagonists searching for a long-lost fragment of the Jesus's cross at the popes' sprawling palace in Avignon. None of the books or movies or travelogues prepared her for Provence's cloudless skies and brilliant sunshine, however. She held up a hand to block the rays as she deplaned, breathing in the briny tang of the sea that surrounded the Marseille airport.

A driver was waiting at the small aircraft terminal with a sporty red convertible. After he'd stashed their bags in the trunk, he made a polite inquiry in French. Blake responded with a smile and a nod.

"Oui."

"C'est bien. Bon voyage."

Grace glanced at him curiously as he slid behind the wheel. "You speak French?"

"Not according to Cecile."

Right. Cecile. The chef who owned the restaurant where Alex and Julie had hosted their rehearsal dinner. The gorgeous, long-legged chef who'd draped herself all over Blake. That display of Gallic exuberance hadn't bothered Grace at the time. Much. It did now. With some effort, she squashed the memory and settled into the convertible.

Blake got behind the wheel. He'd changed into khakis and a fresh shirt and hooked a pair of aviator sunglasses on his shirt pocket.

"Just out of curiosity," she commented as he slipped on the glasses, "where are we going?"

"Saint-Rémy-de-Provence. It's a small town about an hour north of here." A smile played at the corners of his mouth. "A nationwide transportation strike stranded Mother there during one of her antique-hunting trips about five years ago. She used the downtime to buy a crumbling villa and turn it into a vacation resort for top-performing DI employees and their families."

Grace had to grin. That sounded just like her employer. Correction, her mother-in-law. Delilah Dalton possessed more energy and drive than any six people her age.

"The place was occupied most recently by DI's top three welding teams and their families," he added casually. "But Madame LeBlanc indicated we'll have it to ourselves for the next two weeks."

Not so casually, Grace's heart thumped hard against her ribs. The combustible mix of lust and longing she'd had to battle last night had been bad enough. How the heck was she going to get through the next two weeks? Alone. With Blake. Under the hot Provencal sun and starry, starry nights.

Slowly she sank into her seat.

Six

A little over an hour later Blake turned off the auto-route onto a two-lane road shaded by towering syca-mores. Their branches met overhead to form a green tunnel that stretched for miles. The rocky pinnacles of the Alpilles thrust out of the earth to the left of the road. Sun-drenched vineyards and olive groves rolled out on the right, flashing through the sycamores' white, scaly trunks like a DVD run in fast-forward.

As delightful as the approach to Saint-Rémy was, the town itself enchanted Grace even more. Eighteenth-century mansions that Blake called *hôtels* lined the busy street encircling the town proper. Dolphins spouted in a fountain marking one quadrant of the circle, stone goddesses poured water from urns at another. In the pedestrians-only heart of the town, Grace caught glimpses of narrow lanes crammed with shops and open-air restaurants that invited patrons to sit and sip a cappuccino.

Blake noticed her craning her neck to peer down the intriguing alleyways. "We'll have lunch in town," he promised.

"I'd like that."

She studied her groom as he negotiated the busy street. He fit perfectly against this elegant eighteenth-century backdrop, Grace decided. The corporate executive had shed his suit and tie but not his sophistication. Sunlight glinted on the sleek watch banding his wrist and the light dusting of golden hair on his forearm. The aviator sunglasses and hand-tailored shirt left open at the neck to show the tanned column of his throat only added to the image.

"Madame LeBlanc will meet us at Hôtel des Elmes," he added as he skillfully wove through pedestrians, tourists and traffic.

She took a stab at a translation. "The Elms?"

"The Elms," he confirmed. "It used to be called the Hôtel Saint Jacques. Legend has it that the original owner claimed to have invented, or at least improved on, the scallop dish named in Saint James's honor."

Grace had to think for a moment. "Aha! Coquilles St. Jacques!"

"Right. You'll be pleased to know the current chef at the *hôtel* has followed in his predecessors' footsteps. Auguste's scallops au gratin will make you think you hear heavenly choirs."

The easy banter took them up to a pair of tall, wrought-iron gates left open in anticipation of their arrival. Once inside, Grace understood instantly the inspiration for the villa's new designation. Majestic elms that must have been planted more than a century ago formed a graceful arch above a crushed-stone drive. The curving drive wound through landscaped grounds dotted with statuary and vine-shaded arbors, then ended in a circle dominated by a twenty-foot fountain featuring bronze steeds spouting arcs of silvery water.

And looming beyond the fountain was a masterpiece in mellowed gray stone. The Hôtel des Elmes consisted of a three-story central wing, with two-story wings on each side. Wisteria vines softened its elaborate stone facade, drooping showy purple blossoms from wrought-iron trellises. Grace breathed in the purple blossoms' spicy vanilla scent as Blake braked to a stop.

The front door opened before he'd killed the engine. The woman who emerged fit Grace's mental image of the quintessential older French female—slender, charming, impossibly chic in silky black slacks and a cool linen blouse.

"Bienvenue à Saint-Rémy, Monsieur Blake."

"It's good to be back," he replied in English.

After the obligatory cheek kissing, he introduced Grace. She must have been getting used to being presented as his wife. She barely squirmed when Madame LeBlanc grasped both her hands and offered a profuse welcome.

"I am most happy to meet you." Madame's smile took a roguish tilt. "Delilah has long despaired of getting her so-handsome sons to the altar. One can only imagine how thrilled she must be that Alex and Blake have taken brides within a month of each other. *Quelle romantique!*"

"Yes, well…"

Blake's arm slid around Grace's waist. *"Trés romantique."*

His casual comment fed the fantasy of a honeymoon couple. Madame LeBlanc sighed her approval and handed him a set of tagged keys.

"As you instructed, the staff will not report until tomorrow, but Auguste has prepared several dishes should you wish them. They need only to be reheated. And the upstairs maid has made up the bed in the Green Suite and left for the rest of the day. You will not be disturbed."

"Merci."

If the villa's grounds and exquisite eighteenth-century exterior evoked visions of aristocrats in silks and powered wigs, the interior had obviously been retrofitted for twenty-first-century visitors. Grace spotted high-tech security cameras above the doors and an alarm panel just inside the entryway that looked as if it would take an MIT grad to program. The brass-accented elevator tucked discreetly behind a screen of potted palms was also a modern addition.

While Grace peeked around, Blake carried in their few bags and deposited them in the marbled foyer. "Would you like the ten-cent tour, or would you rather go upstairs and rest for a while first?"

"The tour, please! Unless…" Guilt tripped her. "I'm sorry. I zoned out on the plane, but you didn't. You're probably aching for bed."

Something shifted in his face. A mere ripple of skin across muscle and bone. Grace didn't have time to interpret the odd look before he masked it.

"I'm good." He made an exaggerated bow and swept an arm toward the central hall. "This way, madame."

Grace soon lost count of the downstairs rooms. There was the petite salon, the grand salon, the music room, the library, the card room, an exquisitely mirrored ballroom and several banquet and eating areas in addition to the kitchens and downstairs powder rooms. Each contained a mix of antiques and ultramodern conveniences cleverly integrated into an elegant yet inviting whole. Even the painted porcelain sinks in the powder rooms evoked an eighteenth-century feel, and the copper-and-spice-filled kitchen could accommodate cooks of all ages and eras.

The pool house with its marble columns and bougainvillea-draped pergola was a Greek fantasy come to life. The shimmering turquoise water in the pool made Grace itch to shed her clothes on the spot and dive in. But when they went back inside again and started for the stairs to the second floor, it was the painting of deep purple irises displayed in a lighted alcove that stopped her dead.

"Ooooh!" Grace was no art expert, but even she could recognize a Van Gogh when it smacked her between the eyes. "I have a poster of this same painting in my bedroom."

Blake paused behind her. "That's one of my mother's favorites, too. She donated the original to the Smithsonian's Museum of Modern Art but had this copy commissioned for the villa."

He was only an inch or two from her shoulder. So close she felt his breath wash warm and soft against her ear. The sensation zinged down her spine and stirred a reaction that almost made her miss Blake's next comment.

"This is one of the more than one hundred and fifty paintings Van Gogh painted during his year in Saint-Rémy. There's a walking tour that shows the various scenes he incorporated into his works. We can take it if you like."

"I would!"

The possibility of viewing sunflowers and olive groves through the eyes of one of the world's greatest artists tantalized Grace. Almost as much as the idea of viewing them with Blake.

Hard on that came the realization that she had no clue if her new husband was the least bit interested in impressionist art. Or what kind of music he preferred. Or how he spent his downtime when he wasn't doing his executive/corporate lawyer thing. She'd known him such a short time. And during those weeks he, his twin and his indomitable parent had focused exclusively on Molly and the hunt for the baby's mother.

Could be this enforced honeymoon wasn't such a bad idea after all. The main participants in every partnership, even a marriage of convenience, needed to establish a working relationship. Maybe Delilah had their best interests at heart when she'd arranged this getaway.

Maybe. It was hard to tell what really went on in the woman's Machiavellian mind. Withholding judgment, Grace accompanied Blake on a tour of the second story. He pointed out several fully contained guest suites, two additional salons, a reading room, even a video game room for the children of the Dalton employees and other guests who stayed at the *hôtel*. At the end of the hall, he opened a set of double doors fitted with gold-plated latches.

"This is the master suite." His mouth took a wry tilt. "Otherwise known as the Green Suite."

Grace could certainly see why! Awed, she let her gaze travel from floor-to-ceiling silk wall panels to elegantly looped drapes to the thick duvet and dozens of tasseled pillows mounded on the four-poster bed. They were all done in a shimmering, iridescent brocade that shaded from moss-green to dark jade depending on the angle of the light streaming through the French doors. The bed itself was inlaid mahogany chased with gold.

Lots of gold. So were the bombe chests and marble-topped tables scattered throughout the suite.

"Wow!" Mesmerized by the opulence, she spun in a slow circle. "This looks like Louis XV might have slept here."

"There's no record the king ever made it down," Blake returned with a grin, "but one of his mistresses reportedly entertained another of her lovers here on the sly."

Grace couldn't decide which hit with more of a wallop, that quick grin or the instant and totally erotic image his comment stirred. As vividly as any painting, she could picture a woman in white silk stockings, ribboned garters and an unlaced corset lolling against the four-poster's mounds of pillows. A bare-chested courtier with Blake Dalton's guinea-gold hair leaned over her. His blue eyes glinted with wicked promise as he slowly slid one of her garters from her thigh to her knee to her…

"…the adjoining suite."

Blinking, she zoomed out of the eighteenth century. "Sorry. I was, uh, thinking of powdered wigs and silk knee breeches. What did you say?"

"I said I'll be in the adjoining suite."

The last of the delicious image fizzled as Grace watched her husband open a connecting door. The bedroom beyond wasn't as large or as decadent as that of the Green Suite, but it did boast another four-poster and a marble fireplace big enough to roast an ox.

"It's almost noon Saint-Rémy time," Blake said after a quick glance at his watch. "If you're not too jet-lagged, we could reconvene in a half hour and walk into town for lunch."

"That works for me."

Calling herself an idiot for staring at the door long after it closed behind him, Grace extracted her toiletries from her tote bag and carried them into a bathroom fit for a queen. Or at least a royal mistress.

Maybe it was the glorious sun that sucked away her sense of awkwardness. Or the lazy, protracted lunch she and Blake shared at a dime-size table cornered next to a bubbling fountain. Or the two glasses of perfectly chilled rosé produced by a vineyard right outside Saint-Rémy.

Then again, it might have been Blake's obvious efforts to keep the conversation light and noncontroversial. He made no reference to the circumstances of their marriage or Grace's adamant refusal to betray her cousin's trust. As a consequence, she felt herself relaxing for the first time in longer than she could remember.

The still-raw ache of her cousin's death shifted to a corner of her heart. Jack Petrie, Oklahoma City, even Molly moved off center stage. Not completely, and certainly not for long. Yet these hours in the sun provided a hiatus from the worry she'd carted around for so many months. That was the only excuse she could come up with later for the stupidity that followed.

It happened during the walk back to their *hôtel*. Blake indulged her with a stroll through the town's pedestrian-only center, stopping repeatedly while she oooh'ed and aaaah'ed over shop windows displaying Provence's wares. One window was filled with colorful baskets containing every imaginable spice and herb. Another specialized in soaps and scented oils. *Hundreds* of soaps and oils. Delighted, Grace went inside and sniffed at products made from apple pear, lemon, peony, vanilla, honey almond and, of course, lavender. A dazzling display of stoppered vials offered bath oils and lotions in a rainbow of hues.

The clerk obviously knew her business. She sized up the diamonds circling Grace's finger in a single glance. With a knowing look, she produced a cut-crystal vial from a shelf behind the counter.

"Madame must try this. It is a special blend made only for our shop."

When she removed the stopper, an exquisitely delicate aroma drifted across the counter. Lavender and something else that Grace couldn't quite identify.

"The perfumers extract oil from the buds before they blossom. The fragrance is light, *oui?* So very light and yet, how do you say? So *sensuelle.*"

She waved the stopper in the air to release more of its bouquet. Grace leaned forward, breathing deeply. She knew then that whatever else happened in this marriage, she would always associate the scent of lavender with sunshine and brilliant skies and the smile crinkling the skin at the corners of Blake's eyes as he watched her sniffing the air.

He didn't remain an observer for long. Sensing a sale, the shopkeeper dipped the stopper again. "Here, *monsieur,* you must dab some on your wife's wrist. The oil takes on a richer tone when applied to the skin."

With a good-natured nod, Blake took the stopper in one hand and reached for Grace's wrist with the other. His hold was loose, easy. As light as it was, though, the touch sent a ripple of pleasure along her nerves. The ripple swelled to a tidal wave when he raised her arm to a mere inch or so from his nose.

"She's right," he murmured. The blue in his eyes deepened as he caught Grace's gaze. "The warmth of your skin deepens the scent."

Warmth? Ha! She'd passed mere warmth the moment his fingers circled her wrist. And if he kept looking at her like that, she suspected she would spontaneously combust in the next five seconds.

Thankfully, the shop clerk claimed his attention. The distraction proved only temporary, however. Eager for a sale, the woman urged another test.

"Dab a little dab behind your wife's ear, *monsieur*. It is of all places the most seductive."

Grace's internal alarm went off like a klaxon. Every scrap of common sense she possessed urged her to decline the second sample. The sun and the wine and this man's touch were bringing her too close to the melting point. So she was damned if she knew why she just stood there and let Blake brush aside her hair.

The crystal stopper was cool and damp against the skin just below her earlobe. An instant later, her husband's breath seared that same patch of skin. Their only physical contact point was the hand caging back her hair. If the shock that went though her was any indication, however, they might have been locked together at chest and hip and thigh. Thoroughly shaken, Grace took a step back.

The abrupt move brought Blake's head up with a snap. He didn't need to see the confusion on his wife's face to know he'd crossed the line.

The line he'd been stupid enough to draw! He was the one who'd assured her they would work things out. He'd spouted that inane drivel about giving their arrangement time.

To hell with waiting. He ached to drag Grace out of the shop, hustle her back to The Elms and strip her down to the warm, perfumed flesh that was sending his senses into dangerous overload.

"Monsieur?"

The shop clerk's voice cut through his red haze. Before Blake could bring the woman into focus, he had to exercise the iron will that allowed him to appear calm before judges and juries.

She finally appeared, smiling and eager. "Do you wish to purchase a vial for your so-lovely wife?"

God, yes!

At his nod, she whipped out a sales slip. "Do you stay here in Saint-Rémy?"

He knew his address would up the asking price by at least half but was beyond caring. "We're at Hôtel des Elmes."

Her glance sharpened. "Ahhh. I recognize you now. You came to Saint-Rémy last year, *oui?* With… Er…" She broke off, then recovered after an infinitesimal pause. "With your so very charming mother."

Riiiight. Blake seriously doubted his twin had timed a visit to the villa to coincide with one of their mother's protracted stays. Alex and Delilah were both obviously well-known in town, however, so he didn't bother to correct the clerk's misconception.

"We'll take a bottle of that scent."

Beaming, she rattled off the price for a three-ounce bottle. He was reaching for his money clip when Grace gave a strangled gasp.

"Did you say two hundred euros?"

"*Oui,* madame."

"Two *hundred* euros?"

"*Oui.*"

"That's like…"

Blake paused in the act of peeling off several euro notes while she did the mental math.

"Good grief! That's almost three hundred dollars

U.S." Horrified, she closed her hand over his. "That's too much."

A pained look crossed the salesclerk's face. "You will not find a more distinctive or more delicate scent in all Provence. And…"

Her glance cut to Blake. When she turned back to Grace, a conspiratorial smile tilted her lips.

"If I may say so, madame, your husband does not purchase this fragrance for you. He is the one who will detect its essence on your skin. If it pleases him…"

Her shoulders lifted in that most Gallic of all gestures, and Grace could only watch helplessly as Blake dropped the euro notes on the counter.

Seven

Even with Grace's seductive scent delivering a broadside every time Blake turned his head or leaned toward her, he didn't plan what happened when they returned to the villa. His conscience would always remain clear on that point. When he suggested a swim, his only intent was to continue the easy camaraderie established during lunch.

What he *hadn't* anticipated was the kick to his gut when Grace joined him poolside and slipped off her terry cloth cover-up. He'd already done a half dozen laps but wasn't the least winded until the sight of her slender, seductive curves sucked the air from his lungs.

"How's the water?"

Blake tried to untangle his tongue. Damned thing felt like it was wrapped in cotton wool. "Cool at first," he got out after an epic struggle. "Not so bad once you're in."

Oh, for God's sake! Her suit was a poppy-colored

one-piece that covered more than it revealed. Yet he was damned if he could stop his gaze from devouring the slopes of her breasts when she bent to deposit her towel on the lounger. That unexpected jolt was followed by another when she turned to dip a toe in the water and gave him an unimpeded view of the curve of her bottom cheeks.

"Yikes!" She jerked her foot back with a yelp and zinged him an indignant look. "You think this is *cool?* What's your definition of *cold?* Minus forty?"

He grinned and tread water as she dipped another cautious toe. Her face screwed into a grimace. She inched down a step, her shoulders hunched almost to her ears. Eased onto the next step. The water swirled around her calves, her thighs.

"Coward," he teased.

She took another tentative step, and his grin slipped. The water lapped the lower edge of her suit. The bright red material dampened at the apex of her thighs and provided a throat-closing outline of what lay beneath.

"Oh, hell."

He barely heard her mutter of self-disgust. Or felt the splash when she gathered her courage and flopped all the way in. She bobbed up a moment later, her hair a sleek waterfall of pale gold. Sparkling drops beaded her lashes. Laughter lit her eyes.

Something inside Blake shifted. He didn't see the woman who'd lied to him and his family by omission, or the conspirator who'd withheld crucial information about the mother of his child. There were no shadows haunting the eyes of this laughing, splashing water sprite. For the moment at least, no memories constrained her simple pleasure. It was a glimpse of the woman Grace must have been before she took on the burden of her cousin's secrets. An even more tantalizing hint of the woman who might reemerge if and when she shed that burden.

Without conscious thought, Blake realigned his priorities. Convincing his bride to trust him remained his primary goal. Getting her into bed ran a close second. But keeping that carefree laughter in her eyes was fast elbowing its way up close to the top of the list.

"All right," she gasped, dancing on her toes. "I'm in. When does it get to 'not so bad'?"

"Do a couple laps. You'll warm up quick enough."

She made a face but took his suggestion. He rolled into an easy breaststroke and kept pace with her. She had a smooth, clean stroke, he noted with approval, a nice kick. Two laps turned into three, then four. Or what would have been four.

She made the turn, pushed off the wall at an angle and submarined into him. They went under in a tangle of arms and legs. She came up sputtering. He came up with his bride plastered against his chest.

"Sorry!"

Blinking the water out of her eyes, she clung to him. They were at the deep end, in well over their heads. Literally, Blake thought, as her thighs scissored between his. Maybe figuratively.

Hell, there was no maybe about it. He wanted her with a raw need he didn't try to analyze. She must have seen it in his face, felt his muscles tighten under her slick, slippery hands. She looked up at him with a question in her eyes.

"According to our contract," he got out on a near rasp, "any and all physical contact must be by mutual consent. If you don't want this to go any further, you'd better say so now."

After a pause that just about ripped out Blake's guts, she clamped her lips shut and matched him look for look. With another growl, he claimed her mouth.

The kiss was swift and hot and hungry. If he'd interpreted her silence wrong, if she'd tried to push away, Blake would've released her. He was almost sure of that. She didn't, thank God, and he threw off every vestige of restraint.

They went under again, mouths and bodies fused. When they resurfaced, Blake kept her pinned, gave two swift kicks and took them to the wall. He flattened her against the tiles, using one hand to hold them both up while he attacked one strap of her suit with the other. The skin of her shoulder was soft and cool and slick. The mingled scents of lavender and chlorine acted like a spur, turning hunger into greed.

He switched hands, yanked down the other strap. She was as anxious now to shuck her bathing suit as he was to get her out of it. A wiggle, a shimmy, a kick, and it was gone. His followed two heartbeats later.

Her breast fit perfectly in his palm. The flesh was firm and smooth, the tip already stiff from the cold water. He rolled the nipple between his thumb and forefinger and damned near lost it when she arched her back to give him access to her other breast. He hiked her up a few inches, devouring her with teeth and tongue while he slicked his hand down her belly.

"Oh, God!"

Moaning, Grace threw her head back. She'd agreed to this. Had spent more than a few hours tossing around the idea of casual sex with this man. But this—this was nowhere near casual! Blake's mouth scorched her breasts, her shoulder, her throat. And her heart almost jumped out of her chest when he curved his fingers over her mound and parted her crease. She moaned again as he thrust into her and, to her utter mortification, exploded.

The orgasm ripped through her. She rode it blindly, mindlessly, until the spasms died and she flopped like a wet rag doll against his chest.

The thunder in her ears didn't subside. If anything, it grew louder. Only gradually did Grace realize that was Blake's heart tattooing against her ear. Gathering her shattered senses, she raised her head and curved her lips.

The skin at the corners of his blues eyes crinkled as he started to return her smile. Then she wrapped her legs around his hips and his expression froze. Slowly, sensually, she lifted her hips, positioning herself.

"Wait," he got out on a strangled grunt. "We need to take this inside."

"Why?"

"Protection. You need pro…" He broke off, hissing as she angled her hips. "Grace…"

He didn't say it, but she guessed he was thinking of Molly. She certainly was.

"It's okay," she said, breathless and urgent. "I'm covered."

He reacted to that bit of news with gratifying speed. Planting a foot against the tiles, he propelled them toward the shallow end. The sparkling water cascaded over his shoulders and chest as he took a wide stance and hefted her bottom with both palms.

A fresh wave of desire coiled deep in Grace's belly. Eager to give him some of the explosive pleasure he'd given her, she wrapped her legs around his waist. She didn't want slow. Didn't want gentle. When he thrust into her, she slapped her hips into his and clenched every muscle in her body.

He held out longer than she had. Much longer. Grace was close to losing control again when his fingers dug into her bottom cheeks. He went rigid and jammed her against him at an angle that put exquisite, unbearable pressure right where she wanted it the most. With a ragged groan, she arched into another shuddering, shattering climax. This time she took him with her.

Jet lag, a lack of sleep and the most intense sex he'd ever had combined to plow into Blake like an Abrams tank. He remembered helping Grace out of the water and savoring the view before she wrapped herself in one of the villa's blue-and-white-striped pool towels. He vaguely recalled diving back in to retrieve their bathing suits. He wasn't sure whether he'd suggested they stretch out in one of the loungers inside the vine-covered pergola, or she had. But the next time he opened his eyes, the sun had disappeared and hundreds of tiny white lights made a fairyland of the pool area.

He sat up, blinking, and scraped a hand across a sandpaper chin. The movement drew the attention of the woman on the lounger beside his.

"What time is it?" he asked, his voice still thick with sleep.

"I'm not sure. My internal clock is still set to Texas time." She glanced at the canopy of stars outside the pergola. "I'm guessing it's probably nine or nine-thirty."

Blake winced. Great! Absolutely great! Nothing demonstrated a man's virility like taking four or five hours to recharge after sex.

"Sorry I passed out on you."

"No problem." His obvious chagrin had a smile hovering at the corners of her mouth. "I napped, too."

Not for long, apparently. She'd used some of the time he was out cold to change into khaki shorts and a scoop-necked T-shirt. Her hair looked freshly washed, its shining length caught up in a plastic clip.

"Have you eaten?"

"I was waiting for you."

He was still in the swim trunks he'd brought up from the pool. They were dry now and rode low on his hips as he pushed off the lounger and reached out to help her up.

"Let's go raid the kitchen."

The hesitation before she took his hand was so brief he might have imagined it. He couldn't miss the constraint that kept her silent, though, once they'd settled in high-backed wrought-iron stools at the kitchen's monster, green-tiled island. As Madame LeBlanc had indicated, the chef had left a gourmand's dream of sumptuous choices in the fridge and on the counters. Grace opted for a bowl of cold, spicy gazpacho and a chunk of bread torn from one of the long, crusty baguettes poking out of a wire basket. Blake poured them both a glass of light, fruity chardonnay before heaping his plate with salad Niçoise and a man-size wedge of asparagus-and-goat-cheese quiche warmed in the microwave.

He forked down several bites of salad, savoring its red, ripe tomatoes and anchovies, eyeing Grace as she played with her bread, waiting for her to break the small silence. He had a good idea what was behind her sudden constraint. Morning-after nerves, or in this case, evening-after.

She validated his guess a few moments later. Drawing in a deep breath, she tackled the thorny subject head-on. "About what happened in the pool…"

He sensed what was coming and wasn't about to make it easy for her. "What about it?"

"I know we put the possibility of sex on the table when we negotiated this, uh, partnership."

"But?"

She looked down, crumbled her bread, met his gaze again. "But things just spun out of control. I'm as much to blame as you are," she added quickly. "Now that I've had time to think, though, it was too quick, Blake. Too fast."

"We'll take it slower next time."

The solemn promise almost won a smile.

"I *meant* it was too soon. I'm still trying to adjust to this whole marriage business."

"I know." Serious now, he laid down his fork. "But let's clarify one matter. Things didn't just spin out of control. I wanted you, Grace."

Color tinted her cheeks. "I'll concede that point, counselor. And it was obvious I wanted you."

"I understand this is an adjustment period for you, however. For both of us. We've a lot yet to learn about each other."

The deliberate reference to her hoard of secrets brought her chin up. "Exactly. Which is why we should avoid a repetition of what happened this afternoon until you're comfortable with who I am and vice versa."

What the hell would it take to get her to trust him? Irritation put a bite in Blake's voice. "So we just revert back to cool and polite? You think it'll be that easy?"

"No," she admitted, "but necessary if this arrangement of ours is going to work."

He swallowed the bitter aftertaste of anchovies and frustration. "All right. We'll take hot, wild sex off the agenda. For now."

* * *

Grace spent the second night of her honeymoon the same way she had her first, restless and conflicted and alone.

While moonlight streamed through windows left open to a soft night breeze, she punched the mounded pillow and replayed the scene in the kitchen. She'd been right to put the brakes on. The way she'd flamed in Blake's arms, lost every ounce of rational thought... She'd never gone so mindless with hunger before. Never craved a man's touch and the wild sensation of his hard, sculpted body crushing hers.

She'd had time to think while Blake dozed this afternoon, and the fact that she'd abandoned herself so completely had shaken her. Still shook her! She'd witnessed firsthand the misery her cousin endured, for God's sake. Had helped Anne run, hide, struggle painfully to regain her confidence and self-respect. Grace couldn't just throw off the brutal burden of those months and years. Nor could she dump it on Blake's broad, willing shoulders—much as she ached to.

No, she was right to pull back. Revert to cool and polite, to use his phrase. They both needed time to adjust to this awkward marriage before they took the next step. Whatever the heck that was.

It took a severe exercise of will, but she managed to block the mental image of Blake pinning her to the tiles and drop into sleep.

She remained firm in her resolve to back things up a step when she went down for breakfast the next morning.

The villa's staff had obviously reported for duty. The heavenly scent of fresh-baked bread wafted from the direction of the kitchen, and a maid in a pale blue uniform wielded a feather duster like a baton at the foot of the stairs. Her eyes lit with curiosity and a friendly welcome when she spotted Grace.

"*Bonjour,* Madame Dalton."

"*Bonjour.*"

That much Grace could manage. The quick spate that followed had her offering an apology.

"I'm sorry. I don't speak French."

"Ah, *excusez-moi.* I am Marie. The downstairs maid, yes? I am most happy to meet you."

"Thank you. It's nice to meet you, too."

She hesitated, not exactly embarrassed but not real eager to admit she didn't have a clue where her husband of two days might be. Luckily, Blake had primed the staff with the necessary information.

"Monsieur Dalton said to tell you that he takes coffee on the east terrace," Marie informed her cheerfully. "He waits for you to join him for breakfast."

"And the east terrace is…?"

"Just there, madame." She aimed the feather duster. "Through the petite salon."

"Thanks."

She crossed the salon's exquisitely thick carpet and made for a set of open French doors that gave onto a flagstone terrace enclosed by ivy-drenched stone walls. A white wrought-iron table held a silver coffee service and a basket of brioche. Blake held his Blackberry and was working the keyboard one-handed while he sipped from a gold-rimmed china cup with the other.

Grace stopped just inside the French doors to drag in several deep breaths. She needed them. The sight of her husband in the clear, shimmering light of a Provencal morning was something to behold. A stray sunbeam snuck through the elms shading the patio to gild his hair. His crisp blue shirt was open at the neck and rolled at the cuffs. He looked calm and collected and too gorgeous for words, dammit!

She sucked in another breath and stepped out onto the patio. "Good morning."

He set down both his coffee cup and the Blackberry and rose.

"Good morning." The greeting was as courteous and impersonal as his smile. "Did you sleep well?"

Right. Okay. This was how she wanted it. What she'd insisted on.

"Very well," she lied. "You?"

"As well as could be expected after yesterday afternoon."

When she flashed a warning look, he shed his polite mask and hooked a brow.

"I zoned out for a good four hours on that lounge chair," he reminded her. "As a consequence, I didn't need much sleep last night."

And if she bought that one, Blake thought sardonically, he had several more he could sell her.

He didn't have to sell them. The swift way she broke eye contact told him she suspected he was stretching the truth until it damned near screamed.

She had to know she'd kept him awake most of the night. She, and her absurd insistence they ignore the wildfire they'd sparked yesterday. As if they could. The heat of it still singed Blake's mind and burned in his gut.

In the small hours of the night he'd called himself every kind of an idiot for agreeing to this farcical facade. It made even less sense in the bright light of morning. They couldn't shove yesterday in a box, stick it on the closet shelf and pretend it never happened. Yet he *had* agreed, and now he was stuck with it.

It didn't improve his mood to discover she'd dabbed on some of the perfumed oil he'd bought her yesterday. The provocative scent tugged at his senses as he pulled out one of the heavy wrought-iron chairs for her.

"Why don't you pour yourself some coffee and I'll tell Auguste we're ready for... Ah, here he is."

At first glance few people would tag the individual who appeared in the open French doors as a graduate of Le Cordon Bleu and two-time winner of the *Coupe du Monde de la Patisserie*—the World Cup of pastry. He sported stooped shoulders, sparse gray hair and a hound-dog face with dewlaps that hung in mournful folds. If he'd cracked a smile anytime in the past two years, Blake sure hadn't seen it.

The great Auguste had been retired for a decade and, according to Delilah, going out of his gourd with boredom when she'd hunted him down. After subjecting the poor man to the full force of her personality, she'd convinced him to take over the kitchen of Hôtel des Elmes.

Blake had made his way to the kitchen earlier to say hello. He now introduced the chef to Grace. Auguste bowed over her hand and greeted her in tones of infinite sadness.

"I welcome you to Saint-Rémy."

Gulping, she threw Blake a what-in-the-world-did-I-do look? He stepped in smoothly.

"I've told Grace about your scallops au gratin, Auguste. Perhaps you'll prepare them for us one evening."

"But of course." He heaved a long-suffering sigh and turned his doleful gaze back to Grace. "Tonight, if you wish it, madame."

"That would be wonderful. Thank you."

"And now I shall prepare the eggs Benedict for you and *monsieur,* yes?"

"Er, yes. Please."

He bowed again and retreated, shoulders drooping. Grace followed his exit with awed eyes.

"Did someone close to him just die?" she whispered to Blake.

The question broke the ice that had crusted between them. Laughing, Blake went back to his own seat.

"Not that I know of. In fact, you're seeing him in one of his more cheerful moods."

"Riiight."

With a doubtful glance at the French doors, she spread her napkin across her lap. He waited until she'd filled a cup with rich, dark brew to offer the basket of fresh-baked brioche.

"We've got dinner taken care of," he said as she slathered on butter and thick strawberry jam. "What would you like to do until then?"

She sent him a quick look, saw he hadn't packed some hidden meaning into the suggestion, and relaxed into her first genuine smile of the morning.

"You mentioned a Van Gogh trail. I'd love to explore that, if you're up for it."

Resolutely, Blake suppressed the memory of his mother ruthlessly dragging Alex and him along every step of the route commemorating Saint-Rémy's most famous artist.

"I'm up for it."

Eight

Grace couldn't have asked for a more perfect day to explore. Sometime while they'd been over the Atlantic, August had rolled into September. The absolute best time to enjoy Provence's balmy breezes and dazzling sunshine, Blake assured her as the sporty red convertible crunched down the front drive. It was still warm enough for her to be glad she'd opted for linen slacks and a cap-sleeved black T-shirt with I ♥ Texas picked out in sparkly rhinestones. She'd caught her hair back in a similarly adorned ball cap to keep the ends from whipping her face.

Blake hadn't bothered with a hat, but his mirrored aviation sunglasses protected his eyes from the glare. With his blue shirt open at the neck and the cuffs rolled up on his forearms, he looked cool and comfortable and too damned sexy for his own or Grace's good.

"I wasn't sure how much you know about Vincent

van Gogh," he said with a sideways glance, "so I printed off a short bio while you were getting ready."

"Thanks." She gratefully accepted the folded page he pulled out of his shirt pocket. "I went to a traveling exhibit at the San Antonio Museum of Art that featured several of his sketches a few years ago. I don't know much about the man himself, though, except that he was Dutch and disturbed enough to cut off his left ear."

"He was certainly disturbed, but there's some dispute over whether he deliberately hacked off his ear or lost it in the scuffle when he went after his pal Gauguin with a straight razor."

While Blake navigated shaded streets toward the outskirts of Saint-Rémy, Grace absorbed the details in the life of the brilliant, tormented artist who killed himself at the age of thirty-seven.

"It says here Van Gogh only sold one painting during his lifetime and died thinking himself a failure. How sad."

"Very sad," Blake agreed.

"Especially since his self-portrait is listed here as one of the ten most expensive paintings ever sold," Grace read, her eyes widening. "It went for $71 million in 1998."

"Which would equate to about $90 million today, adjusted for inflation."

"Good grief!"

She couldn't imagine paying that kind of money for anything short of a supersonic jet transport. Then she remembered the painting of the irises at the villa, and Blake's casual comment that his mother had donated the original to the Smithsonian.

She'd known the Daltons operated in a rarified financial atmosphere, of course. She'd lived in Delilah's rambling Oklahoma City mansion for several months and assisted her with some of her pet charity projects. She'd also picked up bits and pieces about the various megadeals Alex and Blake had in the works at DI. And she'd certainly gotten a firsthand taste of the luxury she'd married into during the flight across the Atlantic and at the Hôtel des Elmes. But for some reason the idea of forking over eighty or ninety million for a painting made it all seem surreal.

Her glance dropped to the diamonds banding her finger. They were certainly real enough. A whole lot more real than the union they supposedly symbolized. Although yesterday, at the pool...

No! Better not go there! She'd just get all confused and conflicted again. Best just to enjoy the sun and the company of the intriguing man she'd married.

A flash of white diverted her attention to the right side of the road. Eyes popping, she stared at a massive arch and white marble tower spearing up toward the sky. "What are those?"

"They're called *Les Antiques*. They're the most visible remnants of the Roman town of Glanum that once occupied this site. The rest of the ruins are a little farther down the road. We'll save exploring them for another day."

He turned left instead of right and drove down a tree-shaded lane bordered on one side by a vacant field and on the other by tall cypresses and the twisted trunks of an olive grove. Beyond the grove the rocky spine of the Alpilles slashed across the horizon.

"Here we are."

"Here," Grace discovered, was the Saint-Paul de Mausole Asylum, which Van Gogh had voluntarily entered in May 1889. Behind its ivy-covered gray stone walls she glimpsed a church tower and a two- or three-story rectangular building.

"Saint-Paul's was originally an Augustine monastery," Blake explained as he maneuvered into a parking space next to two tour buses. "Built in the eleventh or twelfth century, I think. It was converted to an asylum in the 1800s and is still used as a psychiatric hospital. The hospital is off-limits, of course, but the church, the cloister and the rooms where Van Gogh lived and painted are open to the public."

A very interested public, it turned out. The tour buses had evidently just disgorged their passengers. Guides shepherded their charges through the gates and up to the ticket booth. After the chattering tourists clicked through the turnstile single file, Blake paid for two entries and picked up an informational brochure but caught Grace's elbow once they'd passed through the turnstile.

"Let them get a little way ahead. You'll want to experience some of the tranquility Van Gogh did when he was allowed outside to paint."

She had no problem dawdling. The path leading to the church and other buildings was long and shady and lined on both sides by glossy rhododendron and colorful flowers. Adding to her delight, plaques spaced along the walk highlighted a particular view and contrasted it with Van Gogh's interpretation of that same scene.

A depiction of one of his famous sunflower paintings was displayed above a row of almost identical bright yellow flowers nodding in the sun. A low point in the wall provided a sweeping view of silvery-leafed olive trees dominated by the razor-backed mountain peaks in the distance. Van Gogh's version of that scene was done with his signature intense colors and short, bold brushstrokes. Fascinated, Grace stood before the plaque and glanced repeatedly from the trees' gnarled, twisted trunks to the artist's interpretation.

"This is amazing!" she breathed. "It's like stepping into a painting and seeing everything that went into it through different eyes."

She lingered at that plaque for several moments before meandering down the shady path to the next. Blake followed, far more interested in her reaction to Van Gogh's masterpieces than the compositions themselves.

She was like one of the scenes the artist had painted, he mused. She'd come into his life shortly after Molly had, but he'd been so absorbed with the baby it had taken weeks for him to see her as something more than a quietly efficient nanny. The attraction had come slowly and built steadily, but the shock of learning that she'd deceived him—deceived them all—had altered the picture considerably. As had the annoying realization that he'd missed her as much as Molly had when she'd left Oklahoma City.

Yet every time he thought he had a handle on the woman, she added more layers, more bold brushstrokes to the composite. Her fierce loyalty to her cousin and refusal to betray Anne's trust irritated Blake to no end but he reluctantly, grudgingly respected her for it.

And Christ almighty! Yesterday's heat. That searing desire. He knew where his had sprung from. His hunger had been building since… Hell, he couldn't fix the exact point. He only knew that yesterday had stoked the need instead of satisfying it.

Now he'd found another layer to add to the mix—a woman in a black T-shirt and ball cap thoroughly enjoying the view of familiar images from a completely different perspective, just as Blake was viewing her. How many variations of her were there left to discover?

The question both intrigued and concerned him as he walked with her into the round-towered church that formed part of the original monastery. In keeping with the canons of poverty, chastity and obedience embraced by the Augustinian monks, the chapel was small and not overly ornate. The enclosed cloister beside it was also small, maybe thirty yards on each of its four sides. The cloister's outer walls were solid gray stone. Arched pillars framed the inner courtyard and formed a cool, shady colonnade. Sunlight angled through the intricately carved pillars to illuminate a stone sundial set amid a profusion of herbs and plants.

"Oooh," Grace murmured, her admiring gaze on the colonnade's intricately carved pillars. "I can almost see the monks walking two by two here, meditating or fingering their wooden rosaries. And Van Gogh aching to capture this juxtaposition of sunlight and shadow."

The artist couldn't have hurt any more than Blake did at the moment. The same intermingling of sun and shadow played across Grace's expressive face. The warm smile she tipped his way didn't help, either.

"I know you must have visited here several times during your stays in Saint-Rémy. Thanks for making another trek with me. I'm gaining a real appreciation for an artist I knew so little about before."

He masked his thoughts behind his customary calm. "You're welcome, but we're still at the beginning of the Van Gogh trail. You'll discover a good deal more about him as we go."

She made a sweeping gesture toward the far corner of the cloister. "Lead on, MacDuff."

They spent another half hour at Saint-Paul's. The windows in the two austere rooms where Van Gogh had lived and painted for more than a year gave narrow views of the gardens at the rear of the asylum and the rolling wheat fields beyond, both of which the artist had captured in numerous paintings. The garden's long rows of lavender had shed their purple blossoms, but the scent lingered in the air as Grace compared the scene with the plaques mounted along the garden's wall.

At the exit she lingered for a good five minutes in the spot reputedly depicted in *Starry Night,* arguably one of the artist's most celebrated canvases. The glowing golden balls flung across a dark cobalt sky utterly fascinated her and prompted Blake to purchase a framed print of the work at the gift shop. She started to protest that it was too expensive but bit back the words, knowing the stiff price wouldn't deter him any more than the price of the perfumed oil he'd purchased yesterday.

They stopped at the villa to drop off the purchase, then spent a leisurely two hours following the rest of the trail as it wound through the fields and narrow lanes Van Gogh painted when he was allowed to spend time away from the asylum. The trail ended in the center of town at the elegant eighteenth-century *hôtel* that had been converted to a museum and study center dedicated to the artist's life and unique style.

After another hour spent at the museum, Blake suggested lunch in town at a popular restaurant with more tables outside than in. Grace declared the location on one of Saint-Rémy's pedestrians-only streets perfect for people watching. Chin propped in both hands, she did just that while Blake scoped out the wine list. He went with a light, fruity local white and a melted ham-and-cheese sandwich, followed by a dessert of paper-thin crepes dribbling caramel sauce and powdered sugar. Grace opted for a crock of bouillabaisse brimming with carrots, peppers, tomatoes and celery in addition to five varieties of fresh fish, half-shelled oysters, shrimp and lobster. She passed on dessert after that feast, but couldn't resist sneaking a couple of bites of Blake's crepes.

They lingered at the restaurant, enjoying the wine and shade. Grace was sated and languid when they left, and distinctly sleepy-eyed when she settled into the sun-warmed leather of the convertible's passenger seat.

The crunch of tires on the villa's crushed-shell driveway woke her. She sat up, blinking, and laughed an apology.

"Sorry. I didn't mean to doze off on you."

"No problem." He braked to a halt just beyond the fountain of leaping, pawing horses. "At least you didn't go totally unconscious, like I did yesterday."

A hint of color rose in her cheeks. Blake sincerely hoped she was remembering the wild activity that had preceded yesterday's lengthy snooze. He certainly was. The color deepened when he asked with totally spurious nonchalance if she felt like a swim.

"I think I'll clean up a bit and see what's in the library. You go ahead if you want."

"I'll take a pass, too. I've got some emails I need to attend to."

"Okay. I'll, uh, see you later." She swung away, turned back. "Thanks again for sharing Van Gogh with me. I really enjoyed it."

"So did I."

This was what she'd wanted. What she'd insisted on. Grace muttered the mantra several times under her breath as she climbed the stairs to the second floor.

Tugging off her ball cap, she freed her wind-tangled hair and tried a futile finger comb. When she opened the door to the Green Suite, she took two steps inside and stopped dead.

"Omigosh!"

Starry Night held a place of honor above the marble fireplace, all but obscuring the faint outline of whatever painting had hung there before. The print's cool, dark colors seemed to add depth to the silk wall coverings. The swirling stars and crescent moon blazed luminescent trails across the night sky, while the slumbering village below created a sense of quiet and peace. The dark, irregular, almost brooding shape dominating the left side of the print might seem a little sinister to some, but to Grace it was one of the cypress trees Van Gogh had captured in so many of his other works.

She walked into the suite, took a few steps to the side and marveled at how the stars seemed to follow her movements. Then she just stood for long moments, drinking in the print's vibrant colors and thinking of the man who'd obviously instructed it be hung where she could enjoy it during her stay.

Okay, no sense denying the truth when it was there, right in front of her eyes. Blake Dalton was pretty much everything she'd ever dreamed of in a husband. Smart, considerate, fun to be with, too handsome for words. And soooooo good with his hands and mouth and that hard, honed body of his.

She could fall in love with him so easily. Already had, a little. All right, more than a little. She wouldn't let herself tumble all the way, though. Not with her cousin's memory hanging between them like a thin, dark curtain. As fragile as that curtain was, it formed an impenetrable barrier. Grace couldn't tell him the truth, and he couldn't trust her until she did.

Sighing, she turned away from the print and headed for the shower.

The curtain seemed even more impenetrable when she joined Blake for dinner that evening. As promised, Auguste had prepared his version of coquilles St. Jacques. It would be served, she'd been informed, in the small dining room. *Small* being a relative term, of course. Compared with the formal dining hall, which could seat thirty-six with elbow room to spare, this one was used for intimate dinners for ten or twelve. Silver candelabra anchored each end of the gleaming parquet-wood table. Between them sat a silver bowl containing a ginormous arrangement of white lilies and pink roses.

Blake had dressed for the occasion, Grace saw when she entered the room. She felt a funny pang when she recognized the suit he'd worn at their wedding. He'd opted for no tie and left his white shirt open at the neck, though. That quieted her sudden jitters and let her appreciate his casual elegance.

He in turn appeared to approve of the sapphire-colored jersey sundress that had thankfully emerged from her suitcase wrinkle-free. Its slightly gathered skirt fell from a strapless, elasticized bodice. Earrings and a necklace of bright, chunky beads picked up the dress's color and added touches of purple and green, as well.

"Nice dress," Blake commented. "You look good in that shade of blue."

Hell, she looked good in any dress, any shade. Even better out of one. Manfully, he redirected his thoughts from the soft elastic gathers and refused to contemplate on how one small tug could bring them down.

"Would you care for a drink before dinner?" He nodded to the silver ice bucket on its stand. "There's champagne chilling."

"Who can say no to champagne?"

The wine was bottled exclusively for The Elms by the small vintner just outside Epernay Delilah had stumbled across a few years ago. She got such a kick out of presenting her friends and acquaintances with a gift of the private label that her sons had given up trying to convince her not everyone appreciated their champagne ultra brut.

With that in mind, he filled two crystal flutes, angled them to let the bubbles fizz and handed one to Grace.

"What shall we drink to?"

"How about starry nights, as depicted so beautifully by the print you had hung in my bedroom? Thank you for that."

"You're welcome." He chinked his flute to hers. "Here's to many, many starry nights."

He savored the wine's sharp, clean purity but wasn't surprised when Grace wrinkled her nose and regarded her glass with something less than a connoisseur's eye.

"It's, uh…"

"Very dry?"

"Very something."

"They make it with absolutely no sugar," Blake explained, smiling. "It's the latest trend in champagne."

"If you say so."

"Try another sip. Mireille Guiliano highly recommends it in her book *French Women Don't Get Fat,*" he tacked on as additional inducement.

"Well, in that case…" She tipped her flute. The nose scrunch came a moment later. "Guess it takes some getting used to."

"Like our marriage," he agreed solemnly, then smiled as he relieved her of the drink. "We're learning to be nothing if not flexible, right? So I had another bottle put on ice just in case."

He made a serious dent in the ultra brut over dinner. Grace limited herself to one glass of the semi-sec but didn't debate or hesitate to accept a second serving of Auguste's decadent scallops au gratin. The chef himself presided over the serving tray and forked three shell-shaped ramekins onto her plate. Blake derived almost as much pleasure from her low, reverent groans of delight as he did from the succulent morsels and sinfully rich sauce.

The awkward moment came after dessert and coffee. Blake could think of a number of ways to fill the rest of the evening. Unfortunately, he'd agreed to take wild, hot sex off the agenda. He had *not* agreed to table slow and sweet, but he gritted his teeth and decided to keep that as his ace in the hole.

"I think there are some playing cards in the library. Want to try your hand at gin rummy?"

"We could. Or…" Her eyes telegraphed a challenge. "We could check out the video room upstairs. I saw it had a Wii console. I'm pretty good at Ubongo, if I do say so myself."

"What's Ubongo?"

"Ahhhh." She crooked a finger, batted her lashes and laid on a heavy French accent. "*Come avec moi, monsieur,* and I will show you, yes?"

A month, even a week ago, Blake would never have imagined he'd spend the second night of his honeymoon frantically jabbing red buttons with his thumbs while jungle critters duked it out on a flat-screen TV and his bride snorted with derision at each miss…or that each snort would only make him want her more.

He fell asleep long after midnight still trying to decide how getting his butt kicked at Ubongo could put such a fierce lock on his heart. But he didn't realize just how fierce until the next afternoon.

Nine

When Grace came downstairs, Blake was pacing the sunny breakfast room with his phone to his ear. He speared a glance at her gauzy peasant skirt topped by a white lacy camisole, waggled his brows and gave a thumbs-up of approval.

She preened a little and returned the compliment. He'd gone casual this morning, too. Instead of his usual hand-tailored oxford shirt with the cuffs rolled up, he'd chosen a black, short-sleeved crew neck tucked into his tan slacks. The clingy fabric faithfully outlined the corded muscles of his shoulders and chest. Grace was enjoying the view when he finished one call and made a quick apology before taking the next.

"Sorry. We've just been notified of a possible nationwide transportation strike that could affect delivery from one of our subs here in France. I've got the plant manager on hold."

She flapped a hand. "Go ahead."

That discussion led to a third, this one a conference call with Alex and DI's VP for manufacturing. Although it was still the middle of the night back in the States, both men were evidently working the problem hard. Grace caught snatches of their discussion while she scarfed down another of Auguste's incredible breakfasts.

Blake apologized again when he finished the call. "Looks like I'll have to hang close to the villa this morning while we refine our contingency plan. Alex said to tell you he's sorry for butting into your honeymoon."

Her honeymoon, she noted. Not his.

"No problem," she replied, shrugging off the little sting. "I want to do some shopping. I'll walk into town this morning."

When she left the villa an hour later, she saw vehicles jammed into every available parking space along the tree-shaded road leading into the heart of town. They were her first clue something was happening. The bright red umbrellas and canvas-topped booths that now sprouted like mushrooms in every nook and cranny of the town provided the second.

Delighted, Grace discovered it was market day in Saint-Rémy. Busy sellers offered everything from books and antiques to fresh vegetables, strings of sausages and giant wheels of cheese. A good many of the stalls displayed the products in the dreamy colors of Provence—pale yellows and pinks and lavenders of the soaps, earthy reds and golds in the pottery and linens.

She wandered the crowded streets and lanes, sniffing the heady scents, eagerly accepting free samples when offered. She bought boxed soaps for friends back in San Antonio, a hand-sewn sundress and floppy-brimmed hat exploding with sunflowers for Molly, a small but exquisitely worked antique cameo brooch as a peace offering for Delilah.

She'd thanked the dealer and was turning away when a wooden case at the back of the umbrella-shaded stall caught her eye. It held what looked like antique man stuff—intricately worked silver shoe buckles, pearl stickpins, a gold-rimmed monocle with a black ribbon loop.

And one ring.

Compared with the other ornate pieces in the case, the ring was relatively plain. The only design on the wide yellow gold band was a fleur-de-lis set in onyx. At least, Grace assumed those glittering black stones were onyx. She learned her mistake when the dealer lifted the ring from the case to give her a closer look.

"Madame has a good eye," he commented. "This piece is very old and very rare. From the seventeenth century. Those are black sapphires in the center."

"I didn't know there *were* black sapphires."

"But yes! Hold the ring to the light. You will see the fineness of their cut."

She did as instructed and couldn't tell squat about the cut, but the stones threw back a black fire that made Grace gasp and gave the dealer the scent of a deal in the making. He added subtle pressure by dropping some of the ring's history.

"It is rumored to have once belonged to the Count of Provence. But the last of the count's descendants lost his head in the Revolution and the rabble sacked and burned his *hôtel,* so we have no written records of this ring. No—how do you call it? Certificate of authenticity. Only this rumor, you understand."

Grace didn't care. She'd walked out of Judge Honeywell's office wearing a band of diamonds. Blake's ring finger was still bare. She didn't need a certificate to rectify the situation. Those shimmering black sparks were authentic enough for her.

"How much is it?"

He named a figure that made her gulp until she realized it was a starting point for further negotiations. She countered. He shook his head and came back with another price. She sighed and put the ring back in the case. He plucked it out again.

"But look at these stones, madame. This workmanship."

"I don't know if it will fit my husband," she argued.

"It can always be resized."

He dropped his glance to the sparkling gems circling her finger. His expression said she could certainly afford to have it fitted, but he cut the price by another fifty euros. Grace did the conversion to dollars in her head, gulped again and tried to remember the exact balance in her much-depleted bank account.

She could cover it. Barely. Squaring her shoulders, she took the plunge. "Do you take Visa?"

The velvet bag containing the ring remained tucked in her purse when she returned to the villa. A local official had delivered documents couriered in from some government source, and Blake had invited her to join them for lunch. The woman was lively company and was delighted to learn Blake intended to show his bride Saint-Rémy's ancient Roman ruins. She also warned they must go that very afternoon, as the archeological site could be affected if the transportation unions went on strike the following day as they'd threatened.

Grace couldn't see the connection but didn't argue

when Blake said he was satisfied with his review of the contingency plans and was free to roam for a few hours. Before they left the villa, though, he made sure his mobile phone was fully charged, then tucked it close at hand in the breast pocket of his shirt.

The monuments she'd spotted through the trees yesterday were even more impressive up close and personal. Blake parked in a dusty, unpaved lot filled with cars and what turned out to be school buses. Grace had to smile at the noisy, exuberant teens piling out of the buses.

"I've taken my classes on a few field trips like this one," she commented. "It's always tough to judge how much of what they'll see actually sinks in."

Not much, Blake guessed. At least for the young, would-be studs in the crowd. As both he and his brother could verify, the attention of boys that age centered a whole lot more on girls in tight jeans than ancient ruins.

Boys of any age, actually. Grace wasn't in jeans, but she snagged more than one admiring look from the male students and their teachers as she and Blake joined the line straggling along the dirt path to *Les Antiques*.

The two monuments gleamed white in the afternoon sun. Blake couldn't remember which triumph the massive arch was supposed to commemorate—the conquest of Marseille, he thought—but he knew the perfectly preserved marble tower beside the arch had served as a mausoleum for a prominent Roman family. Luckily, descriptive plaques alongside each monument provided the details in both French and English.

Blake wasn't surprised that the teacher in Grace had to read every word, much as she had on the Van Gogh trail yesterday. Peering over the heads of the kids, she glanced from the plaque to the intricate pattern decorating the underside of the arch.

"This is interesting. Those flowers and vines represent the fertility of 'the Roman Province,' aka *Provence*. I didn't know that's where the region's name came from."

Two of the teens obviously thought she'd addressed the comment to them. One turned and pulled an earbud from his ear. The other tucked what looked like a sketchbook under his arm and asked politely, *"Pardon, madame?"*

"The name, Provence." She gestured to the sign. "It's from the Latin."

"Ah, oui."

Blake hid a smile as the boys looked her over with the instinctive appreciation of the male of the species. They obviously liked what they saw. And who wouldn't? Her hair was a wind-tossed tangle of pale silk, and the skin displayed all too enticingly by the white lace camisole had been warmed to a golden tan by the hot Provencal sun. Not surprisingly, the boys lagged behind while the rest of their group posed and snapped pictures of each other under the watchful eyes of their teachers.

"You are from the U.S.?" the taller of the two asked.

"I am," she confirmed. "From Texas."

"Ahhh, Texas. Cowboys, yes? And cows with the horns like this."

When he extended his arms, Grace grinned and spread hers as far as they would go. "More like this."

"Oui?"

"Oui. And you? Where are you from?"

"Lyon, madame."

The shorter kid was as eager as his pal to show off his English. "We study the Romans," he informed Grace, his earbud dangling. "They were in Lyon, as in many other parts of Provence. You have seen the coliseum in Arles and the Pont du Gard?"

"Not yet."

"But you must!" The taller kid whipped his sketch-book from under his arm, flipped up the lid and riffled through the pages. "Here is the Pont du Gard."

Grace was impressed. So was Blake. He'd visited the famous aqueduct a number of times. The kid's drawings captured both the incredible engineering and soaring beauty of its three tiers of arches.

One of the teachers came over at that point to see what his students were up to. When he discovered Grace was a teacher, he joined the kids in describing the Roman sites she should be sure to visit while in the south of France. He also provided her a list of the architectural and historical items of interest he'd tasked his students to search out at *Les Antiques* and the adjoining town of Glanum.

"What a good idea," Grace exclaimed as she skimmed the Xeroxed four pages. "It's like a treasure hunt."

"The class searches in teams," the teacher explained. "You should join us. You will gain a far better appreciation of this site."

"I'd love to but…" She threw Blake a questioning glance. "Do we have time?"

"Sure."

"We can team up."

Blake gauged the boys' reaction to that with a single glance. "You and these fellows do the hunting," he said easily. "I'll follow along."

List in hand, she joined the search. Her unfeigned interest and ready smile made willing slaves of her two teammates. Preening like young gamecocks, they translated the background history of the first item on the list, and crowed with delight when they collectively spotted the chained captives at the base of the arch representing Rome's might.

Blake found a shady spot and rested his hips against a fallen marble block, watching as Grace and her team searched out two additional items on the arch and three on the tall, pillared tower of the mausoleum. He wondered if the boys had any idea that she let them do the discovering. Or that her seemingly innocent questions about the translations forced them to delve much deeper into the history of the site than they otherwise would have. Those two, at least, were going home experts on *Les Antiques.*

The hunt took them across the street and down another hundred yards to the entrance to Glanum. Unlike the arch and mausoleum, access to the town itself was controlled and active excavations were under way at several spots along its broad main street. Despite the roped-off areas, there was still plenty to explore. The students poked into the thermal furnaces that heated the baths, clambered over the uneven stones of a Hellenistic temple and followed the narrow, twisty track through the ravine at the far end of town to the spring that had convinced Gauls to settle this site long before the Romans arrived.

Grace was right there with her team, carefully picking her way down a flight of broken marble steps to the pool fed by the sacred spring. The fact that she could translate the Latin inscription dedicating the pool to Valetudo, the Roman goddess of health, scored her considerable brownie points with the kids. The delight they took in her company scored even more with Blake.

He could guess the kind of dreams those boys would

have tonight. He'd had the same kind at their age. Still had 'em, he admitted wryly, his gaze locked on his wife.

The hunt finished, Grace exchanged email addresses with her teammates and their teacher before walking back to the car with Blake.

"You were really good with those kids," he commented.

"Thanks. I enjoy interacting with teens. Most of them have such lively minds, although the mood swings and raging hormones can be a pain at times."

Their footsteps stirred the dust on the unpaved path. A car whizzed by on the road to the mountain village high up in the Alpilles. The scents of summer lingered on the still air. Blake grasped her elbow to guide her around a rough patch, then slid his hand down to take hers.

He saw her glance down at the fingers interlacing hers. A small line creased her forehead, but she didn't ease her hand away until they reached the convertible. Blake chalked the frown up to the unsettled nature of their marriage and started to open the passenger door for her. She planted her hip against the door, stopping him.

"I bought you something while I was in town this morning." She fished a small velvet bag out of her purse. "It's not much. But I saw it and thought of you and our time here in France and... Well, I just wanted you to have it."

When he untied the strings, a heavy gold ring rolled into his palm. The fleur-de-lis embedded in its center flashed a rainbow of sparks.

"The dealer said it's an antique. He thinks it once belonged to the Count of Provence, but there's no documentation to support that claim." She looked from the ring to him with a mix of uncertainty and shyness. "Do you like it?"

"Very much. Thank you."

The heartfelt thanks dissolved both the shyness and uncertainty. "You're welcome."

The inquiries Blake had run into her finances told him she must have maxed out her credit card to buy the ring, but he knew better than to ruin the moment by asking if she needed a quick infusion of funds. He showed his appreciation instead by tilting the design up to the light.

"The stones are brilliantly cut."

"That's what the dealer said."

"He said right. You rarely find sapphires with so many facets."

"How'd you guess they're sapphires?"

Grinning, he lowered the ring. "Mother has me take care of insurance appraisals and certificates of authenticity for all her jewelry. She's got more rare stones in her collection than the Smithsonian."

"I don't doubt it. Here," she said when he started to slide it on. "Let me."

She eased the ring onto his finger, then hesitated with the band just above the knuckle.

"With this ring…"

The soft words hit with a jolt, ricocheting around in Blake's chest as she worked the ring over his knuckle. It was a tight fit, but the gold band finally slid on.

"…I thee wed."

Grace finished in a whisper and folded her hand over his. Blake didn't respond. He couldn't. His throat was as tight as a drum.

"I can recall every minute in Judge Honeywell's office," she confessed on a shaky laugh. "I can hear the words, replay the entire scene in vivid Technicolor. Yet…"

She glanced around the dusty parking lot, brought her gaze back to his.

"This is the first time I feel as though it's all for real."

"It is real. More than I imagined it could be back there in the judge's office."

His hand tightened, crushing hers against the heavy gold band. She glanced down, startled, then met his gaze again.

"Let me take you home and show you just how real it's become for me."

Blake had no doubts. None at all. He made the short drive to the villa on a surge of adrenaline and desire so thick and heavy it clamped his fists on the steering wheel.

Uncertainty didn't hit until he followed Grace up the stairs and into the cool confines of the Green Suite. When she turned to face him, he half expected her to retreat again, insist they go back to cool and polite.

He'd never wanted a woman the way he wanted this one. Never loved one the way he did his bright, engaging, sun-kissed bride. The fierce acknowledgment rattled him almost as much as the hunger gnawing at his insides. He could slam on the brakes if he had to, though. It would damned near kill him, but he could do it. All she had to do was…

"Lock the door."

It took a second or two for his brain to process the soft command. Another couple for him to click the old-fashioned latch into place. When he turned back, she reached for the top button on her camisole.

His uncharacteristic doubts went up in a blaze of

heat. With a low growl, he brushed her hands aside. "I've been fantasizing about popping these buttons since you came downstairs this morning."

He forced himself to undo them slowly. He wanted the pleasure of baring the slopes of her breasts inch by tantalizing inch. But his greedy pleasure splintered into something close to pain when he peeled back the cottony fabric and revealed the half bra underneath. With a concentration that popped sweat on his brow, he slid the camisole off her shoulders.

Damn! He was as jerky and eager as any of the adolescents they'd encountered this afternoon. Grace was the steady one. She displayed no hint of embarrassment or shyness when the camisole slithered down her arms and dropped to the carpet.

She reached back and unhooked her bra. The movement was so essentially female, so erotic and arousing. Blake ached for the feel of her smooth, firm flesh against his. But when he dragged his shirt free of his slacks, she copied his earlier move and brushed his hands aside.

"My turn."

Just as he had, she took her time. Her palms edged under the shirt, flattened on his stomach, glided upward. Blake bent so she could get it off over his head. His breath razored in, then out when her hands slid south again. A smile played in her eyes when she found his belt buckle.

"I've been fantasizing about *this* since I came downstairs this morning."

"Okay, that's it!"

He had her in his arms in one swoop and marched to the bed.

Ten

The session in the swimming pool had sprung the beast in Blake. This time, he was damned if he would let it slip its leash. He kept every move slow and deliberate as he dragged the brocade coverlet back and stretched Grace out on the soft, satiny sheets.

He took his time removing the rest of her clothes, and his. As he joined her on the cool, satiny sheets, his eyes feasted on her lithe curves. Tan lines made a noticeable demarcation at her shoulders and upper thighs. The skin between was soft and pale and his to explore.

"Too bad Van Gogh isn't around to paint you." He stroked the creamy slopes and valleys. "You would have inspired him to even greater genius."

"I seriously doubt that."

"Well, you certainly inspire me. Like here…"

He brushed a kiss across her mouth.

"And here…"

His lips traced her cheeks and feathered her lids. "And here..."

Mounding her breast, he teased the nipple with his teeth and tongue until it puckered stiff and tight. Blake gave the other breast equal attention and got a hint of the anguish Van Gogh must have suffered over his masterpieces. He was feeling more than a little tormented himself as he explored the landscape of his wife's body.

She didn't lay passive during the investigation. She flung one arm above her head, brought it down again to plane her hand over his shoulder and down his back. Fingers eager, she kneaded his hip and butt.

Blake felt the muscles low in his belly jerk in response but refused to rush the pace. His palm slid over her rib cage, down her belly. Her stomach hollowed under his touch, and a knee came up as he threaded the dark gold hair of her mound. He slid one finger inside the hot, slick lips, then two, and pressed the tight bud between with his thumb.

Her breath was a fast, shallow rasp now. His was almost as harsh. And when she rolled and nudged him onto his back, it shot damned near off the chart.

She went up on an elbow and conducted her own exploration. Just as slowly. Just as thoroughly. His chin and throat got soft kisses, his shoulder a nuzzle and a teasing nip. She followed by lightly scraping a fingertip down his chest and through hair that arrowed toward his groin.

"Now here," she said with a wicked grin as her fingers closed around him, "we have a real masterpiece."

"You won't hear me argue with that," he returned, his grin matching hers.

She gave a huff of laughter and stroked him, gently at first, then with increasing pressure. The friction coiled him as tight as a centrifuge, but he was confident in his ability to extend this period of mutual discovery awhile longer yet. Right up until she bent down, took him in her mouth and shot his confidence all to hell and back.

His breath left on a hiss. Everything below his waist went on red alert. He managed to hang on for a few moments longer but knew his control was about to blow.

"Grace…"

The low warning brought her head up. Her lips were wet and glistening, her eyes cloudy with desire. When he would have reversed positions, she preempted him by hooking a leg over his thighs. She guided him into her, gasping when he thrust upward, and dropped forward to plant her hands on his chest. The skin over her cheeks was stretched tight. Her hair formed a tangled curtain. Blake had never seen anything more beautiful or seductive in his life.

"Forget Van Gogh," he said gruffly. "Not even he could do you justice."

He shoved his hands through her hair and brought her down for a kiss that was as fierce as it was possessive.

Grace came awake with a twitch. Something rasped like fine sandpaper against her temple. Blake's chin, she decided after a hazy moment. Unshaven and bristly. Deciding to ignore the movement, she burrowed her nose deeper into the warm crevice between his neck and shoulder.

"Grace?"

"Mmmm."

"You awake?"

"Nuh-uh."

"No?"

He shifted, and the chin made another scrape. Grace

raised her head and squinted at the dim shadows wreathing the room.

"Whatimeizzit?"

"Close to six, I think."

"Jeez!"

Her head dropped. Her cheek thumped his chest. She tried to drift back into sleep but laughter rumbled annoyingly under her ear.

"Not a morning person, I take it."

"Not a 6:00 a.m. person," she mumbled, sounding sulky even to herself.

"I'll keep that in mind for future reference."

It took a few moments for that to penetrate her sleepy fog. When it did, she pushed up on an elbow and shoved her hair out of her eyes. She wasn't awake enough to address the subject of the future head-on. Or maybe she just didn't have the nerve. Still a little grumpy, she went at it sideways.

"Are you? A morning person, I mean?"

"Pretty much." An apologetic smile creased his whiskery cheeks. "I've been awake for an hour or so."

She groaned and would have made a dive for the pillows, but he shifted again. She ended up lying on her side, facing him, with her head propped on a hand and her thoughts hijacked by a worry about morning breath. She ran a quick tongue over her teeth. They didn't feel too fuzzy. And her lips weren't caked with drool, thank God! She refused to think about her uncombed hair and unwashed face. Or how much she needed to pee.

Blake, of course, looked totally gorgeous in the dim light. A lazy smile lit his wide-awake blue eyes, and he was tantalizingly naked above the rumpled sheets. He even smelled good. Sort of musky and masculine and warm.

When she finished inspecting the little swirl of dark gold hair around his navel and brought her gaze back to his face, she saw his smile had taken on a different slant. Less lazy. More serious.

"I did some thinking while I was lying here waiting for you to rejoin the living."

She guessed from his expression what he'd been cogitating over but asked anyway. "About?"

"Us."

The arm propping her up suddenly felt shaky. Did he want to alter their still-evolving relationship? Renegotiate the contract? After last night, she was certainly open to different terms and conditions. Still, she had to work to keep her voice steady.

"And what did you conclude, counselor?"

"I want to make this work, Grace. You, me, our marriage."

"I thought we were making it work."

"Bad word choice. I meant make it real."

He reached over to tuck a tangled strand behind her ear. She held her breath until he'd positioned it to his satisfaction.

"I want to spend the rest of my life with you. You and Molly and the children we might have together."

Oh, God! Were they really having this discussion with her teeth unbrushed and her face crumpled into sleep lines? She couldn't fall on his chest again, lock her mouth on his and show him how much she wanted the exact same things.

"Hold on."

Surprise blanked his face at the terse order. A swift frown followed almost instantly as she threw off the sheet.

"I'll be right back."

She spent all of three minutes in the bathroom. When she emerged, he was sitting with his back against the padded silk headboard. The scowl remained, but the fact that she was still naked seemed to reassure him. That, and the joy she didn't try to disguise when she scrambled onto the bed and knelt facing him.

"Okay, I can respond properly now. Repeat what you said, word for word."

He hooked a brow and repeated obediently, "I want to spend the rest of my life with you."

"Me and…" she prompted.

"You and Molly and the children we might have together."

A giddy happiness gathered in her throat, but she had to make sure. "And you can live with the fact that I won't…can't tell you Anne's secrets?"

"I don't like it," he admitted honestly, "but I can live with it."

"Then I say we go for it. Molly, more babies, the whole deal."

The laughter came back, and with it a tenderness that made her heart hurt.

"Whew! You had me worried there for a moment."

"Yes, well, for future reference, you probably want to wait until I've brushed my teeth to spring something like that on me."

"I'll add that to the list," he said as she framed his face with both hands.

She reveled in the scrape of his whiskery cheeks, amazed and humbled at the prospect of sharing the months and years ahead with this smart, handsome, incredible man. Every tumultuous hope for their future filled her heart as she leaned in and sealed their new contract.

* * *

Given the rocky start to her marriage, Grace would never have believed her honeymoon would turn into the stuff that dreams are made of.

Last-minute negotiations averted the threatened strike, so no further business issues intruded and Grace had her husband's undivided attention. As she'd already discovered, he woke early and disgustingly energized. She wasn't exactly a sloth, but she did prefer to open her eyes to sunshine versus a dark, shadowy dawn. They compromised by making love late into the night, every night, and in the morning only after she'd come fully alert. Afternoons and early evenings were up for grabs.

They also spent long hours learning about the person they'd married. Grace already knew Blake liked to read but until now had only seen him buried behind *The Wall Street Journal* or *The New York Times* or the latest nonfiction bestseller. She raided the library on one of Provence's rare rainy afternoons and wooed him away from the real world by curling up with a copy of one of her all-time favorites. He didn't exactly go into raptures over *Jane Eyre* but agreed the heroine did develop some backbone toward the end of the story.

Grace returned the favor by digging into the bestseller he'd picked up at a store in town that stocked books in English as well as French. Although she had a good grasp of American history, she never expected to lose herself in a biography of James Garfield. But historian Candace Millard packed high drama and nail-biting suspense into her riveting *Destiny of the Republic: A Tale of Madness, Medicine and the Murder of a President.*

Aside from that one rainy afternoon, they spent most of the daylight hours outside in the pool or in town or exploring Provence. The Roman ruins of Glanum had fired Grace's interest in the area's other sights. The coliseum at Arles and arch of ramparts in Orange more than lived up to her expectations. The undisputed highlight of their journey into the far-distant past, however, was the gastronomical masterpiece of a picnic Auguste had prepared for their jaunt to the three-tiered Pont du Gard aqueduct. They consumed truffle-stuffed breast of capon and julienne carrots with baby pearl onions in great style on the pebbly banks of the river meandering under the ancient aqueduct.

They jumped more than a dozen centuries when they toured the popes' palace at Avignon. Constructed when a feud between Rome and the French King Philip IV resulted in two competing papacies, the palace was a sprawling city of stone battlements and turrets that dominated a rocky outcropping overlooking the Rhône. From there the natural next step was a visit to Châteauneuf du Pape, another palace erected by the wine-loving French popes to promote the area's viticulture. It was set on a hilltop surrounded by vineyards and olive groves and offered a private, prearranged tasting of rich red blends made from grenache, counoise, Syrah and muscadine grapes.

Each day brought a new experience. And each day Grace fell a little more in love with her husband. The nights only added to the intensity of her feelings. The unabashed romantic in her wanted to spin out indefinitely this time when she had Blake all to herself. Her more practical self kept interrupting that idyllic daydream with questions. Like where they would live. And whether she would transfer her teaching certificate from Texas to Oklahoma. And how Delilah would react to the altered relationship between her son and Grace.

Her two sides came into direct conflict the bright, sunny morning they drove to the open-air market in a small town some twenty miles away. L'Isle sur la Sorgue's market was much larger than Saint-Rémy's and jam-packed with tourists in addition to serious shoppers laying in the day's provisions, but the exuberant atmosphere and lovely old town bisected by the Sorgue River made browsing the colorful stalls a delight.

For a late breakfast they shared a cup of cappuccino and a waffle cone of succulent strawberries capped with real whipped cream. They followed that with samples of countless varieties of cheese and sausage and fresh-baked pastries. So many that when Blake suggested lunch at one of the little bistros lining the town's main street, Grace shook her head and held up the paper bag containing the wrapped leek-and-goat-cheese tarts they'd just purchased.

"One of these is enough for me. All I need is something to wash it down with."

He pointed her to the benches set amid the weeping willows gracing the riverbank. The trees' leafy ribbons trailed in the gently flowing water and threw a welcome blanket of shade over the grassy bank.

"Sit tight," Blake instructed. "We passed a fresh-fruit stand a few stalls back. They mix up smoothies like you wouldn't believe. Any flavor favorites?"

"I'm good for anything except kiwi. I can't stand the hairy little things."

"No kiwi in yours. Got it. One more item to add to our future reference list."

The list was getting longer, Grace thought with a smile as she sat on the grass and stretched out her legs. Other people were scattered along the bank. Mothers and fathers and grandparents lounged at ease, with each generation keeping a vigilant eye on the youngsters tempting fate at the river's edge. A little farther away one young couple had gone horizontal, so caught up in the throes of youthful passion that they appeared in imminent danger of locking nose rings. Their moves started slow but soon gathered enough steam to earn a gentle rebuke from two nuns walking by on the sidewalk above and a not-so-gentle admonition from a father entertaining two lively daughters while his wife nursed a third. His words were low and in French, but Grace caught the drift. So did the lovers. Shrugging, they rolled onto their stomachs and confined their erotic exchange to whispers and Eskimo nose rubs.

Grace's glance drifted from them to the mother nursing her child. As serene as a Madonna in a painting by a grand master, she held the baby in the crook of her elbow and gently eased the nipple between the gummy lips. She didn't bother with a drape or cover over her shoulder, but performed the most natural task in the world oblivious to passersby. Men quickly averted their eyes. Some women smiled, some looked as though they were recounting memories of performing this same act, and one or two showed an expression of envy.

The scene stirred a welter of emotions in Grace she'd thought long buried. She'd prayed during Anne's troubled marriage that her cousin wouldn't get pregnant and produce a child to tie her even more to Jack Petrie. So what did Anne do after escaping the nightmare of her marriage and slowly, agonizingly regaining her self-respect? She fell for a high-powered attorney, turned up pregnant, panicked and ran again. Only this time she didn't run far or fast enough to escape her fear. Anne landed in a hospital in San Diego, and her baby landed in Grace's arms.

Grace had done her damndest not to let Molly wrap her soft, chubby arms wrap around her heart. It had been a losing battle right from the start. Almost the first moment she held Anne's daughter in her arms, she'd started working a contingency plan in her mind. She would keep Molly under wraps while she let it leak to friends that she was pregnant. Once she was sure word had gotten back to Anne's sadistic husband, she would take a leave of absence from her job and play out a fake pregnancy somewhere where no one knew her. Then she'd raise Molly as her own.

Instead, her dying cousin had begged Grace to deliver the baby to her father. Grace had conceded. Reluctantly. She understood the rationale, accepted that the child belonged with her father. The weeks Grace had spent with the Daltons as Molly's temporary nanny had only reinforced that inescapable fact. But the bond between her and Molly had become a chain around her heart. She'd dreaded with every ounce of her soul breaking that chain and walking away from both the child and the dynamic, charismatic Daltons. Now the chain remained intact.

Drawing up her legs, Grace rested her chin on her knees. She still needed to put a contingency plan into operation. She couldn't take the chance that Anne's sadistic husband might discover Grace had married a man with a young baby. Petrie would check Blake out, discover he wasn't a widower, wonder how he'd acquired an infant daughter just about the same time Grace came into his life.

She would contact a few of her friends in San Antonio, she decided grimly. Imply she'd met someone late last year, maybe during the Christmas break, and had spent the spring semester and summer vacation adjusting to the unexpected result. Then Blake Dalton had swooped in and convinced her to marry him.

Those deliberately vague seeds would sprout and spread to other coworkers. Eventually some version of the story might reach Jack Petrie. It should be enough to throw him off Molly's scent. It had to be!

Lost in her contingency planning, she didn't hear Blake's return until he came up beside her.

"One strawberry-peach-mango combo for you. One blueberry-banana for me."

She moved the sack with the tarts to make room for him on the patch of grass. Legs folded, he sank down with a loose-limbed athletic grace and passed her a plastic cup heaped with whipped cream and a dark red cherry. They ate in companionable silence, enjoying the scene.

The Sorgue River flowed smooth and green just yards away. The young lovers were still stretched out nose-to-nose. The father was hunkered down at the river's bank within arm's reach of his two laughing, wading daughters. His wife held the baby against her shoulder now and was patting up a burp.

Grace let a spoonful of her smoothie slide down a throat that suddenly felt raw and tight. This baby looked nothing like Molly. Her eyes were nowhere near as bright a blue, and instead of Mol's golden curls, she had feathery, flyaway black hair her mother had obviously tried to tame with a jaunty pink bow. Yet when she waved tiny, dimpled fists and gummed a smile, Grace laughed and returned it.

Blake caught the sound and followed her line of sight. Hooking an elbow on his knee, he watched the baby's antics until she let loose with a burp that carried clearly across the grass. After another, quieter encore, her mother slid her down into nursing position.

When Grace gave a small sigh, Blake studied her profile. He wasn't surprised by what he saw there, or by the plea in her eyes when she turned to him.

"I've had an incredible time in Provence," she said slowly. "Every day, every night with you has been a fantasy come true."

She threw another look at the baby, and he read her thoughts.

"I miss Molly, too," he admitted with a wry grin. "Let's go home."

Eleven

His mind made up, Blake moved with characteristic speed and decisiveness. While he and Grace threaded through the crowded market to their car, he used his cell phone to run a quick check of flight schedules for Dalton International's air fleet. The corporate jet was on the wrong side of the Atlantic, so he booked first-class seats on a commercial nonstop flight to Dallas leaving late that afternoon. With the time differential and the short hop to Oklahoma, they would get home at almost the same hour they departed France.

That left Grace barely an hour to throw her things together and say goodbye to Auguste and the rest of the staff. Blake's farewells included exorbitant gratuities for each member of the staff and a promise to bring madame back for a longer stay very soon.

The rush of leaving and her eagerness to get back to Molly carried Grace halfway across the Atlantic. Having Blake beside her in the luxurious first-class cabin staved off fatigue during the remainder of the trip. His low-voiced, less than complimentary commentary on the action flick they watched together had her giggling helplessly and the other passengers craning to see what was on their screens.

Fatigue didn't factor in until after the plane change in Dallas. Fatigue, and a serious case of nerves about coming face-to-face with Blake's mother again. Delilah had let loose with both barrels at her last meeting with Grace. The note from her that Alex delivered in San Antonio had much the same tone. She hadn't been happy about the hurry-up wedding and warned that she'd have something to say about it when the newlyweds returned from France.

Grace couldn't imagine how the redoubtable Dalton matriarch would react to the altered relationship between her son and his bride. Delilah must have known Blake proposed for strictly utilitarian reasons. Mostly utilitarian, anyway. Would she believe his feelings could undergo a major shift in such a short time? Probably not. Grace could hardly believe it herself.

By the time they turned onto the sweeping drive that led to Delilah's Nichols Hills mansion, dread curled like witches' fingers in her stomach. Then the front door flew open and she saw at a glance she'd underestimated Delilah. The older woman took one look at them and gave a whoop that boomed like a cannon shot in the brisk September air.

"I knew it!" she announced gleefully as they mounted the front steps. "No one can resist the fatal combination of Provence and Auguste. Especially two people who were so danged hot for each other."

"Don't you ever get tired of being right?" Blake drawled as he bent to kiss her cheek.

"Never." Blue eyes only a shade lighter than her son's skewered Grace. "And that's something for you to remember, too, missy. Now get over here so I can give my newest daughter-in-law a hug."

Enfolded in a bone-crunching embrace and a cloud of outrageously expensive perfume, Grace made the instant transition from employee and former nanny to member of the family. She was so grateful to this fierce and occasionally overbearing woman that she found herself battling tears.

"Thank you for trusting me with Molly and for…and for…everything."

"We should be thanking you." The hug got tighter, Delilah's voice gruffer. "You brought Molly to us in the first place."

Both women were sniffling when they separated. Embarrassed by her uncharacteristic descent into sentimentality, Delilah flapped a hand toward the stairs.

"I expect you want to see the baby. She's up in the nursery. I just heard her on the monitor, waking up from her nap."

The last time Grace had climbed this magnificent circular staircase was as an employee in Delilah's home. She couldn't quite get a grip on her feelings as she ascended them alongside Blake, anxious to embrace the baby now making come-get-me noises from the room on the left at the top of the stairs. Nerves played a major role. Excitement and eagerness bubbled in there, too. But mostly it was sheer incredulity that she now had the right to claim this man and this child as hers.

When they swept into the nursery Delilah had furnished so swiftly and so lavishly, Molly was standing up in the crib. Her downy blond hair formed a spiky halo and her blue eyes tracked their entrance with a touch of impatience, as if asking what took them so long.

Grace's heart melted into a puddle of mush at the sight of her. It disintegrated even more when Molly gave a gurgle of delight and raised her arms.

"Gace!"

Half laughing, half sobbing, Grace swept the baby out of the crib.

September rolled out and October came in with a nighttime temperature dip into the forties and fifties. As the weeks flew by, a nasty little corner of Grace's mind kept insisting this couldn't last. Sometime, somehow, she would pay for the joy she woke up with every morning. But her busy, busy days and nights spent in Blake's arms buried that niggling thought under an avalanche of others.

Their first order of business was finding a house. Rather than move Molly's nursery to Blake's bachelor pad during the hectic process of inspecting available properties, they accepted Delilah's invitation to occupy the guest wing of her mansion. So naturally both Molly and Delilah went with Grace to check out the possibilities when Blake got tied up at work. Julie, too, when she wasn't flying or distracted by the business of setting up the home she and Alex had recently moved into.

Grace worried at first that Delilah might try to push her toward something big and splashy, but her mother-in-law was motivated by only one goal. She wanted her granddaughter close enough to spoil at will. So she was thrilled when Grace settled on a recently renovated half-timbered home less than a mile from the Dalton mansion. The two-story house sat well back from the street on a one-acre lot shaded by tall pines. Grace had fallen in love with its oak floors and open, sunny kitchen at first sight, but balked at the five bedrooms until Blake convinced her they could convert one to an entertainment center and one to an exercise room unless and until they needed it for other purposes.

Once the house was theirs, Grace faced the daunting prospect of filling its empty rooms. She thought about tackling one room at a time, but Delilah graciously offered the services of her decorator to coordinate the overall scheme.

"Take her up on it," Julie urged during a weekend brunch at their mother-in-law's.

The two brides lolled on the sunlit terrace, keeping a lazy eye on Molly in her net playpen while their husbands checked football scores in the den. Delilah had taken her other guest to the library to show him some faded photographs she'd unearthed from her early days working the oil fields with her husband. Grace found it extremely interesting that Julie's irascible partner, Dusty Jones, had apparently become a regular visitor to the Nichols Hills mansion.

"The decorator is good," her new sister-in-law asserted. "Really good."

Grace could hardly disagree. She'd lived in these opulent surroundings for several months as Molly's nanny. The Lalique chandeliers and magnificent antiques suited Delilah's flair and flamboyance, but Grace had lived in constant dread of Molly spitting up all over one of the hand-woven Italian silk seat cushions.

"Trust me," Julie urged. "Victor will help you achieve just the look you want. He understood right away that I wanted to go clean and uncluttered in our place. I've agreed with almost everything he's suggested so far."

"Surprising everyone concerned," Grace drawled, "yourself included."

"True," the redhead agreed, laughing. "I do tend to formulate strong opinions about things…as Alex frequently points out."

Marriage agreed with her, Grace thought. She looked so relaxed and happy with her auburn hair spilling over her shoulders and her fingers playing with the gold pendant Alex had given her as an engagement gift. The figure depicted on the intricately carved disk was the Inca god who supposedly rose from Lake Titicaca in the time of darkness to create the sun, the moon and the stars. Julie, who'd spent several years ferrying cargo in and out of remote airstrips in South America, had told Grace the god's name but she could never remember it.

"Might as well bow to the inevitable and give Victor a call," Julie advised, stretching languidly. "If you don't, Delilah will just invite him for cocktails one evening and make the poor guy go over your house plans room by room while she pours martinis down his throat."

"Okay, okay. I'll call him."

The two women sat in companionable silence. They'd known each other for only a few months but had become friends in that short time. Marrying twins had solidified the bond. It had also given them unique perspectives into each other's lives.

Grace had worried that her being the one to provide indisputable proof that Blake was Molly's father might drive a wedge between the brothers. Or between her and Alex. Until those final DNA results had come back, the preponderance of evidence had pointed to Alex as the most likely father. He'd taken the baby into his heart and had rearranged his life around her. The home he and Julie had just moved into had been bought with Molly in mind.

Alex appeared to have adjusted to being the baby's uncle instead of her father. He was just as attentive, and every bit as loving. Still, Grace struggled with a twinge of guilt as his wife got up to retrieve the stuffed turtle Molly had chucked out of her playpen.

"Tell me the truth," she said quietly when Julie dropped into her chair again. "Did Alex resent me for keeping my cousin's secret?"

"He did, for maybe a day or two after Blake showed him the final DNA results. He's a big boy, though. He worked through his disappointment." Her eyes took on a wicked glint. "I might have helped the process by redirecting his thoughts whenever I thought they needed it."

"Yes, I bet you… Oops, that's Blake's phone. He said something about expecting a call from Singapore. This may be it."

She scooped up the device he'd left on the table and checked caller ID. The number was a local one.

"Guess it's not Singapore."

Evidently the caller decided his message was too urgent to go to voice mail. Grace had no sooner set the phone down than it buzzed again, this time with a flashing icon indicating a text message.

"I'd better take this in to him. Keep an eye on Molly for me."

"Will do."

Phone in hand, she followed the sound of football fans in midroar to the den. Hoping it was the Dallas Cowboys who'd precipitated that roar, Grace shifted the phone to her other hand.

She honestly didn't mean to hit the text icon. Or read

the brief message that came up. But a single glance at
the screen stopped her dead in her tracks.

Have an update on Petrie. Call me.

Ice crawled along Grace's veins. The hubbub in the
den faded. The papered walls of the hall seemed to close
in on her. She couldn't move, could barely breathe as
Jack Petrie's image shoved everything else out of her
mind. Smooth and handsome at first. Then smooth and
sneering, as he was the last time he'd allowed Grace
to visit his home. *His* home. Not her cousin's. Not one
they'd made together. The house was his, the car was
his, every friggin' dollar in the bank was his, to be doled
out to *his* wife penny by penny.

The ice splintered. An almost forgotten fury now
speared through Grace. Caught in its vicious maw, she
let an animal cry rip from her throat and hurled the
phone at the wall.

The Dalton men came running almost before the
pieces hit the floor. Alex erupted from the den first.

"What the…?"

"Grace!" Blake shoved past his brother. "Are you
okay?"

She didn't answer. *Couldn't* answer. Fury still clawed
at her throat.

"Has something happened to Molly?" He gripped her
upper arms. "Alex! Go check on Julie and the baby!"

He could have saved his breath. His brother was already pounding down the hall.

"Talk to me, Grace." Blake's fingers bit into her
flesh. "Tell me what's happened."

"You got a call. That's what happened."

"What?"

She wrenched out of his hold. With a scathing look, she directed his attention to the shattered phone. He frowned at the pieces in obvious confusion.

"It was a text message." She fought to choke out the words. "My thumb hit the icon by mistake. I didn't intend to read the message. Wasn't intended to read it, obviously."

"What are you talking about? What message? Who was it from?"

"I'm guessing your friend, the P.I. What's his name? Jerrold? James?"

His jaw went tight. "Jamison."

"Right," she said venomously. "Jamison. He wants you to call him. For an update on Petrie."

"Oh, hell."

The soft expletive said it all. Spinning, Grace stalked down the hall and almost bowled over the two who emerged from the library. Any other time she might have noted with interest that a good portion of Delilah's crimson lipstick had transferred from her mouth to Dusty Jones's. At the moment all she could do was snap a curt response when Delilah demanded to know what was going on.

"Ask your son."

She brushed past them, wishing to hell she'd pocketed the keys to the snazzy new Jaguar Blake had insisted on buying her. She needed to get out. Think through this shock. But the keys were on the dresser. Upstairs. In the guest suite. Grace hit the stairs, grinding her teeth in mingled fury and frustration.

By the time she reached the luxuriously appointed suite, she'd added a searing sense of betrayal to the mix. She snatched the keys off the dresser, digging the jagged edges into her palm, staring unseeing at other objects scattered across the polished mahogany.

"Going somewhere?"

She jerked her head up and locked angry eyes on her husband. "I'm thinking about it."

"Mind if I ask where?" he asked calmly.

Too calmly, damn him! She'd always admired his steady thinking and cool composure. Not now. Not with this hurt knifing into her.

"I believed you," she threw at him. "When you said you could live with my refusal to betray Anne's trust, I actually believed you!"

"I am living with it."

"Like hell!"

His eyes narrowed but he kept his movements steady and unhurried as he turned, shut the door and faced her again.

"When you wouldn't trust me with Anne's secrets…"

"I couldn't! Some of us," she added viciously, "hold to our promises."

"When you *couldn't* trust me with Anne's secrets," he amended, his mouth thinning a little, "I had Jamison keep digging. I know now her real name was Hope Templeton."

The telltale signs that he was holding on to his temper with an effort took some of the edge off Grace's own anger. The hurt remained.

"I only had one cousin. Her birth is a matter of record. I'm surprised it took your hotshot P.I. so long to discover her real name."

"I also know she got married at the age of seventeen."

"How did you…? I mean, we…"

"Altered the record? I won't bother to remind you that's a crime."

He was in full lawyer mode now. Legs spread, arms crossed. Relentlessly presenting the evidence. The two of them would have to have this out, Grace realized. Once, and hopefully for all.

Reining in the last of her temper, she sank onto the bed. "Go on."

"What my hotshot P.I. did not find was any record of divorce. I can only assume Anne was still married when she and I met. I can also assume the marriage wasn't a happy one."

"And how did you reach this brilliant deduction?"

He shrugged aside the sarcasm. "The fact that Anne had left him, obviously. And that she used an assumed name, presumably to prevent him from finding her."

Grace could add so much more to the list. Like Anne's aversion to public places for fear Petrie or one of his friends would spot her. Her bone-deep distrust of all men until this one. Her abrupt disappearance from Blake's life, even though she must have loved him.

"I had Jamison check out her husband," he said, breaking into the dark, sad memories. "According to Texas Highway Patrol records, Jack Petrie is a highly decorated officer with two citations for risking his life in the line of duty. One for dragging a man and his son out of a burning vehicle. Another for taking down a drug smuggler who shot a fellow officer during a routine traffic stop."

"You didn't contact him, did you?" Grace asked with her heart in her throat.

"No. Neither did Jamison. But he made discreet inquiries."

She breathed in, out. "And?"

"Jamison came away with the impression Petrie was a devoted husband who liked to show off his pretty young wife. Rumor has it he was devastated when she walked out on him."

Blake waited for her to deny the rumor. When she didn't, he got to the real issue. "That leaves Molly."

"She's your child, Blake!" The exclamation burst out, quick and passionate. "Not Petrie's!"

"I know that. Even without the DNA evidence, Jamison's sources confirmed Anne left her husband almost a year before she and I met. Still, they were married when she gave birth to Molly, and under the law…"

"To hell with the law! You've run the tests. If it ever came to a legal battle, you've got more than enough evidence to support your paternity."

She came off the bed, pleading now.

"But it doesn't need come to a battle. Anne's dead. Petrie has no idea she had a child. Just leave it that way."

"What are you so afraid of, Grace? What was Anne afraid of? Did Petrie hurt her? Use his fists on her?"

"I…"

"Tell me, for God's sake!"

She almost broke down then. She would have given her soul at that point to share the whole, degrading truth, but her promise hung like an anchor around her neck. All she would respond to was one specific question.

"It wasn't physical. Not that I know of, anyway. But mental cruelty can be just as vicious."

"All the more reason for me to protect Molly from this jerk."

He had the training, the extensive network of connections to enact all sorts of legal sanctions. She knew that. She also knew the mere fact he'd had an affair with Anne would drive Jack Petrie to a jealous rage. The man was a sadist. He'd strangled his wife with a warped kind of love that others mistook for devotion. Anne was beyond his reach now, but her child wasn't. Or her lover.

"You've just proved my point," Grace countered with a touch of desperation. "You think Anne's husband won't want vengeance? He'll try to milk you for millions. Drag a paternity suit out in court for years. Have you thought of that?"

"Of course," he snapped. "I'm not afraid of a fight, legal or otherwise."

Okay. All right. She had to breathe deep. Slow down. Remember she wasn't dealing with someone as unbalanced as Jack Petrie.

"Put your own feelings aside for a moment, Blake. Think what a long, drawn-out court battle could do to Molly. When she's older she'll be curious about her mother. All she'd have to do is surf the Net. You can imagine the headlines she'll stumble across. Billionaire's Love Child Center of Vicious Paternity Dispute. Decorated Police Officer Calls Wife a Whore. Secretary Hooks Rich Boss with Sex And…"

"I've got the picture."

He got it, and he didn't like it. She didn't, either, but they couldn't ignore it.

"Don't dig any further, Blake. Please! In a year, two years, everyone outside our immediate circle will just assume Molly's our child. Petrie won't have any reason to question it."

He looked as if she'd punched him in the gut. Or square in his sense of right and wrong. His eyes went cold, his voice flat and hard.

"So you want to live a lie. Like your cousin."

For Molly's sake she gave the only answer she could. "Yes."

Twelve

"She just can't bring herself to trust me."

Blake gripped his beer and ignored the buzz from the crowd gathered in the watering spot a few blocks from Dalton International's corporate headquarters. He and his brother had wrapped a bitch of a meeting with senior executives from Nippon Steel earlier that evening, then taken their Japanese visitors to dinner at one of Oklahoma City's finest steak houses. The Nippon execs had taken a limo back to their hotel, leaving Blake and Alex to lick their wounds over a beer and a bucket of peanuts before heading home to their respective spouses. Despite the round of tough negotiations, it was Blake's spouse who occupied his mind more than the Japanese.

"I accept that Grace promised to keep Anne's secrets," he said, stretching his long legs out beneath a tabletop littered with peanut shells. "I respect her for holding to that vow, but Christ! We've been married almost a month now and she still doesn't think I can handle this character Petrie."

Shrugging, Alex attempted to take the middle road on the subject he and his twin had already beaten into the ground a number of times. "Grace knows Petrie. We don't."

"We know enough! The bastard terrorized his wife and forced her into a shadow life. Now he's doing the same thing to *my* wife."

Frustration ate like acid at Blake's gut. It was doing a serious number on his pride, too. He yanked at the knot of his tie and popped the top button of his shirt before downing a slug of beer.

"Mother says Grace stays in the background at the charity functions she's involved her in and ducks whenever a photographer shows up. She does the same when we attend a concert or some black-tie affair. The woman is fixated on maintaining a low profile until our marriage is old news."

"So? You don't exactly chase after the spotlight yourself."

"Dammit, bro, you're not helping here."

"You wanted a sounding board, I'm doing my best board act." Peanut shells crunched as his twin leaned his elbows on the table. "I've told you what I really think."

"Yeah, I know. You think I should take a quick trip to San Antonio and confront this guy. Let him know who he'd be dealing with if he got any smart ideas."

"Correction. I think *we* should take a quick trip to San Antonio."

"It's my problem! I'll handle it."

"You're doing a helluva job with it so far."

Blake's lips drew back in a snarl. He managed to choke it off. Barely. Alex knew damned well he was spoiling for a fight. Obviously, his twin was prepared to step in and draw the punches.

"Well, at least you've got Jamison's sources keeping an eye on Petrie," Alex commented.

"I'm getting regular updates."

"Does Grace know?"

"She knows."

That had caused another rough scene. Grace argued that Petrie was a cop. Sooner or later he would pick up on a surveillance, become suspicious, track it to the source. Blake countered with the assertion that Jamison and his associate in San Antonio were pros. They wouldn't tip their hands. In either case, Blake flatly refused to turn a blind eye to a potential threat.

Grace had conceded that point. Reluctantly, but she'd conceded. Still, the fact they were living with this guy Petrie's shadow hanging over them locked Blake's jaw every time he thought about it. He'd promised his wife he wouldn't confront the man without talking it over with her first. That discussion was fast approaching. In the meantime, he and Grace each pretended they understood and accepted the other's viewpoint.

"I get that Grace saw firsthand the hell Petrie put her cousin through," Alex said, attacking the matter from another angle. "What I don't get is why she doesn't want to take him on. I didn't know Anne all that well, but I do know Grace. My sense is she's much stronger than her cousin was."

"Stronger, and a whole bunch more stubborn," Blake agreed with a grimace.

"She's also got us to do the muscle work. All of us. Mother and Julie want in on this. Dusty, too."

Momentarily diverted, Blake raised a brow. "Yeah,

what's with that? The old coot's at Mom's house just about every time I stop by there these days."

"They're consulting," Alex replied, deadpan. "As Julie's business partner and coowner of one of Dalton International's subsidiaries, Dusty prefers to talk shop with someone who worked the same oil patches he did."

"Oh, Lord! I'm not going to tell you the image that just jumped into my head. But…" Blake raised his beer. "Here's to 'em."

Grinning, the brothers clinked bottles. Alex signaled the waitress to bring two fresh ones before returning to the issue digging at them both.

"Back to Grace. She's got to know she can count on you, on all of us, to protect her from this asshole Petrie."

"She knows," Blake said grimly. "The problem is she thinks she's protecting us. Or Molly and me, anyway."

His brother winced. "That's got to stick in your craw."

"Like you wouldn't believe."

He didn't go into further detail. As a kid Alex had been the one to wade fist-first into battle. Blake had always had his brother's back, though, and Alex his. The fact that his wife didn't trust him to have hers rubbed him raw. Feeling the grate yet again, he circled his beer bottle on the littered table and sent a shower of peanut shells to the already carpeted floor.

"So how long are you going to play this by her rules?" Alex wanted to know.

Blake's head snapped up. The uncompromising answer came fast. "The rules change the moment I sense so much as a hint of a real threat."

Grace was perched on one of the kitchen counter stools when she heard the muted rumble of the garage door going up. She'd put Molly down for the night at seven-thirty and indulged in the sybaritic luxury of an hour-long soak in scented bath oil that evoked instant memories of Provence's hot sun and endless lavender fields. Barefoot and supremely comfortable in a well-washed, black-and-silver San Antonio Spurs jersey that came almost to her knees, she'd curled up with a biography of Van Gogh before deciding to treat herself to a bowl of double chocolate fudge ripple. After so many years of busy days in the classroom and nights grading papers, she loved having the time and the freedom to read whatever struck her fancy. She loved even more reading to Molly, which she'd started doing before they'd moved into the house Grace was having such fun furnishing.

All in all, her days were perfect. The nights came pretty darn close.

Grace had gotten past her anger over Blake directing his P.I. to dig into the past her cousin had tried so desperately to escape. She'd also recovered—mostly—from the stinging sense of betrayal that he'd done it after she'd begged him to let that past stay buried. She understood his rationale. She didn't agree with it, but she understood it.

Unfortunately, a difference of opinion on something so crucial couldn't help but affect their continually evolving relationship. The strain it had caused was like a small but irritating itch they'd mutually decided to ignore.

Despite the itch, they still took pleasure in discovering new facets to each other's personalities. The quirks, the unconscious gestures, the ingrained habits. What's more, they still shared the sheer joy of Molly.

And Grace's pulse still bumped whenever her husband walked into a room.

Like now. She swiveled the stool, cradling her bowl of double chocolate fudge ripple, and felt the flutter as Blake entered the kitchen through the utility room connected to the garage. He moved with the athletic ease she so admired and looked as classy as ever, although the open shirt collar and the tie dangling from his suit coat pocket added a definite touch of sex to the sophisticated image.

They hadn't reached the stage of casual, hello-honey-I'm-home kisses yet. Grace wasn't sure they ever would, although she knew darn well they couldn't sustain indefinitely the searing heat they'd ignited during their honeymoon. She felt it sizzle now, though, as he nudged her knees apart so he could stand between them and cupped her nape.

"Did you and Alex get your Japanese execs all wined and dined?"

"We did."

His palm was warm against her skin, his eyes a smoky blue as his head bent toward hers. Tipping her chin, Grace welcomed him home with a kiss that left her breathless and Blake demanding a second one just like the first. She gave both willingly, as greedy as he was, but had to jerk back when the fudge ripple threatened to slide into her lap.

Blake eyed the bowl's contents with interest. "That looks good."

"Sit down, I'll get you some."

"I'll just share yours."

"Hmmmm." Her brow furrowed in a mock scowl. "In the 'just for future reference' category, I don't usually share my ice cream. Or my fries."

"Noted. But you'll make an exception in this instance, right?"

Since he was still wedged between her thighs and didn't look as though he planned to move anytime soon, she yielded the point.

"Okay. Here you go."

He downed the heaping spoonful in one try, prompting a quick warning.

"Whoa! You'll get a brain freeze gobbling it down like that."

A slow, predatory smile curved his mouth. "No part of me is liable to freeze like this."

He moved closer, spreading her wider. The Spurs jersey rode up, and Grace felt him harden against her.

"I see what you mean," she got out on a gasp when he exerted an exquisite pressure at the juncture of her thighs. "No danger of frost down there."

Or anywhere else!

The pressure increased. The muscles low in her belly clenched. He splayed his hands on her hips to keep her anchored, and the wild, throbbing sensation built with each rhythmic move of his lower body against hers.

"Blake!" She tried to wiggle away but the counter dug into her back. "We'd better slow down. I can't… You've got me too…"

"Hold on."

Like she could? Especially when he spanned her waist and lifted her in a smooth, easy move from the stool to the counter. She didn't even realize she still held the now-melted ice cream until he took the bowl and let it clatter into the sink. Then the jersey came up and over her head. Her bikini briefs got peeled off. Her mouth was level with his now, her hips in line with his belt. She should have felt completely, nakedly exposed. All she experienced was the urgent need to get him naked, too.

"Your jacket… Shirt…"

He shed the top half of his clothing with minimum movement and maximum speed. The bottom half stayed intact as he buried a fist in her hair, and took her mouth with his.

There was something different in this kiss, in the maddening pressure he exerted against her. He was a little rougher, a little harder, yet somehow more deliberate. As though he could demonstrate some sort of mastery over her if he wanted to but chose to restrain himself. Or not. Grace didn't register more than that hazy impression before he replaced his lower body with his hand and drove everything resembling rational thought out of her head.

She came mere moments later in a burst of bright colors and pure sensation. The explosive climax arched her spine and brought her head back. She slapped her palms on the counter to support her taut, shuddering body, but her arms folded like overstretched elastic.

Blake scooped her off the counter before she went horizontal and carried her limp and still quivering with pleasure to the bedroom. When he shed the rest of his clothes and joined her in bed for the grand finale, he was so gentle and tender Grace completely forgot that odd moment in the kitchen.

It came back with a vengeance less than a week later.

Yielding to her mother-in-law's indomitable will, she strapped Molly into her car seat to drive her over to the Nichols Hills mansion for some grandmother-granddaughter time. Grace herself had been instructed to shop for a cocktail dress for the big-dollar fundraiser

Delilah insisted her sons and their wives attend the following evening.

"Which I really do *not* want to go to," she said via the rearview mirror to the infant happily banging a teething ring against the side window.

Her eyes on the baby, she had to jam on the brakes to avoid an SUV cruising past the end of the drive. The near miss rattled Grace and reminded her to keep her attention on the road. The brief visit with Delilah didn't exactly soothe her somewhat frayed nerves.

"You should get your nails done while you're out," her mother-in-law suggested after a prolonged exchange of Eskimo kisses with a joyously squealing Molly. "Your hair trimmed, too."

"I look that bad, huh?"

"You look gorgeous and you know it." She hitched the baby on her hip and skewered her daughter-in-law with one of her rapier stares. "Just not as glowing as you did when you got back from Provence. Don't tell me you and Blake have taken the sex down a notch already."

"I won't," Grace countered coolly.

"Don't get on your high horse with me, girl. If it's not sex, it has to be that business with Jamison. Look, I don't like to meddle in my sons' lives but…"

She paused and waited with a reluctant grin for Grace to finish snorting.

"Okay, okay. Meddling is my favorite occupation. But I thought you and Blake had come to an understanding on that matter."

"We have. More or less."

The older woman let Molly play with her sapphire-and-diamond wrist bangle and skinned Grace with another serrated look. "I'm only going to say this once. I'll never mention it again, I swear."

Grace believed that as much as she believed her former employer could keep her nose out of her sons' affairs. Once Delilah got the bit between her teeth, she kept it there.

"You did right standing by your promise to your cousin," she said, "but she's dead and you're married now. You need to decide where your loyalty lies."

Grace went rigid, her eyes flashing danger signals. They bounced off Delilah's thick hide.

"Go," she ordered brusquely. "Shop, have your nails done, and for God's sake think about what I just said."

Grace fumed all the way to the exclusive boutique she and Julie had discovered some months ago. She pulled into a parking slot two doors down and killed the Jag's engine, then sat with her fists gripping the leather-wrapped steering wheel.

She didn't need Delilah to lecture her about loyalty, dammit! She'd spent what felt like half her life and every penny of her income shielding Anne from her sadistic husband. If she closed her eyes, she could still see her cousin fighting desperately for her last breaths. Hear her rasping plea for Grace to take Molly to her father and please, *please* don't let Jack know about her.

Her knuckles whitened on the wheel. She stared at the shop window in front of the Jag. The window was bare except for a For Lease sign, but Grace barely noticed the empty expanse of glass and darkened interior.

Maybe...

Maybe the habit of protecting her cousin had become too ingrained. Maybe she'd been following instincts tainted by Anne's bone-deep fear when she should be trusting Blake's. He was calm and cool in a crisis. And more intelligent than any six people she knew. He could also wield resources every bit as if not more powerful than Jack Petrie's. Most important, he was Molly's father. He'd strangle anyone who tried to harm her with his bare hands.

Groaning, Grace dropped her forehead to the wheel. Heart and soul, she ached to hold to the promise she made her cousin. She couldn't. Not any longer. Delilah was right. She had to let go of Anne's past. Her future revolved around Molly and Blake. With a silent plea to her cousin to understand, she raised her head and fumbled in her purse for her cell phone.

She pressed one speed-dial key. Her husband's superefficient executive assistant answered before the second ring.

"Blake Dalton's office."

"Hi, Patrice, it's Grace. Is Blake free?"

"Hi, Grace. Sorry, but he's in the middle of a conference call with the Association of Corporate Counsel's executive committee. They want him to chair the next symposium, you know."

"Yes, I do."

"Shall I pass him a note to let him know you're on the line?"

"No, just tell him… Tell him I was thinking about my cousin and…"

Hell! She couldn't put what she wanted to say on a yellow call slip.

"Just tell him I called."

"I will."

"Thanks."

She tapped End, feeling much like Julius Caesar must have when he brought his legionnaires across the Rubicon. She couldn't go back now. She didn't *want* to go back. She'd charge full steam ahead with Blake and Molly and a life without the specter of Jack Petrie hanging over it.

She was still riding the relief of that decision when she emerged from Helen Jasper's boutique some time later. As usual, the shop owner's eye had proved as unerring as her taste. She'd purchased the entire line of a young Oklahoma designer she was sure would make a splash in the fashion world. Grace ended up buying not only a tea-length cocktail dress in dreamy shades of green, but two beaded tops and a pair of slinky palazzo pants with accessories to match. She'd also had Helen bundle up the outfit she'd worn into the store and now felt very autumnal in heavyweight linen slacks in cinnamon-brown, a matching tank top and a pumpkin-colored silk overblouse left unbuttoned to show off a faux lizardskin belt as wide, if not as clanky, as Delilah's.

Smiling at the thought of Blake's reaction to the backless and darned near frontless cocktail dress, she bunched her shopping bags in one hand and fumbled in her purse for the car keys. She popped the door locks, dropped her purse on the front seat and was about to add the shopping bags when a black SUV wheeled into the slot next to hers. The idiot driver cut into the space so sharply she had to quickly yank on the open door to avoid having it dinged.

Mentally giving him the bird, she bent to retrieve the tissue-stuffed bags her quick move had sent tumbling to the floor mat. When she straightened, she caught a glimpse of the other driver from the corner of one eye. He'd exited his vehicle but hadn't moved away from it.

A prickly sense of unease raced along her spine. He

was standing close to her Jag. Too close. A half dozen tips from the various self-defense articles she'd read crowded into her mind. She went with the only one she could.

Jamming her car keys between her fingers, she closed her fist to form a spiked gauntlet and started to turn. She didn't get even halfway around before something hard rammed against her shoulder blade and her world turned red.

Thirteen

"She doesn't answer her phone."

Blake paced his brother's office on the twentieth floor of Dalton International's headquarters. Wall-to-wall windows offered a different perspective of downtown Oklahoma City than that in his own office at the opposite end of the long corridor bisecting the CEO's suites. But Blake had no interest in the sweeping panorama of the round-domed capitol building in the distance or the colorful barges meandering along the river in the foreground. He took another few paces, his fists jammed in the pocket of his slacks.

"I've left three voice mails. The first was around ten-thirty, the last one a half hour ago."

Although it was now just a little past two, Alex understood his brother's concern. He'd spent several tense hours himself when Julie took off in search of a missing Dusty Jones, her cell phone died and Alex didn't know where the hell she'd disappeared to. When he reminded Blake of that knuckle-cracking episode, his brother shook his head.

"I thought of that, but her phone was sitting in the charger next to mine when I left the house this morning. It's fully juiced."

"And Mother didn't know where Grace was heading?"

"Not specifically. Just that she was going shopping and maybe to get her hair or nails done."

"That sure narrows it down," Alex said drily as he reached for the phone on the broad plane of his desk. "I'll call Julie. I remember her mentioning some boutique or other that she and Grace really like."

Luckily, he caught his wife on the ground between crop-dusting runs. Julie had come to a reluctant decision to quit flying agro-air, worried that its high concentration of chemicals could affect the baby she and Alex had decided to try for. She was in the process of training a replacement now—and acclimating the poor guy to the challenges and dubious joys of working with Dusty.

Blake tried to suppress his nagging worry while his brother explained the situation to his wife and scribbled a couple of numbers on a notepad before promising to call back once they'd located Grace.

"She said to try a boutique owned by a woman named Helen Jasper." Alex punched in the first number. "Also a nail salon on… Hello? Ms. Jasper? This is Alex Dalton."

He listened a moment and smiled.

"Yes, I am. Very lucky. So is my brother. That's why I'm calling, actually. We need to get in touch with Grace, but her cell phone's not working. She was going shopping, and Julie said to try your place." His glance cut to Blake. "She did? All right, thanks."

Some of the tension riding Blake's shoulders left when Alex reported his wife had spent several hours and what sounded like a big chunk of change in the boutique.

"She left a little before noon. Maybe she stopped somewhere for a leisurely lunch."

"Maybe." The tension ratcheted up again. "But I can't see her lingering over a long lunch without calling to check on Molly."

"Let's try this nail place. She could have…"

Alex broke off, frowning when the door to his office opened. His executive assistant sent him an apologetic look as Delilah swept in pushing Molly's stroller, unannounced as usual. The matriarch of the Dalton clan—and nominal president of DI's board of directors—saw no reason why she had to wait for an underling to grant her access to either of her sons.

She halted the stroller in front of Blake. "Your assistant said you were here with Alex."

He barely had time to absorb her knee-high boots, black leggings and rust-colored tunic cinched with a monster leather belt decorated with an assortment of dangling, clinking zoo animals in silver and gold before Molly gave a joyous screech.

"Da-da!"

His heart turning over, Blake responded to his daughter's outstretched arms by unclipping the stroller's safety belt and gathering her in his. She brought with her that ever-fascinating, always changing combination of baby smells. Today it was powder and strained peaches and a faint, yeasty scent he couldn't identify.

"Have you heard from Grace?" Delilah demanded while Molly planted wet kisses on his cheek.

"No, but we know she left her favorite boutique a couple of hours ago."

"I was just saying she may be treating herself to a late lunch," Alex put in.

"She wouldn't do that," Delilah asserted flatly. "Not without giving me a call first to check on Molly."

The skin at the back of Blake's neck stretched taut. His mother had just confirmed his own thoughts.

"Patrice said Grace left a message for you earlier," she continued. "She didn't communicate her plans for the rest of the day?"

"Just that she wanted me to call her."

"That's it?"

"No." Blake's jaw tightened. "After she didn't reply to my second voice message, I grilled Patrice. She said Grace mentioned wanting to talk about her cousin, then changed her mind and just asked Patrice to tell me she called."

"Her cousin?"

Despite the distraction of Molly's palm slapping his cheek, he didn't miss the sudden flicker of guilt in his mother's eyes.

"What do you know that I don't?"

"Well…"

With a sudden premonition of disaster, Blake passed Molly across the desk to her uncle and locked on his mother. "Tell me what you did."

"I didn't *do* anything," she huffed. "I merely suggested to my daughter-in-law that she might want to think about whether she owes her loyalty to her dead cousin or her very much alive family."

"Dammit! I told you not to interfere in this."

"You're raising a daughter," she fired back. "You

should know by now that being a parent gives you the inalienable right to interfere when necessary."

Too furious to counter that broadside, Blake strode to the windows. He knew damned well that Grace *did* think about where her loyalty lay. Continuously. The matter twisted her in as many knots as it did him.

Had she gotten fed up with the pressure he and now Delilah had put on her? Was that why she hadn't responded to his return calls? Had she decided she needed some downtime, away from the Daltons, mother and son?

Christ! Would she just disappear? Walk out of his life as Anne had?

The thought put a hard, fast kink in his gut. Just as fast, Blake unkinked it. There was no way Grace would do that to him. She had too much integrity, too strong a sense of fair play. They'd argued over this whole mess, sure, but she knew he loved her too much to let her just disappear from his life.

Didn't she?

Brought up short, he tried to remember if he'd articulated the actual words. Maybe not, but he'd sure as hell showed her how he felt. The fact that he couldn't keep his hands off her spoke louder than words. As if it were an implied-in-fact contract, the attorney in him asserted, she could certainly infer his feelings from his actions.

Right, the less legalistic side of his mind sneered. Just as he could now infer why she hadn't returned his calls.

Well, there was one possible reason he could address right now. Cell phone in hand, he brought up the address book and hit Jamison's number.

"It's Blake Dalton," he said tersely. "I need an update on Petrie."

"Got a report a half hour ago," the P.I. informed him. "I was just going to email it to you."

"Give me the gist."

"Hang on, let me pull it up. Okay, here it is. Electronic surveillance of Petrie's residence showed him returning there yesterday afternoon at fourteen-thirty hours. My associate checked with his source in his highway patrol unit. Petrie and his partner testified in court in the morning. Reportedly, he felt queasy afterward, said he was coming down with something. He took the rest of the day off and called in for sick leave again this morning, saying he had a doctor's appointment. Surveillance showed him leaving his residence in civilian clothes at oh-six-fifteen."

Blake's eyes narrowed. "Pretty early for a doctor's appointment."

"That's what I thought, too. I've got my guy digging deeper."

"Call me as soon as... Wait. Back up a minute. You said Petrie testified in court yesterday morning?"

"Right. On a drug-stop case that crossed state lines and involved the feds. I've got the specifics here if you..."

"I don't need the specifics. Just tell me which court."

"Bexar County, 73rd Judicial District," Jamison reported after a moment. "Judge Honeywell presiding."

It might not mean anything. Honeywell heard dozens of cases every week. But the possibility, however remote, that Petrie might have picked up something about Grace from the judge or his assistant put the crimp back in Blake's gut.

"Call your associate in San Antonio. Tell him to put everything he's got on this. I want him to know Petrie's exact whereabouts, like fast."

"Will do."

He palmed the phone and was just turning to update the others when Alex's intercom buzzed. Shifting Molly to his right arm, his twin reached for the phone. Blake felt a surge of hope that Patrice had forwarded a call from Grace to his brother's office. That hope sank like a stone when Alex flashed him a quick frown.

"Yes, I'll take the call." He jiggled Molly, waited a moment and identified himself. "This is Alex Dalton."

Blake cut across the office. He pressed against the front edge of Alex's desk as the groove between his twin's brows dug deeper.

"Right. Thanks for calling."

"What?" Blake demanded before Alex had dropped the instrument back on the hook.

"That was Helen Jasper, the woman who owns the boutique where Grace shopped this morning. She just went out for a late lunch break and spotted Grace's car parked a couple doors down from her shop."

His voice was as grim as his face.

"She looked in the Jag's window. Said she could see the bags from her store spilling off the front passenger seat. Grace's purse is on the floor with them."

Delilah took Molly back to her house while her sons set out across town. Alex navigated, and Blake drove with a fierce concentration that was only minimally directed at the road. He tried to tell himself there were a number of reasons Grace might have left the Jag parked outside the boutique for so long. But none of reasons he dredged up explained her leaving her purse inside, in full view of anyone tempted to smash a window and empty it of wallet and credit cards.

"There's the boutique," Alex said when Blake pulled into the parking lot of an upscale strip mall. "And there's Grace's Jag."

Blake screeched into a slot beside the midnight-blue sedan and jammed his own vehicle into Park. He carried a spare key to the Jag on his key ring and was aiming it to beep the locks when Alex put out a restraining hand.

"There could be fingerprints or fibers or other evidence."

Like blood. He didn't say it. He didn't have to.

"Sure you want to contaminate the scene?"

"I've driven this car dozens of times. My prints, clothing fibers and DNA are all over it, but I'll be careful."

As it turned out, the doors weren't locked. Blake used the underside of the handle to open one. The baby seat sat empty in the back with some of Molly's toys scattered beside it. The front passenger seat held a jumble of shopping bags. Additional bags had obviously tumbled off the seat onto the floor. Grace's purse lay half-buried amid the silver tissue paper and pale blue bags. Her cell phone was clearly visible in the purse's side pocket.

Jaw clenched, Blake moved to the rear of the vehicle and used the key to pop the trunk. His breath escaped in a hiss of sheer relief when he found it empty. Alex gave him a silent, sympathetic thump on the shoulder. Blake knew he'd imagined the worst, too, although the empty trunk provided only temporary respite from those grim scenarios.

"I'll call Harkins," Alex said curtly.

Phil Harkins was a friend as well as a supremely competent chief of police. Alex had his phone out when Blake yanked on his arm.

"Wait!"

He ducked under the raised trunk lid and came back up with a half-folded sheet of paper he'd missed on the first, anxious sweep. The message inside was scrawled in bold black ink.

You took my wife. I took yours. If you want to see the bitch alive again, you'd better keep this between you and me. A rich prick like you shouldn't have much trouble finding us. We'll be waiting for you.

Blake swore savagely and passed the note to Alex. His brother was still reading it when Blake's cell phone pinged. He checked caller ID, saw it was Jamison and cut right to the chase.

"What have you got?"

"Petrie flew out of San Antonio on a oh-seven-ten flight direct to Oklahoma City. He landed at eight-twenty, picked up one checked bag and rented a black Chevy Traverse from Hertz, Oklahoma tag six-three-two-delta-hotel-eight."

"Does the rental have a vehicle-tracking device?" Blake bit out.

"It does, but Hertz wouldn't give me access to their system."

"I'll take care of that."

He skimmed his contacts and pulled up Phil Harkins's number. The DA was in his office, thank God.

"Hey, pardner," he said with the affable geniality he showed to everyone except the worst of the bottom feeders his office prosecuted. "How's it hanging?"

"I need a favor, Phil. Fast, with no questions asked."

"Shoot."

* * *

Ten nerve-twisting minutes later, Harkins delivered.

"Hertz just transmitted the GPS tracking data. Your boy departed the airport, drove to your neighborhood and cruised your street. Didn't stop, but made a sharp U-turn at nine-fifty-four and drove to Nichols Hills."

Hell! He'd been following Grace. Blake was sure of it.

"He idled a block from your mother's place for eighteen minutes," Harkins recited, "then drove to your present location, where he sat for almost two hours."

Watching Helen Jasper's boutique. Waiting for Grace.

"Do your people have a lock on him now?" Blake asked, his insides ice-cold.

"Roger. He's heading south on I-35, three miles from the Texas border." Harkins hesitated. "I don't know what you have going on here, but I can ask the Texas Highway Patrol to make a stop."

Blake couldn't chance it. Petrie was a Texas state trooper. He could have his radio with him and be listening in on their net.

"No, don't alert the troopers. Just keep tracking him and let me know if he deviates from I-35." He shot his brother a fast look. "I'll be in the air."

Alex was punching the speed call number for his chief of air operations before Blake disconnected.

"What have we got ready to go?" He listened then issued a terse instruction. "Top off the fuel tank on the Skylane. We'll be there in fifteen minutes."

Blake didn't question the choice of a single-engine turboprop over one of Dalton International's bigger, faster corporate jets. Alex could put the Skylane down in a cow pasture if he had to.

* * *

They were in the air less than a half hour later. Alex laid on max airspeed and made a swift calculation.

"We should catch them between Austin and San Antonio…if that's where the bastard's headed."

Blake nodded, his eyes shielded by the sunglasses he'd put on to protect them from the unfiltered sunlight. He kept his narrowed, intent gaze trained on the wide ribbon of concrete cutting across the rolling hills and checkered fields below.

Petrie was down there, a thousand feet below and almost two hours ahead, driving a black Chevy Traverse. Blake could only pray he'd stuck to his end of the deal and had Grace sitting alive and unhurt beside him.

Fourteen

Grace shifted in the bucket seat, biting down hard on her lip when the SUV jounced over a rut. With her arms cuffed behind her, the ache between her shoulder blades had magnified to sheer torture in the interminable hour since she'd regained consciousness.

She turned her face to the window to hide a wince and searched for a landmark, any kind of a landmark. All she could see was a dense forest of stunted live oaks poking above an impenetrable wall of scrub. Refusing to give in to the desperation squeezing her chest like a vise, she faced front again and forced herself to speak coolly.

"Where are we going?"

Buzz-cut, tanned and clean-shaven, the outwardly all-American guy in the driver's seat wrenched his gaze from the single-lane dirt road ahead and shot her a look of smiling malevolence.

"I told you. You'll know when we get there. Now unless you want to talk to me about that rich bastard who screwed my wife..."

Grace set her jaw.

"That's okay, cuz. You'll be squealing soon enough. Now shut the hell up. I don't want to miss the turn."

This was how it had gone since Grace had come to, dizzy and nauseous and aching all over. Petrie had refused to tell her how he'd found her. Refused to do more than smile with amused contempt when Grace warned he wouldn't get away with snatching her off the street.

She knew without being told that kidnapping wasn't all he intended. He was a cop. He wouldn't leave a live victim to bring him down. She also knew he intended to use her as bait to get to Blake.

She'd been so careful! How had he made the connection between Blake and Anne? No, not Anne! Hope! She had to think of her cousin as Hope again, use that name when referring to her, or she'd feed into the rage smoldering behind Petrie's careful facade.

Ten minutes later Grace caught a glimpse of blue water through the screen of trees. Five minutes more, and Petrie slowed to a near crawl, then turned onto an overgrown dirt track. Grace had no idea how he spotted the track. There was no mailbox, no scrap of cloth tied to a bush, nothing but two sunken ruts cutting through the heavy underbrush.

Thorny vines and ranches scraped the SUV's sides. He was doing one helluva number on the paint job, she thought with vicious satisfaction, then gritted her teeth as the SUV bounced over the ruts and white-hot needles stabbed into her aching shoulders. She wanted to sob with relief when the brush finally thinned and the dirt track gave onto a clearing that sloped down to a good-size lake.

A cedar-shingled cabin sat at the top of the slope, well above the waterline. Cinder blocks supported a screened-in porch. Additional cinder blocks formed columns to hold up the roof that shaded the porch. Grace whipped her gaze from the cabin to tree-studded opposite shore and spotted two or three similar structures. Most looked as if they were boarded up. None was within screaming distance.

Petrie pulled well off the track, killed the engine and got out. Leaving his door open, he extracted something from the floor behind his seat. A rifle case, Grace saw. Hand-tooled leather. Padded handle. Housing for the high-powered hunting rifle she'd seen him clean at his kitchen table more than once.

The case terrified her. Not for herself. For Blake. He would come after her. Find her somehow. Walk right into Petrie's gun sight.

The terror spiked again when Petrie got out and propped the rifle against the fender before extracting a soft-sided pistol case from his door's side bin. The case was half-zipped, providing easy access to the blue steel semiautomatic he slid out. It wasn't his service weapon. Grace had seen his state-issued black leather holster and Sig Sauer often enough to recognize the difference. This had to be a throwaway, one of those weapons reportedly confiscated during traffic stops that somehow never made it into evidence logs. Untraceable to the man who now coolly ejected the magazine and checked to verify a round was chambered before snapping the magazine back in place and thumbing the safety lock.

Just as coolly, he settled the pistol in the waistband of his jeans and picked up the rifle case. Grace's heart was racing when he rounded the hood, yanked open the passenger door and popped her seat belt.

"Let's go."

He hooked a hand around her upper arm and dragged her out, firing the pain in her shoulders to white-hot agony. It took every ounce of will she had not to moan as he hauled her up to the cabin. The screen door screeched when Petrie pulled it open, then groped above the main door for the key he obviously knew was there.

When he shoved Grace inside, the stink of old, dank blankets and used fishing tackle hit like a slap to the face. Grimacing, she inspected the dim interior. Bunk beds lined one wall. A rough-plank picnic table, a worn sofa with mismatched cushions and a lumpy armchair took up most of the remaining floorspace. The kitchen consisted of a counter with a sink, hot plate and half-size fridge. An unpainted door hung on its hinges at the far end of the room and gave a glimpse into a cubbyhole of a bathroom.

"Nice place you got here," Grace commented with a credible sneer.

"Belongs to a friend of mine. He's invited me up here a couple times to fish and drink. I know it offends your delicate sensibilities, but it'll do fine for what I have in mind, cuz."

"Stop calling me that, you dog turd. You and I are in no way related, thank God."

"You always were the feisty one."

She didn't like the slow, up-and-down look he gave her.

"I might just have to train you to heel, like I did Hope."

"You want to bet that's gonna happen?"

The face her cousin had once rhapsodized about being so strong and stamped with character now radiated nothing but amused contempt.

"We'll see how full of piss and vinegar you are when I'm done with you."

Dragging her across the room, he spun her so she was nose to nose with the rolled-up mattress on one of the top bunks. She felt him working the cuffs on her left wrist, felt it spring free and the screaming agony when her arm dropped to her side. She knew she had only three or four seconds to whirl and claw and fight for her freedom, but before she could do more than curl her numbed fingers Petrie had spun her around again. In a quick move he snapped the free end of the cuff to the metal pole supporting the upper bunk. Steel rattled against steel as the cuff shimmied down the pole.

"Make yourself comfortable, cuz. I figure we've got some time before the fun starts."

With unhurried calm, he placed the tooled leather case on the table, unzipped it and began to assemble his hunting rifle.

Grace watched him, her arms dangling uselessly at her sides. They felt as though they'd parted company with her aching shoulders. When the blood finally pulsed back into them, she angled around as far as the cuff would allow and yanked at the rolled-up mattress on the lower bunk.

"All right, Jack," she said after she sank onto the dank ticking. "You may as well tell me. I know you're itching to rub my face in it."

"How I found you, you mean? Or how I found out about my whore of a wife and the rich dick you married?"

"Both."

"Took some doing," he admitted as he snapped the rifle's bolt into place. "I've been searching ever since Hope walked out on me. Checking state and county

court records, making calls to various police depart-
ments, screening NamUS—the National Missing Persons Data System," he clarified gratuitously.

Grace knew damned well what NamUS was. The
data system was open to anyone with a computer. She'd
screened it regularly herself for updates on her cousin.

"It wasn't until your marriage license popped in the
Texas Vital Statistics database that I finally got a solid
lead, though. I saw Judge Honeywell had married you
and talked up his assistant. She gushed about what a
handsome couple you'd made, how the judge and the
Daltons went way back. I went right home from the
courthouse and got on the computer."

He lifted his gaze, gave her a mocking smile.

"Found plenty of coverage about the Daltons of Oklahoma City but didn't see much mention of you. Made
me think you were keeping a low profile for a reason,
so I dug deeper and found a petition filed with the Oklahoma County clerk's office to establish paternity of the
infant referred to as Margaret 'Molly' Dalton."

The smile took a hard twist.

"So I made some calls, cuz, and discovered a
woman matching your description showed up at Dalton's mama's place almost the same day as the infant. I
knew the kid wasn't yours. I'd been watching you too
close. So there could only be one reason why you'd take
a leave of absence from your job to work as a nanny."

The mask slipped, releasing the fury behind it.

"The brat is Hope's, isn't it? My whore of a wife had
a kid by this guy Dalton, and noble, do-gooding Cousin
Grace rushed to the rescue just like she always did."

"Jack…"

"Shut up! Don't even try to lie your way out of this.
The kid's birth certificate was included in the pater-

nity petition. Didn't take a genius to link her birth to the death certificate filed in the same California courthouse."

He shoved away from the table, the hate now a living thing. Grace tried not to flinch as he stalked across the room.

"She died out there," he raged. "Hope died, and you didn't even let me bury my wife."

"Jack, please. She…"

"Shut up!"

The backhand exploded against her cheek and slammed her head against the metal pole. Tasting blood, Grace fought to blink away the black spots blurring her vision.

"You're going to pay for what you did, bitch. You and Dalton."

With that implacable promise, Petrie went back to the table and picked up the rifle. Grace was still swallowing hot, coppery blood when the door banged shut and the screen door screeched behind him.

Her head swam. The whole side of her face hurt. She slumped against the metal post until she gritted her teeth and forced herself to think through the pain.

The cabin sat on a high slope that gave a commanding view of the only road in. Anyone approaching by boat would be similarly exposed. Grace couldn't wait for Petrie to pick Blake off. She wouldn't!

Breathing through her nose, she twisted to look up at the bunk above her. Its mattress was rolled up, too, revealing a crosshatch of springs hooked through the rectangular metal frame bolted to support poles.

No, wait! She blinked again, praying her still spinning head wasn't registering a blurred image. The frame wasn't bolted. With the first thrill of hope she'd felt since she'd regained consciousness, Grace saw the frame fit into Y-shaped supports.

If she could lift the frame out of the supports…

Slide the cuff up and off the pole…

She stretched out on the dank mattress and listened for any sound indicating Petrie's return, but all she could hear was the thunder of her own heart. Keeping a wary eye on the door, she rolled up on her hips and planted her feet against a corner of the frame above her.

It didn't budge. Jaw clenched, she pushed again. There was a squeak of rusted metal, an infinitesimal shift. Grunting with effort, Grace applied more leverage and got the frame half out of the support. The cry of the screen door made her drop it and her legs instantly.

"Had to set up a few electronic trip wires," Petrie informed her when he entered. With brutal nonchalance as he dropped some kind of a battery-operated device on the table. "We don't want your husband to burst in on us unannounced, do we? Now all we have to do is wait."

Neither Grace nor Petrie had any way of knowing his electronic sensors would work against, not for, him.

She lay in stark terror for what felt like hours, alternately praying the black box wouldn't beep and praying it would signal the arrival of an entire SWAT team. When the box finally gave two loud, distinctive pings, her heart stopped dead in her chest.

Then everything seemed to happen in fast-forward. She didn't have time to think, barely had time to choke back a sob before Petrie grabbed the rifle and charged for the door. He left it open, giving her a partial view of his body shielded by one of the concrete block columns and the rifle nested snug against his shoulder. Frantic, she rolled onto her hips and jabbed her feet at the upper bunk's metal frame.

"That you, Dalton?"

The answer came just as Grace got the corner of the frame off the supports.

"It's me. I'm coming in."

The frame dropped at a sharp angle, its rusted edges almost slicing into her face. She rolled out from under them just in time and somehow managed to keep the handcuffs from making more than a brief rattle. Petrie didn't hear it, thank God. His focus and his aim were both on the figure climbing the slope.

"Walk slow," he bellowed, "and keep your hands in the air."

Panting with fear and desperation, Grace eased off the bunk and then slid the cuff up, off the metal pole. The steel bracelet dangled from her other wrist as she searched frantically for a weapon, any kind of a weapon. The only thing within reach that wasn't nailed down were the fishing rods. If nothing else, she could slash and whip one of them. She scooped one up and was frantically trying to disengage it from the others when Petrie bellowed a warning.

"You can stop there."

Grace could see Blake now, unarmed, more than close enough for a high-powered hunting rifle to drill a hole through his heart.

"I got a score to settle with you, Dalton. I'm going to do it slow, though. I think maybe I'll put the first bullet in your kneecap."

"You can put a bullet wherever the hell you want, Petrie. Just let my wife go first."

"I don't think so, pal. She's got as much to answer for as…"

Two loud pings stopped him cold. Instinctively, he tilted his head an inch or two toward the intrusion detection device still sitting on the table. Grace knew that was all the break she'd get. She lunged through the open door, arm raised, fist wrapped around the rubber handle of the fishing pole, and lashed into Petrie's face with everything she had.

"Sunuvabitch!"

He flung out an arm, caught her broadside and sent her crashing. She slammed into the hard ground and caught only a brief glimpse of Blake hurtling past her in a flying tackle. She was rolling onto a hip, dazed and shaken, when a second figure burst out of the brush on the opposite side of the clearing and raced for the cabin.

Alex pounded past her onto the porch. Blake didn't need his brother's help, Grace saw as she staggered to her feet. He had Petrie on his back, straddling his hips while he smashed a fist into his face with lethal precision.

A dazed corner of her mind wondered how a corporate attorney could take down a trained cop. Then she remembered the tales Delilah had recounted about her sons' rough-and-tumble childhood in Oklahoma's oil fields and saw firsthand the rage her husband put into every blow.

Finally, Alex had to intervene. "That's enough. Jesus, you'll kill him."

He caught his brother's arm and hauled him off a now almost unrecognizable Petrie.

"He's... He's got another gun." Still winded from her fall, Grace steadied herself with a hand on the cinder blocks and gasped for breath. "In his waistband, at his back."

Blake rolled the man over and took possession of

the pistol. Thumbing the safety with practiced ease, he passed it to his brother.

"If the bastard tries to get up, blow his head off."

Then he was beside her, his blue eyes savage when he took in the bruise she knew had flowered after Petrie's backhanded blow.

"I'm okay," she said before he could spin around and add to the punishment he'd already inflicted. "Just winded…and scared."

"Me, too," he admitted hoarsely, cupping her unbruised cheek with a bloody palm. "God, I was terrified we wouldn't get here in time."

She didn't ask how he'd found her. The details didn't matter now. All she needed, all she wanted at that moment was to lean into his hard, welcoming body.

He held her off and looked down at her with grim intent. "I never told you I love you. That ripped at me the whole time we tracked you."

She managed a shaky smile. "Well, now that you're here…"

"I love you, Grace. I'm sorry it took almost losing you to make me realize how much. Maybe someday you'll forgive me for that."

"I will. I do. And you have to forgive me for almost letting my promise to Anne blind me to the promise I made you."

"I will. I do."

She went up on tiptoe and brushed her mouth over his—very carefully.

"I love you, too." She put her whole heart into the simple words. "So much I can't remember what it was like to *not* love you. Now take me home so we can clean our scrapes and bruises and start our marriage over."

Epilogue

Delilah insisted on celebrating her granddaughter's first birthday with her usual flamboyance and flair. As one of the Oklahoma City Zoo's most generous bene-factors, she chose that as the venue for the momentous event and marshaled her entire staff to prepare for it.

Her social secretary drew up the guest list, which in-cluded fifty of Delilah's closest friends—all potential donors for a new exotic bird aviary—as well as every child enrolled in the Oklahoma City Special Olympics.

Louis, her majestic butler, came up with the design for the colorful invitations. They featured a talking par-rot who squawked out the delights in store.

Her chef baked the six-layer jungle-themed main cake himself but graciously allowed a caterer to han-dle the rest of the menu items.

Naturally, Delilah also marshaled her daughters-in-law for party duty. She brushed aside the fact that Julie had turned over crop-dusting operations to her partners and the two additional pilots they'd brought on board. Julie's current responsibilities as director of flight operations for Dalton International kept her twice as busy, but Delilah blithely announced she could take the necessary time off to help with this once-in-a-lifetime event, as could Blake and Alex. Grace, who had delayed going back to teaching for a year or two, was totally immersed in the early preparations and event itself.

When the big day arrived, Delilah assigned her daughters-in-law the job of welcoming invitees and handing out goody bags crammed with beak-billed ball caps, macaw whistles, parrot sunglasses and canary-shaped marshmallow bars. Alex she put to work matching golf carts with drivers for kids who had difficulty walking. Blake had been tasked to assist a Special Olympics coordinator organize games suitable for children with varying disabilities. Bow-legged Dusty Jones and various volunteers from DI manned the lemonade, popcorn and cotton-candy stands set up throughout the zoo.

Even Molly participated. Spouting gibberish only she could understand, she played pat-a-cake with anyone who would reciprocate and toddled on wobbly legs after brightly colored beach balls in the infants' roller-derby. She also locked her arms around several other kids and refused to let go.

"She's at the hugging and kissing stage," Grace explained apologetically as she disentangled her daughter from a red-faced three year old. "C'mon, Mol-i-gans, it's time to blow out your candle and cut the cake."

Molly came into her arms with a smile so joyous that Grace's chest squeezed. She could see more of her cousin in the baby now. Not the frightened, cowed woman Hope had become, but the happy, laughing girl Grace had skated and played hop scotch and made mud pies with. Tears stung as she stood for a moment amid the bird calls and colorful chaos, nuzzling the squirming infant.

Oh, Hope! She's so bright and beautiful. Just like you.

Then she spotted her husband weaving his way through the crowd. A grinning boy in leg braces rode on his shoulders, waving energetically with one hand while he kept a death grip on Blake's hair with the other. When they reached his mother, Blake dipped so she could lift her son down and stopped to exchange a few words with her.

Grace's chest went tight again. Could her life be any fuller? Could her heart? This kind, thoughtful, incredibly sexy man filled every nook and cranny of her being. He and Molly and the child just beginning to take shape in her belly. She'd never dreamed she could feel such all-consuming happiness—and such a sharp stab of panic as when Molly gave a joyous cry and all but launched herself from her arms.

"Dada!"

Experience had taught Grace to keep a secure lock on the chubby little legs, thank goodness. Laughing in delight at her neat trick, Molly hung upside down until Blake righted her.

"Think you're pretty smart, don't you?"

"Smart," she echoed from the nest of his arms, adding to her growing vocabulary of one-syllable words. "Molly smart."

"Yes, you are. Very smart."

He angled her against his chest and slipped his free arm around Grace's waist. "Mother texted me with orders to convene for the cake cutting."

"Me, too. Guess we'd better comply."

They met Alex and Julie where the paths to the aviary converged.

"Un-ca!"

Molly reached out imperious arms and was duly passed to her uncle. While he and Blake led the way to the tables groaning with cake and other goodies, Julie fell into step with Grace.

"When are you going to tell Delilah you're pregnant?"

"We were thinking after the party might be a good time. She'll be too pooped to rush over to our house and start redecorating the nursery."

"Ha! Don't bet on it." The auburn-haired pilot hesitated for a moment, a rueful smile in her unusual eyes. "Listen, sweetie, I don't want to steal your thunder, but... Well..."

"Julie!" Grace swung around. "You, too?"

"Me, too, unless the stick I peed on this morning is defective."

"Omigod! This is wonderful! Delilah will have to divide her energy between the two of us!"

Julie burst out laughing. "I thought that advantage might occur to you. It certainly did to me."

They waited to spring the news on their mother-in-law until after the last of the guests had left. The family sat amid the party debris to catch their breath before pitching in to help the clean-up crews. Molly was sound asleep in the stroller parked between Grace and Blake. Alex sprawled long-limbed and loose at a picnic table with Julie beside him. Delilah drooped in a folding chair, sighing in ecstasy when Dusty pushed his battered straw Stetson back on his head and began to knead her shoulders. Weariness etched lines in her face but she essayed a smile as she surveyed the deflating balloons and animal-shaped confetti littering the scene.

"The party went well, don't you think?"

"I'd say so," Blake agreed lazily. "How much in pledges did you strong-arm out of your friends?"

His mother's smile turned smug. "Just over a hundred thousand. They could hardly balk when I promised my sons would match them dollar for dollar."

Neither son so much as blinked at this blithe reach into their pockets.

"Half goes to Special Olympics," Delilah continued, wincing a bit as Dusty's gnarled fingers found a knot. "The other half should cover the new exotic bird aviary. The Zoo Director was thrilled at the news."

Grace and Julie exchanged glances, then both women telegraphed unspoken signals to their husbands. Blake took the cue first.

"Grace and I have some exciting news, too."

Delilah shot upright and skewered Grace with keen blue eyes. "I knew it! You're pregnant!" Chortling, she twisted to give Dusty a triumphant grin. "Didn't I tell you that wasn't the flu that had her tossing up her break-fast last week?"

"Yep, you did."

The matriarch faced front again and trained her laser eyes on Julie. "What about you? I figure there was a reason you quit working with chemicals six months ago. You and Alex trying for a baby?"

"Not trying," Julie admitted. "Having."

"Whooeee!"

Dusty's gleeful shout made Molly jerk in her stroller. Startled, she puckered her lips and blinked once or twice, then settled back into sleep while the crop duster danced a quick jig.

"I'm gonna be a three-time grandpa. Not honorary, either," he added when he spun to a stop. Under his bushy white brows, his glance turned to Delilah. "Guess this would be a good time we tell 'em our news, Del."

"Guess so."

The sapphire bangle she always wore winked on her wrist as she reached for the thorny palm he held out to her. She didn't have to go into detail, though. Both sons and daughters-in-law were already on their feet.

"About time you made an honest man out of him," Alex said with a wide grin as he pulled her out of her chair and wrapped her in a fierce hug. He yielded his place to Blake, who echoed his brother's sentiments.

"We've been wondering when you two were going to come out of the closet. Literally."

To the amazement of all present, Delilah blushed a rosy red. Dusty merely beamed while Julie enveloped his bride-to-be in another hug.

"I'm so happy for you." Her laughing glance went to her former partner. "And if anyone can keep you out of the casinos, you old reprobate, it's Delilah."

Grace waited her turn, her heart so full it was almost a physical ache. She'd promised during Hope's last, anguished hours to deliver Molly to her father and make sure she was loved.

She is, Hope. So very loved.

So was Grace. She felt its embrace when she walked

into Delilah's arms and met her husband's eyes over his mother's shoulder.

Whatever happened, whatever came in the years ahead, this was one promise she and Blake would always keep.

* * * * *

The Royal Cousin's Revenge

Catherine Mann

Mills ❤ Boon™
pure reading pleasure

One

Javier Cortez walked onto the private jet as coolly as he'd walked out of Victoria Palmer's life a year ago.

Seeing him, Victoria gripped the armrests, her short fingernails digging into the butter-soft leather. If only there were other passengers inside the luxury craft. If only the pilot wasn't behind a closed door to the cockpit.

If only she'd had some warning Javier would be on this flight, too.

But he'd caught her unawares and unprepared. And without question, she needed all her defenses in place around this man.

He noticed her then and his eyes locked on hers, his expression as enigmatic and unreadable as always. Javier rarely showed emotion.

Except when he'd made love to her.

Her eyes tracked her former lover as he strode toward her.

What was he doing on this flight? Why was he even in Boston instead of at home in Martha's Vineyard?

She'd contracted to be a private nurse for his uncle on his family's private island off the Florida coast—the post she'd had when she'd met Javier more than a year ago. She'd agreed to work for his uncle for only a week this time, balking at stepping back into this family's world. But the old man had offered her quite a sum...and she couldn't afford to say no. She needed the money to pay her brother's lawyer.

Javier shifted his briefcase from one hand to the other, tucking the monogrammed case beside a seat. Defined muscles rippled under his wool suit—vicuña. She still remembered the feel of the exclusive texture in her hands as she tore the clothes from his body.

She couldn't seem to stop looking at him. His coal-black hair was swept back from his broad forehead. The sharp angles of his face spoke of his aristocratic heritage. Javier Cortez had—no kidding—royal Medina blood coursing through his veins. His uncle had ruled a small island country off the coast of Spain until a violent coup more than twenty-five years ago.

The Medinas and their Cortez relatives had lived in anonymity until recently when the press had caught wind of their royal roots.

Not that she'd cared a bit about his blue blood—not then, and not now. She'd cared about the man. The recent media exposé on his family had etched stress lines in the corners of Javier's eyes. Not that he would ever admit to any vulnerability.

His family may have relocated to America, but his

regal Castilian heritage couldn't be denied. And his raw magnetism couldn't be missed.

A shiver of awareness, of desire, skittered up her spine. How would she maintain the necessary distance from him until they reached Florida?

Her mouth went dry as he stopped beside her seat. The spicy scent of his bay rum soap drifted along the recycled air.

"Why are you here?" he demanded.

"You remember me?" She couldn't resist the jab, given how unemotionally he'd walked toward her.

"Don't be ridiculous." He waved aside the barb with an autocratic flick of his hand. "And don't be coy. Why are you here?"

Irritation simmered.

"I live in Boston. If anything, I should be asking you the question."

"This is a Medina plane, and you, Victoria Palmer, are not a Medina."

"But I am, once again, on the Medina payroll. Your uncle hired me to help with his nursing care. With his sons visiting, he wants to make the most of his time with them."

Enrique Medina was slowly dying of liver failure caused by injuries he'd suffered while on the run from the rebels who'd ousted him from his homeland of San Rinaldo. The deposed king still lived in isolation on an island off the coast of Florida, where she'd cared for him the first time. Where she and Javier had begun their affair.

A Medina cousin, Javier worked for Enrique's son on Martha's Vineyard as head of security for their resort. A year ago, he had been visiting his uncle's mansion to check on the island's safety.

One look at the brooding Javier and Victoria had fallen for him. She'd changed jobs to relocate and live near him. Their affair had lasted four months. But she'd let sexual attraction blind her to how wrong they were for each other. How very unbending and arrogant the man could be.

He'd broken her heart. He'd wrecked her family.

She wouldn't be a fool for him again.

"You should sit so we can take off," she said coolly.

Victoria pulled her romance novel from beside her in the seat, hoping he would get the message and leave her alone.

The scent of his soap intoxicated her all the more as he slid onto the sofa across from her, his knees almost brushing hers.

He snapped his seat belt on smoothly, without once looking away from her. "Why wasn't I told of your arrival?"

A dry smile tugged at her lips. "Maybe your uncle didn't want to listen to you gripe about having me around."

A lone eyebrow rose arrogantly. "He asked me to make upgrades to his security. That means I have to know everyone who comes and goes from the island. Anything I may or may not feel is of no significance."

Sheesh. Now, didn't that just put her in her place? Anger knocked against her ribs. Anger, not attraction, particularly since he'd just made it clear he didn't care about her either way.

"Well, now you know. I'm going to the island." She put on her headphones and opened her novel.

And nearly groaned as she realized her bookmarked place stopped right at a particularly steamy love scene.

Javier Cortez hated surprises. He'd experienced firsthand the high price of being caught unawares and unprepared, ousted from his homeland as a kid, chased by rebels who'd killed his grandparents and his aunt. Settling deeper into his seat as the private plane soared upward, he studied his ex-lover reading her novel—or pretending to read, since her page-turning was suspiciously random. He was a man who liked to be in control, and Victoria Palmer was one huge jolt to his system. She dulled his instincts and rattled his focus. She was also still hot as hell. He wouldn't be able to stand up anytime soon without revealing just how much she still affected him. Her blond hair was gathered in a sleek ponytail that trailed over one shoulder. He ached to ease that simple cloth band down the length of her hair and free the silky strands to tumble all around her.

Her chest rose and fell faster and faster, her full breasts pushing against her white cotton shirt. Even her semi-uniform of the simple blouse and khakis she wore appeared elegant. She had a Scarlett Johansson–type lushness to her. No, his attraction to her hadn't dimmed one watt in the past year.

If anything, abstinence had made the gnawing hunger all the more fierce.

Desperate to regain his equilibrium, he searched for a subject that would put a damper on the chemistry crackling between them strong enough to start an in-flight accident. He raised his voice to be heard over her headphones. "How's your brother?"

Her violet-blue eyes snapped up from her book. She yanked out the ear buds. "I see you're as heartless as ever. My brother is still in the juvenile detention center where you put him."

Her brother had come to live with her when his parents had given up trying to control him. But the change of venue hadn't done a thing to alter the delinquent teen's attitude, and Timothy's behavior had begun to border on criminal. Finally, when Timothy had committed vandalism at a Medina resort where Javier oversaw security, there'd been no choice but for Javier to have him arrested.

He knew it had been the right decision, even if it had meant incurring Victoria's wrath. God, she was hot when she got mad.

"Your brother put himself in juvie by pretending to be a valet so he could take joyrides in high-priced cars, just to name one of his stunts that you dismiss as a 'prank.' I happen to call it criminal activity. Having people make excuses for him certainly doesn't help."

"Are you saying it's my fault he's in jail?" She slapped her book down. "I took that job in Boston to be closer to you and now I'm stuck there to be near my brother in jail. What do you think of that?"

"It does not matter what I think." He shrugged with a nonchalance he didn't feel. In fact, blood surged south as she leaned forward. "I am only here to do my job, as are you."

"My job?" She yanked her seat belt off and stood sharply, her signature temper sparking in her eyes. "Convenient that you're finally remembering that now. How about we stick to the professional and stop talking about my family?"

He nodded. Why had he provoked her with the reference to her brother? He wasn't sure. In fact, mentioning Timothy Palmer only made him angry about how much trouble the teen had caused his sister, the kind of danger he'd brought to Victoria's doorstep.

What Timothy had cost them all.

Victoria stood in the middle of the plane, glancing left and right as if searching for an escape hatch. Rather tough to find even on a luxury plane.

He gestured toward the back. "There's a bed if you wish to nap."

A bed? Not the smartest thing to mention with so much awareness searing the air.

Her eyes went wide with an answering arousal just as the plane bounced on a pocket of turbulence. He reached for her, but she jerked to the side, bracing a hand on the leather seat. The jet bucked again. Victoria's feet shot out from under her.

And she landed squarely in his lap.

Two

Her heart plunged to her stomach as the plane lurched and she landed in Javier's lap. She grabbed his shoulders before she toppled to the floor. The jet bounced along another pocket of turbulence, thrusting her against the solid wall of his muscular chest.

And the thick arousal straining against his pants.

Oh. My.

She searched his hot brown eyes and her skin tingled. The scent of him—bay rum and manly musk—triggered memories of the two of them tangled up naked together in bed. She knew well how much pleasure waited for her if she dared to ditch her panties, free his erection and straddle him here, now.

A year ago she would have done just that. After all, they were alone in the airplane cabin, the pilot ensconced behind the door. Javier had avowed he enjoyed her impetuous nature. She'd never told him how he drove her to cast aside sexual inhibitions in a way no other man had before.

Their affair had been filled with impulsive, uninhibited hookups. While making love, Javier shed his cool demeanor as quickly and fully as his clothes. The attraction between them had been combustible, distracting them from the differences they'd both tried so hard to ignore.

But those differences had eventually—inevitably—driven them apart, shattering her heart in the process. She reminded herself that nothing had changed.

She wriggled to slide free of the man, the temptation.

He clamped onto her hips, his jaw tight. "Victoria, for God's sake, hold still."

His ragged request turned her shaky knees even weaker. His mouth was a mere whisper away. So easily she could angle her lips against his and without question the flames would ignite.

Less than a half hour in his company and she was already prepared to repeat the same mistakes.

She sagged against his chest even as her mouth demanded, "Let me go."

"I'm trying." His fingers twitched against her hips. With restraint? Or frustrated desire? "Believe me, woman, I am trying."

The heat of his words flowed over her face, soaked into her soul, which had hungered for him so very desperately this past year. Why did he have to be here? Now? For the past year in Boston, she'd half feared, half hoped she would run into him on the street. He worked on Martha's Vineyard for his Medina cousin, but it wasn't that far away.

As the anniversary of their breakup approached, she'd known she had to do something to get him out of her heart once and for all. The temporary stint subbing for Enrique Medina's regular nurse had seemed like a sign, a chance to prove to herself that she could now walk in Javier Cortez's world unscathed.

But this plane ride had proven that she couldn't. Only, she couldn't afford to back out, not when she so desperately needed the money to pay her brother's lawyer for the appeal that could free him on his eighteenth birthday rather than his twenty-first.

She also couldn't afford to forget for a minute that Javier was the one who'd put her brother behind bars for what amounted to a series of teenage pranks.

Tears stung her eyes and before she could hide them, Javier knuckled one away with surprising tenderness. God, having his hands on her again was heaven and hell.

The sound system crackled a split second's warning before the pilot's voice filled the luxurious space. "The weather isn't cooperating with us today. We have storms ahead for most of our trip. Please return to your seats and fasten your seat belts."

Javier's hands slid enticingly down her arms before settling on her hips again as he lifted her. But he didn't let go. His steadying grip stayed on her waist.

She braced her palms against his chest, a hard wall as unyielding as the man. "Javier." Her voice was so shaky she cleared her throat and tried again. "When we arrive at the island, I think it best that we avoid each other."

"If you have no feelings for me, then seeing each

other isn't a problem." His fingers skimmed up her spine, drawing her closer.

"Of course I have feelings for you." She kept her hands on his chest, her arms maintaining at least a modicum of distance between them. She put ice into her words. "You infuriate me. It hurts my heart just to look at you. I hate the way my body seems to want you in spite of everything. But I am a nurse. I understand it's just biology."

"I would call it chemistry." His eyes smoldered.

"Chemistry notwithstanding, I don't want you in my life. So I would appreciate it if you would please keep your distance."

He stared into her eyes for so long she feared he would argue. Or maybe even kiss her, which would only prove just how quickly chemistry would trump her logic.

Finally his hands fell away and he let her go. "It's a large island. The king's mansion is huge. Staying apart shouldn't be any problem at all—although you're free to let me know if you change your mind."

As she made her way across the aisle, she watched him calmly pull a laptop from his briefcase as if she didn't even exist. How could he compartmentalize his emotions so easily?

Her legs folded under her and she dropped into her seat, her body still on fire from the feel of Javier's hands.

Javier went through the motions of working on his computer, but his real focus was the woman across the aisle from him. She'd given up trying to read and had fallen into a fitful sleep. Dark circles stained the delicate skin under her eyes, attesting to long-term strain. Most likely caused by that damn fool brother of hers. Javier had hoped putting the kid on the road to reform would ease the pressure on his sister. He'd tracked the boy's behavior since Timothy entered the juvenile detention center and the teen seemed to be keeping his nose clean.

Javier had kept track of Victoria, too, which made it all the more surprising to find her here today. He should have known, damn it.

Could the aging king—his uncle—have set him up? The ailing man was physically near death, but his mind was still sharp as ever.

If so, Javier didn't appreciate being manipulated. If he wanted Victoria in his life again, then he would take action.

A niggling voice in his head reminded him of all the times he'd covertly watched over her in the past months. He'd been living his life in limbo. Very atypical for him. But then, the way he felt around Victoria was far from "typical."

Without a doubt, he had unfinished business with this woman. And he had a weeklong window at his uncle's island to find closure....

Or find his way back into her bed.

Three

Victoria stared out the small round window as finally, finally the flight neared an end. Between the crummy weather and the looming presence of Javier across the aisle, her nerves were knotted tightly. At least she would have work to occupy her soon.

In the distance, an island rested in the middle of the murky ocean. The storm front gave the world a fuzzy haze that deepened as night began to fall. Palm trees spiked from the landscape, lushly thick and so very different from the leafless snowy winter that gripped Boston.

She'd been to the island before, but the magnitude of it still threatened to steal her breath anew. The Medina compound was a small city unto itself, a surprise splash of lights in a sea so vast, like a holiday design on the water left past the season.

As the plane powered through the bumpy airspace,

the island began to take shape. A dozen or so small out-buildings dotted a semicircle around a massive struc-ture—the main house bathed in floodlights.

The white mansion faced the ocean in a U-shape, constructed around a large courtyard with a pool. She could distinguish few details in the encroach-ing dark, but she recalled from her earlier visit how highly protected the place was—a gilded cage for En-rique Medina's sons, to say the least. Even from a dis-tance she couldn't miss the grand scale of the sprawling estate, the sort befitting royalty.

Yet the former ruler chose to cut himself off from the top-notch medical facilities his fortune could so easily buy. She would do her best for him, but his criti-cal condition would be better monitored in a hospital, something she intended to remind him of as politely and firmly as possible. Often.

She was here for Enrique Medina, and any problems with the deposed king's nephew needed to be put on hold. Her hormones needed to be put on hold.

The intercom system crackled a second before the pilot announced, "Attention please. We're anticipat-ing a rough landing. Weather only worsens the longer we're in the air, so we're going to put this thing down on the ground as soon as possible. Prepare yourselves for a rapid descent."

Her heart bolted up into her throat. Before she could stop herself, she reached for Javier's hand.

Javier's hand was numb from how hard Victoria had squeezed it during the entire hazardous landing. He'd kept his calm, even though his own gut had twisted at the thought of her in danger.

Now safely on the ground, he held the umbrella over her head as they raced through the sheeting rain toward the Porsche Cayenne four-wheel drive waiting for them. He needed to get her inside the car and safely to the mansion.

He nodded to the armed security guards and waved for the Porsche to be brought closer.

Lightning split the inky sky. Thunder clapped fast on its heels. Too fast for his peace of mind. He hooked an arm around Victoria's waist and pulled her to his side. His feet pounded faster on the paved lot alongside the airstrip, each step splashing in deeper puddles as the downpour increased.

He yanked open the passenger door and guided her inside before racing around the hood to settle behind the wheel and start the SUV. The finely tuned engine purred to life as guards loaded the luggage in back.

Seconds later Javier steered out of the parking area and onto the narrow two-lane road lined with palm trees.

Victoria plucked at her soaked khakis. "I feel awful dripping water all over such an incredible car."

He cranked up the heater. There was a nip in the air despite the subtropical climes, worsened by the damp of the rain. "No worries about the water. The car's just a thing."

"To you, maybe. To me, this sucker costs more than I make in a year."

"The seats will survive a little water." Although his sanity might not survive the sight of her soaked to the skin, her nipples pressing against her shirt. The white blouse had gone sheer when wet, giving him a too-clear view of her lace bra.

"Eyes on the road, please."

"Right." He looked away fast, mentally kicking himself for becoming distracted, especially in such crummy weather. The Porsche's top-of-the-line shocks worked double-time to absorb the bumps of rolling over downed branches littering the road.

But his mind kept returning to what Victoria had said about the Porsche. He'd never considered that his family's money might make her uncomfortable. His portion of the royal cache was in the millions, but he'd chosen to earn his way in the world, to have a profession. He'd assumed he and Victoria had that work ethic in common, and now he realized she'd never thought anything of the sort.

Lightning ripped the sky in half just as a realization thundered through his brain. What else had he missed about Victoria while he was too caught up in the incredible sex to look deeper?

The sky lit up again. A crack sounded, differently this time.

"Damn!" He jerked the SUV left. Hard. Right when a towering tree split in half.

The Porsche skidded sideways to a stop just shy of the tree as it crashed across the road in front of them. Rain hammered the rooftop, the only sound in the aftermath.

He turned fast. "Victoria?"

"I'm okay," she said.

Her face was pale, but otherwise she seemed unharmed.

"Thank heavens you reacted so quickly, Javier. Now we can just take an alternative route."

Alternative route? If only it could be that simple. He

knew this island like the back of his hand. He had to in order to keep the Medina family safe.

"There is no other road to the house from here. We're going to have to turn back."

Her eyes went wide with dawning shock. "But the king? He's waiting for me."

"He will have to make do with a mansion full of staff and an entire clinic at his disposal. And his other nurse won't leave until you arrive." His mind churned with options…and enticing possibilities. Hadn't he wanted to find closure with her? Maybe he just needed to get her out of his system. "We should get somewhere safe and dry soon."

Somewhere alone.

She eyed him suspiciously. "Where?"

"No worries. I know every inch of this island."

Because he'd just decided on the perfect place to take Victoria to have her all to himself.

Four

Victoria shivered inside her wet clothes even with the SUV's heater blasting. Her skin still tingled from the way Javier had devoured her with his eyes. And now they would be spending the night together, whether she liked it or not.

He was on his cell phone informing the main house of their status so the king wouldn't worry.

"Right," Javier answered the person on the other end of the line, his Bluetooth headset glowing in his ear. "Since the road is blocked, we're going to hole up at the greenhouse for the night. No need to risk sending anybody after us now that you've hunkered down for the storm…. Of course…I'm sure…. I'll check in first thing tomorrow."

And that fast, he ended the call as if it was nothing more than a business dealing—rather than sealing their fate. Sealing them together, alone, for the next twelve hours. How would she resist him? Suddenly the air felt altogether too hot. Her body flushed with desire.

Decelerating, Javier rounded a corner, leaving behind the road and lines of towering palms and entering a clearing. Headlamps striped over the glass structure of the greenhouse. Only a small gazebo and a sprawling oak stood between them and the conservatory.

He pulled up beside the front door, turned off the engine and twisted toward her. "This is the greenhouse I told you about. It also has a café area, so we should be able to find something to eat. There's even a sofa and shower in the back office."

She drew in a deep, bracing breath and reached for the door handle. "Then I guess we should head inside." Racing out before he could come around with the umbrella, she sprinted toward the front entrance. Rain pelted her skin. Javier charged alongside her up the stone steps that led inside. He threw open the double doors, startling a sparrow into flight in the otherwise deserted building.

As he closed the door, a cloak of darkness and heavily perfumed air enveloped her.

Slowly her eyes adapted until shadowy images took shape. In contrast to the crowded nurseries she'd visited in the past, this space sprawled like an indoor floral park, and included gathering areas and benches for reading or meditation. Lush ferns dangled overhead. Tiered racks of florist's buckets with cut flowers stretched along a far wall. Potted palms and cacti added height to the interior landscape. An Italian marble fountain trickled below a darkened skylight.

Water spilled softly from a carved snake's mouth as it curled around some reclining Roman god.

She spun slowly in the cavernous room, immersing herself in the thickly intoxicating scents. Vines grew tangled and dense over the windows. Moonlight filtered through the glass roof, muted by rivulets of rain. "This island has everything."

She shouldn't have been surprised—the island had not only medical and dental clinics, but a chapel, guesthouses and stables.

And a very sexy man who was all hers for the night. Amber moonbeams streaked over his broad shoulders. His jet-black hair glinted with raindrops, calling to her fingers to skim over his head with the familiarity they'd once shared.

"Everything? Very close. My uncle did his damnedest to give his three sons a 'normal' childhood after they left San Rinaldo, as much as he could, short of letting them off the island. The king wanted to make sure his family had everything so they wouldn't want to leave."

She slowed in front of him, feeling the weight of Javier's gaze as he stopped beside wrought-iron screens twined with hydrangeas and morning glories.

"What about you?" she asked.

"I grew up in Argentina," he answered, his handsome face impassive. "We were the decoy family. We may be cousins, but we looked enough like the Medinas for the king's purposes."

She gasped in horror. "How awful."

"My family was only alive because he financed our escape." He stroked a hydrangea bloom nonchalantly.

"The danger we faced in Argentina was less than anything here."

Victoria approached him warily. How had she not learned this about him? She should have pressed him about his background once they grew serious, but there was so much secrecy around his family and he'd insisted she was safer not knowing.

Now that the Medina secret had been revealed to the world by Javier's cousin Alys, however, there were fewer restraints. Maybe now she could understand him better, find a way to make peace with their heartbreaking relationship.

Thinking of Alys, she said, "After being forced into seclusion, used to divert danger, it's easy to see how your cousin might resent the Medinas."

"Don't try to justify what Alys did." The vine snapped between his fingers abruptly, his fist crushing the bloom. "She betrayed the Medinas by leaking their secret to the press. Alys is not as closely related to the king and his sons as I am. She hoped to marry a prince and gain all the perks and the fame that came with it. Only the worst kind of person betrays family for money."

"Just like my brother?" She took a step toward him, anger sparking. "Is that what you're trying to say?"

His chin tipped—stubborn, uncompromising. "Read into my words what you will."

"I really hate it when you do that." She plucked at her clammy clothes, her skin hot and too tight for her body. Damn him for the way he unsettled her.

"Do what?" He towered over her.

"Never answer my questions." She stood her ground. She knew he'd never harm her the way he'd crushed that fragile bloom in his fist. "Why can't you ditch the whole regal air and simply give me a straight answer?" He studied her for so long she wondered if he might just walk away, ignore her altogether. Then something shifted in his expression, his brown eyes turning smoky.

"Because—" he slid his hand up to cup her cheek, the hydrangea petals soft and fragrant between his palm and her face "—when you stand so close to me, I can only think of kissing you."

Five

Javier had known he had to kiss Victoria from the second he saw her spinning under the skylight, muted moonbeams washing over her. The way she embraced life had drawn him to her from the start.

Now she stood only a breath away. Her tongue peeking out and touching her top lip was all the encouragement he needed to follow through. He slid a knuckle under her chin and tipped her face to his. After a year apart, a year of aching to have her, she was in his arms again.

Pulling her to him, he sealed his mouth to hers as she opened for him with a sigh that tasted of pure Victoria. Raw desire seared through his veins, firing hard and low.

She looped her arms around his neck and arched against him. Her damp clothes clung to his, fabric warmed from her body. From their passion.

He delved deeper into her mouth, relearning the feel of her, the texture, what made her respond and wriggle closer. Her breasts pressed against his chest, stirring memories of his hands curved around their creamy softness. The pounding storm overhead echoed the drumming of his pulse in his ears.

His hands stroked down her back, then lower until he cupped her bottom to bring her more fully against the length of him. "God, Victoria, I want you so damn much it hurts."

"I know," she whispered against his mouth. "I feel the same way. It's been too long. A whole year without you, without this…"

Her hand slipped between them and over his arousal. His head fell back, his eyes sliding closed. He ground his teeth in restraint until he feared he'd crack a crown. He drew in a bracing breath. The scent of her fabric softener released by the rain mingled with the heavy floral scent of the conservatory, drugging him.

He'd chosen the greenhouse deliberately. It was the most private and romantic locale he could think of at a moment's notice. He could have pushed for the local head of security to send someone to retrieve them. But he couldn't give up the opportunity to be alone with Victoria.

Suddenly a horrible thought occurred to him…. He'd manipulated her, brought her here without explaining there were alternatives, without giving her a choice. He hadn't been fair. He might be autocratic, but he prided himself on his integrity. Even when it had cost him her love last year. Even if it cost him this second chance.

Gripping her shoulders, he eased away with more

than a little regret. She swayed under his hands, her eyes fluttering open to reveal dazed desire and a hint of confusion.

"Javier?" She fisted her fingers in the lapels of his damp suit coat.

He skimmed a strand of her blond hair from her face. "There's never been any question how much we want each other. But we need to be honest."

"You want to talk? Now?" Her voice rose with incredulity.

His libido echoed her objection. But if they were going to take this further, he had to be up front with her. "We don't have to stay here tonight. I can make a call and have someone take us to the mansion."

"But the storm? I thought the roads were blocked?"

"The main roads are out, yes. But there are some four-wheel-drive options. The weather makes things difficult, but not impossible."

Realization slid over her face, her eyes going wide. "You're saying you brought me here on purpose?"

Was she angry? He couldn't tell. At least she hadn't pulled away, so he pressed on.

"Yes, I chose this place so that we would be alone together. I planned to romance you with flowers." He plucked a hydrangea petal from her hair. "All the same, that kiss caught me by surprise...."

"Me, too," she admitted wryly.

"I also didn't expect how fast things would spiral out of control between us. Though I should have anticipated it, given our past." He cupped her face and held her gaze with his. "If we go beyond one kiss, if we stay here for the night, I need you to be one hundred percent certain it's what you want."

She stared at him for so long he prepared himself for the increasing possibility that she would turn him away. And this time it would be for good. There would be no more chances with her. This woman, her beautiful blue eyes, her scent, her touch, would haunt him for the rest of his life.

She unfurled her fingers from his suit coat, and regret slammed through him so damn hard he almost rocked back on his soaked heels. Could he really let her go again?

She dusted her hands along his jacket, brushing off more hydrangea petals that clung to the fabric. And he realized she wasn't pushing him away at all. In fact, her hips were nestling closer in a perfect fit against him.

"Javier—" she stroked her finger along his neck to his jaw "—no one should drive in this weather when we have a safe place to stay. I am exactly where I want to be."

Relief flooded him, more than he expected. He knew there were still more things they should discuss, more issues to be aired and resolved....

Like the full extent of the role he'd played in her brother's incarceration.

She sketched her fingertips along his lips. "Let's stop talking and make the most of this night together. We'll deal with the rest tomorrow when the storm clears."

He couldn't miss the surety in her voice. And while he questioned the wisdom of letting sex distract them as it had so often in the past, he couldn't resist this opportunity to be with her.

Extending his hand, Javier stepped back toward

the office, which he happened to know conveniently housed a shower. "I think it's time we got out of these wet clothes."

Six

Victoria fit her hand in Javier's, committing to the moment. She pushed aside thoughts of the times she'd harbored dreams of committing her life and heart to him, as well.

Tonight they would make love again. She hadn't forgiven him for what he'd done to her brother, but she couldn't deny herself this chance to be with Javier, to ease the ache that had been building for an entire year.

She needed to have one last time with him. Although there weren't a lot of flat surfaces here to choose from. "Where are we going?"

Leaves brushed her legs as she walked past a climbing vine.

He smiled, his dark eyes lit with promise. "The office has a full bathroom. I have fond memories of how we used to shower together."

"This place has a tub?" Her thumb grazed the inside

of his wrist along his strong, steady pulse as she envisioned floating rose petals.

"Gardening can be messy business." He backed her around a potting station with terra-cotta urns in a neat line, bags of soil stacked under the table.

"Makes sense, I guess. And wonderfully smart of you to think of that."

He reached beyond her to open the office door. "If I was as smart as you give me credit for, I would have thought of this long ago."

"Shhhh…" She pressed a finger to his mouth. "No more talking."

She replaced her finger with her lips, and thank heaven he took the hint. His hands returned to her body, making fast work of the buttons down her blouse. And she had no intention of lagging behind. She skimmed off his jacket, her hands remembering how best to undress him, until their clothes left a trail into the bathroom.

Skin to skin, she fitted herself more fully against his body, sighing with a deep satisfaction from just the feel of him. With another sigh she let her head loll back, and she looked around them….

Wow…this wasn't just some tiny powder room.

Her eyes took in the tan travertine tiles, the thick towels and, most important, the spacious spa shower with an assortment of floral soaps stacked on shelves built into the wall.

Her visions of floating roses shifted to fantasies of lathering each other with soap flecked with lilac, gardenia, jasmine or honeysuckle. "I just wouldn't have expected anything so luxurious in a greenhouse."

"My uncle does not scrimp." He reached past her to turn on the water.

She trailed her fingers down Javier's bare chest, reveling in the flex of muscles under her touch. "No complaints here. One last question…" Her stomach twisted in apprehension. "Do you have birth control? We didn't exactly plan for this."

"I have it taken care of," he vowed. "I would never leave you unprotected. The bathroom on the corporate jet is fully stocked, and when we were on the plane I took what we might need." He bent to snag his pants from the floor and dipped a hand into his pocket. "I didn't want to be caught unprepared."

"Thank goodness." She stood in the open shower, one hand braced on the wall. "How many did you bring?"

He devoured her with his eyes as he backed her inside and placed the stack of packets in the soap dish. "Ambitious plenty."

Warm pellets of water sluiced over her naked body, but his bold confidence seduced her even more. "For once, I like your arrogance."

Their bodies melded under the heated spray, which was pooling around their feet. She kissed, nipped and sipped along his neck, along his shoulders. His hands were all over her, so perfectly stroking her breasts in just the right places she realized he hadn't forgotten a second of their time together, either.

Then he soaped up a lather between his palms, the scent of lilac clinging to the steam so potently she was sure that fresh flowers were pressed into the bars. And then he drove all thought away as his fingers slicked between her legs.

She rediscovered his body as fully as he explored hers until she thought she would shatter, right there, right then in his arms. "I need you inside me. No more waiting."

His low growl of approval rumbled against her chest. She barely registered how quickly he sheathed himself, and in an instant he had her against the tiled wall. Cupping her behind the knees, he lifted her, hooking her legs around his waist until he was perfectly positioned to…thrust.

She hugged him closer, dug her heels tighter into his flanks as he moved and she met him. They synced, reclaiming their rhythm as the past twelve months evaporated with the steam. As if all those nights she'd lain alone in her bed hungry for him hadn't happened. As if she hadn't dreamed of having him just this way.

Except with those dreams, she never finished. She woke unfulfilled, aching and lonely for him. There had been so many good times before the end….

She pushed away thoughts of her brother, of her horrible last argument with Javier, and focused on the feel of him within her, his arms and impassioned words all around her. His hard, muscled chest brushed against her breasts, the light rasp of hair teasing her to pebbly tight peaks.

The gathering need tingled inside her, prickling along her skin, hotter than the water vaporizing around them until… Her release rocked through her, showered through her, pulsing again and again just as he did.

His hoarse shout of completion twined with hers and she could have sworn the ground vibrated around them. Maybe it was more thunder, but regardless, she'd been rocked by the force of their coming together.

Her legs slowly slid down to the tile floor again, but she doubted she could have stood on her own. She held on, her face buried in his neck as he gathered her closer.

She couldn't hide from the truth any longer. Being with Javier was different, special. She would always want him, the man who had demanded she do the one thing she never could.

Turn her back on her brother.

Seven

Inhaling the scent of flowers, Victoria and their love-making, Javier pulled her closer to his side on the makeshift bed on the floor under the skylight. After their shower, he'd found some blankets and pulled pillows from the sofa. They'd made love throughout the night, catnapping in between.

Well, she napped. He watched her sleep, a pleasure he'd missed over the past year.

And now their night was coming to an end and he had to act decisively to make her his, because he couldn't walk away from her again. He nuzzled the top of her head, savoring the silky texture of her hair splashed across his chest.

The rain had stopped; the sun was just beginning to pinken the horizon.

Victoria stirred against him and sighed. "We should get dressed soon."

"We should. And we will." Sometime before dawn he'd put on his trousers and run out to retrieve their suitcases from the Porsche. Then he'd quickly gotten naked with her again. He trailed his fingers along her silky arm. "But just because we're leaving this place, you have to know I won't let you go as easily this time."

Avoiding his eyes, she slid her leg over his intimately. "Let's talk about something else. Let's do something else."

He clamped a hand on her thigh, forcing down his body's instinctive reaction to her nearness. "Why are you really on the island? You had to realize I would hear you'd returned, even if we didn't run into each other."

She pulled away. "Are you accusing me of setting this up?"

"No need to get bristly." He grazed his hand up to her waist. "I'm glad we had this night together."

She tugged the silky afghan around her and walked to the edge of the fountain, where he'd placed their suitcases. "I'm here because I didn't have any other way of making enough money to pay my brother's lawyer."

"You're here for your brother?" His body chilled. He sat up, following her with his eyes.

"Your uncle offered me a temporary fill-in job." She opened her paisley bag and tugged out a stack of clothing, her movements fast and jerky. "He said there aren't many nurses he trusts, especially since the Medina secret was splashed all over the papers."

"Your parents should be taking care of your brother's expenses." And if they hadn't given up and dumped their son in her lap, life would have been so different for all of them. "I'm only trying to protect you."

"He's my brother." She yanked on pink panties and a bra with quick, angry hands. "Family means something to me."

"Are you making a dig at my cousin?" He would have stood and walked over to her, but he was still too damned turned on by her. "I can't trust her, and I refuse to justify that to you."

She pulled on a fresh pair of khakis and a white button-up before sagging to sit on the bench around the fountain. Sighing, she put her face in her hands. "Would you please put some clothes on? My brain short-circuits when you're naked."

Now, that was a victory at least. He silently shoved himself to his feet and tugged on slacks and a shirt. "You can open your eyes."

She peered between her fingers with a begrudging smile. "Okay, I'll acknowledge your point. Your cousin is a security risk to the rest of your family, but she's also an adult. Timothy is a teenager." Standing, she faced him, ready to go toe-to-toe. "If his whole family walks away, who will he turn to?"

He gripped her arms. "That's my whole point, damn it!"

"What do you mean?"

He pivoted away sharply, stunned at how she'd knocked him off his game so easily. "Forget I said anything."

"I can't do that." She stepped around in front of him, her hands on her hips. Her jaw jutted stubbornly. "I will not abandon him, no matter what he does."

He could see she wasn't going to back down, even if she followed her brother right into harm's way.

And for the first time, he considered that he might have played a role in that by not telling her everything that had happened around her brother's arrest. He'd been trying to protect her.... And he'd royally screwed up.

He had to fix that, starting now. "Your brother wasn't guilty of just simple vandalism." He pushed out the truth he knew would crush her, but it would also keep her safe. "Victoria, he was part of a street gang."

"A gang?" She gasped in horror, in shock. She held up a hand of denial and backed away. "That's not true."

"Yes, it is." He started to reach for her, to comfort her, but her eyes stopped him short. He stuffed his hands into his pockets. "His lawyer knew it, because I gave him the proof. Surveillance cameras picked it up. He was being pressured to commit those acts—stealing cars, lifting jewelry—as initiation."

"Why wasn't I told any of this?" Anger snapped in her eyes.

Clearly any answer he gave to that was only going to make her angrier, so he deflected with "Why do you think his lawyer and I cut a deal? I wanted your brother safely tucked away. Your parents couldn't handle him, and you have to face that you couldn't, either. He was out of control. Juvenile detention wasn't just the place he deserved to be, it was the safest place for him to be."

Her lips pursed tight, her body rigid. "What gave you the right to decide all of that without consulting me? Obviously you didn't trust me...." She held up her hand. "Never mind. Let's put this conversation on hold. This is all too much, too fast, and I'm too...mad and confused to even speak to you. The rain has stopped. We should leave."

He saw the determination in her eyes and couldn't help but admire how hard she fought for Timothy, how she put herself on the line for people she cared about. She was fiery and fearless, impetuous and idealistic in a way that touched him, no matter how much those qualities could stir trouble for her. And for him, too.

Yes, he could read her eyes well. While she was willing to forgive her brother anything, she wasn't so willing to extend that forgiveness to him.

What a damned inconvenient time to realize just how much he loved her.

Eight

Victoria held back her tears all the way to the Medina compound. Hurt, anger and betrayal warred inside her as she stood in front of the massive front doors. How could Javier have kept something so important from her?

And how could her brother have gotten himself tangled up with such a dangerous group without her having a clue?

Her head was spinning so fast she barely registered the lush landscape, the towering Spanish-style mansion she'd first seen over a year ago. She could think only of the man standing stonily beside her. How could she even consider renewing their relationship when he was every bit as intractable as ever?

And yet realizing how much harder it would be to walk away from him a second time made the tears burn even hotter behind her eyelids.

Before she could blink her vision clear again, the butler directed them to go around back where the king waited on the veranda. She walked alongside Javier on the landscaped path, past the pool in the courtyard. The citrus scent of orange trees heavy with fruit hung in the air. She rounded a corner, passing armed guards just before she spotted Enrique Medina.

Confined to a wheelchair, he was thin, gray and weary. Still, no matter the sallow pallor and thinner frame, Enrique's face was that of royalty. His aristocratic nose and chiseled jaw spoke of his ages-old warrior heritage. And while his heavy blue robe with emerald-green silk lapels was not the garb of a king in his prime, the rich fabrics and sleek leather slippers reflected his wealth.

Enrique greeted them both with a regal nod, then turned to his nephew. "Javier, could you walk down to the beach for a moment?" It was more of a demand than a request, his Spanish accent as thick as she remembered. "I wish to speak privately with Victoria. You and I can talk later."

Javier raised an eyebrow before pivoting away toward the beach—leaving her alone with the deposed king. Victoria couldn't help but notice how Javier purposefully retreated now after her demand that they not discuss her brother. She needed time, and from the way he'd accepted the old king's dictate without comment, she sensed Javier was giving her that space.

Sea breeze wrapping around her, she stepped forward, already assessing Enrique's health from a professional perspective. She hadn't received an update from the previous nurse yet, but the patchwork of veins prominent on the backs of his hands told her he'd been receiving IV medications often. "How are you feeling, sir?"

"Still stubborn about calling me Enrique, I see." His body might be weak, but his voice still commanded attention—it was as firm and constant as the roar of the waves crashing against the shore. "Thank you for agreeing to come."

She forced her focus to stay on him rather than on the man striding along the shore. "I am so very sorry you still require nursing care."

He waved aside her words of sympathy. "Have you and Javier made up?"

Her gaze snapped firmly to Enrique. "Pardon?"

"You spent the whole flight and last night together. I would hope the two of you have stopped being fools and repaired your relationship."

A suspicion flickered in her brain. With her nerves so raw, she blurted, "Did you send for me just so I would be with Javier?"

He lifted a gray eyebrow. "Even I cannot command the weather. But yes, I arranged things so you were on the same flight. I am running out of time to see my nephew settled. Something needed to be done."

Indignation starched her spine. She'd had her fill of this royal family maneuvering her life without consulting her. "What made you assume it was your place to do that, sir?"

Gripping the arms of his wheelchair, he sat up straighter. "Because I was once young and foolish. I thought I had forever to be with the woman I loved." He studied her with piercing brown eyes that reminded her of his nephew. "Sit down and stop looking at me as if I am the enemy."

His autocratic tone took as much getting used to now as it had last year, but she read the genuine caring in his eyes. The older man was dying and wanted to ensure that the people he loved were happy.

Slowly she took the seat across from him. "I'm listening."

"Good." He nodded regally. "If you and Javier don't have feelings for each other, then I have done nothing more than give you the chance to reflect on a past romance."

Her eyes trekked to Javier standing on the shore with his hands in his pockets, tall and handsome against the sunrise.

"Yes, I have…feelings for him…." She loved him. God, how she loved him, so deeply it had haunted her for the past year.

"He fears for your safety, you know, and with cause."

"My brother—"

"No… Javier is overprotective because of the way he was forced to grow up, always watching over our shoulder. Our family has been on the run, living in seclusion under assumed names for so long. It is difficult to throw aside those fears just because the world now has learned our secret."

Unbidden, images of Javier living as part of a decoy family for the Medinas came to mind. He had put himself in harm's way for the sake of family. Hardly the kind of man she could accuse of not caring about his relations. Regret for that comment she'd snapped at him niggled along her conscience.

Her heart ached for the young boy Javier had been, for the way it had marked the man he was today. "How do I get through those walls he has built around himself?"

He patted her arm. "My dear, be tenacious with him, just as you are tenacious when it comes to your brother."

His words sank in, bringing so much of her relationship with Javier into focus. She'd fought for her brother, was willing to forgive him even his criminal behavior. Yet she hadn't fought for her relationship with Javier, a man who'd gone to the mat for her family. For so long she'd been able to depend only on herself, her parents letting her down—letting her brother down—again and again. Somewhere along the line she'd forgotten how to trust, and how to work as a team.

Her eyes sought Javier, the man who'd offered her everything. The time had come for her to be brave enough, bold enough to fight for him.

Javier watched Victoria stride down the beach toward him, her shoes in her hand, the wind streaking her long blond hair behind her. God, he wanted her with him, always. He would never give up trying to persuade her, but he understood that ultimately the decision had to be hers. He'd powered his way through life up until now, but steamrolling this woman wasn't fair—and it wouldn't work.

She stopped alongside him, staring out over the ocean.

He studied her for some sign of what scrolled through her mind. "What did my uncle have to say?"

A smile tugged her full lips. "That he brought us both here to work out our problems."

Not surprising. The king structured his world obsessively as if he could protect them all still. Javier had always admired his uncle's wisdom, the caution he exercised to protect his family. "I suspected as much. Sorry about the whole royal take-charge thing. It's in our blood."

She laughed softly. "Only you would apologize for being related to a king."

"Only you wouldn't give a damn that my family is royal and obscenely wealthy." He had never once needed to wonder if she cared about him because of his family tree.

"Actually," she said, "I'm glad your uncle did it."

Now, that did surprise him. "Even though I'm still the same jerk I was a year ago?"

She turned to face him, scraping back the wind-swept hair that streamed over her cheeks. "You're not a jerk. Assertive sometimes, but I'm beginning to understand that everything you do is for others."

While he didn't totally buy into her altruistic picture of him, he sure as hell wasn't going to argue. "Victoria—" His voice sounded ragged even to his own ears. "I need you in my life."

"Damn straight you do." She slid her hand into his and squeezed. "I think the separation was as tough on you as it was on me. Last year you wouldn't have admitted to taking me to the greenhouse on purpose. You gave me an out if I wanted it."

"It wasn't easy." An understatement, to say the least. He gathered her against his chest and inhaled the scent of her shampoo, the scent of her. "More than anything I want us to be together, not living even a couple of hours apart. I like my job in Martha's Vineyard, but

I have the financial security to go elsewhere if you're intent on staying in Boston—"

She placed her fingers over his lips. "I don't want us to spend even one more day apart. I'm a nurse. I can work anywhere you are, and Martha's Vineyard is still close enough for me to help my brother get his act together."

Her brother. Her family. His family now, too, through Victoria.

He looked back up at the mansion, the U-shape layout wrapping around them, a protective cocoon of family present to help them resolve their differences and find the happiness they'd struggled to capture on their own. Being a Medina might have come with strings attached, but they were also the kind of ties that tethered him. Grounded him.

She curled her arms around his waist and pressed her cheek against his chest. "What are we going to do about my brother?"

"We?" He tipped her face up. "That's the first time you've asked for my help, you know."

"I can't give up on my brother, but I admit, my old way of dealing with his problems wasn't effective." She looped her arms around his neck. "Perhaps we could talk through some tough-love alternatives for him. We could work together. You don't have to carry the worries of the whole world all by yourself. And neither do I anymore, thanks to you."

He smiled. "I can definitely live with that. On one condition…"

"And that would be?"

Looking into her beautiful blue eyes, Javier said the words he'd been waiting to share since the day he'd met her. "Marry me. Be my wife, my lover, the mother of my children. Share your life with me so I can show you every single day just how very much I love you."

Her smile shone brighter than the sun rising over the ocean. "Yes, yes, yes and a million times yes to everything. I love you and will marry you, and I look forward to waking up with you every morning for the rest of my life."

He sealed his mouth to Victoria's as firmly as he sealed his promise of forever loving her.

* * * * *

Desire

IN-STORE 16TH AUGUST

Available Next Month

A Scandal So Sweet Ann Major
More Than He Expected Andrea Laurence

The Cinderella Act Jennifer Lewis
A Man Of Privilege Sarah M. Anderson

Gilded Secrets Maureen Child
The Highest Bidder: The Gold Heart, Part 1 Barbara Dunlop

Strictly Temporary Robyn Grady

In-store
August 2012

The Bodyguard
Various Authours

Three captivating stories featuring our favourite protective Alpha heroes.

Outback Proposals
Margaret Way

Two heartwarming tales of love and passion straight from the Australian Outback.

Greek Affairs: To Take A Bride
Various Authors

These sexy, rich, ruthless and passionate Greek men are about to sweep these women off their feet and into their beds!

Innocent In The Desert
Various Authors

These hot-blooded, hard-hearted kings of the desert have chosen their queens!

Order now at millsandboon.com.au

Get hooked with this great new series...

Castonbury Park

A new seductive Regency read every month — for lovers of Downton Abbey.

The Wicked Lord Montague
August 2012

The Housemaid's Scandalous Secret
September 2012

The Lady Who Broke The Rules
October 2012

Lady Of Shame
November 2012

The Illegitimate Montague
December 2012

Mills ♥ Boon™

Find out more about our
latest releases, authors
and competitions.

 Like us on facebook.com/millsandboonaustralia

 Follow us on twitter.com/millsandboonaus

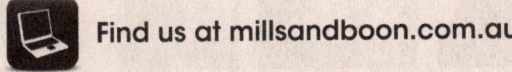 Find us at millsandboon.com.au